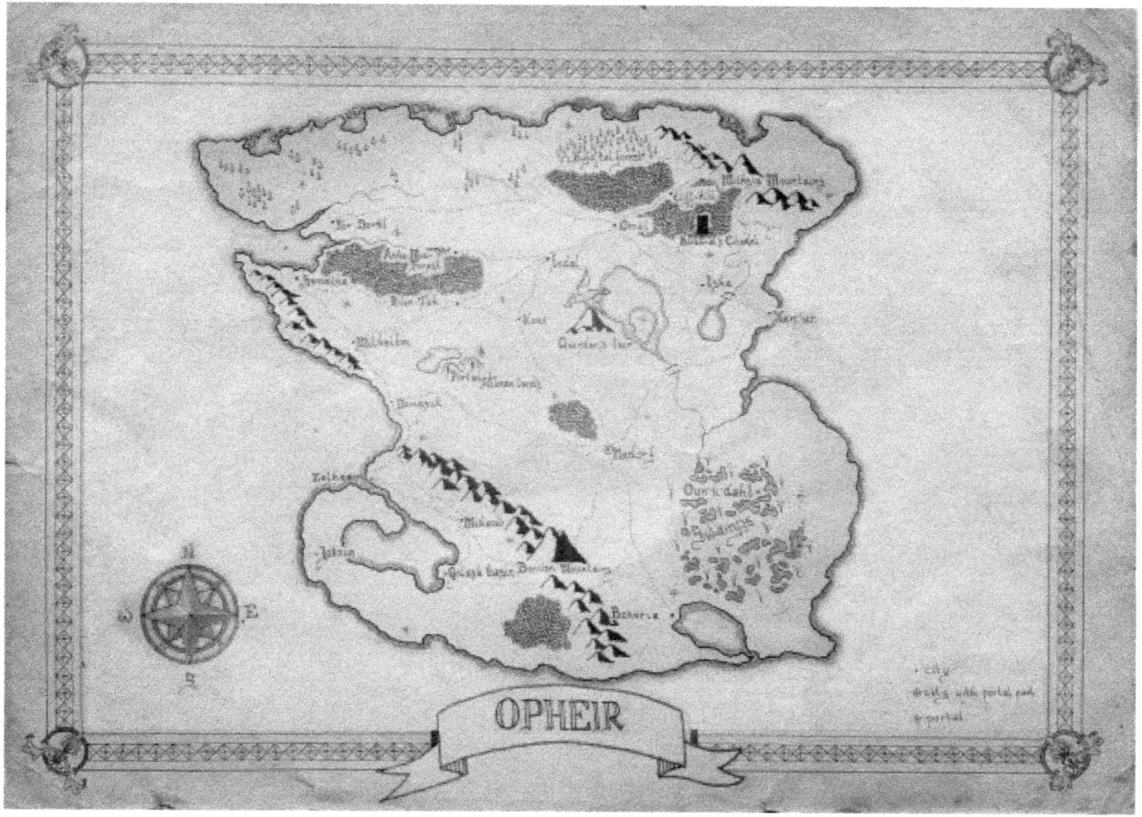
OPHEIR
N
E
W
S

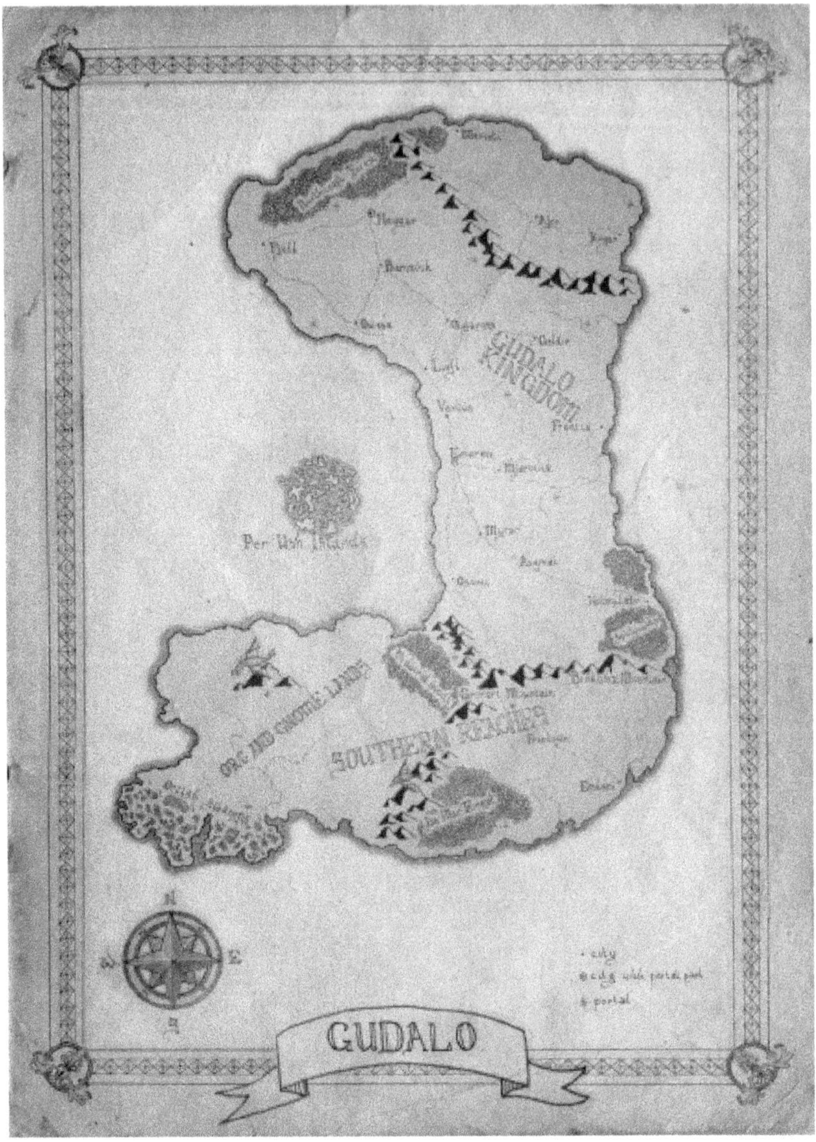
GUDALO KINGDOM
ORC AND GNOME LANDS
SOUTHERN REACHES
N
E
W
S
city
portal
GUDALO

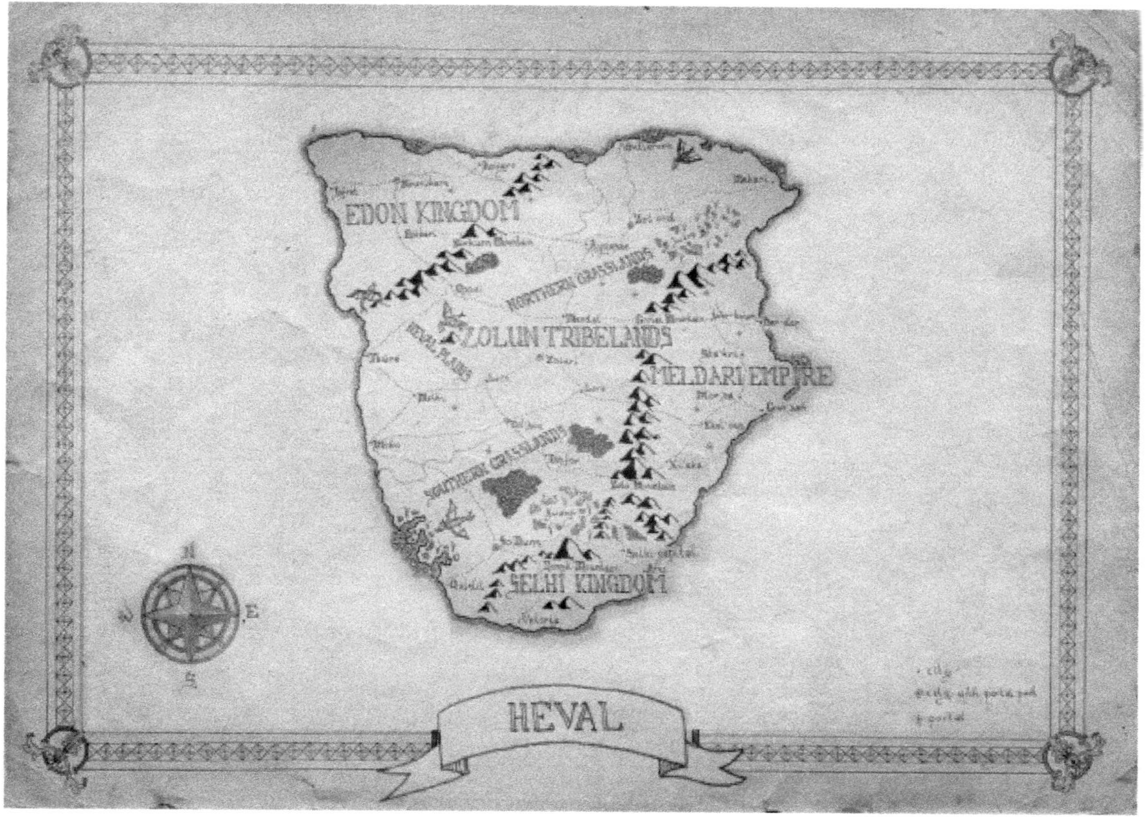

EDON KINGDOM
NORTHERN GRASSLANDS
ZOLUN TRIBELANDS
MELDARI EMPIRE
SOUTHERN GRASSLANDS
SELHI KINGDOM
N
E
S
HEVAL

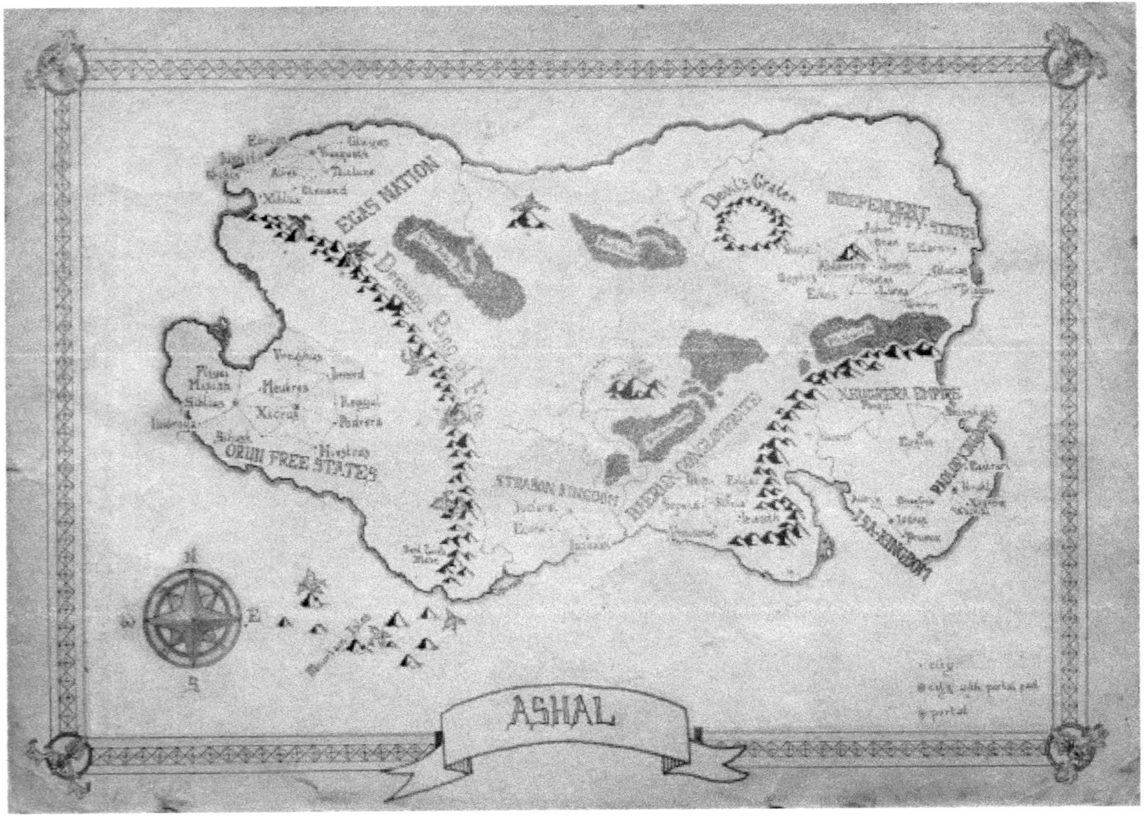

ASHAL
EGAS NATION
Devil's Crater
INDEPENDENT CITY STATES
N
S
E
city
portal

Want a bigger map of Emerilia and the continents? Check out **http://theeternalwriter.deviantart.com/**

Character Sheet is located in the back of the book for reference.

Emerilia

Time of Change

Chapter 1: Forward

Josh looked around the table surrounded by Dwayne, Kim, Suzy, Lucy, Jules, Dave, King Alkao, Aleph Council Leader Hamdir, and Overseer Rendar.

"Okay, so the first piece of business is what to do with the prisoners we have. Lucy, could you begin?" Josh looked to her.

"We currently have nearly a hundred and fifty thousand prisoners who are to serve out a sentence for seven years and then pay for their freedom after the fact. We have gone through their contracts and magical bindings with Overseer Rendar and they meet with the mage's guild and college's guidelines. We are currently determining proficiency and skills to figure out where they would be best at. We want to extend their services to the people of Devil's Crater and the Aleph. Spring is fast approaching and Devil's Crater would be able to clear and farm more land with their assistance. They would be good for different jobs with the Aleph and we will make their information available to you if you would desire to have some of them to fulfill their contracts in your residences," Lucy said.

"Devil's Crater would be very interested in taking on some of their contracts. However, it will take us some time to build the correct facilities for them to live in." Alkao tried not to seem too excited by the prospect.

The Devil's Crater population had been cut nearly in half by the fight with the Demon Horde. They were now armed, armored, and better trained than ever before, but they had more people in the DCA than they did working in Unity or the different sectors of their crater.

Having laborers and people who would be willing to work the jobs that Demons had been told were below them for years would be a great help.

"I will have to bring this up to the council. As you know, we are pretty insular. Having people who fought our forces in our cities is sure to rub some people the wrong way," Hamdir said.

Josh nodded, expecting as much. The Aleph might be looking to make allies and get to know other people and races, but they were very careful about who they let into their facilities and cities.

"Dave, how are we looking?" Josh asked.

Dave made to speak, but yawned instead. "Sorry, uh, okay, so, we've been carving out homes and places all across Terra. In the week since the fight against Esamael's forces, I think all of our allies have asked for a place in Terra. We've got most of their embassies up. The trading district is nearly complete and the industrial sector is coming online. The refinery is at full capacity and I have plans to add another power plant in the city for redundancy. The first green tower is complete and three others have been positioned and are being fed power now. They should be complete in a week or two."

"So, when can we start bringing more people in here?" Josh asked.

"We can start moving them in now if you want. Shard?" Dave seemed to ask the air.

A Dwarf and Elf Halfling appeared in the middle of the table.

"Dave?" Shard asked.

"How are we looking with our systems?" Dave asked.

"I am eighty percent installed within Terra and everything looks to be going according to plan. I was able to speed up refinery times, as well as tweak power generation and better coordinate the underground traffic system."

"I thought we were going to build our own AI?" Dwayne said.

"I thought about it, but instead I gave a binding contract to Shard. Even though he'll be running things here, he won't have complete access. The contract also creates some compartmentalization that will prevent him from sharing what he learns with those outside of the guild leadership," Dave said.

"It is also very difficult to make an AI," Hamdir said.

"Yeah, I went through the Aleph's information on it." Dave shook his head with a pained expression on his face.

"We talked about it before and I okayed it," Josh said. "You were still dealing with the prisoners."

Dwayne nodded in understanding.

"Okay, Lucy, Suzy, how is the network coming along?" Josh asked.

"We have been working with the Aleph. The onos and terminals are ready to go," Suzy said.

"Ono?" Josh asked.

"One-directional teleport pads. We didn't want to call them teleport pads because they're very different, so we're calling them onos and, before you ask about the terminals," Suzy held up a hand to stop him, "we figure that we can do the same thing that we had with Devil's Crater in the beginning. Hamdir can probably better explain it."

"Thank you, Suzy. As you know, the terminals are how we do most of our transactions, except more sensitive materials or larger contracts. With the terminals, it means that people needing just simple goods won't need to go to Terra all the time. We will be providing the upfront cost as well as a fee for sending goods through your ono network. We will also be able to provide the services of a bank, holding onto people's items for a fee or holding their wealth for withdrawal or use. However, our method of wealth will not be gold and silver, but rather soul gems. For us, we've got power plants and stations, but we're using all of that power for various things. People who can produce more Mana will become richer. This means that there will be more power available and people will train to increase their Willpower and Intelligence to become stronger, making Emerilia and the people in it stronger. The terminals will also work as control panels for the onos. If someone wants to come through the ono, they pay the fee with gold, or soul gems, or other items. The terminals will notify Shard that a ticket to Terra has been purchased, and he in turn will notify the teleport pad's controllers. As people travel between the two locations, they will be checked to make sure the trip was paid for and then be teleported to Terra," Hamdir finished.

"Well, that certainly fixes a lot of issues we've been having," Dave said.

"Exactly. In major locations, we will have Florence's people and the terminals. In remote locations, we will have just the onos and terminals," Suzy said.

"How are we looking for time scale on everything?" Josh asked.

"Right now, our production capacity is of five new ones a day. The most time-consuming aspect of this whole thing is going to be actually going from town to town and placing drop pads." Lucy looked to Suzy, who nodded.

"Okay, let's get that started as soon as possible," Josh said.

Dave raised his hand.

Josh pointed to him.

"In the beginning, we're not going to be able to have that many teleport pads here to take in people, so it will be easy to manage the people coming in." Dave gave Josh a look.

Josh hid his wince. It was a good cover while there were other people around, but the truth was that even with all of the resources, they were going to get from Selhi and Gudalo, the costs of making Terra and the ono network wasn't small and teleport pads still cost nearly ten times the price of one ono.

The treasury was looking pretty scarce. Getting the various allies in their embassies and traders renting their spaces and selling their wares would bring in some much-needed wealth.

With the Aleph using soul gems as currency, we can build up some wealth there with the power station facility and the secondary power plant. Also, food always sells, so the greenhouses will be good. Having the free labor from the prisoners will allow us to build our reserves a bit more, Josh thought.

Rendar raised his hand.

"Please speak, Overseer Rendar," Josh said.

"Thank you for letting me sit in on this meeting and overlook the transition of the prisoners to their new accommodations. I have been greatly impressed with the way in which you have handled everything," Rendar said.

A pop-up blurred in Josh's vision.

Your standing with the Mage's Guild has increased from Neutral to Friendly.

Your standing with the Mage's Guild has increased from Friendly to Ally.

"Thank you for your kind words." Josh bowed his head slightly.

"I was wondering what you mean by this ono network? My curiosity has been piqued and I'm always interested in learning more." Rendar smiled.

"Well, I guess the rest of the world is going to know soon enough. The Aleph have been making simplified versions of the teleport pads, which we are going to be placing in every city, town, and point of interest across Emerilia. Terra will act as a hub to move people and goods across Emerilia at great speeds," Josh said.

"That is quite the undertaking," Rendar said. "Will it not disrupt trade?"

"It will disrupt some trade. Big items such as crops will still be cheaper to move by wagon and ship. We are also going to be needing a lot of people from those shipping and merchant companies to be assisting in moving items around Terra," Josh said.

"It seems that Emerilia will become a much smaller place." Rendar had a thoughtful look on his face.

"The mage's guild and college are both welcome to make an application to rent residences here. It will probably be easier for the office of the Overseers to be in a location that they can move across Emerilia in a matter of seconds," Josh said.

Rendar nodded. "That would indeed be beneficial. I know that there are many contracts with the mage's guild that I could pass along."

"I know that someone would be interested and we are going to have a number of Players and adventurers coming through here," Josh said.

Rendar nodded his head.

He's seen the possibilities. I have no doubt he'll pass the information up higher. Josh hid his smile.

There were no other large discussions for the meeting, so it quickly ended.

Some guild members went off to deal with their different jobs, or talk to various people. Josh went to his office where he found Cassie waiting for him, looking out over Terra.

"Hey." He closed the door behind him.

"Hey, Josh!" Cassie looked away from the window.

"Enjoying the view?" He gestured at the city beyond.

"It's nice, but we might need to slow down on increasing the size of the place. I know you've got plenty of plans, but with everything, we're very nearly scraping the bottom of the guild's coffers," Cassie said with a severe look.

"Lucy tells me it enough for five people. I don't need you to tell me as well," Josh complained, moving to his seat and slumping into it.

Cassie sat on his lap. He made to kiss her, but a finger stopped him.

"Business first," Cassie said.

"Okay, business first."

"You have Suzy and Dave running the business and development side of things for the most part. It's mostly a cover for Lucy, who is using it to manage her spy networks. They might be great fighters, but how do they know how to run all this? It's getting way too complicated."

Josh snorted. "Trust me, Dave and Suzy aren't even going full out. Dave's ideas might be a bit expensive up front. He was the one who talked me into making Terra what it is and not just some two apartment blocks. Though, look at his growing towers, the power station he and Malsour made, or the refinery. We're generating more power than ever, power that the Aleph just said that they would accept in lieu of gold and silver. The gardens are coming up on their first harvest. We've already got buyers interested in Devil's Crater. Cliff-Hill Industries, from their smithies to their factories, will be putting up places in Terra to sell products and services. Florence has the Exdar's trading halls ready to go. The last piece is the onos and terminals. Once those are in place, then we can wait and build up our reserves."

"Why do you have so much faith in Dave and Suzy?" Cassie asked.

"They're good friends of mine and I know that on Earth, they're really good with managing these kinds of things."

"You're not going to tell me who they are on Earth, are you?" Cassie asked.

"They left that life alone to become who they are now. They're E-heads to the core."

"Well, ready to add another E-head to that roster?" Cassie smiled.

"Are you sure?" Josh asked, holding back his excitement. Becoming an E-head was a big deal.

"I'm bored of all the publicity, the damned meetings, wearing skimpy clothes to get more followers. This is where you are and I prefer to be here with you." Cassie blushed and looked at her hands.

Josh laughed, hugging Cassie to him, and kissed her. She didn't stop him this time.

***

Dave walked into the training area. It had some of the strongest magical coding written into the walls as some of the most powerful Players on Emerilia duked it out here.

It didn't take him long to find Deia and Anna fighting it out. They were using swords and magic. With their Abscondita armor, a full-powered blast could take out half of their power reserves. With a charge of two million, their strength was becoming scary.

And we haven't even reached the level of some of the more famous POE adventurer groups. Dave smiled. There was always someone stronger. He had but stepped upon an incredibly long path.

The Council of Anvil and Fire had been meeting nearly every day with the ongoing Dwarven tournaments. He had been watching some of the fights that his fellow Master Smiths talked about. It seemed as if the hidden stars of Emerilia had come out to show off their strengths.

Some of the arenas had needed to be rebuilt after some of the preliminaries.

Dave had wanted to join in on the fights, but he had too much work to do and he didn't want to give away his new fighting style.

An orb seemed to materialize in his hand.

He had multiple metal orbs circling him at all times, but with their stealth runes, he was the only one who could sense them. He'd been working on the magical coding more and more, trying to reduce all signs of them.

The orb disappeared again, floating around Dave as he once again looked to the fight.

Some of the Stone Raiders had been able to get into the tournament. Steve, Kol, and Gurren were off watching it while Malsour was working with Dave on their secret projects with Suzy. Induca was off in Devil's Crater visiting with Fornau, Quindar, and their children.

Alkao entered the side of the arena. His eyes found Dave and he waved to him. Dave waved back to the large Demon King. He waited at his spot as Alkao made his way over.

"Come to see your girlfriend duke it out?" Dave asked as Alkao got close enough, the two of them clasping forearms.

"It's fun to see her beating up other people." Alkao grinned.

"Yeah, I've heard that you two have been having *private* training sessions." Dave grinned.

"A man has to keep some of his dignity. She beat my red ass across the damn arena." Alkao sighed.

Dave clapped Alkao on the shoulder. "That I can understand—the trouble with going out with a strong woman. Damn stubborn and one hell of a fighter!" Dave laughed.

Alkao chuckled. "The strength of your partner reflects well on you. Better to rise together than dominate the other."

"Damn, looks like she might have actually knocked some knowledge free in there, or do you have a concussion?" Dave looked at Alkao as if he were injured.

Alkao rolled his eyes. "I saw that you are now making those floating orb items. What are their uses?"

"My cast time with complicated objects takes a long time, like with the armor. Hell, nearly fried my damn brain making everyone armor back in Devil's Crater." Dave's voice turned sober at the thoughts of all those who had died. *If only I had been faster—if I could have come up with the idea before...*

"It was a great loss, but without you, many more of my people would have died." Alkao seemed to read through Dave's thoughts, his voice neither condemning nor carrying pity.

Dave looked to Alkao. The two of them shared a moment before Dave turned to the fight.

"Well, much like the bracelet, I needed to have things set up that I could call in an instant. I used the idea of Shard and Steve's runed spheres. With a little movement, the orbs can carry out multiple different spells and orders. With the originals, I conjured them." Dave had one of the orbs appear. "These, I made out of real materials and placed a soul gem core at the center. All I do is conjure metal inside, move the inner parts to the correct formation and send it off to carry out what I want. Instead of memorizing and casting a huge spell, I just need to change a few runes and move a few pieces."

"Never fight Dave, even when it seems there's nothing around. Got it," Alkao said, releasing the orb. It faded into nonexistence.

"We've fought some powerful enemies and I've recently figured out just how powerful some of our opponents are going to be." Dave turned thoughtful. "Our path moving forward is not going to be easy. We're going to need every trick that we can come up with."

Alkao nodded in silent agreement.

They watched Deia and Anna fighting. Their powerful attacks cancelled each other out. The air around Anna was distorted, taking on the white windy appearance of the sky guardian that she had used against Esamael's forces.

Deia's flames seemed to make wings from her back and under her feet.

After seeing the strength Anna gained with augmenting her body with Air, Deia had been working harder on her augmentation. Denur's lessons had sunk in: use less Mana, but in a focused way, to alter her battlefield and the way in which she fought.

"Deia is powerful when attacking, but lacking in defense. Whenever her momentum is halted, she tries to attack harder instead of waiting for an opportunity to regain the offensive," Alkao said.

Dave doubted that the Demon King would have said that a year ago.

"Anna is calm and calculated, but she is using the same attacks and feints as before. Her movements are really simple when you break them down, but she constantly uses them in different combinations. With her processing power, it's hard for someone to beat her unless they have overwhelming power. I wonder if this is the power of an artificial intelligence inside the body of a Beast Kin?" Dave said.

"It does make for an impressive fight, but there are always people beyond the predictable."

The two fighters sped up and their blows rang out. The barriers flared slightly from the fallout of the two women's attacks.

"If someone is able to fight faster than Anna or just faster than her mind, then her plans would be thrown into chaos."

Dave nodded. "You raise a good point."

It made Dave think about his own stats. He had a really high Intelligence, but his Agility was comparatively low.

At first, he had been fighting on the front lines with Steve, Anna, and occasionally Deia, but since Lox and Gurren had joined Party Zero, there were five, sometimes six melee fighters, out of the nine party members.

Dave's strength was his ability to support others. Add an enchantment here. Give a person a weapon there. Drop a Mana bomb there. While he was fighting, he needed to split his thoughts, to focus on fighting.

He wanted to be at the front, to be fighting toe-to-toe, but as he continued to ponder on this, he came to the conclusion his biggest impact would be as a rear support.

My Vitality hasn't ever been the strongest. Now Deia and Anna can take it out with two hits. What's going to happen if something we fight gives me three hits?

Steve was a pure tank. His hit points were high and his Mana barrier was stronger than Deia, Suzy, Anna, and Dave's Abscondita armor combined.

Gurren and Lox had been training hard. Although their Strength and Agility were still less than Dave's, their Vitality, training, gear, and classes were all directed to make them stronger fighters. They were specialized Dwarven tanks.

Dave could trust them to take the front. He wasn't going to try to change his weapons master class. It was still a great boost to his stats and if he did stay back, there might be a time when he needed to run forward and cut down those who put pressure on his front-line teammates.

"You look rather deep in thought," Alkao said.

"I just thought that I should stop fighting at the front. Sure, I'm decent at it, but with my orbs and my knowledge, I'm better at conjuring items to support my people. I'm a walking, talking, magical coding and enchanting machine. 'Bout time I started thinking and fighting like it."

Alkao grunted. "I've learned that sometimes it is harder to stay in the rear than be among the fighting."

Deia's blow went too high; Anna jetted from one side and then back in and under the attack in a blur. Her sword stopped just centimeters from Deia's front.

Deia jumped back, pausing before she lowered her weapons. She bowed to Anna slightly. She was showing now. Dave had altered the armor so that it would change with her as she and the baby inside her continued to grow.

Wish she would take it easier. Dave frowned.

Anna and Deia looked over to where Alkao and Dave stood in the bleachers.

Alkao and Dave waved.

"Guess we should get down there." Dave made his way to the stairs leading down into the arena.

"After you." Alkao followed him down to the arena floor. Deia and Anna were talking and gathering up the gear that they had put to the side.

"How did the meeting go?" Deia asked as Dave greeted her with a kiss.

"Good. Looks like the mage's guild and college are happy with us. Also, seems like Alkao and Devil's Crater are going to be getting a lot of laborers in the near future," Dave said.

"It won't be long until winter is gone. There's plenty of work to be done," Alkao said.

"You decided to come and watch, trying to pick up hints on how to beat me?" Anna teased.

"One day, I will get through that stubborn shell. Though, for today, I will settle for taking you out to get some lunch." Alkao smiled. The two of them only had eyes for each other.

Dave wrapped his arm around Deia as she rested her head on his shoulder.

"What are you two looking at?" Anna said, noticing their looks.

"Will you go out already!?" Dave said. Deia gave Anna a look that agreed with her fiancé's words.

"This again?" Anna groaned.

Alkao smiled and put a teasing arm around her. She let it settle there and the corners of her mouth curled upward.

"Will you join us for lunch?" Anna asked.

"No can do. We've got a checkup," Dave said.

"Looks like you've got him well trained."

"He remembers this stuff more than me. I feel like I'm some kind of prize-winning cow!" Deia said.

"I would never say such a thing!" Dave looked to Alkao for support.

"You best not or else I'd be kicking you out of bed," Deia threatened, nestling her head into his neck.

"I don't think you can sleep without your body pillow," Dave said with quiet confidence.

Deia looked up at him with thinned eyes. Dave's stoic expression broke into a smile and Deia's lips quivered for a moment before she looked away, trying to hide her amusement.

"All right, well, we'll get together sometime later," Anna said as she and Alkao started to walk away.

"Have fun!" Dave led Deia in another direction, toward their apartment.

"I thought we were going to the appointment?" Deia intertwined her fingers in Dave's.

"We are, but you've been fighting with Anna for a few hours."

"Oh." Deia sniffed her pits. "You might have a point," she said, blinking as if she were about to pass out.

Dave shook his head at her antics.

***

Jules looked up from her desk. She had been working for four days straight after the battles in Gudalo. There were wounded streaming in from everywhere it seemed, from their allies and Stone Raiders, to Esamael's people who were found broken on the ground.

With magic, they had been able to save a great number of people, though not everyone had survived. The streets and apartments of Terra had been filled with the worst cases. The Stone Raiders' allies sent their healers to help.

Jules had turned to looking after the people left in her care or taking time to recover. Those with lost limbs took more time to heal due to the cost of magic and the toll on the person regrowing the limbs.

When Dave knocked on her door with Deia in tow, Jules's face lit up.

"Come in!" she said with a wide smile. Dealing with so many injuries had put her in a rather somber mood. Having Dave and Deia there with her expecting brought some much-needed happiness into her day.

"Hey, Jules." Deia walked into the room. Dave closed it behind them.

"Hello, Deia. How are you feeling?" Jules moved to the examination table, tapping it.

Deia jumped up on it as Jules rubbed her hands together to get them warmed up.

"Good. The nausea has reduced. I've been training some." Deia paused at Jules's severe look.

"Oson'Deia, I told you to calm down on the training. You do it or else I'll damn well hound you down at the arena!" Jules's eyes bore into Deia.

"Okay," Deia said in a small voice.

"Good. Simple exercise is fine, but heavy strain on your body is only going to hurt you and your baby. You Elves give birth faster so you're nearly halfway through your pregnancy. Just another three months and your boy or girl will be out and ready to bug you two." Jules pushed Deia back onto the table and moved her shirt out of the way as she ran her hands over her stomach.

A smile reappeared on Jules's face as she could see the tiny baby within Deia moving around. The baby gave a slight kick, making Deia and Jules smile and giggle a bit.

Jules's eyebrows rose as she examined the child. "Do you want to know if it will be a boy or girl?"

"No, we'd like to keep that a mystery," Deia said.

"Very well." Jules nodded, checking things once again and then taking her hands away.

"Okay, well, you both look healthy as far as I can tell. Also, the baby is going to be pretty damn powerful on the magical side."

"Good—need someone to compete with Deia." Dave smiled.

Jules moved to her table; Deia and Dave took seats in front of her table.

"Okay, for the next three months, take it easy. Don't use more than fifty percent of your magic. Try to keep away from big fights, definitely not on the front lines. Also, tone down the training. Stress on your body and the baby is doing no one favors," Jules warned Deia.

"I'll tone it down on the rigorous stuff and the fighting."

"I'll make sure she does," Dave reassured Jules.

"Good!"

"What am I going to do for three months?" Deia moaned.

"Well, could see your family some, read, visit the Aleph and Demons. I know that they'd be interested in learning some fighting skills from you. Also, we can go see the Dwarven tournaments or go on a few scouting trips," Dave said.

"Okay, maybe a break would be fun," Deia said, touching her jaw.

"Could see your mom and your sister as well. After all, your mom's in a similar situation." Dave grinned.

"Still weird how Elven mothers and daughters will be pregnant at the same time as if it's natural." Jules shook her head.

***

King Sigaird finished signing the final proclamation. Lord Orkan of the Orcs and Gnomes to the southwest and Lord Fea'Iso of the Elves to the southeast put down their own quills.

The pieces of paper seemed to turn together; light filling the room as they combined into one single scroll.

A pop-up appeared in front of the leaders and their people.

People of Gudalo! A treaty has been signed between the Gnomes, Orcs, Elves, and Humans of the continent, revoking the borders to the south of the country. All hostilities will cease immediately. A forum made up of the best and brightest will be made from the citizens of Gudalo.

Applications and testing will begin in one month.

Together, Gudalo will become stronger than before!

"Well, it looks like we're finally done!" Sigaird looked to the other leaders.

"What will you do now?" Fea'Iso asked.

"Well, make sure that it is a smooth transition from my reign to the new leaders of our nation, clean up any of the remaining mess left behind by Esamael and then retire as a King." Sigaird stood. "Oh, and start adventuring again with my wife."

Sigaird grabbed Lady Merguine's hand. She let out a shriek as he pulled her close and kissed her. To any who were analyzing her, her last name fell away, changing to Sigaird.

"Strong man does what he wants, not what he is told," Orkan said with approval.

"How were you able to hide your identity that well?" Fea'Iso asked Merguine.

"Think of it as a blessing." Merguine smiled.

The Lady of Air had been the one to bless her. Her aim had been to unite Gudalo, but Esamael had started to move. Still, she had not left her two champions to their own devices. It seemed that she had a role to play in getting the Stone Raiders to act.

With the information that the Stone Raiders were able to gather on Esamael and his people, little effort was needed to root out his supporters among those with power and positions of nobility.

Once they were gone, there were few who openly opposed this move to unite the continent. Sigaird's hope was that with the unification of the people under one government and the integration of all cultures, Gudalo would never again return to such polarity.

I never thought that I would be happy about Esamael's greed, though it will certainly aid in paying the Stone Raiders.

They had saved Gudalo and given them a path forward. Esamael, who had been taxing all of the people around him, as well as the businesses selling to Per'ush and the teleport pad in Emaren, had amassed a large amount of wealth—wealth that was returned to the crown.

Sigaird had lowered the cost of entering Gudalo and people were flooding in.

Gudalo had seen the darkness of greed, but now with the rot cut away, they could once again grow and prosper into something that would make the world look at them with respect.

Chapter 2: Projects' Room

Malsour sighed and tapped his jaw in thought as he looked at the items in front of him. He had been spending the last week modifying the lab. Now, it was one large room, two stories tall.

There were tables and different workstations around the room. In one corner, there was the humming sphere that Dave was calling his mini-sun. The damn thing gave off enough power to make Malsour pucker up and he'd been around Lady Fire for a large part of his life.

Then, there was another machine that took in heavy metals and then pushed out diamond crystal Mana wells. They were moved to another machine that took them and put them into control boxes that could safely drain power from them.

Then, there was a soul gem growing factory, magical coded pieces of various kinds, bags of holding, different bracelets, rings, and necklaces over four tables, and then a suit of armor that had no visible way to get into it, right next to one that had been taken apart and cut open. Some items were together, others apart and strewn across desks.

To many, it was pure chaos.

To Dave and Malsour, it was paradise.

There was a flash of light and three people appeared at the front of the room.

Malsour instantly recognized Lady Fire and Bob.

The other tall man with a beard seemed to reach out for something.

"Don't touch that!" Malsour barked across the room.

The man's eye met Malsour's with an annoyed expression.

"We're not sure if that will destroy everything in a ten-foot radius or plant a forest for ten miles!" Malsour yelled.

"Bob, what the hell is this place?" the man asked.

"Well, good of you to ask, Water." Bob smiled as he walked over to Malsour.

Fire looked pale as she crossed her arms protectively over the very visible stomach bump.

"What the hell are all of these things doing in the same place and what is that over there?" She pointed right at the "sun" and Mana wells.

"Damned bomb factory in here," Malsour muttered.

"Malsour Dracul, you will explain what you are doing with such dangerous magic!" Fire demanded just as the door to the lab closed. Dave and Deia walked in.

"Bob! What the hell, dude? This is supposed to be a *secret* lab! Not a damned tourist attraction!"

"I wanted to show them the stuff we've been working on. They're some of the oldest people after me and they do have a lot of knowledge about magic," Bob said.

Dave's face went slack. "You were bored and you wanted to show off," he deadpanned.

"Hi, Deia. What are you doing in this place?" Fire disregarded what the other two were talking about as she side-hugged Deia.

Malsour shook his head and went back to studying the information in front of him.

Bob tried to convince Dave that he wasn't showing off, but Dave wasn't having any of it, seeing through the Grey God's bluff.

Water made his way over to Malsour, careful not to touch anything.

"So what is this place?" Water asked.

"Bob didn't brag about it?" Malsour snorted.

Water gave him a look that seemed to ask, "what the hell do you think?"

Malsour gave a half-smile, shaking his head as he looked over the room. "We're working on projects for items that might let us face what's coming out from Bob's prison and the Jukal, if they attack us."

"Okay, though I don't see how one lab could do all of that," Water said.

"Over there, we've got a reactor that can generate more power than an entire island of Per'ush mages' combined strength in about ten minutes. There, we've got a Mana well that will give off residual Mana for a few million years. Over in that area, we're working on armor sets. Dave is trying to determine how to make an armor set to augment a person's abilities. Then, we've got all manner of weapon augmentation and defense coding. We've got a few Aleph automatons in the back." Malsour waved to a large storage room off to the side. "Right now I'm working on incorporating grand workings with Dwarven artillery."

"What? What do you mean by incorporate?" asked Water.

"Well, we found that while you can activate grand workings anywhere, they don't last forever, so using them close to the enemy is the most effective way. We had a fight where someone sent a person in with a grand working. The closer it is when it goes off, the more destruction it'll bring down. So, what if we don't need to be right next to an army to activate the working? How about if you launch it from Dwarven artillery? Or, what if you changed the grand working so that it goes for maximum destruction over targeting? It could reduce the Mana used for the transmission and control of the spell, and more used to give the spell power?" Malsour smiled.

Water looked pale as he looked from the artillery pieces to the grand working parts and finally to Malsour.

"You're the Lord of Water, right?" Malsour held out a hand.

"Yes, and sorry, I didn't catch your name. You're...?" Water held out his hand.

"Malsour Dracul." Malsour smiled.

"Shadow Eater." Water shivered slightly as he shook Malsour's hand.

"Oh, that is an old nickname," Malsour said with a cold smile.

"You killed off everyone who attacked the Wood Elves you were living with," Water said.

"They killed my friends and a woman I had feelings for." Malsour sounded tired. "That was almost four hundred years ago."

"I have a good memory and I was still only about a century or so old at the time," Water said.

"Sure is enough to make me feel old," Malsour replied. Silence stretched between them while Bob and Dave went off to inspect some defensive items. Deia and Fire sat down in chairs, rubbing their backs.

"You know that the items in here could change Emerilia as we know it," Water asked.

"Good. We're going to need to change it and fast if we hope to survive."

Water studied Malsour for a few moments. "Well then, that is something that we both agree on. Can you tell me what your different projects are? I might not know as much as Fire, but I can still be some help." Water smiled.

"Well, I was looking at enchantments or clothing to encapsulate people so that they could go into any environment." Malsour guided Water away from his table.

***

"Okay, so, you got me to help you out in making the reactor, but now what do you want it for?" Bob asked as he and Dave made it closer to the power creating and storage area of the laboratory.

"The power generators and facilities that the Aleph use are really good, but we need something that can give off more power in a shorter amount of time and doesn't burn as much material for a larger power output."

"Okay, yeah, so the fusion reactor does make more power for less materials, but I don't see why you would need that. You have a power station right outside that can give off nearly two times the power of this thing." Bob gestured to the rune-covered metal sphere.

"Right now, we're stuck on this planet. Essentially, we are a big ole sitting duck for the Jukal's countermeasures. When they come for us with their battle fleets, we're going to need a way to deal with them," Dave said.

"Okay, so what? Massive planet-to-space cannons?"

"I'll put that on the list, but they'd be a pain in the ass to make, material wise. No, I was thinking something else." Dave shared his interface with Bob.

A hologram of what looked like a smaller version of the Aleph cities but was capped off at either end with rounded ends appeared.

"Seriously, can you just tell me what the hell you're working on and not play Mister Mysterious Peekaboo," Bob complained.

"Well, you were the one who wanted to show off the lab to your friends," Dave joked.

Bob looked over the image again, sighing as he looked at it closer and moved through the hologram. "Thirty meters long and five across." Bob opened his hands, the hologram coming apart into parts. "You've got gravitational magical coding, then a fusion power plant. A system to move items from the center of the thing to the front. That sphere there looks like a part of Shard."

Bob stopped talking and looked at the different parts. "It's a ship." Bob looked to Dave.

"Correct. It's a fighter prototype. The power system will probably be a scaled-down version of the reactor we have here, or a Mana well if we can get a larger output from it. Weapons, we're still working on, and coding the gravity drive is proving to be a pain in the ass."

"So, more prototype than real?" Bob surmised from Dave's words.

"At this point," Dave admitted.

"Well, one thing I can tell you—you're missing somewhere for the pilot or pilots to control the ship from." Bob waved to the hologram.

"Kind of. It's part of what we're working on here. You know how bags of holding distort the weight or size of items?"

"Yes." Bob nodded.

"Well, we've found a way to automatically pull from bags. So instead of having a large magazine for the weapon systems, we just have bags of holding that the ship's loading system pulls from. Also, if we can figure out how to put a person in them and exert commands onto the ship, it would work perfectly. We could go damn fast and not have to worry about turning the crew to mush as they're not in the same physical world as the ship!" Dave grinned.

"I'm still saying that we use the Human bags of holding for the armor and then find a way to link the Mirrors of Communication to the ships," Malsour said. Water was beside him as they joined in on the conversation.

"That would be much easier to do," Bob said.

Dave had a thoughtful look on his face before he shrugged. "I've been thinking about setting up a factory to make Mirrors of Communication. They're pretty expensive to make material wise and they need people to watch over them. It's worth a shot."

"What is this armor you're talking about, and bags of holding?" Water asked.

"The Stone Raiders have a number of members who are POEs. If they die, they don't come back. Dave had the idea of trying to make something to protect them. At first, his idea was to make really strong armor," Malsour started.

"Then, I found that the armor I wanted to make would just be really heavy and annoying to move around. I wished that there was a way to just code the inside of the armor instead of having a person in there," Dave added.

"I heard him talking about having something smaller in a large space, kept on talking about Doctor Who, whatever that is." Malsour shrugged. Dave looked as if he wanted to say something, but held it in. "Anyway, I talked about the bag of holding and Dave had a lightbulb moment."

"We're still working on it, but we know that putting things into a bag of holding makes it heavier, even if slightly. It shows that the contents of the bag of holding can have an effect on this physical world. So, if we were able to put a person into the armor, but they don't take up all the room in the armor, I can fill it with all kinds of enchantments, boosting their defensive and offensive power. If their armor is about to fail or they're dangerously close to using up their power reserves, they get ejected from the armor. Inside the bag of holding, an enchantment is activated and they're returned to preset teleportation coordinates," Dave said.

"The people using your armor wouldn't have to fear death. They might be POEs, but they have the power of a Player," Bob said.

"To get to that point, we have to figure out a way to do that bag of holding transfer of commands. Then we've got to figure out a teleportation spell or enchantment, then all of the magical coding that will work to increase their power," Dave said.

"Just having the ability to act like a Player would probably do enough. Boosting their power could come secondary," Water said.

"One thing at a time—don't need to go the full distance in one go," Bob agreed.

Dave nodded.

"So what is your most important project? We should probably start with that and then move forward," Water suggested.

"Someone's excited to get to work." Bob grinned.

"Well, it's not every day that you get the chance to build something that could change Emerilia's reality." Water tried to sound stoic even as he fought off a smile.

"Well, the first would be over here." Dave led the group over to a Mana well encapsulated in a glowing soul gem. Embedded around the Mana well and covered by the soul gem were magically coded cylinders that grew in size until they blew up into a circular pad. It bore many resemblances to a teleport pad.

"This is our ono prototype." Dave gestured to the unit. "It's a single location teleport pad... It is powered by a combination of a Mana well and a soul gem matrix. The well gives off power continuously while the gem matrix stores it when not in use. This also allowed us to add a shield, powered by the stored Mana. They cost a considerable amount in both gold and resources and we don't want them to be destroyed, so we've added in a secondary command circuit to the magical coding."

"If this secondary command circuit is tripped by us, then the onos will generate overlapping Mana barriers to protect against physical and magical attacks," Malsour said.

"So, one really powerful Mana barrier. Your locations are going to be heavily defended," Water said.

"Emerilia will be heavily defended," Dave corrected as he opened up his interface and sent out a map to Water and Bob.

They looked at the information and their eyes went wide.

"Damn, half measures really aren't your thing!" Bob snorted.

"Well, we're going to need a good defense first, then we can go on the offense," Dave said.

Bob's view was filled with a new screen.

Event: Of Myths and Legends

3 Creatures of Power have escaped their imprisonment and have arrived back on Emerilia.

The Event: Of Myths and Legends has begun!

Kill the Creatures of Power to gain rewards and experience. If you fail to kill the creatures, then Emerilia could be forever changed.

Creatures of Power located on Emerilia: 3

Creatures Killed: 0/3

The Jukal people have voted to release:

Khanundra

Melhoun

Akatol

Bob looked away from the screens as a silence filled the laboratory. Everyone finished reading the screens and looked to Bob.

"Looks like the event is upon us," Bob said simply.

"I thought that we still had four more months!" Fire said.

"I thought so as well, but these are powerful monsters. I had to wake them up beforehand or else the Jukal Empire might think something was up. It looks like they voted for the creatures to be released. I wasn't told of this," Bob said.

"What's done is done. Do we know which creatures were released?" Water asked.

"Khanundra, Melhoun, and Akatol," Bob said with a stony expression.

Malsour balled his fists up. His fingers whitened as he looked to Fire.

"I need to tell Denur and the rest of the Dragons. She is not going to be happy that her genocidal husband is back," Fire said in a biting tone before she disappeared in a flash of Fire.

"Dave, I am told that you can craft fine weapons. I would like to procure a number of them for my people. It seems that we cannot wait until the end of the Dwarven tournament to arm ourselves with Weapons of Power. I must return to my Merpeople. If Melhoun once again moves through the seas of Emerilia, he will undoubtedly target the Merpeople once again or try to enslave them." Water seemed to rise up from the floor, covering the Lord of Water. As the water fell away, the old man had disappeared.

"Who is Khanundra?" Dave asked.

"Khanundra is the leader of the Lady of Light's Angels, a Level 1,000 creature." Bob shivered slightly. "There's no telling what kind of monster she will become if the Lady of Light turns her into a Champion as well."

"Well, then, we best get to work on what we've got in here. It looks like we're going to be needing these projects working sooner than we thought," Deia said.

Chapter 3: Dwarven Tournament

Steve ignored the looks he was receiving as he walked with Gurren and Lox through Donsk Mountain.

Many Giants and members of the larger races tried to make themselves look bigger as they puffed up their chests and walked as if their invisible lats were pushing out their arms.

"Are they trying to look like idiots or pass out from flexing so long?" Steve asked in a bored tone.

"I thought they were all trying to flirt with you. You know, doing the whole 'I'm a big man, I'm awesome as hell, and I'll beat your ass if you say different,'" Lox said.

Gurren snorted and drank from his tankard.

"You got something to say to me, say it!" one of the Giants who had been flexing challenged Lox.

"It's my day off, yeh twerp. Go rub yerself in cooking oil somewhere else!" Lox yelled before he burped loudly.

He made to drink from his tankard, but found it strangely empty. "Hurhh, well, where's the next beer stall?"

"Do you not know of the mighty Elsoa! What are you doing, running away?" Elsoa yelled.

"So, you're bloody Elsoa. Whatever—knowing your name ain't gonna get me beer!" Lox yelled. Gurren and Steve followed him.

"You coward!" Elsoa yelled.

Lox stopped so fast that Gurren and Steve ran into each other.

"Gurren, hold my mug." Lox held it out.

Gurren sighed, taking it as Lox turned around.

"Look—the little coward is coming back!" Elsoa said.

Steve actually looked at the Giant; it seemed as if he had something like a posse that laughed at his jokes. They looked like the kind of people who liked picking on those weaker or smaller than them.

"Baby, don't hurt the widdle Dwarf too much," a woman wearing entirely too little clothing to be out in public said, rubbing herself against the giant of a man.

"Okay, princess, I'll do my best." Elsoa grabbed her backside, his fingers disappearing up her skirt for a moment.

Lox was just five feet away. With just one look at him, people who had been going down the street moved out of the way of the Dwarf and the Giant who stepped away from his girlfriend.

Lox didn't stop walking. The Giant yelled out; his body became covered in some kind of armor as he swung his fist with all his Strength. But, Lox simply ducked under the blow and moved with a speed that belied his size and build. His fist slammed into the Giant's head, breaking the armor that had formed over his chin, and sent him ten feet to the left.

Elsoa dropped to the ground, clearly unconscious.

"Baby!" The girl ran to the Giant.

"Couldn't even take a punch. This is a tournament, not a place for a brawl. We're here for some entertainment!" Lox turned around and headed back to Steve and Gurren.

"Looks like there's a drink stall up ahead." Steve pointed up the street.

"Good! We should catch this afternoon's game. I heard it's two Level 70 shield and sword types who will be duking it out!" Gurren handed back the mug as the trio headed toward Donsk Mountain without even looking back.

***

After being cleared by Krenua, Alkao and Anna stepped out of the teleport pad and into Donsk Mountain. Krenua, Alkao's old second-in-command and now the head of the Black Hands, was in charge of protecting Alkao and Anna.

Waiting for them on the other side was a delegation of Dwarves. One of them moved forward.

"My name is Indi. We welcome you to our mountain. My lord wishes to extend his greetings to you. At this time, he is taken up with the Dwarven tournament, but he has extended an invitation for you to both to join him in his private box," Indi said in his deep, rolling voice.

"Thank you, Indi. We are indeed thankful for the invitation. If time will permit it, we would indeed like to speak to Lord Ulon under the Donsk Mountain," Alkao said with a slight tilt of his head.

"I will pass on your words. Please enjoy your time in the mountain."

With that, Indi and his group moved away as Alkao moved out of the teleport pad's square.

People watched and muttered to one another. There were a few Demons and Beast Kin competing, but most of them were in Grorart or Aldamire Mountains. They were legendary races, leading to more than one person muttering about them as they passed.

Still, no one tried to approach them as they walked through the square. Their very actions had proved that they weren't known as some of the fiercest fighters just because of half-remembered legends.

They had defended against a Demon Horde numbering in the millions; therefore, they were not an unknown race and group.

Krenua and his people were constantly looking for a threat.

Alkao snorted and a small smile reached his lips.

"Getting in the festive mood?" Anna asked.

"Just wondering how Krenua's eyes are still connected with him looking around so much," Alkao responded.

Krenua growled, relieving some of the tension in the air.

"So, where are we going to eat?" Alkao asked.

"Gurren, Lox, and Steve are here. They suggested a tavern a bit out of the way," Anna said.

"Lead on." Alkao smiled.

She grabbed his hand and pulled him away. Alkao's smile widened. She glanced back, quickly turning back around as she caught his eye. Her tail moved a bit quicker as she continued to guide him and their guards.

She might be stubborn, but that tail of hers always gives away her true thoughts and feelings.

***

Steve, Lox, and Gurren met up with them at dinner. The place was as friendly as it was boisterous; the tournament had put everyone in an excited mood. Laughter and cheers rang through the room.

Alkao had enough drinks to make him feel a bit drunk. Anna watched over them and Krenua watched everyone else who might be a threat.

After dinner, they headed to one of the nearest arenas.

"Now this is what I'm talking about!" Lox yelled as they exited the walkways and came out into the seating that surrounded the arena.

Already, there were two people fighting it out on the stage.

A Fire mage and an Earth mage were locked in a brawl. The Fire mage was moving around the arena on flames, while the ground underneath turned into spikes at a moment's notice. The burly Earth mage ran at the Fire mage; rocks shot up from the ground to create steps for him.

Alkao whistled at the show of not only skill but the depth of their Mana pools that the two fighters must have to put on such a fight.

"This way!" Steve wandered to their seats as people moved out of his way. They found their seats, not bothering to sit down as they looked down on the fight.

Alkao winced as he saw a pebble dart out of nowhere and slam into the Fire mage.

Sensing it at the last second, the Fire mage dove out of the way of the projectile, which would have shattered his ribs. However, the Fire mage wasn't quite fast enough. With the sickening sound of breaking bone, the Fire mage let out a cry as he landed.

The Earth mage, thinking he had hit his opponent's ribs, darted forward, eager to end the fight. A spear of earth grew in his hands. As he let out a yell, the spear was sent whistling through the air.

The Fire mage turned, using the flames on his feet to shift out of the way of the Earthen spear.

Disguising his movement, the Fire mage raised his good arm. Quickly opening his hand, he released a condensed blue flame toward the Earth mage.

The Earth mage barely had time to look surprised as he caught the spell in the face and went flying backward. A Mana barrier flared around his body as he crashed on the ground.

The Fire mage cried out as he landed on his bad shoulder, but it was clear he was still in the fight.

"The winner is Peter the Red!" a Dwarven announcer yelled.

The Earth mage was fuming, but it was clear that without the Mana barrier that he would have been killed.

"What just happened?" Alkao asked.

"Earth mage got his arse kicked!" Gurren said, coming through the crowd with armfuls of tankards. He handed them out as he explained.

"All of the fighters are wearing a Mana barrier. It's made so that people don't die and they can go full out. Well, most of them. The stronger fighters and group fights are going to be in the Mirror of

Communication just because no one wants to pay for those kinds of damages! Once the barrier receives an amount of damage that would be lethal, whether obvious or in the judges' opinion, they stop the person from fighting. Then, the other person wins. Or, they submit. If you submit, then the other dude wins, naturally." Gurren shrugged as he drank from his tankard.

Alkao drank from his tankard as well. A smile appeared on his face. *I could get used to this and going full out in the Mirror of Communication. I'm looking forward to those fights. Might be interesting to try that out with the DCA.*

"The problem with fighting in the Mirror of Communication is that you take in all of your skills and relative strengths, but while you're in there, your physical body doesn't improve. Just your reactions. In reality, your body is just standing there touching a mirror," Anna said, as if reading Alkao's mind.

"Good for showing off your skills and current abilities without worrying about the damage. Bad if you actually want to grow any," Lox surmised.

"Also, really helps with making things that are *really* dangerous." Steve sighed.

"Sounds like you have something on your mind," Anna said.

"Let's just say that I'm happy that Dave has all of his lessons on magical coding in a Mirror of Communication conference room. We'd have quite a few craters in Emerilia with all the experiments people have been doing!"

Alkao watched the ground as it was refreshed in a matter of minutes. There was different terrain all over the place, allowing any and all Affinities to be used. There was even light and dark cycles.

Big screens floated in the air, showing off the fight up close even if it moved farther away.

Alkao had no trouble seeing it with his eyesight.

"Up next! We have the hidden expert Shoshin from Isefor, a master swordsman known to end his competition in less than ten hits! Facing him will be Al'abir, from Levte! A spearman known for facing down a cave of trolls and holding them still for two days and three nights! Who will last?" The Dwarven announcer's voice rolled through the arena as gates opened on either side of the arena.

"Begin!"

The swordsman left a trail of dust behind him as he ran at his target, his hand on his sheathed sword.

Al'abir took a running jump, grunting as he landed near the Fire area of the arena. He moved his spear around, but he got in just two turns with it before Shoshin was on him. With a yell, Shoshin's sword was free from his scabbard, almost too fast for the eye to follow.

"Shoshin has finally drawn his blade and Al'abir barely escaped the draw strike! What will he do!" the announcer cried out.

Blade rang out against spearhead. The shaft was made of a bamboo-like material, flexing as Al'abir moved it around his body, as well as back and forth, dodging out of the way of the swordsman.

His movements were quick and slow at the same time: moving with just enough speed so that Shoshin's blade didn't hit, but slow enough that he retained control of his spear.

Al'abir jumped backward; Shoshin pushed him hard as he made it inside Al'abir's reach. His spear might be long, but once Shoshin was within his reach, his advantages were cut down.

"Swordsman and spear fighter—this is an interesting fight!" the announcer said.

"Need more people who fight with an axe," Steve complained.

Alkao laughed, seeing Steve was entrapped with the display of martial might in front of him.

"Swordsman without a shield—odd." Lox's voice made it sound as though it was downright *unnatural.*

"So, stick toucher or the sword-wielding weirdo?" Gurren asked, looking around.

"Stick toucher." Anna took a drink from her tankard.

"You have some odd nicknames." Alkao shook his head.

"What do you mean, stick toucher? The sword weirdo is inside his reach!" Lox said.

"Yes, but dipshit ten strokes is in long pole's area," Steve said.

"He lured the swordsman into the Fire area. Isefor is between swamplands, cold and wet or humid and wet. He pulled him into the desert territory, dry and burning hot." Krenua looked around. "Shoshin kills people in less than ten hits; he's quick and fast in bursts. Al'abir stood in a cave, facing trolls for three nights and two days. He lives in the Heval plains—they're hot all the time and damn dry. Al'abir is conserving his energy. His spear is flexible and allows him more movement and can increase his power with the momentum created at its tip."

"Good eye," Anna said.

Krenua nodded his head slightly, a small smile on his face.

Alkao was glad that the two of them got along. Krenua was the closest thing he had to a friend before he had come back to Emerilia.

They watched the fighters, talking about their moves, what they should have done or what had impressed them. They talked about what they had been up to, what plans they had. For the first time in a long time, Alkao felt a sense of calm. It was as if he had taken a deep breath and as he let out his breath, all his worries had gone with it.

As Krenua called it, Shoshin started to weaken with time. His Endurance was nothing like his opponent's.

Al'abir was like an elusive fly. He might give ground but he turned or avoided every attack with a violent grace that showed off his skill.

Getting angry and tired, Shoshin rushed inward, screaming as he did so. Al'abir should be at a disadvantage with Shoshin being in his spear range, but he still smiled slightly. Alkao felt the coldness in his eyes—the coldness of a predator. Alkao grinned, hiding his teeth as he drank from his tankard.

Al'abir jumped backward and spun his spear.

Shoshin, expecting Al'abir to flee, continued forward, right as Al'abir dropped, planting his spear. The point jutted out in front of Shoshin's neck.

Shoshin's barrier acted, flaring up. If not for the barrier, then Shoshin would have opened his own neck.

"Al'abir is the winner!" the announcer yelled out. People cheered and groaned; money was exchanged while some people celebrated with slamming their tankards together. Others downed them in regret.

"This fighting is indeed interesting," Krenua allowed.

"Well, when you have a day off, then we'll show you some real fighting in Devil's Crater. There are some fun little dungeons we've been cycing for a while!" Lox clapped Krenua on the back. He might be too short to hit the Demon's shoulder, but the heavy hits still made Krenua tilt forward with the strength behind it.

"I would like that," Krenua admitted with the same hunter's grin that Alkao had shown before.

"We'll join." Anna put her hand on Alkao's shoulder. It looked odd with the lithe and shorter wolf Beast Kin putting her hand on the dominating Demon.

If only they knew who was the strongest out of us. Alkao chuckled to himself.

"The mages might be off doing their thing and Dave is keeping Deia restrained because of the child she bears, but I say it's time that us melee types had some fun!"

Just then a screen, appeared in everyone's face.

Event: Of Myths and Legends

3 Creatures of Power have escaped their imprisonment and have arrived back on Emerilia.

The Event: Of Myths and Legends has begun!

Kill the Creatures of Power to gain rewards and experience. If you fail to kill the creatures, then Emerilia could be forever changed.

Creatures of Power located on Emerilia: 3

Creatures Killed: 0/3

"Well, looks like you ask and it happens," Gurren said.

"Shit," Anna hissed.

A pillar of pure Light illuminated the night's sky.

"Where was that?" Gurren said.

"Markolm, the Elves' island and the Angels' original home." Anna closed her eyes, smelling the air as if to try to sense something.

"Khanundra!" Anna spat.

"What?" Alkao asked.

"That aura—it's Khanundra's, the matriarch of the Angels, born from the Lady of Light's very flesh."

"Why can't gods just, you know, do something else? Where is the damn rulebook that says they have to watch over us? Could just go play a round of golf or get a massage. I swear, they're more tense than the wonky spring in my left leg!" Steve complained.

"I think that I will need to go to Devil's Crater. If there are more creatures coming from Bob's prison, we need to be ready." Alkao pulled out a healing potion. In a gulp, his warm and fuzzy feeling was replaced with cold logic.

"I'll come with," Anna said.

"With recent events and announcements, we have decided that we will be hosting the rest of tonight's games tomorrow! I say again..." The announcer went on, giving his message again.

Chapter 4: The First of Many

Josh stood before a large table in the guild's command room. The table highlighted three areas, places of the event emergence.

Khanundra had returned in Markolm, but then immediately went into hiding. Melhoun was last seen between Gudalo and Heval. Akatol seemed to have appeared over Ashal, crying out in anger as he stepped forward.

"We have reports that the Merpeople and the Dragons are responding to Melhoun and Akatol respectively."

"The Players in Markolm are looking for Khanundra, but can't seem to find her. We suspect that the Lady of Light has pulled her into her hall," Lucy said from where she was working with multiple information screens in front of her.

"Pass that information onto the other embassy leaders and ask that they send military representatives here to liaise information. Looks like we'll finally put this operations center to its intended use." Josh tried to stay calm.

"How powerful are these three creatures?" Dwayne asked.

"Enough to change the landscape of Emerilia all by themselves. They're probably rated as strong as Demigods." Lucy shook her head.

"Okay, so what can we do?" Josh asked.

"Do?" Lucy looked to Josh. "Josh, these creatures are nothing like what we've fought before. It would be like a Level 10 fighting a Level 300. They've had time to perfect their magic and it is damn powerful. Khanundra was made *from* a god; Fire created Akatol as the second of his species. Besides being the father of the Dragon race, he wanted to be exalted as a god so he started killing people to show his power. He killed off three of his own children and twelve of his grandchildren before he was imprisoned. When Melhoun lived, nothing could move through the seas. He became bored and started ravaging the coasts of populated lands, demanding tribute to appease his temper. He tortured, killed, and ate those sacrificed to him and then continued on to destroy everything, sacrifice be damned. Water came down to kill him, but Melhoun fled around the world, wrecking everything in his path. At one point, Gudalo and Heval were connected, but he cut through them to escape Water. The destruction went on for three days before Melhoun seemed to disappear."

A chill ran down Josh's spine with a mix of excitement and fear: excited that he might be able to fight such creatures and fear at the loss of his levels, gear, and resources. *This is what it means to be a gamer—to fight onward, knowing that you might fail, but determined to do it again and again till you succeed.*

"Well, if we can't beat them now, then we're going to have to get stronger!" Josh said with a fire in his soul as he smirked. He looked to the rest of the Stone Raiders in the room.

"Now you're talking my kind of language." Dwayne let out a deep laugh and tapped the hilt of his sword.

***

The Lady of Light opened her eyes; golden light spilling from them. Power seemed to surge through her hall, drawing the gaze of people who had been tending to their tasks toward their goddess.

With her Endurance, she only needed a few moments of rest to stay awake for months.

Now, her aura filled the hall and home of her most loyal followers.

"Daughter," Light said, a half confused whisper, half hopeful breath.

She raised her hand and pointed it to the ground before golden light filled the room. The light seemed to grow. It was soft and comforting, but even the lights of the hall couldn't keep up with its brightness. In the middle of the Lady of Light's hall, a being descended: a woman with polished golden armor and hair that fell down her shoulders.

On her hip, she wore a sword; the other hip held a shield's handle. On her back, bright white wings were curled up. Although they looked soft, their brightness had an oppressive feel, making it hard to look at her for any extended period of time.

Her feet touched the floor. The golden auras of Light and the angel dominated the room.

"My Lady of Light, I have returned." The Angel's voice seemed to calm all those who heard it and made them feel drawn to her. It flowed with grace, but was precise in its pronunciation.

"Khanundra, the leader of my Angels. I have missed you," Light said softly.

She had created the Angels as tools, a way to defeat the Demons and tear power from the rest of the Pantheon. She had amassed a great power when she sent her Angels on a holy war to cleanse Emerilia of those who did not worship her.

The Angels had been torn from the world and held prisoner by the Grey God. Now, with Khanundra's return to Emerilia, it was only a matter of time before the rest of her Angels returned.

"I am honored by your words, my lady. However, I do not sense the rest of your legions," Khanundra said, confusion in her voice.

"It has been many years since you last walked Emerilia, Khanundra. The Angels were captured by the Grey God, but soon all of your brothers and sisters will be returned to us. We will tear down those who took you from me and then I shall ascend to my position as the matriarch of the Pantheon," Light said with complete confidence.

Khanundra prostrated herself on the floor. "Command me and I shall carry out your will," Khanundra begged, complete confidence and faith in her creator.

A cold smile formed on Light's lips. "Go, and clean yourself up. Learn from my people what happened to Emerilia in your absence. In three months' time, the remaining Angels will join us and we will be prepared." Light's voice was firm and sure.

"As you command, my goddess." Khanundra got off the floor and backed away out of the hall, bowing the entire time.

It seems that she is looking to come back onto my good side. She feels as though she has let me down. That will be useful to me in the future. A creature wanting to prove its worth will do much more than one that simply does it to gain more power for themselves. Light relished in the power that Khanundra fed her from the moment she was returned to Emerilia.

She briefly closed her eyes, imagining the power that she would feel with all of her Angels returned. She had not felt that strong in centuries.

***

Fire appeared at her balcony and looked down at her gathered Dragons.

Due to their shared bond, they could faintly tell what the other was thinking. It seemed that Akatol's return had not gone unnoticed.

"Where is he?" Fire looked to Denur, who was perched on her own ledge next to Fire's home.

"Opheir; it seems that he took over Quindar and Fornau's old home." Denur let out a snort, her nose flaring.

"We will set for the mountain immediately. We need to put him down before he restarts his blood rituals and subjugation of the People of Emerilia," Fire said.

"*I* will go, but *you* will remain here," Denur said.

"Denur," Fire said, her tone dangerous.

"Fire, you might be my mother, but right now you're pregnant. There is no way I'm letting you go into battle while carrying a child," Denur said.

Fire could count on one hand the times when her Dragons were angry with her and as she looked out upon them, she realized that Denur had the support of all her children.

Fire knew that she shouldn't be going, but she was the one who had given Akatol life, given him power. She had hoped that he would grow out of his delusions. Instead, he fell into them more. She felt responsible for him and his actions. She felt a kick in her belly and her hand moved to it.

She sighed and closed her eyes. "Fine, but if you're going, I'm going to make you my Champion." Fire looked to Denur.

"I accept." Denur lightly jumped from her balcony. As she descended, her body became smaller and shifted into a Human. Just before she landed, her large wings were the last thing to combine into the cloak that she wore. She knelt before Fire, her head lowering.

"Denur, mother of Dragons, and my daughter, I offer to you the position of my Champion, to go forth and protect those who seek the path of knowledge and punish those who use that knowledge for nefarious uses. Do you accept?" Fire asked.

"I do." Denur looked to the ground.

Fire summoned up power within her body, pulling from her personal Mana pool. Flames grew over Fire's body, her aura enough to make the Dragons take pause. Her eyes were like twin blazing orbs.

Fire lowered her hand and touched Denur's head. Flames grew to envelop both of them before receding into Denur's body. The air became thick with Mana as Fire transferred power into Denur, awakening her abilities and removing the limits upon her body.

Fire was familiar with Denur's body, having made Denur herself. Fire altered and changed Denur, opening up new pathways for her Mana to flow, reinforcing her body.

Denur grunted, shifting under the flames that now covered her. They turned from red to yellow to blue, flowing from Fire to her.

The power left Fire; the flames around her and Denur faded away.

You have created a Champion of Fire

You have blessed Denur Dracul, turning her into a Champion of Fire. As your vessel, she will carry out your orders across Emerilia.

Denur Dracul has undergone powerful changes.

Unknown stat increase

Unknown abilities unlocked

Class awarded: Champion of Fire

Fire dismissed the screen, watching as Denur dismissed her own screens.

"Ugh, sometimes I hate this system. It can't even give me a correct reading on what you did," Denur complained.

"More powerful, blah blah, Champion, blah." Fire waved her hand and smiled at Denur, who rose from her kneeling position with an amused look on her face.

"Now go and deal with Akatol. Protect this family and Emerilia." Fire looked into Denur's eyes. There was a sadness there. Akatol and Denur had raised many children together, but his past kindness did not free him from the slaughter he visited upon the People of Emerilia.

He had killed tens of thousands of Emerilians in horrific sacrifices to increase his power. Even as he became stronger from the bloody rituals, his fanaticism grew. Through this, he was able to dominate any and all creatures under the power of a god or goddess. The Dragons had been but playthings in his eyes as he continued his slaughter. This was why Bob needed to step in to remove the threat of Akatol, who was highly overpowered and unbalanced compared to the others within Emerilia.

Fire felt fear creep up her spine. Denur and her children were powerful; she just didn't know that over the time that Akatol had been sealed away that they had been able to attain the same power as he had.

"I will see to it." Denur nodded, her eyes filled with stony resolve. She walked toward the balcony, expanding into her Dragon form. It had grown with the newfound power that ran through her body. With a powerful flap of her wings, she rose, moving off the balcony, and headed for one of the exits.

Dragons lifted off from their perches within the volcano, following their matriarch, joining those who were already outside, their numbers unable to fit within the volcano.

All of them had heard the stories and the warnings of Akatol as children. He was the monster that they could become. To protect Emerilia, to protect their family, they had to kill the father of Dragons.

"Good luck," Fire whispered, scared for them as she unconsciously moved her hands over her belly.

***

Dave entered the emergency meeting with the Council of Anvil and Fire. There were concerned faces around the table. The normally rambunctious and jovial mood was replaced with a serious one.

Now was not the time to talk about their trade. Now, their job was to protect the Dwarven people and face the hardships that had come to light.

Ankol sat at the head of the table. Everyone took their seats, waiting for him to talk.

"I believe it is time that we elected someone to a governor position on the council," Ankol started.

A Dwarven governor was only elected in times of chaos to lead the council and make the decisions that needed to be made.

"Many of us have fighting experience, but none more than Endur. I believe that a Dwarf who not only knows the people, but the shield bearers who defend our homes would be best for the position," Ankol said.

There were nods and noises of agreement.

Dave looked to Endur; the Dwarf's face seemed to harden.

"I thank you for the nomination," Endur said.

"Are there any other nominees?" Ankol looked around.

The Dwarves might have big egos, but here in the council, they had learned to work together. They were the leaders of the Dwarven race. If they were to fall into squabbles, then their race would fall apart.

"Okay, Endur will take over as governor after this meeting." Ankol smacked his hammer on the table. "Three creatures have been released from their imprisonment. We know that one is a Water Dragon hiding in the Dragon mountain in Opheir. The other descended in a golden light over Markolm before disappearing. We do not know what or where the third creature is."

Dave raised his hand.

"Dave?" Ankol gestured for him to speak.

"It is the Angel Khanundra, Dragon Akatol, and Water serpent Melhoun," Dave said.

The expressions around the room were grim with the news.

"It is time to spread the Weapons of Power," Sola said. There were grumblings of agreement and disagreement.

Ankol looked to Endur.

"I guess I will be stepping into my role a bit earlier?" Endur looked around the table. This was why he was elected. There was little time for in-fighting and debate.

"We will continue with the tournament. At the same time, we will open our mountains to the people around us. They will have to buy a residence and we will not deal with shanty towns outside our cities. Disease will kill us as sure as any blade. We will contact our allies to talk about our plans for the event. When the tournament is completed or when our military judges pick someone from the fights, if the Grey God agrees, we will guide them to our Weapons of Power vaults. We will not show preference to Dwarves or other races or groups. At this time, we need to get those weapons into the hands of the most capable. We will bring the war council into the Anvil and Fire's meetings. It is imperative that there is no confusion between us." Endur looked around the table, his eyes hard.

Dave felt a chill run down his spine. With these words, the Dwarven war machine would turn. With but a word, Warclans would assemble as the time of peace was broken. This was a war council.

Endur's eyes locked on Dave. "Dave, we will take up the offer from the Stone Raiders and open an embassy in Terra as soon as possible. We will have two Warclans from each of the mountains ready at all times to move: to either defend our homes, or move to Terra on assaults that will be organized there."

Dave nodded in agreement. He knew that Josh would agree with Endur.

Endur looked to the rest of those gathered there. "Raise the Warclans, all of them. Check our stockpiles of grand workings and make sure the mountains are secure. We will talk to the Aleph about assisting in arming and armoring our people. It's time these myths and legends remember why the Dwarves and their allies are to be feared."

Chapter 5: Above Opheir

Lucy was looking through various Player feeds.

Players in Opheir showed video of Akatol descending out of the sky. He seemed to be as large as the mountain he landed on. He let out a bellow that shook the very land.

Across the forums, Players were grouping together. Guilds were offering gold and items for information on the creatures that had arrived in Emerilia.

Of the three, the only one that seemed to be within their reach was Akatol, who was now occupying Quindar's old lair.

People were rushing through Cliff-Hill and Nadorf to face off against the Dragon. With the surprise event, people were rushing online.

As the Dragons from Densaou Ring of Fire were using the air currents to bring them up and over the sea between Ashal and Opheir, they were taking hours.

The Players were using teleport pads within Nadorf or Cliff-Hill and then using their powerful beasts or the like to travel toward Opheir. The luckier Players were already in Opheir, some actually seeing Akatol land at the mountain.

Many of these people moved to the mountain at their best speed.

While Players raced to Opheir, the POEs were running away from the mountain, getting as much space between them and the Dragon as possible.

His aura was strong enough to be felt in Kono. The city was quickly evacuating; most of the people staying there were vendors excited to make money off the incoming Players.

A video popped up at the top of the forum.

Lucy clicked on it; it was from a group of Players in Egas Nation. Above them, dozens of Dragons were headed toward Opheir. They didn't seem as large as Akatol, but there were a lot of them.

Just thinking about the destructive power of the Dragons was a scary thought. She'd been looking over Dragon videos of Players who had gone Dragon hunting.

They seemed like impossible creatures. Few items even affected them. Their strength and magical power were incredible—the definition of Creatures of Power.

Players raced in from every direction, but they charged toward Akatol's new home without a clear plan, excited to see what Akatol was made of. Many of them had broken through the hundred ranks. Thinking that they were all-powerful, they reached the entrance of the mountain lair.

Lucy found an ongoing stream. The comments were going wild, up and down the side of the screen. She ignored them, watching what was going to happen.

They slowed their advance and actually moved into something resembling a formation. Players at their level instinctually started classifying one another, their strengths and weaknesses, based on appearance and gear.

They moved into the dark cave which spiraled down into the ground. The Players bunched together, taking a bit more caution.

Some charged ahead.

Lucy watched on the Players' mini-maps as they continued downward. Small groups charged forward, eager to gain the glory.

Some of the more veteran Players stayed back, continuing down slow and steady.

The first dots seemed to stop down the mountain, moving around in a large area before fading out. Lucy hissed; none of them had their streams going.

Lights bloomed around the main group that was descending into the mountain, pushing back the darkness that started to make it harder to see.

More Players joined or moved forward; one such group charged downward on their beasts.

Lucy found one of them with a stream; the group raced down the spiraling corridor, eager to be the first to the bottom. The group reached a large open area, a dim light in the ceiling and coming from a pit off to the side. On the other side of the room, there was a large pool of water.

They looked around, trying to find where the Dragon was. Several cried out as icicles seemed to appear above them. The icicles stabbed through the riders and mounts, impaling them to the floor. Icicles and rain drops moving so fast that they blew people apart upon impact moved around the room.

"Feels like they're being herded," Lucy said, trying to get as much information as possible from the stream. They were all going to die but they'd be back in a few hours, even if it was with less stat points and a reduced rank.

It was a large setback for those who had higher ranks, and even more so if they had equipment that wasn't soul bound to them.

"Well, there's a reason that few people try to fight Dragons." Lucy shook her head.

"How goes the information gathering?" Josh looked up from the map, he, Cassie, Esa, Kim, and Dwayne were standing around.

"Looks like a bunch of people rushed to Quindar's lair, which I guess we should call Akatol's lair now. Getting turned to mincemeat down there, but still no idea where Akatol is. Seems he went in there, but no signs of him," Lucy said.

"I wish we could be there," Dwayne growled.

"Soon enough; we know our own strength and fighting Dragons is outside of it. We just need some time and we can fight Akatol and whatever comes out with the event," Josh said.

"Okay, so we've got the basics for a raid into Alturaran lands. They're pretty powerful, but we can deal with them. Then we've got another raid possibly for that portal in Gudalo that leads to the Xelur's realm. We have dungeons within Devil's Crater and scouting quests around Devil's Crater," Kim said, bringing their attention back to what they could do.

They were setting up different locations and areas for the guild members to join parties and work on improving their skills.

"Okay, good, because I've been looking at quests from the mage's, adventurer's, and trader's guilds. They've got a ton of quests that the guild members can double up on. Getting better rewards for what they find as well as getting more experience to increase their levels," Cassie said.

"We shouldn't forget the Mirror of Communication school. While we might have really impressive stats, knowing how to use them is important." Esa looked to Josh.

"Okay, if we can get some Mirrors of Communication for cheap, or we can build them, then we'll make a hub for people to join into the school and learn in there." Josh looked to Kim. "I sure as hell don't want some of their experiments blowing up in our faces."

Kim muttered under her breath, but it was too quiet to be heard.

"Something's happening!" Lucy shared the stream she was following of the semi-organized Players moving down to the bottom of the mountain.

All of them watched on their interfaces.

Lights were sent out across the room, illuminating it. Some people threw up or gagged from the sight. There must've been around fifty bodies impaled into the floor with icicles.

Blood was drawn across the floor of the lair.

"What is this?" one of the Players in the stream asked.

"I don't know, but it doesn't feel good," another said.

"Stick together and get more lights up. We need to know where this bastard's at," the leader of the group said.

Lights moved out, illuminating the room.

"Is that blood in a formation?" a Player asked.

"Looks like some kind of magical circle written in blood," a mage Player said.

"What the hell. I thought it was a Water Dragon—this is some necromancer shit!"

"Hey, just 'cause we use corpses doesn't mean we're bad people," a necromancer complained.

"Yeah, just creepy as fuck," another muttered.

"Sounds like Jake." Dwayne snorted.

Lucy looked at him and shook her head.

"Pay attention, will you?" Josh sighed. It was hard for them to ever be serious.

It was cool, but it was just a game. Even if these people all died, they could come back again in six hours and play again.

Their attention returned to the party that was moving into the Dragon's lair.

The ground was bare rock with a heated area of sand to the right side and a rather large pond of water to the left that went back into the mountain.

They were halfway into the room when the large pond seemed to erupt into motion. A massive head peered out of it.

"You will suffice," the Dragon said.

The Players broke out of their shock. The ranged attacks let loose while the mages fired off their prepared spells. Melee types rushed forward in a yell. Buffs and curses were cast. The Dragon glowed slightly as the Players seemed to light up the room they were in.

The Dragon chuckled. It was dark blue, almost black, with bright-blue lines that almost looked electric running over his body and filling his eyes.

It stretched out of the pond, its body filling the room. The attacks seemed like nothing to it as it inhaled, pulling the air and the Players in the room toward it.

Its breath came out in what looked like icy flames. The very air froze as it cut through the Players. There wasn't anything that they could do against its monstrous power.

Akatol waved his hands pillars of ice formed impaling those that entered his lair.

There was no room for mercy or time to react.

Blood-red energy drained from these sacrifices. Their power seeped into Akatol, who shuddered in excitement, his eyes having a crazed look to them.

The stream went blank. The room seemed to be silent as everyone took in what they had seen.

"What level were they?" Josh asked.

"Level 100, roughly. Some might be stronger as they were passing through Opheir," Lucy said.

Esa took a sharp intake of breath and shook her head as she gripped the back of a chair.

The others in the room were also lost in their own thoughts. *Level 100 Players and they hadn't been more than a minor obstacle to Akatol.* "It looks like the other Dragons are just a half hour away from the lair." Lucy watched another video that had showed up only a few minutes ago. It showed Dragons all aiming for Akatol as they flew over the sea separating Ashal and Opheir. They would cross over the Iska in less than an hour.

It was nearly dawn as their massive bodies sailed through the air, their every motion speaking of the power they wielded. Each and every one of them looked determined.

After seeing what one of them could do, Lucy felt a thrill at seeing them.

"I hope that Dave is right in saying that they're going to fight Akatol," Josh said.

No one needed to say anything; they all agreed.

***

Denur flapped her wings. It had been a long time since she had the freedom to fly around unobstructed. In the realm that Bob had put them in, they had freedom to do as they wished. In Emerilia, they liked to keep to themselves, flying within the ring of fire so that they didn't come into conflict with anyone else.

In any other situation, she might have felt joy. Now, she felt a coldness in her actions. There was no need to speak with the rest of her family.

They flew in a V formation, riding off one another's air streams. People looked to the skies, remembering the tales of Dragons, their indomitable strength of magic and will.

"We must not give Akatol any time to create spells. He is a master at spell formation. Given enough time and the resources, he is sure to make a barrier or realm that only he controls. Make sure that you don't give him time to act," Denur said to the others through their bond.

They understood and agreed as they headed over Iska, banking slightly to bring them on a heading for Quindar and Fornau's old lair.

They didn't teleport because power usage for such massive creatures over such a large distance would have been massive. Thus, they took to the skies, using the air currents that circulated around the sea between Ashal and Opheir in a counterclockwise motion.

If they were to go straight, they wouldn't have the aid of the wind and instead be fighting it the entire time, making them tired when they got to their destination.

***

"Ah, dear wife—still she cannot see the issue with letting these creatures wander across Emerilia. We, who are stronger than the gods themselves, should be praised as such. I will show her and my family the way. Once I have cleansed Emerilia of all but the beasts, then we will be free," Akatol said to himself.

His tail connected the last circle around him. It had been written with the blood of his foes.

Nearly a hundred bodies lay around him. Many were weak, but there had been some rare talents among them. Their power now flowed through him as he closed his eyes. Light started to gather in the lines around him. Growing in their brilliance, the power in the air seemed immeasurable.

The bodies lay on their spikes, lighting up as power was pulled from them and into the vast magical circle.

"It's crude, but it will serve as a good test for things that are to come." Akatol poured out his monstrous magical reserves.

The air around him lit up with blue light. It flowed into the bloody spell formation. The light given off was visible from the entrance to the mountain.

"Absolute domain," Akatol called out. A flash of power rippled out from the mountain, spreading out over an area of ten kilometers wide in every direction.

***

"No!" Denur raged, diving toward the mountain. She saw the pass of magic; a cold and familiar feeling ran through her scales. She had seen this working before.

With her vision, she saw the magical forces finish, reaching outward. Then it seemed to recoil back inward.

Everything that was within ten kilometers was stripped of water in seconds. Trees and plants crumbled. Creatures and people died. The ground collapsed and fell apart. The lake near the mountain drained, the creatures within it having all of the water within them forcibly removed.

The water rushed toward the mountain, swirling into a sphere when it reached its top. All heat was quickly drained from it, turning it solid ice.

Denur let out a screech, turning away from the scene in front of her while the rest of her family followed.

"Mother, what do we do now?" Gelimah asked as they hovered in the air, watching the devastated area around the now ice-encapsulated mountain.

"We watch, grow our strength and find a way into his ice palace," Denur hissed.

"What is the spell he used?" Renver asked.

"It's a mix between Total Domination and Ice Palace. He cast Total Domination to take control of the land, then ripped all of the water and Mana in the area toward himself, creating an ice palace. His domination will grow in power, making his palace stronger and stronger with each passing day," Denur growled.

"The Total Domination will also make it so that anyone who goes into its area of influence will not be able to draw upon Mana from the area they are in. You can only use the Mana reserves you have. Seeing as the ice palace would take all of our power reserves and quite a bit of Fire's, anyone who broke through would then have to deal with Akatol, who will be rested and stronger than ever. Akatol gains strength as things are killed within his domain. He probably killed thousands of plants, animals, people—anything with a life-force, you get experience for killing. As his domain grows, so does his personal levels," Gelimah said with clear frustration.

All of the Dragons listened to him. He was one of the most knowledgeable; he and Malsour spent their lives learning and hiding from the world to understand the secrets of magic.

"Five of you will stay here. We will have five Dragons nearby; more will stay at the edge of the Mithsia Mountains in case they are needed and we will hollow out a mountain at the edge of Egas Nation in case we need more people to help. I will tell Fire what happened," Denur said.

"We should seek Malsour's council," Gelimah admitted.

Denur raised an eyebrow. Gelimah and Malsour were highly competitive with each other. Hearing Gelimah say that Malsour might know more than him was irregular.

"He and Dave have been working on various projects. Malsour has tried to hide it, but I have seen his interest in multiple areas. It might be an idea to see what they think. They might have something that could help us," Gelimah said.

"It looks like you are finally growing up, my son," Denur said with a slight smile.

Gelimah snorted, hiding his embarrassment.

"Once I talk to Fire, I will seek out Malsour," Denur agreed.

Chapter 6: Opening Terra

"So, we're agreed?" Josh looked to everyone who stood in the command center. Over the last two days, they had received information on the three creatures that had appeared in Emerilia, and they had planned out different ways to keep the guild entertained and working to get stronger.

Now, they were dealing with their biggest issue: opening Terra.

They had planned to do it in a few weeks, but with the sudden arrival of the three creatures from their imprisonment, it became clear that it would be better to do it sooner rather than later.

Allies and other foreign powers had approached them, looking for an embassy in Terra. They also agreed to lend a portion of their forces if they were needed for the defenses of the other nations that were allied with the Stone Raiders.

Some of them did not agree to this condition, and as such, Josh didn't believe they should be given the opportunity of joining Terra.

No one disagreed with what Josh was saying.

"Lucy, see that the messages are sent out: Terra is open to those who have rented a place here. It's time we brought this place alive." Josh smiled.

He wished that it was under a less tense circumstance, but needs must.

"Can do." Lucy opened her interface.

The others seemed to breathe a sigh of relief; they were now committed.

"Damn, it feels like we should be doing more," Dwayne complained.

"What are we going to do but make these creatures more powerful if we face them in our current state?" Kim asked.

"I know, but damn, we're the strongest guild in Emerilia and even with the other top four supporting us, we couldn't take down these beasts. Hell, we don't even know where two of them are at!" Dwayne rubbed his face and sat back in his chair.

"Dwayne, this event isn't going anywhere. We're going to have plenty of fighting later on. Now is time to do some level grinding, get our gear sorted, get used to Terra and everything that's going on. Sure, we've got some big threats lying around Emerilia, but unless they act, we get time to relax a bit. We've been fighting in the Aleph cities and facilities, then Devil's Crater and we just showed Emerilia our power. I like fighting as much as the next person, but right now, it is time to take a bit of a break. We've got a few months until the events start opening up for real. We're going to have raids going around the clock, parties out fighting and only logging off to sleep and eat and come back on." Josh smiled to Dwayne.

"Well, I can't say that doesn't sound like a hell of a lot of fun," Cassie said.

The other Stone Raiders agreed.

"The developers say that this war could even change the way that Emerilia looks, so, might be worth checking out the sights you haven't seen already. They might get messed up," Kim said.

"Well, I do have some animes to catch up on, so that would be nice," Dwayne admitted.

"See! Wait, which animes are you watching?" Josh asked with a curious glance.

"Annnd, we lost them." Lucy shook her head with an amused smile on her face.

The others chuckled as Lucy turned back to her interface. Her smile fell away.

No one noticed it, but Lucy looked nervous and scared, as if she feared that something was going to go terribly wrong. She looked as if she was scared for the POEs who might fall in the face of the prisoners' and Players' actions.

***

Kol walked through the teleport pad in Terra, turning and grumbling to those behind him. "Keep up, you lot."

The smiths of all races followed Kol as he led them out of the control room. They talked about the simple craftsmanship and the work that was around the control room. Their grumbles and complaints came to an end as they exited the control room and stepped out onto one of Terra's main streets.

They looked out over the spinning city.

There was a simple park with a small pond in it. Glowing growing towers made of soul gems dotted the city space. Apartment buildings, looking like spokes in a wheel, reached across the empty space to touch opposite walls of the cylinder. Industrial plants were turning over here and there. People were moving into the city. It was slowly coming to life, but it was clearly not complete.

Soul gem buildings were still growing here and there. In other places, Aleph automatons were making rooms, elevators, and all of the infrastructure that would be required.

The buildings were of various sizes so that one wouldn't feel contained or cramped. It truly was a growing city.

Kol smiled proudly, thinking of all that Dave had done to make this sight a reality and proud of his grandson Gurren for being a part of the guild that called this achievement their home.

"Hah! Never thought that seeing someone else's work would shut you lot up! Wait until you see what Master Grahslagg has done for our smithy!" Kol called out, continuing on his way as the smiths talked among themselves.

They moved through the streets, watching as a soul gem walkway grew between two buildings, meeting in the middle, hanging right over the main street where traders were already checking out potential storefronts.

Kol laughed as he started to smell food already being cooked, demonstrating that Dave wasn't the only entrepreneur of the lot.

Down the street, the smiths talked excitedly about the soul gem buildings, comparing them to the soul gem building that was currently taking over the Devil's Crater Smithy.

Confusion could be seen across their faces as Kol stood before a six-story soul gem building.

"Well, you going to stand there all day or are you going to get to know your new workplace a bit better?" Kol demanded, walking into the smithy while hiding his wide grin at the excited noises as the smiths rushed toward the smithy.

***

Dave and Deia walked through Terra.

"Feels like it was a lot quieter this morning," Deia said to Dave as they walked down the main street. Where there had just been open windows and bare buildings, there were now people moving about. Traders were on the streets, marking out where they would put up their stalls and sell their wares. With this many Dwarves around, taverns were already opening their doors, unable or unwilling to waste the business.

It was a busy atmosphere and a few people were frustrated, but for the most part, they were excited.

The event had shaken some people who had seen the creatures emerge, but people being people, regardless of what sub-race they were, had adopted an out-of-sight, out-of-mind mentality. They didn't think that the creatures that were currently hiding would ever come for them.

Even though there were three extremely powerful creatures loose across Emerilia or hidden in it, Dave felt an odd calm. He knew that he should be freaking the hell out, but instead he was walking through Terra, looking at what he had created in just a few months, smiling as he saw the bustle of people moving into their homes.

Among them, he saw the indentured prisoners were being moved through the city, broken up into smaller groups and given menial jobs. They had spent their whole lives training for war, but those skills didn't necessarily translate into running a city. Until they proved their abilities and that they could be trusted, manual labor was their lot.

"I think you might be right." Dave saw Deia eyeing a stall that was roasting skewers of meat. "You want one?" Dave walked over to it, patting Deia's hand that rested on his arm.

"Maybe just one," Deia admitted.

Dave laughed, smelling the sweet and savory aroma coming from the street vendor stall.

"Ah, customers! Could I interest you in some meat skewers or our other snacks?" The boy tending the stall smiled. He looked to be in his teens, but by his manners, he was well versed in how to operate the stall.

"I'll take three, please," Dave said.

"That will be three coppers, please," the boy said.

Dave pulled out the three coppers. The boy pulled three meat skewers, wrapping them and exchanging them for the money.

"Have a nice day and we look forward to your return business!" the boy said with a big smile.

Dave nodded to him and passed a skewer to Deia. She nibbled it as they walked the streets.

The walkways above would provide even more room for people to sell their wares or advertise them. The city had been designed with visitors in mind, accommodating to the needs of those just passing through.

People and supplies were flowing into the city. Already, Player and POE adventurers had come in and looked around. The idea of

Terra was great; being able to go to a city that catered to the needs of adventurers had a big pull.

"So, when will the first onos be installed?" Deia asked.

"We're going to start in a few days. We've got quests out for people to move drop pads into position within different cities. We're targeting the different places within Ashal first. They have more goods of higher quality to move faster and with the cities' limited room to grow crops, there is a real interest in not only our weapons, but our ability to supply food and crops," Dave said.

"Seems your inner businessman has come out." Deia smiled at Dave.

"That's a nice way to say I'm nerding out slightly." Dave leaned into her.

She gave him a quick kiss, placing her head against his shoulder for a second before eyeing the second skewer he was holding.

Silently, he handed it over.

"I do wonder why I got that third skewer. It was as if I knew someone who couldn't admit when they wanted more than one," Dave pondered aloud.

Deia hit Dave with the side of her hip playfully.

They walked along for a while, talking about different things. Finally, Deia asked a question as they neared the smithy.

"Do you think that your machines and creations can defeat the creatures that come out through the event?"

"I don't think that we can win with just them. Sure, there are some really powerful things that I'm working on and they could give us an advantage, but there are some that I'm hesitant to use," Dave admitted.

"Why?" Deia asked.

"We're limited in what we can do because of the Jukal. If we use something too powerful and it trips the Jukal AI, then they're going to start looking more closely at us. If they do that, they might figure out that we're not just playing their game." Dave's voice turned serious.

"I know that you're building some pretty powerful weapons and artifacts, but we use some pretty powerful magic that is comparable to what you are making," Deia said, trying to reassure him.

A heavy silence fell over them.

"A brilliant man, one of the geniuses of Earth, once said when talking about the weapon of mass destruction he had made, that the problem laid in the heart of mankind. That, if he knew what he was building, what it was to become, he would have been a watchmaker. Right now, I'm making these things, saying that I need to break the Jukal's control over our lives. I could go and pass out these weapons to people across Emerilia—a simple farmer with the strength to kill everything in five kilometers, or a person with twenty times their original power and without fear of dying. What will happen when Players find out that they're not playing a game?" As Dave's mind worked, his Intelligence took him to a dark place.

Deia squeezed his arm to try and reassure him. "So, what will you do?" Deia asked, her voice low. She knew that leaving Dave to stew in his own thoughts would lead him down a sad path.

"I will follow what countless Dwarven Master Smiths have done. I will create Weapons of Power, but I will make sure that they are limited in their number and that they are the ones to pick their users."

Deia took in a sharp breath. So far, Dave had made items that were comparable to Weapons of Power, but with one significant difference. Weapons of Power were not only created by a Dwarven Master Smith's smithing art, they were combined with the soul of the master who created them. This meant a drastic increase of power in the weapons. It also added in a fail-safe that they wouldn't work for someone who used the weapons for nefarious circumstances. Though the cost was not inconsiderable, it actually took a part of the Dwarven Master Smith's soul, much like how a summoner made a contract with the creatures bound to them. The Weapons of Power exerted their own will to create contracts with those who might use them.

Deia wanted to argue with him. Using part of his Willpower, his very soul—it was not a decision to take easily. From the look on his face, Deia knew that he had already made the decision and a part of her was proud of him. He was a brilliant man and the things that he was creating in Emerilia could bring wanton destruction. This was one way to safeguard the people of Emerilia and the future of the people.

"I understand," Deia said in a soft voice.

Dave seemed to deflate; it seemed that he had been ready for a fight. "You do?" he asked, relief in his voice.

"Yes. You are a good man, Dave Grahslagg, to not only care about the creating of weapons, but what their purpose will be. It makes me proud to call you the father of our child." She pulled him close.

He turned to face her, the two of them looking into each other's eyes.

Deia could see the stress that had been tearing Dave up from the inside. She hugged him as he pulled her close, as if fearing to ever lose her.

"Thank you," Dave said.

Those two words held emotions that made Deia bite her lower lip at what Dave's mind had been torturing him with.

"The path we walk will not be easy and we will make mistakes, but as long as we do everything in our power to make Emerilia a place for our children to live, and we can live knowing the means that we used, we will make it out of this," Deia said into Dave's ear.

He took a deep breath and nodded. "I needed that, love."

They pulled apart and looked at each other.

Deia gave him a quick kiss. "I love you."

"I love you, too," Dave said. The two of them savored hearing the other say the words.

"Now, let's go and look at that smithy of yours!" she said with a proud smile.

"This way, milady." Dave held out his arm; she wrapped hers in it, staying close to him.

***

Fornau stepped through the teleport pad, leaving Devil's Crater and arriving in Terra. "Malsour!" he said.

His great-uncle waved as he exited into Terra proper.

"How are you doing, Fornau?" Malsour wrapped him up in a hug.

"Good, good!" Fornau smiled.

"How is that sister of mine faring with your younglings?"

"She's got her hands full, but she's been a great help. Quindar needed a bit of break from it all and she's enjoying teaching the DCA aerial force how to use their abilities.

"They're getting much stronger. Yoalin has expressed an interest to come and help us as a maid and we've taken up her offer. She should be in Devil's Crater in a few days." Fornau smiled.

"Ever since Likal died, she's pined for children, but never brought herself to get another partner," Malsour said sadly. "It will be good for her to be around some younglings."

"Yes, and put Quindar's mind at ease about leaving," Fornau agreed. His eyes looked upward, finding a city above him. His eyes moved around, studying the city. It was confusing and complex and he started to get a nauseous feeling about it.

His eyes fell on growing towers and parks, soothing his mind as he took a breath. "This is incredible," Fornau said. His nausea fell away as he took in the sights of the city.

"Thanks. Come on. I've got some food and drink at my place." Malsour chuckled.

Fornau returned the smile. He had not just come here for pleasantries.

They took some of the underground carts that moved things through the city. In just a few minutes, they were at the Stone Raiders towers. They got off; magical scanners checked them as they walked into the apartments.

They made small talk until they reached Malsour's apartment. He closed the door and activated a magical code he'd made into the apartment.

"So, looks like dear old Dad is back," Malsour growled. Some of his aura leaked out as he took a seat.

"I was told that Great-grandmother messaged you?" Fornau asked.

"Yes, and she was asking for a way to defeat Dad's Total Domination and Ice Palace." Malsour sighed and rubbed the bridge of his nose.

"Well, she sent me here to check up on you. You seemed to allude to something, but never said anything specifically," Fornau said.

Malsour looked at Fornau, studying him before he sighed again. "Do I have something that might be able to break Ice Palace and kill dear old Dad? Yes. Can I give it to you? No."

"Why not?" Fornau leaned forward.

"As I was trying to explain to Mom..." Malsour paused, as if finding the words. "The two items that would be used to clear Dad from Emerilia would have a massive impact on Emerilia. There are a few things to take into account. For us Dragons, Akatol is a stain on our honor. I understand that, believe me. I was there when we tried to stop him from sacrificing half of the people on Ashal!" Malsour let out a frustrated sigh. "But this is just the start, the first round. If we use these things now, then the moderators who govern Emerilia through the Grey God will notice and they will be the ones acting. This magic is powerful. So, I cannot give you or the rest of our family these tools to end dear old Dad. That said, there are other items that we could use to weaken him."

"What?" Fornau asked.

"A magical link," Malsour said.

Fornau frowned.

"Our problem right now is that it would take so much power to take down the ice palace that it would drain our Mana reserves before we cracked it, and we can't give up on attacking it or else it will recover. We also can't recover our Mana while in the area of Total Domination. What I am suggesting is using a system similar to what the Stone Raiders use. We store energy in vault-classed soul gems. We have some Dragons outside the area of Total Domination, fueling the soul gems, while others are inside, directly attacking the ice palace, drawing from the soul gem. They can increase their Mana pool and get a symbiotic regeneration of their Mana," Malsour said. "So, one gives their power to the soul gem outside of the area of Total Domination, passing that power to the other so that they can continue their attacks and replenish their Mana."

"Exactly. Then as one Dragon gets tired, they pull back, switching out with the other, so that everyone has energy when the ice palace falls." Fornau nodded.

"It will take longer than the other option, but then we can hold those stronger powers in reserve for when we need them," Malsour pointed out.

"Why didn't you tell this to your mother?" Fornau asked.

"She wants to end Akatol here and now. She doesn't care that much about the outcome after. If you come to her with a reasonable request, she'll hear you out. I can't leave here right now; I've got work to do. Sometimes, things just have to be said and discussed in person. Also, she'll want to see this before moving ahead." Malsour pulled out a soul gem the size of his forearm and two enchanted amulets, passing them to Fornau.

"I've always wanted to be a carrier pigeon," Fornau said, sarcastically.

Malsour snorted as a small smile appeared on his lips.

***

It had been a constant rush of people and supplies moving into Terra. Few had ever been able to see inside an Aleph city. With Terra, they were able to see inside one of the legendary cities.

The soul gem buildings, roving parks, and the budding trading district made more than one noble household or trading company decide to put down roots in Terra as soon as possible.

At the same time, military units from all across Emerilia marched, rode, and sauntered into the city.

Embassies were in the same district, placed into various towers. Areas for their fighting forces had been set aside, allowing their people to train even as they stayed inside the city.

Businesses were starting out and already hawking their wares. Players from other guilds and leaders from various POE guilds came to check out the city; a number of them bought up items or visited the Grahslagg Corporation's smithy.

It boasted the membership of several Dwarven Master Smiths as well as their understudies. They could repair any item, make custom weapons and armor, and they were one of only two businesses that had buildings made from soul gems—the other being Exdar's Traders' building.

It bordered between the Stone Raiders' guild towers and the intersecting main roads, and then led out to the surrounding businesses.

Lucy smiled, thinking about Florence. She was acting not only as the manager of the trading side of the Stone Raiders in Terra, but also managing all of the leases that were being bought up across the city. She had become one of the hardest people to meet with.

"Shard, how are we looking?" Lucy had her own people out around Terra, making sure that everything went well and to deal with any difficulties from the shadows.

"It seems that everything is going relatively smooth. There have been some nobles who think a bit too highly of themselves. Also, a few brawls and some people trying to pressure others into moving to get their place. I have dispatched automatons to deal with these issues. It might be some time until people start understanding that this is a fair city and that they can't pressure and extort people as they might in other cities." Shard sounded pleased with himself.

"What about the embassies and the military forces?" Lucy pursed her lips.

"They are showing off with one another. There have been a few fights here and there, but I've issued warnings. It seems that none of the powers want to cause an incident. Having them all come in as one as you suggested has created an interesting circumstance where they are playing off one another to show that they are more committed to this cause. It has also led to quite a number of back room talks. I have not been listening in but it seems that with the constant information about the creatures that have come to Emerilia that they have started to push old issues away. The military commanders are at least having quiet talks regarding their neutrality to one another. I do believe that they are coming together," Shard said.

Lucy smiled with the praise. "I just hope that they will all work so well together, but hopefully together we can save Emerilia."

She wished like the others that they were off and fighting against the escaped prisoners. She knew the time would come and that there were battles planned for next week.

"It is one hell of a sight." Lucy grinned. Terra was coming alive. They had built it with their achievements and abilities. It made her giddy inside to see what they had done, and reassured her with what she wanted to do in the future.

Chapter 7: Class of Hard Knocks

Alkao grunted under the impacts of Anna's Air blades against his shield. He rolled to his side, using his sword to cut through her latest Air blade. A flap of his wings threw him forward.

Anna danced out of the way of his attack, bringing her sword across her body to hit him in the side.

Alkao pivoted, his wings flapping as he defended with his shield. *Right back where I started,* Alkao complained in his head.

"Okay," Anna said.

Without dropping his guard, Alkao peeked his head over his shield and saw Anna standing there, with barely any sign that she had been training for the last three hours.

"Damn minx, faster than me with your Air Affinity," Alkao grumbled. He wiped sweat from his brow before he sheathed his sword and put his shield down.

"Well, I have been practicing a lot longer than you; got some more tricks." Anna smiled impishly.

Alkao let out an amused huff and pulled out a water canteen. "You off to start training the aerial forces?"

"Yeah. Quindar is coming over to help out. How are the ground forces going?" Anna asked.

"Well, Dave sent me a message asking if Deia can teach them. Seems she's not happy with sitting still, even if she is pregnant. Also, Gurren, Lox, Induca, and Steve are heading off with Krenua and a bunch of his people to scout around Devil's Crater and go find some dungeons."

"While Dave and Malsour are messing around with magical coding and anything they can find that could cause damage." Anna rolled her eyes.

"They're your party," Alkao said with an amused look.

"Yeah, so I know just how crazy they are!" Anna said in frustration.

Alkao laughed at Anna's expression. "I think that we will soon have need for both strong and crazy people," Alkao said after a few moments.

"How go the preparations?"

Alkao picked up his shield, hanging it over his shoulder. "With all of the people coming through Devil's Crater to go to our dungeons or venture into the wilds of Ashal, we have thankfully made quite a bit of money. I've already placed a number of orders with the Aleph, mage's guild, and Dwarves for different items to increase our defenses, from grand magical workings, to Dwarven artillery and Aleph Mana bombs.

"Dave and Malsour are working on an idea for a series of Mana barriers to protect the keeps, Unity, and settlements and a grand barrier the likes of which hasn't been seen before to cover all of the crater from long-range attacks."

"They certainly love to make different items," Anna agreed.

Alkao could see the curiosity on her face. "Wondering if they can make you another wondrous blade or set of armor?" Alkao teased.

"I have all of the gifts that I might need, but they are constantly coming up with new weapons," Anna said with a troubled look.

"Makes me happy that they're on our side," Alkao said.

Anna made a noise of agreement. "Well, I'm off to train some more thick-skulled idiots. Have fun being King," Anna said with a suddenly bright smile.

"Thank you." Alkao's voice was dry. He had been made the King of Devil's Crater in their time of crisis and he understood it. Though he had gained his prestige through fighting, not by doing paperwork that currently threatened to choke him, he understood the need to complete it and dutifully fulfilled his role as his people followed him.

***

"Morning!" Lox said as he, Gurren, Induca, and Steve walked up to the group of fighters with Krenua.

"Ready to go dungeon spelunking?" Steve asked.

"Steve, that's when people climb through caves, crevasses, and that stuff. We're dungeon clearing." Gurren sighed.

"Yes, we are ready," Krenua said to Lox, as he and his four other leaders moved to join them.

"Good! We'll head northwest through the hunting grounds and then into the dungeon there. Probably take us a few hours to get through the hunting areas," Lox said.

"How are you lot for gear?" Induca asked.

"We have rations, armor, and our weapons," Krenua said.

Induca shared a look with Gurren and Lox.

"Can spring for some Health and Mana potions. They've got low Mana pools and their armor is decent enough if we go to some low-level dungeons," Gurren said, having a conference with the others. Steve kicked the dirt, bored.

"We couldn't take your potions. There is no way that we would be able to pay you back," Krenua said, embarrassed by his own words.

"Gurren and I have been shield bearers for nearly forty years combined. We've got plenty of gold. This is supposed to be training. For that, you need the proper gear," Lox said. It was clear he wasn't going to be overturned on this.

"Thank you," Krenua said. He meant it. He would owe them a favor, but having Health and Mana potions was not something that they could buy with their salaries yet.

"Always love a bit of shopping!" Induca smiled.

The rest of Party Zero groaned.

Lox, Gurren, and Steve continued having a quiet and annoyed conversation as they headed for Unity's marketplace.

Induca dropped back to meet Krenua and his people. "So, any of you magic users?"

"I have some limited ability. Josen is a beginning healer and Edlai uses Earth magic to enhance her Strength," Krenua said.

"Good! Looks like I can pass some tips and tricks on to the younger generation as well!" She winked at them.

Krenua looked at Induca and frowned slightly. She looked as though she were just twenty years old.

"Don't you know it's rude to try to guess a lady's age?" Induca caught his eyes.

"I'm sorry—just, it's hard to think of you as being older than twenty."

"Oh, you're so cute!" Induca said.

Krenua blushed and scratched his head awkwardly.

Induca looked highly amused, but stopped herself from teasing him more. "Okay, so first of all, let's see you use your basic spells, one at a time. Then, we can figure out a way to increase your power." Induca watched their spells as they walked through Unity.

The city had exploded outward: houses ran in orderly lines, and four roads led out of the city, through the gates and out into the different sections of Devil's Crater. Building within the original area of Unity would be complete in a month or two. Already, some Dwarven contractors and Fornau were looking at adding another ring around the city separated by the moat, creating a layered defense.

Walking through the city, one ran into high-leveled Players and adventurers. Guild buildings dotted the landscape, with people from all races moving between the buildings.

Devil's Crater offered protection and access to dungeons and high-leveled beast hunting that few other empires, kingdoms, nations and city states of Ashal could provide.

The marketplace was filled with hawkers selling their goods. People were everywhere and traders were doing a brisk business of buying rare items and resources, selling all common items that people might need, as well as supplies for adventurers.

Induca watched the three who were working on their magical talents.

"Okay, there are three main components to spell casting: first is Willpower, second is your knowledge, and third is your Intelligence." Induca's playfulness from earlier had turned into a no-nonsense lecturing mode.

"All three of these things are inextricably linked. To cast a spell, you need to first know the spell, then you need to have the mana pool to fuel it and the willpower to recover that mana and not go into mana fatigue from casting it. The more knowledge you have of the spell, then the more you can change it to have a greater or lesser effect or even change that effect. With more willpower, you can cast more spells of high mana cost faster. With a high intelligence, you can cast more powerful spells."

Induca looked to Krenua. "Krenua, you have a low Mana pool, but you have a high natural Intelligence which means you have a larger mana pool and it's easier for you to understand more complex ideas. You have limited confidence in spell casting and haven't practiced it enough to become comfortable with it. Use simple spells as much as possible, constantly if you can. It will increase all three aspects of spell casting and will allow you to have insights into other spells you can mutate off your own."

"Insights into spells we can mutate?" Josen asked in a confused tone, as if not understanding what the words were trying to allude to.

"Oh, I do so love dealing with new students!" Induca clapped her hands with a big smile on her face. "So, where do spells come from?" She looked at her group.

"From other mages," Edlai said.

"Where do mages get their spells from?" Induca asked.

"Old texts, awakening to their Mana, and watching natural processes of the world?" Krenua sounded unsure.

"These are all ways to learn spells, but these spells will not be as strong as a spell that you come up with yourself," Induca said.

"Ourselves?" Josen asked.

"Okay, so take your healing magic for example. When you heal someone, what do you do?" Induca asked.

"I cast the spell, supplying as much Mana as it needs to heal the wound." Josen shrugged.

"Jules would have a fit if she heard you say that." Induca shook her head. "Yes, you can use a general spell that speeds up recovery, though if you focus on the broken parts of a person you can heal them faster." Induca looked at the five DCA officers who stood in a circle with her, all their attention on her.

"If I have a broken bone through the skin, if I was to have the bone set, then used a spell that promotes just bone growth, it would be much more effective and cost less Mana. Then, another spell can heal the muscles, another for blood vessels, another for tendons, and another for skin. All of these spells are derivatives of that original healing spell. It is their precision that has changed. You use less Mana and instead of trying to focus on a large spell to do everything, you're using a series of limited spells. Much easier to have confidence in putting small things together instead of everything in one go!"

"How can we refine our spells and change them?" Josen asked.

"You need to practice. Go check out people who are wounded, look over books on medical information, and study spells that heal people and compare it with your own spells. Take what you know, adapt it to what you need and test it out," Induca said.

"What about other spells that don't deal with healing?" Edlai asked.

Induca frowned before she held up her hand. A ball of flame appeared.

"This is a simple Fire spell, but if I adjust it," Induca's flame extended out into a spear, "then you can make it change forms at will. Mana is a fuel source for anything and everything you can create with magic. Spells are the way to direct that fuel. Many are scared to modify their spells because of backlash. This is why practice is important! The more you practice, the better you will come to understand the spell you are using. If you do not understand it, then how can you expect to go onto higher and stronger spells? When you are training with weapons, do you not train your body first so that when you pick up a sword, you already have the basics of movement and fighting to draw from?"

Krenua rubbed his chin in thought. His most basic and familiar spells were a basic flame spell that he could create on his forefinger and a shadow spell that he could use to cover his hands.

The Fire spell was good for lighting fires and the shadow spell was one of a series that he had bought in order to become a better stealth fighter. He had gathered a number of these shadow spells, spending a small fortune on them. Now, with Induca's words, he understood how to adapt the spells outside of their normal uses. He looked at his hand. Shadows seemed to creep out from between his fingers. He closed his eyes and focused on the spell's formation.

As he did, he tried to understand and test out the spell some more. He realized that it didn't feel familiar. He knew how to cast it, but it was as if he had a third limb that was working on its own. He had little understanding of how the spell worked.

He opened his eyes and looked to Induca.

"Having a conference?" Lox asked as Steve and Gurren followed.

"Just a little bit of magical intervention. We need to make one more stop." Induca led them down the street.

"While we walk, I've got presents!" Steve said.

"You've got presents? You couldn't fit in the damn doorway!" Gurren complained good-naturedly as he pulled out Health potions.

Krenua's eyes went wide as he looked at the Health and Mana potions. They were high-grade potions, capable of bringing someone back from life-threatening injuries. Each person got two of the high-grade healing potions and a half-dozen larger potion bottles that carried a medium-grade healing potion, and then four of the medium-grade Mana potions.

They all thanked the trio, storing the items away in their pouches of holding. The Aleph had used their manufacturing expertise to reduce the cost and increase the speed of manufacture of simple items of holding and the DCA had taken advantage of this fact.

Things had certainly changed in Unity.

They quickly arrived at the mage's college building that was attached to the mage's guild.

Induca went in, quickly coming out with five spell books. "Read these." Induca passed the books out.

They took them gingerly. Spell books were a rare commodity still for the DCA.

"Induca, this is too much," Krenua said.

"Ah, just give it a read. We've got plenty of gold and not much to really spend it on. You all listened to the ramblings of an old lady and this is your reward. Also, it will help develop your magical ability faster." Induca crossed her arms and tapped her foot. "Now, you going to keep me waiting?" she demanded, trying to look cross but it was clear she was joking.

Krenua opened the spell book.

Spell Book: Arcane Sight

Do you wish to learn the spell: Arcane Sight?

Y/N

"Yes," Krenua and the others said as the prompt came up. The pages started to turn, slow and then faster. Ideas and thoughts raced through their minds. The back of the book closed with a crash and turned to dust, the magical resources of the book now spent.

"Good. Arcane sight is the basis of a good understanding of magic. It will also help to keep your soldiers who know magic in line." Lox moved forward. Gurren, Steve, and Induca followed while watching the DCA officers blinking and rubbing their heads at the sudden influx of information.

"Try out the arcane sight. We're pretty safe in here to try it out; just don't look at Steve too much!" Induca said.

"My handsome face really is too much for some to handle." Steve looked back and gave them an exaggerated wink.

"Seriously, why do we keep on bringing this lump of scrap metal around?" Induca joked.

People moved out of their way, staring at the members of Party Zero and the DCA officers. Krenua hadn't noticed the looks that Party Zero gathered before.

They were some of the most powerful fighters in the Stone Raiders, if not the strongest. They were a bunch of goofs who lived to train and fight, but they were also just people. To those they passed, they were idols or famous figures.

Yet, the four of them didn't care for the looks or mutterings as they passed. Krenua felt their excitement as they joked and played around. What was fame if they couldn't play? They were excited to clear the dungeons!

"Arcane sight," Krenua said. He had not yet come to call on spells without an incantation or a pre-made spell formation. His world seemed to change as he slowed his pace, lest he run into something.

The light of the world dimmed as clouds of blue Mana energy moved through the air. It was focused in people and in magical objects, showing Mana moving through people's veins and stored within their bodies. As he looked closer at magical items, he could see the runes that made the items work.

He and his fellow officers looked around in wonder at the world of magic. It was as if a whole new realm had been opened up to them. It was a beautiful display, leaving them all stunned.

"Now that you've got that sight working, test out your spells. If you don't have a spell, let me know and I can give you a simple one." Induca looked to them.

All knew some simple spell, whether through a magical awakening or through a spell book. Everyone thought of being some great magician or powerhouse, so it was natural to dabble in magic, even if it was just for a few tricks.

Krenua followed, not paying attention to the outside world, following their four guides blindly as he called up his Fire spell. Krenua let out a sharp breath. Not only was there flame, but there was a small spell formation that revolved around the tip of his forefinger.

He studied the different symbols. He didn't truly understand what they did, so he started increasing his Mana input and decreasing; he watched as the symbols changed. He increased and decreased the size, applying multiple different effects on the flame.

It was incredible! Now he understood how people could spend centuries studying the mysteries of magic, trying to figure out its secrets and propagate their own ideas. It was amazing to see.

Krenua looked up from his flame, feeling a headache come on from using the arcane sight and flame spell for so long. He looked to the Party Zero members. Lox and Gurren's armor practically glowed with runic lines of power.

His eyes moved to Induca. Her skin seemed to radiate power, the Mana in her so dense that it made Krenua wonder what manner of spells she could call on. Then his eyes moved to Steve. At first, there were just a few tracings of runes, concentrated on the joints of his body. Then the arcane sight pierced through those layers.

Krenua nearly fell over with the brightness of the runes that made up Steve. It was as beautiful as it was powerful.

Krenua looked away, his eyes burning as he deactivated his arcane sight.

"When your Mana pools fill back up, you can start checking out your spells again. Unless we're eating or sleeping, work on your magical perception. With you Demons, you have great Strength and Agility, but where other races gain ten points to their Mana pool for every increase in Intelligence, you only get five. Work on that precision! Also, these will passively work on your Mana pool and get you used to Mana drain." Induca tossed them necklaces.

"Induca, you have given us many gifts. How can we repay you?" Krenua held the simple amulet with runes on it.

"Get stronger. We're going to be facing a lot of enemies in the future side-by-side. It's been awhile since we've trained people and you look like a good bunch of candidates. The stronger you are and the more you learn, the more you can pass onto the rest of the DCA and strengthen it. You're our allies. Would it not be natural that we wished our allies were as strong as possible, especially in these dark times?" Induca asked.

Gurren and Lox looked backward.

“And don’t worry, we’ll show you how to really fight with those swords and shields,” Lox said with a wide smile.

“Thank you,” Krenua said.

“No worries. It’s always good to be able to pass on our secrets and training others is good fun. Think of your debt already paid if you are able to learn something on this trip.” Lox smiled and the others nodded.

“Very well. Then I guess we should get a move on for this dungeon!” Krenua smiled, excited by the possibility to increase his own strength.

“That’s the spirit!” Steve yelled.

“Follow me!” Lox picked up into a jog. Even though he was nearly half the height of the Demons, Lox’s speed was high even with all his gear on.

The rest of Party Zero and the DCA officers took off at a run, quickly exiting Unity and heading out of the cleared area around it and into the largely untouched forest that lay in the northwestern section of Devil’s Crater.

The sounds of the city were left behind as the sounds of nature—animals running between cover, hunting, or becoming still as they passed—surrounded them. The air was colder, with a touch of dampness in the slightly swampy area.

Krenua and the other officers thought that they had good Stamina, but they were breathing heavy within five minutes under Party Zero’s speed.

Suddenly, they slowed to a crawl. They all stopped, gathering around and getting low.

“I’ve got this one.” Steve’s arm turned into a bolt thrower as he moved off. Even with his size, he was able to move almost silently through the forest.

Krenua watched in bewilderment.

Moments later, there was the sound of the bolt thrower firing. A creature's roar tore through the forest before stopping midway.

"Got it." Steve stood up from behind some cover. He swept forward, and the others moved with him.

"Check to make sure that nothing sneaks up on us," Lox ordered.

Krenua pointed to two officers, pointing in directions for them to watch. They nodded and disappeared into the underbrush, looking for any other animals that might be attracted by the spilled blood and noises.

Krenua shifted to the other side, moving around the beast that had been slain. His eyes went wide at seeing the Level 93 asamp.

They clung to trees, looking like branches. When prey passed, they swung down and would shoot out a razor-sharp projection from one end, stabbing into its victim. Barbs would keep them attached as the asamp injected venom and pulled its sucker up, drinking the life blood of its victim.

They were hard to spot and harder to kill, with their bodies being as hard as rock.

Steve's bolt had come in along the side of the tree, hitting the asamp where it connected with the tree and its brain was located.

A Level 10 asamp was a great source of materials for alchemists and crafters. *A Level 93?* Krenua whistled, thinking of how much the creature could reach at auction.

Lox and Gurren talked with each other as Steve bagged the asamp.

"Okay, let's move out. We've been given a quest to clear out a path through this region as well as a number of bounties for different creatures around here. Hope you brought your A-game. If we can get this done, then there's some good gold in it before we even get to the dungeons," Lox said.

Krenua and the other DCA officers smiled.

They had decent pay from the DCA as well as room and board, but the government didn't have all that much gold to spare. If they were able to gain some gold and resources from these bounties and such, it would help them get their own custom weapons and work on their fighting skills or get better meals.

"We're going to rotate people through positions. Induca and Steve will be scouts. Gurren and I will take down the creatures. All of you DCA types will rotate through." Lox's voice was loud enough so that the scouts who were out around the area where the asamp had died could hear. "Good! Krenua, sort out who you want where. We'll move out in ten minutes!"

Induca and Steve moved in the dungeon's direction, taking over the scout's positions while Krenua raced back to give his people their new positions.

***

Lox and Gurren walked through the forest, joking and laughing. The DCA officers had been on edge since the first asamp; they'd encountered a number of them since the first. Lox and Gurren took a DCA officer up each time, studying the creature and then letting them have the first attack on it.

The Dwarves both carried heavy crossbows in their bags of holding that could break through even the normal skin of the asamps, not just their weak points.

It had restored confidence in the DCA officers and they had learned a lot from the veteran warriors.

Induca showed the scouts different ways to detect the enemy but mainly focused on magic. Steve joked around and talked about magical coding.

The four of them had a great background of information; being able to share it was exciting to them.

"Damn, I'm going to be a weapons trainer in my old age," Lox snorted with a smile as they walked past the three-quarter marker between where they had entered the forest and the dungeon they were aiming for.

"What did you say?" Gurren blinked. The map rapidly updated with different landmarks. Gurren had used his surveyor skill to update their maps.

"It's actually kind of fun teaching others about fighting. Satisfying, you know," Lox said.

They had been warclan leaders and shield bearers what felt like a lifetime ago. There was nearly ten years between their ages, but with the long lives of Dwarves, it was normal to have much older and younger friends and that was what they had become. Through their training of Stone Raiders in Cliff-Hill, to their battles side-by-side and adventures across Emerilia, they had become as close as brothers.

"Making me feel old for you." Gurren harrumphed.

"We're all getting old," Lox complained.

"Not me!" Gurren said proudly.

Lox snorted. "Remind me of that brash Max."

"If only I was so lucky," Gurren said with a sad smile, remembering Max, who'd died at Boran-al's Citadel.

For a bit, they walked in silence as their newest students joined them.

"Okay, now let's see how you fight!" Lox pushed the sad thoughts away.

***

"Dungeon, I'm home!" Steve singsonged as they exited the woods to the clearing around the dungeon. This one wasn't in the cliffs around Devil's Crater like many, but was simply a sloping path that rose up into a clearing in the forest.

They had killed a number of rare creatures and gathered some herbs that they had seen on the guild's quest boards.

The Stone Raiders' Guild needed gold with their expansion and with the DCA officers getting some good spending money, it would make more units think about going out into the wilds to increase their skills and their fortunes.

Lox might look like a simple gruff Dwarf, but he was a thinking Dwarf!

"I swear, if you start singing that damned seven Dwarves crap, I'll break your actuators so you can only walk on your tiptoes!" Lox hated Steve's tone-deaf singing that would make a baby rabbit want to cry.

"I would be the prettiest ballerina," Steve said in a dejected voice.

"Why do we always get the metal-brained monkey?" Gurren sighed. He pulled out a helmet from his bag and put it on his head.

"'Cause we got hit on the head too many times as children," Lox said in a sorrowful voice.

Steve snickered at this. He changed his arms through their different functions to make sure that they all worked before he grabbed the axe on his back. It came free with a scraping on metal.

All of the DCA looked at the massive weapon.

"Hello, honey. You missed me? I know you have. Coochie, coochie coo." Steve moved his finger on the back of the large axe head as if petting the underside of a kitten's chin.

The DCA officers looked to the Party Zero members.

Induca shrugged while Lox and Gurren checked their swords and shields and then one another's armor as if they had done it thousands of times before.

"What you looking at? You some master mages in disguise or real fighters?" Lox ground out. "Now, you've been supplied with these weapons and armor. Are you going to let down Devil's Crater and let it go to shit? Front and center, one line, arm's breadth apart! Weapon and armor inspection!"

Lox might not be their commander, but the way he talked seemed to overwrite the officer's way of thinking as their bodies moved into position without conscious thought.

Induca lightly stretched, checking the potions and gear in her belt and hot bar before she went over to Steve to see whether he needed anything checked.

Lox and Gurren moved through the five DCA officers, giving a lesson on how to properly perform inspections on gear, what were flaws, how to do minor repairs and maintenance. It took an hour before they were done, and now the officers saw their weapons and armor in a whole new light.

"Okay, now I think you're ready to venture down." Lox looked to Gurren, who nodded.

"This is how we're going to do it: three of you up front, one of us behind you. We will advance slowly and carefully, discover the enemies, make a plan and carry it out. You will be up at the front, so don't rely on us to save you if we run into a situation. This dungeon hasn't been scouted, so slow and steady through here."

With that said, Lox looked around at them all. His stoic expression turned into a grin. "Well, let's clear us out this dungeon then!"

Krenua advanced at the front with two of his officers on either side. Behind them was Steve. He smiled as he moved his axe back and forth slowly.

They advanced into the dungeon. It had a faint musty smell; water could be heard dripping in the distance. It quickly became darker in the dungeon as it went lower.

Krenua held up his hand as he heard a noise ahead of him. He moved up slowly, careful to not make a sound.

A corner blocked him from seeing what was ahead. He peeked past it to see that the tunnel opened up into a larger cavern with three different tunnels breaking off from it.

The tunnels were secondary to the fourteen timber wolves that had made the intersection their home, burrowing into the walls to make their dens.

At their lowest stage, timber wolves were just slightly larger than regular wolves. They had some control over Earth magic to enhance their strength and their hide. Their coats were colored brown, with flecks of green. At higher levels, they grew to a monstrous size. Their fur could harden to look like the bark of a tree and they could call on vines and branches to grow from their body to help them in a fight. They were stronger, faster, and they could interact with their Earth magic by instinct.

These were only mid-grade timber wolves at Level 120, nearly sixty levels lower than the lowest DCA officer in the party.

"Timber wolves; looks like this is their den. About fourteen of them that I can see," Krenua said into the party chat. They could talk as loudly as they wanted to through the party chat without fear of anyone hearing them and also blocking outside noises to a degree when they were fighting.

Krenua started using his arcane sight; it had come to him by reflex now. Even with a day of practicing the spell, he had come to have a much higher understanding and appreciation of what was needed to be a mage.

"Good. Pull back," Lox said.

They reached the rest of the party waiting for them a few meters back.

"These are easy opponents for you lot." Lox gave them a confident look. "Three of you across the dungeon—use your shields and swords. Slow and easy."

In minutes, Krenua and the two officers who had been scouting with him were moving up toward the timber wolves. Edlai and Josen were behind them, with Steve and the rest of the party behind them.

They were half the way up the tunnel from the bend that they had scouted from when three bolts tore through the air. Steve's bolts took out two timber wolves and wounded a third.

"Charge! Momentum is winning—losing it is death!" Lox yelled out.

The officers yelled and pushed forward.

The wolves let out their howls, rushing to meet the attackers who had entered their homes.

The DCA officers barely stayed on their feet as their shields crashed into the timber wolves. Only by running forward were they able to have enough momentum to stay upright.

"Get down low! Second rank, get your shields over top of them. In battle, it's not going to be all hit and run. Sometimes you will just have to fight it out!" Lox barked.

"Three inches of your blade is your enemy's death. Four inches of steel means you don't have a weapon!" Gurren yelled.

Krenua heard their calm voices. Even though they were fighting for their lives right now, their confidence and calm made him relax as his sword continued to dart out.

His original apprehension and fear dimmed as he stopped simply reacting according to the training he had gained with the DCA and started to think about his actions. The timber wolves' fighting style was to pounce on their enemies. As such, their forelegs got caught on the DCA officers' shields, leaving their stomachs open to the officers' blades.

"Aim where you're hitting. Don't just stab wildly—you'll only anger them more." Krenua tried to imitate the calm of Lox and Gurren's voice.

In minutes, the last of the wolves were put down, their green-brown pelts now red with blood.

Krenua and his officers stood from their fighting stances, a look of relief on their faces.

"You killed the animals and now you're taking a break. When you've killed something on the field of battle, are you just going to stand around holding your privates, thinking you're the gods' greatest gift? There's three entrances to here. Who knows what these wolves woke up or alerted?" Lox asked, his voice firm.

The officers winced at their own actions, quickly organizing themselves and moving to watch the three corridors.

"Steve, Induca, and I will take your spots," Lox said after a few minutes of letting them reflect on what they had done. "Go, see Gurren."

The officers moved to Gurren as quickly as possible, trying their best to look like the professionals they were.

"Who here knows how to field dress a kill?" Gurren asked.

Josen and her fellow Beast Kin Gola put up their hands.

"Good—get started on those ones. Waste not, want not. They'll catch a pretty penny in Unity. Also, when you're in the field, having a bit of fresh meat is sure to rally the troops after days or weeks of moving through forests and rough terrain," Gurren said. "Now, the rest of you, watch here."

Gurren taught them how to check the creatures, remove their offal and talked about ways to use them in the field.

Then, they moved forward again through the leftmost corridor. If they always took the corridor to the right or left, then they would always know their way out of a place without having to check their mini-map.

They killed more timber wolves and a selection of devil wisps, creatures that looked like red floating motes of light and attacked with lightning. Three of the officers had been stunned before Induca finished the wisps off in a single attack.

The entire time, they were learning. It wasn't like when they had worked in formations or lessons. Everything that Party Zero talked about had been tried and tested. They were veterans in their field.

The DCA officers were all part of the Red Hands force. They were meant to be the best of the best. They were the strongest who had earned a place in the Black Hands and then their fellows' admiration had raised them to officers. They lived to be out in the field, to be putting their skills to use and developing new ones. Even if they were tired, they pushed forward, eager to show off their strength and abilities.

They had been moving through the dungeon for a number of hours when Lox called a break.

"Get some food and water into you. Remember that you and your people are only mortal beings. You can't go forever and neither can they. You need to stay in top condition at all times. Down here, not being rested and ready can lead to a fatal mistake." Gurren pulled out a sandwich.

"I'm going to scout ahead," Induca said.

"I'll come with. Maybe we'll run into a big beastie." Steve had no need to eat and Induca's Endurance was so high, hunger didn't really affect her.

Chapter 8: Devil Crater's New Residents

Quindar floated in mid-air as if it were as natural as standing. DCA aerial troops moved in formation through the sky. Different groups practiced aerial formations through mock combat.

Others dove over a designated drop zone, using their armor's ability to create spearheads to safely practice dropping Mana bombs. Others fought one another with their swords and weapons built into their armor and forearms.

"Looks all a bit chaotic." Anna floated over to Quindar with a smile on her face.

"Yeah, it looks that way at least."

To the untrained eye, it would look like madness but to Quindar and Anna, they could see the various formations working together to pull off the complicated movements within the air.

"Nothing is as bad as how my family are when they get to training outside. Now, that is one hell of a sight to see." Quindar grinned.

"Oh, I bet," Anna said. Wind curled around the lower half of her body, keeping her aloft.

"Their aerial movement isn't bad but they are getting a bit overconfident. I'm thinking of facing them off against some experienced ground forces to make the point that even if more mobile, they are still quite vulnerable," Quindar said.

"Agreed. There is a growing rivalry between the two groups. Tempering that, so that they push one another forward to outdo the other, would be advantageous," Anna agreed. "I'll get with Kala and see what she says."

A shadow passed over the sun as Efri and Malkur's flying forms moved to greet the two instructors. Their large wings flapped beside them as they came into a hover next to them.

"So, what new training are we going to be putting our people through?" Malkur asked.

"We're going to have you face off against the ground forces to see how you do. I see a lot of smiles out there. Nerves will keep your people alive—overconfidence will get them killed as fast as diving into the ground," Quindar said.

Malkur nodded solemnly. "Understood," he said, straightening up in mid-air.

"Good. Then we'll go and see what Kala thinks. It's been some time since I saw that ornery old bear!" Anna laughed.

Quindar smiled as the air shifted around her and distorted with heat. Barely visible flames appeared on her feet as she shot forward through the skies; Anna tilted, following as Malkur and Efri's wings beat rapidly to keep up with the two trainers.

They had been training outside of Unity. If their people missed, they didn't want them to hit any of the surrounding buildings or people who moved through the city. There was also a lot of air traffic with a large amount of the population having the ability to fly.

Kala and her forces were also outside of Unity for similar reasons. They had training camps in every sector of Devil's Crater to get her people used to the different terrains.

They had also become much stronger in their fighting, meaning they needed to keep them away from civilians who might try to fly overhead or pass the training barracks in Unity—they could easily be killed by the secondary effects of her troops.

Quindar used her far sight to watch the troops. Kala was with a group fighting in the farming section of Devil's Crater. They were moving with shields over their heads, closing between two groups, trying to use their strength to overpower the other.

Then there were individual sparring areas where people were fighting in small groups. In the largest training area, DCA soldiers patrolled the border between the farms and the hunting area of the crater.

She watched as a group of soldiers stalked their patrolling fellows. It would lead to the patrols being more attentive and allow the stalkers to improve their ability to follow the enemy and strike when they were weak or distracted.

"Seems the more I watch the DCA, the more similarities I see with hunters instead of simple soldiers," Quindar said.

A massive bear walked up and down the fighting square where groups were clashing. She had a large war hammer on her back as she yelled out instructions.

Anna led the way, moving over to the training area.

Kala looked up. Seeing the four arrivals, she gave instructions to her officers who moved among the fighters, giving pointers and watching them to see how they could improve. Kala stepped away from the fighting, drinking from a canteen on her hip as the four came in to land in front of her.

"So, what brings you bunch of bird wannabes over to my fine establishment?" Kala asked with a happy grin.

"Good to see you, too, Kala," Anna said dryly.

"Been awhile since I saw you. We've got to spar sometime soon. I've been working on ways to tan your ass," Kala said with confidence.

"Like you've been able to do that in four hundred years!" Anna crossed her arms.

"Hey! I was asleep for nearly three hundred of them! But, seriously, you coming over to teach this lot how to fight with their Affinity?"

"I'm still bogged down with teaching people how to fight in the air, though I know that my friend Deia might be over. She's getting a bit stir-crazy with not doing anything. She's a really damn fine swordswoman and she uses her Fire element in her attacks. She's as good as me, if not better," Anna admitted.

"Oh, is that so?" Kala cocked her head to the side. Anna was not one to waste praise on someone.

"She uses her Affinity as if it's an extension of herself. She's not as fast as me, but I think that she will reach my stage with enough time. It will be good for your people to get some more training from her, and she can grow her understanding of her fighting."

Kala made an interested noise. "I will definitely look out for her in the future."

"We also came to see if you and yours would be interested in fighting the aerial forces. They're getting a bit cocky and cocky can lead to them making mistakes. Might also be a good point to bring them down a few notches," Quindar said.

"I thought you were one of those cocky air lovers. Seems that I was wrong." Kala smiled.

"Ah, well, *I* could beat you rocks anytime of the day, but not everyone can be as powerful as me." Quindar smiled daintily.

Kala let out a laugh. "Come, us ladies have lots to discuss. You two, don't fall over in a stiff breeze. Go and start sparring with each other. All that paperwork is making you soft," Kala said to Efri and Malkur.

"We have a lot of work to..." Malkur started.

"Go spar, or else I'll remind you of just how well I trained you lot." Kala's face hardened.

Malkur and Efri straightened their posture. Kala might be the same rank as them, but she was still their trainer who had engraved the fear of higher ranks and her own temper into their very souls.

"Yes, General Kala," Efri said.

"Good. I will be watching. Give it your all. Make a good demonstration for this bunch." Kala waved to her people who were training across the fields.

Chapter 9: Wasn't This Supposed to be Easy?

Lox looked over the officers as they advanced through the dungeon located in Devil's Crater.

Right now, they had to watch out for the officers. With being in actual life-and-death situations, they were able to put their different skills and spells to the test. The chance that they could die was high, but it made for the best training situation. They could go further than before with the confidence of Party Zero's people being there, but they had to be careful to not exceed their limits.

A screech rang out through the tunnels they were walking through; a howl of a timber wolf followed as Lox gripped the hilt of his sword.

"What the hell was that?" one of the officers asked.

"Timber wolf and goblin." Gurren looked to Lox.

The Dwarves' hatred toward goblins was an almost ingrained instinct. There had been many times when goblins had broken into Dwarven tunnels and mountains, creating havoc with their large numbers and twisted bodies.

The timber wolf and goblin came into sight.

Goblin rider

Level 241

Timber wolf mount

Level 210

"Damn, is everything in here in the top tier of strength?" Lox muttered under his breath.

The timber wolf's hide was turning from its earthern colors to a bark-like texture. Stirrups had formed in the wood for the goblin to ride.

The goblin was straighter, with a hint of intelligence in its eyes. It carried a crude spear, but Lox could see that the material was not as rudimentary as those that the goblins around Mithsia Mountains used.

"It's got an ebony spearhead," Gurren hissed.

"Well, then we're just going to have to liberate it from the goblin." Lox turned his sword in his hands. "Steve," Lox called out.

Steve braced himself and his arm changed to his bolt thrower. He let loose, but the goblin ducked down lower on the wolf.

The wolf's hide was broken and scratched in places, with only a few of the bolts making it through and sticking into the timber wolf.

"Freaking running tree!" Steve yelled out.

"Brace yourselves, dammit!" Gurren yelled. They wouldn't make it out in front of the officers before the wolf reached them.

The officers braced themselves as the timber wolf rushed in.

It hit like a battering ram, throwing two of the officers as the goblin's spear darted outward.

Induca created an explosion, throwing an officer back so that they were hit in the shoulder instead of having the spearhead open their neck.

The goblin and timber wolf were pushed to the side, crying out at the heat and force of the explosion.

Lox and Gurren charged forward. Gurren's shield stopped the goblin's spear cold before it tried to impale another officer.

Then the goblin was past them; it used its feet to get the wolf to turn and face them again.

The wolf had a faint green hue around it as it channeled its Earth Affinity. Its muscles bulged and its hide became harder as it turned and leaped forward at the party. With a squeal from the goblin, the timber wolf surged forward.

Lox and Gurren turned, bracing themselves next to each other. Their shields clanged together and then slammed into the ground. They had lived with their swords and shields for the majority of their lives, standing next to each other for nearly a decade. Their minds operated as one.

"It's going to buck up over us. Steve, be ready!" Lox called out.

The wolf seemed to hear them and added on more speed.

The goblin chittered angrily, riding its wolf with one hand, the other holding its spear ready.

The wolf slammed into their shields. Lox and Gurren easily kept it at bay. Their blades flashed forward as one, cutting the timber wolf's rear legs as it went up their slightly angled shields and over the top.

Steve let out a roar; his axe flashed as it came across on the timber wolf.

The goblin had the presence of mind to hold off trying to penetrate the Dwarves' shields and instead his spear darted out to hit Steve in the head.

The wolf's hit points hit zero as it crashed down to the ground.

The goblin's leg was trapped under the timber wolf. It made to escape as a bolt of flame cut through its head, leaving a cauterized hole through its forehead. It slumped over, dead.

"Check for injuries. Steve, watch that hallway. Induca, support!" Lox moved to the officers, who were getting off the ground.

***

Krenua quickly moved to check on his people.

He had been tossed aside by the strength and speed of the timber wolf. Unlike the Dwarven shields, theirs did not stick into the ground to aid them. They were much simpler, made to move fast and be agile more than a defensive wall.

He felt a little dizzy, but he could go on. He stumbled, gathering up his gear before he checked on Edlai, who had also been thrown.

Josen stopped him and looked in Krenua's eyes. "Concussion," Josen diagnosed.

"Give him a good swig of the medium Health potion; be right as rain." Lox moved to Edlai. "Okay, I'm going to have to set this, then I can get you a potion and you'll be right as rain."

"Su-ure, wait!" Edlai yelled as there was a sickening noise of bone being put back into place. Edlai cried out as Lox held the arm steady and poured Health potion on it.

The arm started to heal rapidly, and Edlai's yells lessened as the pain fell away.

"Be good to go in a few minutes," Lox said in a reassuring voice.

Josen gave Krenua a Health potion. Krenua took back a good swig of it. He felt fine, but he was a bit fuzzy, though he wasn't about to go against Lox's instructions. He handed the potion back to Josen, who capped it and put it back in his pouch of holding. Krenua felt as if a pressure on his brain was lifted as things became clearer.

Just then, there was a growling noise from down the tunnels. Howls followed it. It seemed that their fight had drawn some attention.

"Induca, officers, support! Come on, you two, let's greet our guests!" Lox said, a fire in his eyes and an excited smile on his face.

Krenua understood that smile. Lox was excited to test out his skills against an opponent that might actually be able to challenge him.

The tunnel heated up. Josen finished inspecting the other officers as they pulled themselves together.

The tunnels were filled with the sound of scratching and howls that were getting closer. Finally, the goblins and their timber wolf mounts were visible in the tunnels. There were seven timber wolves and their goblin riders.

"Ranged!" Lox called out. The officers used their ranged attacks, causing some of the wolves to tumble. Those behind them were nimble enough to get past them, slowing them by just the smallest of margins.

Steve's arm changed into a bolt thrower. It fired rapidly; the sound of the drawstring and the mechanical components rang through the tunnel.

Lox and Gurren fired their crossbows. Their bolts hammered home, breaking through the timber wolves' hard hides and taking the goblins in the face and chest, throwing them from their mounts if they were hit.

"Advance!" Lox called out.

Induca let loose with her magic. A spark of fire ran to meet the incoming goblins and timber wolves. It touched the leading timber wolf, exploding outward and down the tunnel.

Krenua reeled from the sound of the explosion.

"Double time!" Lox called out. The sound of Steve's bolt thrower decreased.

Krenua looked up to see that the seven goblins and their mounts were critically injured or dying. The aftereffects of Induca's spell quickly tore away any remaining hit points they had.

Krenua knew his ears were messed up from the high-pitched whistle he heard. He followed the rest of the party as they rushed forward.

A party of four goblin riders was taken out in mere minutes, bolts taking them down in quick succession.

Lox and Gurren's Strength allowed them to easily pull back their powerful drawstring. Krenua doubted Alkao was at the same level as them in terms of pure Strength.

As the whistling in Krenua's ears started to normalize, he heard howls not only in front of them but also behind them.

"We can't slow down or else they'll be able to bring more of their riders to attack us," Gurren yelled over the noise.

They came to an open area with two tunnels. They took the one to the left and kept going.

The tunnel started to grow in size, with Lox, Gurren, and Steve being able to run beside one another. They came out into a room filled with whips, riding gear, and different prods.

The goblins looked at the party as they entered.

To Krenua's eye, it was clear that these were goblin beast tamers.

Where the goblins paused, looking at the party in shock, Party Zero didn't hesitate. Lox and Gurren let out their war cries and their auras burst forth.

This is the power of a Level 200 aura?

Krenua and the officers staggered under the power of the two Dwarves' aura.

The goblins, being between 100 and 200, were dropped to the ground in a cold sweat. Only the highest were able to move, their movements slow and uncoordinated.

Induca watched, providing support here and there. She wasn't needed much as Lox, Gurren, and Steve tore through the goblins.

Lox hit so hard with his shield that the goblins' internal organs ruptured, making them cough blood as they fell to the ground. Lox's sword darted out, taking a head. He ducked and pivoted, his shield's grounding spikes eviscerating another.

His sword flashed out like a mechanical press, piercing through armor and bone to penetrate another goblin's heart. He kicked out; his monstrous strength broke the goblin's knee as he turned. His sword flashed out to slap an arrow out of the air that was aimed at Gurren's back.

Steve might be a giant of metal, but he had earned his spot among the Stone Raiders and Party Zero. Even with just his massive axe, he was able to defend, attack, and move forward. He didn't feel pain from the hits on his body. The goblins could only leave scratches as his hits turned them into a pulped green mass or tore them apart. He moved forward, his axe taking someone from their armpit up to their opposite trap. He used the flat of his blade, stopping an attack and hurling the goblin across the room. It was as if he were a child smacking a flower with a stick.

Gurren flowed in, stopping an attack on Steve's leg; his blade came down, plunging through the goblin's neck and into its chest. His blade came free in a spray of green blood; his shield slammed against a crude dagger, breaking the attacker's arm and stopping their attack dead. Gurren's sword flashed forward, punching into and out of the goblin so fast it didn't know it was dead before Gurren was taking down his next victim.

"You need an invite?" Lox barked out.

Krenua gripped his sword and shield, letting out a yell. The officers ran forward, joining into the fray.

It was brutal and dirty fighting. The goblins used anything and everything to fight the party. Krenua and the Demon officers were used to the brutality. A part of their baser instincts took over. Krenua allowed himself to move toward his berserker stage, his body becoming light and powerful as he used his shield, feet, claws, sword, and even forehead to break the goblins' defense and kill them.

Time seemed to have no effect on them as they fought, looking out for the others and slaughtering the goblins.

Krenua lowered his sword some time later, wiping the green blood that fell from his forehead.

"Looks like there's some fire in your bellies!" Lox said. The pressure of Party Zero's powerful auras fell away.

The howls through the tunnels seemed closer and there were a lot of them.

Gurren made to greet them.

Induca put a hand on his shoulder, stopping him. "Why fight them when we can get their untrained beasts to do it?" She pointed to a crude door made from strong timber with a heavy piece locking it.

"I like the way you think," Gurren said, his smile that of a hunter's.

They moved to the door and opened it. Inside there, a number of beasts were all locked up. They ranged in levels and in breeds.

"They have two ogres and a damn troll?" Lox said in an annoyed tone.

"Good thing we got in here to deal with this mess," Gurren said.

Lox grunted, looking unhappy with it all.

"It's like the world's weirdest and creepiest zoo," Steve said.

"I'll put simple spells on the locks that will break them open in a few minutes. We've got to be gone by that time." Induca touched the metal or wood locking mechanisms in the large holding area.

"Well, there's a door over there." Edlai pointed at a large gate off to the side.

"Good eyes!" Lox jogged over and checked the door. He waved for the others to follow. Induca finished touching the different locks; there was now a brand that seemed to have been burnt into the materials.

"Huh, well, looks like these goblins like their sports," Lox said.

The howls and noises of the goblins could be heard in the room where the beast tamers had been.

"Time to go!" Steve barged open the big door, revealing a grate made of bones.

"Edlai, do what you can to seal that door," Lox said as they rushed through the gate.

Steve moved like the juggernaut he was, picking up speed before he hit the bone gate.

Magical runes flared and then gave way as Steve broke through. The gate that had kept countless creatures at bay was nothing to Steve's strength.

Edlai's magic went to work, making the wood door fuse together into a single wooden plank. It wouldn't be enough to hold the goblins at bay for long but it would slow them down.

A timber wolf and rider moved into the creature pens. The goblin let out a screech; other timber wolves and their riders appeared.

The locked-up creatures let out their battle cries and slammed their bodies against their cages, eager to join in on the fight.

Induca held out her hand and the locking mechanisms on the different cells and cages in the room broke.

The first creature escaped its cage, looking stunned for a second before its instincts took over. It raced to meet the goblins and timber wolves.

More creatures were released as the riders were halfway through the beast stable.

The animals fought anything they came into contact with, even fighting the other creatures they had been imprisoned across from.

"Let's go!" There was no more time to watch the scene as the holes in the crude gate grew over.

The party ran out of the gate, finding themselves in an arena fifty meters long and wide. It had a muddy floor, with bodies in various states of decomposing, being left where they had fallen.

Lox and Gurren leaped from the arena floor, jumping for the stands. Krenua and the Demons used their wings.

"Ready?" Steve grabbed the two Beast Kin and jumped, soaring through the air and coming down in a crash on the rough stone seating that had been carved out around the arena.

Induca used fire to fly to the stands.

Gurren and Lox slammed into a door in the stands. They came out into what looked like the goblins' living area.

The goblins let out screeches as they went to meet the intruders. There had to be nearly a hundred of them.

Induca stepped out. Lox and Gurren's auras had been heavy on the soul. Now, Krenua had a hard time staying up as Induca seemed to be covered in flames as she floated a few feet off of the ground.

"I'll keep them distracted a bit!" Induca yelled out. A half-dozen flames spread out in front of her, growing, turning and burning brighter, until they became flame atronachs.

They flew through the air, leaving red streaks of fire as they unleashed Fire spells from above, drawing on the energy that animated them.

Induca fired out fireballs, killing goblins here and there, but their main function was to break up the goblins into small packets.

"On me!" Lox called out, surging forward. The officers and Gurren followed while Steve stayed to protect Induca.

There was nothing to do but fight. The atronachs supported and Steve sent out bolts, his axe breaking anything that dared to close with Induca.

Induca controlled the goblins' actions, keeping them off-balance and opening them up for attack by the rest of the party.

They didn't even need to communicate more than a few words. Their coordination was so impressive after the countless battles they had fought together.

Krenua and the officers were drained as they finished off the last group of goblins. Their Stamina had hit zero long ago, but not wanting to let down the others in their party, they pushed themselves beyond their limits.

Induca focused her fire on their last group of opponents.

There were several riders on high-level timber wolves that seemed to be made from living trees due to their high level but they didn't draw the eye.

Hobgoblin

Level 287

Hobgoblins were an oddity of the goblin race; they were stronger and smarter. They were usually the leaders of goblins and shouldn't be underestimated.

Induca called down a firestorm on the creatures. The heat in the room jumped upward as Krenua covered his face, trying to get away from it all.

The flames died down as Steve appeared among the final group of goblins.

He yelled as his axe came upward. It was deflected by the hobgoblin's tree trunk.

"Focus on the small creatures! I've got this one!" Steve said.

Krenua swore that he saw the damned idiot smiling!

They downed their Mana potions and a few Stamina potions that Gurren and Lox had handed up, tossing them aside and charging into the fight.

They were bone-tired. All of them had taken wounds and they were covered in goblin gore. Krenua and the officers grouped together. They couldn't fight the remaining goblin riders and their mounts one-on-one.

A being of flames appeared in a red streak. Around her, her flame atronachs defended their master, their arms turning to blades of blue flames while they breathed fire from their inner white flames.

Induca looked like a goddess looking down upon a battlefield. Her flames struck out from her hands, overwhelming the creatures' defenses until they tore through them.

Krenua and the officers took on a formation that bowed out toward the enemy. The goblins moved around on their timber wolves as if they were connected by the mind.

They slashed at the officers as they passed, getting tangled up with the Party Zero fighters who could deal with them one-on-one.

They reacted and fought; the directions that Lox, Gurren, Steve, and Induca had passed on unconsciously sunk into their minds.

They had changed in their fight through the tunnels. It wasn't a complete reversal or overwhelming change, but just by a few degrees. A few degrees that allowed them to truly use their abilities, to put forth their best attacks and if not kill a timber wolf and its goblin rider, they could seriously wound them.

Horria took a nasty cut up her arm to her shoulder. She cried out, her shield coming to the side to dislodge the goblin's spear.

Krenua moved up, taking her position as Josen poured healing potion into the wound that went all the way to Horria's bone.

Their armor didn't extend down their arms, as it would make them slower at fighting. It was why they didn't have much armor around their hips and knees. They were made to be mobile, not to stay in one position and defend. Though, facing stronger opponents and in an enclosed area, it was not possible for them to move around and strike their opponents.

They had to endure.

Steve let out a roar. His left arm's shield extended out as Steve backhanded the hobgoblin in the face with the edge of the shield.

The hobgoblin was tossed several feet, landing on the ground with a dazed look on its face and a large gouge down the side of its face.

Steve jumped; the dazed hobgoblin looked to him as if he were drunk. Steve arched back like a drawn bowstring in the air. His body suddenly became straight as his axe whistled through the air. Streaks of white from the disrupted air showed on either side of his axe as he brought it down on the hobgoblin's head.

Its legs twitched and the creature went still.

Steve pulled out his axe, flicking it to the side to clear the blade.

It flicked out again in a blur of speed, taking half of a goblin off its mount. He threw his axe, burying it in another rider and wolf.

The rest of the goblins and their mounts were quickly finished off.

No one talked for a bit, recovering their energy. Even Lox and Gurren looked tired from that battle.

"Well, this will be a really good training ground. I hope that the goblin mobs don't respawn too fast." Lox took a swig from his canteen.

"Respawn? Mobs?" Krenua asked, confused.

"You have a lot to learn about dungeons, especially with so many of them in your crater!" Gurren smiled.

"Mobs are monsters that spawn in certain locations. In dungeons, they can respawn after a certain amount of time so you can fight them again and again. These are some really high-leveled and powerful mobs. They should have a slow respawn rate of a few hours so that when you're leaving, they don't come back as you're exiting. That said, this is Ashal and there are more rare resources and creatures here than anywhere else," Induca said.

Krenua rested against a rock pillar. "So, they can come back again and again and we have to fight them?"

"Well, you don't have to fight them, but if you don't, then sometimes they can create kiddos or get to a high enough level that the dungeons can't hold them anymore and attack things outside of the dungeon," Lox said.

Krenua's expression became serious. These children from the mobs and the higher-leveled mobs were now the creatures that roamed the hunting grounds to the northwest of Devil's Crater. They were less in number than in the dungeons, but if they were able to grow in numbers, then it could lead to a large problem for those living in Devil's Crater.

"I think I now understand why having adventurers clearing out dungeons is a good idea," Krenua said.

"Yeah, especially with the number of dungeons you've got in Devil's Crater. It only makes sense," Steve said.

"Now, let's get this loot sorted out and then get out of here. That's enough training for tonight and I need to get all this crap off my armor and take a shower!" Lox said.

"You're telling me! Seriously, you're the smelliest roommate I've ever had," Gurren complained.

"You woke yourself up by farting last night!" Lox shot back. Like that, the seriousness from moments ago fell away as they relaxed.

Gurren closed his mouth on his retort, a sheepish look on his face. "That was one time," he muttered to himself.

"Krenua, have scouts posted at the entrance and the arena. We don't know if some of those creatures got loose in here. Going to need to send a bigger party down here to clear it out," Induca said.

Krenua gave the orders, wearily. He'd learned a lot today, but he was bone-tired from all the fighting that they'd done up to this point.

Chapter 10: A Meeting of Forces

Malsour and Fornau exited the Cliff-Hill teleport pad. Malsour greeted a few people and headed off toward Dave and Deia's home. Fornau followed him.

They went into the basement, using the teleport rune to reach the seeder and then took the secret exit from the seeder to come out a number of miles outside of Cliff-Hill. From there, they changed into their Dragon forms and headed for where Denur had taken up residence in Mithsia Mountains.

People pointed to them as they arced through the skies. There had been more Dragons seen in the last couple of weeks than ever before. Most thought that there were just a handful in Emerilia.

Malsour's Dragon form was nearly three times Fornau's. As Dragons aged, they continued to grow. Now, he was about the size of four busses, with a wingspan of nearly six.

Malsour flapped his wings, faster and faster. It had been months since he was able to return to his Dragon form. He raced ahead, banking from side to side, bringing his wings in and dropping as he spun; his wings shot out, catching the wind around him once again and he surged forward.

"This is refreshing," Malsour said to Fornau, his voice deep and powerful as if he were a mountain range given life.

With his power, he felt as if anything was possible. He had been in his Human form so long that he hadn't understood how much his power as a Dragon had increased. His Human form could barely handle a tenth of his total power as a Dragon.

"Feels good to change every so often," Fornau agreed. His voice was less powerful than Malsour's but would make nearly any other creature bow their head in fear and respect. They were the untouchable rulers of the beasts within Emerilia, much like how the lion was the king of the African plains on Earth.

Malsour took in the feeling of flying. With his eyes, he could pick up the sight of Dragons standing like statue golems on different peaks of the Mithsia Mountains.

They kept away from the main mountain in the range where the Dwarves lived. The Dwarves kept an eye on them, but it seemed that they were fine with having Dragons around as long as they didn't get too close.

Seeing his family standing upon the peaks of these mountains, Malsour could only smile. To him, it had not been long ago that they were sealed within the desolate realm that Bob had been able to sneak them into.

They had only one another. Some had flown away to try to escape, but those who stayed—they had become incomparably close.

Most people were family by blood, but they were family in their hearts. They would do anything for one another without a second thought.

That was true love and devotion to one's family.

The Dragons saw their elder uncle returning. Many were called elder brother within their family; simply calling them cousins was an understatement of their feelings. Uncle and aunt monikers were given to those who had not only shown their strength, but become pillars of their family.

The Dragons, seeing Malsour, let out greeting roars as they raised their mouths to the sky and unleashed their Dragon breaths in salute.

More and more saw Fornau and Malsour, greeting them as they passed. Creatures in the area cowered in fear, lowering themselves to the ground in prostration. Those far enough away fled in fear of somehow insulting these Dragons.

Malsour pulled in air; a vortex of wind formed around his mouth. The closer it came to his mouth, the darker it was. He let out a bellow; his black flames reached out for two hundred meters in greeting. Fornau let out his green flames.

From within the Mithsia Mountain range, a truly massive Dragon stretched her wings. To many, it would look like a small mountain stretching out.

Denur flapped her wings and rose into the air. Her children rose with her, coming out of their newly made caves to greet their elder uncle.

It didn't take long before Malsour and Fornau met with the oncoming party. A few stayed behind at the mountain, ready to assist those who were circling Akatol's domain and ice palace.

"Son, I see that Fornau was able to pull you away from your experiments," Denur said.

Malsour could only smile. It was as if he could sense her happiness; his own heart beat in happiness as he looked at his gathered family. There were few ways to express what he felt.

"It was a bit difficult—Uncle gets too involved in his work," Fornau jested.

The Dragons laughed.

"I'm sorry I haven't been able to visit earlier. I've been so busy." Malsour tilted his head away awkwardly.

"No worries. We are excited for all you have been able to do. My half-sister was certainly happy with meeting you. Seems that you and your sister Induca have found a good place," Denur said, clearly excited for her son.

"Thanks, Mom," Malsour said with feeling before his expression fell. "I wish I came under better circumstances, but I might have a way for you to open the ice palace so we can stop Akatol." Malsour no longer thought of Akatol as his father and in reality, he was now much older than his father, who had been sealed away for so long.

"Let us talk somewhere a bit more comfortable," Denur said, becoming serious. She and Malsour had fought side-by-side to defeat Akatol the first time.

She turned toward the mountain. Malsour took up position behind her right wing, the oldest and most powerful at the lead of the formation to break the wind easier for the ones behind them.

They quickly arrived at the mountain range. Malsour greeted his family with nods and smiles, promising to talk to them later as he and his mother as well as Louna moved into the largest cave.

They collapsed their size, reducing their power but allowing themselves to move easier.

"Okay, so what is this idea?" Denur looked to Malsour.

"We siphon power from some of our family in to the people who are attacking the ice palace. We have the ones with the highest

Willpower outside Akatol's domain; they wear an amulet which will drain them of Mana into a vault soul gem. Then our family with the best attack spells get in close to the ice palace, attack it with their magic while being supplied with Mana from the vault soul gem."

"Are you sure it will work?" Denur asked in a serious voice.

"With the Stone Raiders, it is common practice to have an amulet to drain power when you're not fighting; then, if we get into a fight, we reverse the amulet to draw in power. It allows us to go past our limits. It can lead to Mana fatigue, so we're going to need to change people who are in Akatol's domain out," Malsour said.

"Are there any other options? The longer that Akatol is in there, the longer he has to come up with something," Denur said.

"There is another option that would defeat Akatol within a few moments. The problem is that it would lead to much more powerful forces watching Emerilia closely and we will be severely limited in what we can do. I hope to keep those kinds of measures hidden for as long as possible." Malsour hoped that he had been as vague as possible so that his words hadn't been picked up by the AIs watching Emerilia. He knew that Bob was running some interference, but he didn't know how effective it was. After all, Melhoun, Akatol, and Khanundra had been released into Emerilia without his consent.

Denur held Malsour's eyes for a while. She nodded, having complete confidence in her son. If he said that this was the best way, then she would try it out. "Very well, let us see if this works."

Malsour changed his hand so that it was slightly more Human, allowing him to open his spatial ring and pull out a vault soul gem and two identical runed amulets.

***

Lord under Mithsia Mountain, Fend, watched as the Dragons had greeted two who seemed to come back from the direction of the Dragon's lair in Opheir. He didn't know who they were but it was clear that they were greeted with excitement by the rest of the Dragons. Fend scratched his cheek before stroking his beard in thought.

The Dragons had left them alone for the most part. They'd set up a home in the edge of the Mithsia Mountain range, about as far from his Dwarven city as they could get. They'd kept to themselves, the two groups making a silent agreement to not mess around with one another.

Now, with the arrival of these two Dragons, he felt something was about to change. He had heard the reports on the ice globe and the dead ground around where the Dragon's lair rested.

The dead land apparently stopped Mana from being regenerated and it was slowly growing, at about a meter per day, killing low-level beasts and wildlife.

Elven rangers watched the lair. Lord Fend, Evo'Mael of the Ku-fo'tel forest, and King Hierca of Opheir had been talking to one another about possible action that they could take against the lair. Even the elves of Asha-moor had made it clear that they would assist if it was desired.

"That was one of the biggest Dragons I've ever seen. It seems that it might be one of the older ones," Wrole, Fend's old friend and advisor, said after Fend had been lost in thought for a number of minutes.

"They're all bloody massive and old," Fend growled.

"Movement!" a spotter called out.

Fend moved back to the telescopes and cast far sight as he watched the Dragons once again moving. "It looks like they're going for the ice globe."

There were a number that were staying behind, but several of the largest ones were following behind a massive Dragon who could only be compared to a mountain in size.

"Denur," Fend whispered in reverence. The massive Dragon could only be one creature: Denur, the mother of Dragons.

Quickly, the Dragons gained altitude and headed toward the ice globe that now lay to the south.

"What do you want us to do?" one of the Dwarven warclan commanders asked.

"Make sure that no one pisses off the Dragons and keep training! If this has shown us anything, it's that we're going to have to fight much stronger opponents in the future." Fend looked away from the telescope.

"Yes, Lord Fend." The warclan leader bowed slightly before he opened his interface to send the messages out.

***

Malsour watched as Denur, Gelimah, Louna, and several of his younger family members flew toward the total domain that Akatol had created.

Malsour flapped his wings, the trees and forest around him blowing away with the massive wingbeats.

He settled down on the ground. He checked the amulet around his neck and pulled out the vault soul gem. It already had a slight charge held in it, growing with every second as power was drawn out from Malsour.

He watched as his family members got within a few hundred meters of the ice palace. They unleashed their attacks as one: their elemental breaths, their strongest attack.

It hit the ice palace from every direction; in places, parts were melted off or broken away. It wasn't much, but it certainly had an effect.

The vault soul gem stopped increasing in stored power as Denur let loose her breath attack, her consumption of Mana at the same rate that the amulet took power from Malsour.

Her blue flames made the outside of the ice palace melt where her breath hit. Waves of heat came off the ice palace that was colder than the coldest part of the north and south poles.

After a few minutes, Denur and the other Dragons left, taking to the skies.

Malsour watched as the ice palace quickly worked to repair the damage that had happened to it.

The only way to destroy the ice palace was from the inside, or by constantly hitting from outside with strong destruction spells. The power that was needed was incredible. Few creatures other than the Dragons could be able to do it. Even they would need to do it for several weeks before they cracked the palace open.

Malsour took to the sky, headed to meet back up with the rest of his family.

The vault soul gem and amulets had been a success. It looked as if they had a way to crack the ice palace without being dangerously close to Mana fatigue.

***

The room was silent except for the atmospheric exchanger that constantly moved air through the Deq'ual system station.

Chairwoman Wong, Engineer Edwards, and Commander Sato were the only occupants.

Edwards held his tongue even though it looked as if he were ready to burst, his eyes darting between Sato and Wong.

Wong sat parallel to her desk, looking at the wall as her left forefinger rested on the desk and tapped it lightly.

Sato was expressionless as he watched Wong.

Wong finally moved after ten minutes. She looked as though she had aged a year, but her expression was firm. "Sato, by the power invested in me, I give you permission to continue with your ship and weapon advancement programs," Wong said. It seemed to have taken an effort of will to get those words out.

"People are going to think that we're idiots; that we should just hide out for the rest of our lives here. Now we can confirm that the Jukal Empire is still functioning and very much active and that they have genetically altered and imprisoned a planet of humans for their own sadistic entertainment. I want you to work to increase our abilities so that we are able to create a fighting force that can rescue the people on Emerilia and fight the Jukal. I am going to remove the restrictions on birth rates as well as the amount of people within the military. I ask that you continue to talk to the other Human stations and see if we can send people to check on their situation. If at all possible, I want to scout them. Get as much information as you can get from our contacts in Emerilia," Wong said.

"Understood, Chairwoman Wong." Sato nodded.

Even Edwards kept his mouth shut, feeling the weight of the decisions made in this room.

Chapter 11: A Craftsman's Power

Dave finished the very last rune on the metal sheet. He lined it up with the other paper-thin sheets. There were four sheets but they were large and covered in tiny and exact runes. He had needed to use his conjuring art to remove the metal so exactly. Even then, it had been hard to get everything exactly right.

He rubbed his eyes. He had been working on it for a couple of days between his different classes, conferences, and signing various items that Suzy brought to his attention.

He looked around. He was in one of the workshops within the Mirror of Communication school. There were a number of people looking over at him, quickly turning back to their work. This was a magical coding lab. People from all over Emerilia had tried their hand at magical coding in here. With every week, more people were in Dave's classes.

Dave heard someone yell out in excitement in the distance. The lab was the size of a football field.

He quickly opened his quest interface.

Quest: Skill Creator Level 10

Personally teach 3,200 people your Skill (3,051/3,200). Or help your students reach the level of Apprentice (149/200). Or help your students reach the level of Journeyman (0/1).

Rewards: Unlock Level 11 Quest

Increase to stats

Active Skill: Teacher

Level: Journeyman Level 7

Effect: You can teach people skills that you have prior knowledge of, up to your level of ability. Your students are 10% more likely to understand what you're teaching them. Teaching on subjects you have a higher knowledge on will yield higher results. Teaching skills you have mastered or created give higher chance for students understanding your lessons.

Dave smiled. It seemed that they had just made it into the Apprentice level.

He looked to his own coded work. It wasn't even a centimeter thick, with runes covering it in what seemed to be a haphazard mess. There were hundreds of thousands of runes on those simple sheets.

He opened up his interface, changing the settings of the area he was in slightly so that he could record much more information than others could. With his Bleeder Class, he found that he was able to see more options within Jukal technology, as it now recognized him as a Jukal and therefore allowed him more access.

He closed the interface and started to feed the rune sheets with a vault soul gem. It took a considerable amount of power.

He looked around, making sure no one was too close to see his work in front of him. Happy with it, he activated the magical coding within the sheets. It seemed to move a foot to the right before it fell down, smoking as the sheets melted.

Dave grinned to himself.

A new notification flashed in his face.

Active Skill: Teleportation

Level: Master Level 3

Effect: Able to create a device to teleport across distances.

Dave did a little dance, silently doing the cha-cha slide in front of his worktable.

"Who is that weirdo?" someone in the Novice phase asked their lab partner.

"Shh, keep your voice down. That's Dave Grahslagg. You know, the guy who *made* magical coding," the other hissed back.

"What? But why's he dancing?"

"He always gets a little excited when he gets a breakthrough or when someone else figures something out," the second lab partner said, shaking his head.

"So, he just had a breakthrough? What was he working on? I didn't even see anything happen!" The first looked over to Dave, trying to see what he was working on.

"I don't know, but with him, if it's something he's just figured out, we'll probably see Emerilia change again. It's said that he and Steve made those onos—you know, those teleport pads that just go to Terra?"

"How can someone have so many accolades already?" the first complained.

"By working at it and not complaining about what others have been able to do," the second said angrily, not looking up from the runes he was working on.

"Oh, sorry," the first said sheepishly, looking to his own metal sheet he was coding before he glanced up at Dave again. He swore that the metal sheet in front of him was just a mass of melted metal.

Maybe it was so warm from heat discharge after using the soul gem power that it came apart?

Dave didn't pay any attention to the mutterings of the students as he deleted what he was working on and then exited the Mirror of Communication.

After leaving the Mirror of Communication, he found his physical body trapped with Deia's leg over his; her head rested on his chest and her hands were wrapped around his arm.

She let out soft breaths, drooling on him.

Dave snorted at the sight.

"Demigod and she's slobbering on me," he whispered to himself, kissing her forehead.

She moved, tightening her grip on him before she relaxed, a pleased expression on her face before it once again flowed into sleepiness.

Dave's free hand moved to Deia's stomach. Even if he might have figured out how to create his own magically coded teleporter, it was by no means his greatest achievement.

"I'm looking forward to seeing what you can do," he whispered, focused on Deia's stomach.

***

"How is this possible?" Quino asked Kol. All of the Dwarven Master Smiths working in Terra were in the conference room of Terra's smithy.

The noises of work could be heard in the background. All of the DCA soldiers had been issued and fitted with armor. Now the smithies under the Grahslagg Corporation were working on their own projects and there were a number of them. People from all over Emerilia were coming to them with rare weapons to be repaired or forged. They were a household name, with their smithies being synonymous with quality.

"Dave has his mine manager class at a really high level. Also, we got lucky," Kol said. It was clear that he was keeping something to himself.

The other smiths were interested, but they trusted him.

"But, so much Mithril. Hell, the amount of ebony you have here! That's more output than most Dwarven mountains over five years!" Jesal said.

"Well then, we best put it to good use, like repairing the Stone Raiders' weapons. If you wish to buy materials to work on your own projects, you are allowed, but there is a limit to the number that you can purchase. Everyone will be allowed the same amount," Kol said. "You can pay for it with time from repairing or making items, or you can pay for it with other precious materials or soul gems. From now on, all Grahslagg smithies will only be accepting these two items in payment."

A stir went through the smiths.

"Why not copper, silver, and gold?" Quino asked.

"Copper isn't that useful for us right now, and we've got tons of it. Silver is useful for magical coding. Gold is used to make things pretty. Here, we want weapons first, appearance second. Soul gems we can use to buy and sell items with the Aleph, Devil's Crater people, and Terra. Also, they power this place and we can use them to power the magical coding in weapons," Kol answered.

"What about wages?" Jesal asked.

"We're going to be switching that over to soul gems, simply put. They're becoming the new money for Stone Raiders and their allies. With Terra trading in them, nearly everything in two of our three locations, people are using the gems to buy and sell items," Kol said.

"Okay, we agree—now, what about these projects that Dave has given to us? Can we do those as we want?" Sola asked.

"Okay, so for those, there is a bounty. He has a bunch of projects but he can't work on all of them. If you can find a solution to his problems, then there is a list of rewards that you will gain in resources," Kol said.

The Master Smiths leaned in with interest. Money, fame—all of it was second to their own smithing. Finding solutions to Dave's problems would stretch their minds and they could get items to make their own projects!

Grins broke out on the rough, scarred, and bearded faces of the Dwarven Master Smiths taking up the challenge.

***

"Dave!" Malsour yelled as he entered the lab.

"What?" Dave yelled back, not looking away from his work as a bag of holding evaporated in his hands. Burns seemed to form on the material in the shape of runes and Magical Circuits before the bag was burned up.

"I need thirty amulets and fifteen vault soul gems!" Malsour said.

"Huh?" Dave looked at Malsour, his eyebrows coming together in a frown.

"My family needs them to break open the ice palace in Opheir and get at Akatol," Malsour explained.

"I've got three soul gem factories going—two in Terra, one in the seeder—but you know I'm using those soul gems for our extra projects," Dave said.

"I just want fifteen just in case, but if I can get the amulets and a few coded vault soul gems, it would be good," Malsour said.

"That I can do. Check in the material storage locker—take the charged ones. Also, I'm going to need you to increase the draw from the fusion plant. I want to really test it out. For that, I need to send the power somewhere," Dave said.

"I thought we agreed to not play with the bomb in the back of the room?" Malsour yelled as he moved to the materials room. It was a simple room with chests that looked to be more pieces of art than having any actual function. Newer ones were simple metal gray.

Dave had a special order to get a number of the spatial chests. He needed them for moving materials with his factories, smithies, and his various projects, as well as just storing them in place.

Malsour called up what he wanted out of the organized chests. Once they appeared in mid-air above them, Malsour put them into his ring.

"Hey! I needed to step up the Mana well production! For that, I needed some irradiated materials that I can get really easy by using the big bomb, as you call it!" Dave yelled so that he could be heard in the storage room.

"How many you trying to do in a week?" Malsour yelled back as he closed the chest. He moved to another and checked his inventory.

"Well, right now we're at a Mana well every five days. I think I can get one every two days. I'm working on an assembly line to combine the Mana well, soul gem matrix, and the onos. However, I think I might give it over to the Aleph; they'll be able to do it better." Dave trailed off, the last a thought to himself.

"Sounds like a good idea, spread the work around a bit. Dave, where's the damn amulets?"

"Third from the far right, box all blue and gold weirdness," Dave yelled back.

"Thanks!" Malsour opened it up and found the amulets. He grabbed them and walked back out into the lab.

Dave was floating in mid-air in his spinning chair. Around him, there were various spatial items and things of holding.

Malsour stopped and looked at Dave. He used his arcane sight without any conscious thought.

Dave was manipulating the gravity of the room to move the various items. They moved in elliptical orbits around him, though there were some places where there weren't items. But Malsour's gut told him that there was something.

"How is the work with the armor going?" Malsour asked, cancelling his arcane sight.

Dave turned in the air, a thoughtful look on his face. "With the enchantments and magical coding that I can do on the armor, they're going to be some of the scariest things I've ever made. I'm thinking of making them for Lox and Gurren, though I'm still working on these damned items of holding. It won't work if I have the armor filled with coding plates and find they can't fit in it."

"Why don't you ask Bob about it? He might have an idea or two," Malsour said.

"Good idea." Dave opened his interface.

Malsour smiled. When Dave was working on a project, he had a one-track mind.

"Oh, and I'm going to bring Steve in on all of this. He might act like a goof, well, all the time, but he's smart as hell when it comes to coding and figuring things out," Dave said.

"I saw some of the coding on the onos; getting his help would be good." Malsour turned to leave, but stopped. "Wait, you said you know what you're going to be coding in the armor already? What about the power consumption? The layering armor and the interlinking coding plates? That should have taken months?"

"Well, I have a very willing workforce. I might have overstepped by saying it was done, but I offered a contest to the Dwarven Master Smiths working in my smithies. Each of them is working on a part, competing with one another to make their best work. As a reward, I'll give them some resources that are hard for them to get." Dave had a devilish grin on his face.

Other than Dave, the Dwarven Master Smiths had been working with magical coding for the longest time.

They'd also been making weapons and other items with Magical Circuits for years. They were probably only second to Dave, only due to Dave coming up with crazy ideas and breaking down so many Magical Circuits that he was a moving repository of runes from dozens of different languages.

Malsour let out a breath. Dave had boldly declared that he would make the suits of armor as true Weapons of Power, using his smithing art and imparting a piece of his soul onto each of them. He would be greatly increasing their power and also giving them something that could test and check the user and their intents.

If Dave had made it by himself, it would have been a great achievement, a true Weapon of Power. But now, he was getting nearly a dozen Master Smiths to create the various components. Where Dave might make a general coding to make the item function, each of the Dwarven Master Smiths would pour their heart, soul, and creative talents into their work, making each piece of coding, layer of armor, and power consumption runes the strongest they could be.

Chapter 12: A New Challenge

Deia stepped through the teleport pad's event horizon, leaving Terra and entering Devil's Crater.

"Deia!" Anna said with a wide smile, hugging Deia, careful to not squeeze her too hard.

"So, I heard that you need a weapons trainer?" Deia smiled.

"Getting a little cabin crazy?" Anna laughed as she led Deia away.

"A bit; not being able to go on dungeon raids or check out new ruins and locations is a bit wearing. Dave's been trying to distract me with coding. I find it interesting and he's got a lot of interesting projects, but I really just want to work on my fighting skills. Seeing as I can't," Deia patted her stomach, "I guess I'll teach some people how to do it."

"Well, we've set up something of a fight between some of the aerial and ground troops of the DCA: try and humble them a bit, see how to improve them and get some good ole fashioned rivalry between them!" Anna grinned.

"I haven't been able to get to the Dwarven tournaments. You and Alkao should come with Dave and I for some of the later ones," Deia said.

"Okay." Anna sighed in resignation.

They chatted and walked through Unity. It didn't take them long to leave the growing city behind and head out toward the training area where the training fight was supposed to take place.

Deia floated into the air, her feet glowing with fire. "Sorry, ankles get a bit swollen with walking and it's much easier to do this."

"It's fine with me." Anna easily stepped into the air beside her.

"You really were suppressing the hell out of your wind attribute," Deia said ruefully. She was a demigod by blood, but Anna was truly a wolf Beast Kin with the mind and thoughts of an AI.

She'd had to train it to this level and her ability was incredible as wind seemed to embrace her as if a part of her very being.

Anna gave a sly smile as the two of them continued with their old conversation, moving through the air. They quickly arrived at the training area, no longer held back by the speed of their legs.

Kala stood in front of the perfect rows of DCA soldiers. They all had slight changes to their weapons and armor. Their movements were subtle to keep blood flowing in their bodies.

Malkur stood in front of the aerial troops. They were moving around a lot more, not used to staying in one place for long. Those who had wings moved them around slightly, as if keeping them warm to immediately take off.

Deia looked at them with the eyes of a woman who had seen combat for nearly three centuries. As much as her father had looked to protect her, he had not kept her from going beyond Kufo'tel forest and searching for her own path.

Her aura detection was rather high after having worked with the Stone Raiders and Party Zero, making it a game to find someone's aura, or to hide it.

Looking at them now, they were true soldiers. Before, when they had been fighting the Demon Horde, they had come together, putting their differences and their old barbaric system of upward progression behind them. They had clothes, but few to no weapons and armor.

Now, they were all outfitted with gear. Their base training had been developed on and they were well on their way to refining it.

"If I was to make a guess, I would say that they're on average twenty to thirty percent stronger than when we were defending Devil's Crater." Deia's eyes moved from person to person.

The two groups stared at one another across the training area.

Quindar stood on a podium some distance away. The eyes of the soldiers looked to Anna and Deia as they seemed to descend out of the heavens.

As one, they all seemed to lower their heads. The members of Party Zero were heroes of Devil's Crater. Deia had earned the title of Fire Blessed by the people of the DCA. Many had seen her power as she unleashed all of her strength to cover their retreat and take out as many of the Demon Horde as possible.

Deia was stunned for a second. A small smile appeared on her face as she nodded back to them.

Their heads moved back upward, looking to their opponents and the three women on the podium at the head of the two formations.

"Most of their strength comes from finally working with their talents. Once they specialized, doing what they were the best in and what they wanted to learn more about, their strength took off like a rocket," Anna said.

"It will make for an interesting match, Aunty." Quindar smiled at Deia.

"You make me feel old!" Deia gave Quindar a slight nudge. There was already a feeling of familiarity between the two as they smiled, the spark of instant friendship ignited.

"Shall we let them begin and we can continue our talk as we observe?" Anna asked.

"Let's," Quindar said.

Deia nodded.

"Today, we will be looking at how you've advanced in the last couple of weeks. Remember your training! We will be having Kala's trainees against Malkur's trainees, aerial against ground. You have ten minutes before the fight will begin. Kala, Malkur—see to your forces!"

Anna's voice died down as Kala's officers barked out commands. The forces moved out in groups for the rough unaltered training area where they would be fighting.

Malkur's officers called out orders; their people listened to them intently as they spread out, moving their wings to prepare for flight.

A number of Krenua's high-ranked officers stood behind the three women, moving to the different groups. They were the strongest of the Devil's Crater Army. For this, they would be the referees making sure that no one got badly injured and helping if they did.

"Their flight time isn't too long and they stay grounded as long as possible so that they have more energy in the air," Quindar said.

"They'll get the strength eventually. I've been working on coding up a training aide that would simulate flying at different heights to give them a better idea of their limits and how to act at higher and lower altitudes as well as in calm and hard winds," Anna said.

"You're attending the coding classes as well?" Deia asked.

"Well, I've been reading Dave's information manuals. I can't digest the information as fast as Steve or Shard, but I'm still pretty fast at it," Anna said.

"And very modest as well," Quindar quipped.

The forces moved out onto the field.

"Shall we follow?" Anna asked.

"Certainly," Quindar said. The air picked her up as it had with Anna.

"So, how are the children?" Deia asked as she, too, took to the air.

"Accident prone, mischievous, and amazing." Quindar smiled. The corners of her eyes wrinkled in delight, thinking of her babies. "I will say, having an extra pair of hands is a godsend," Quindar said as they hovered fifty feet off of the ground.

The ground troops had broken down into units of ten and were all looking ready to move outside on the training area. They were spread out over a massive area and staggered so that they didn't cluster.

"Yoalin might not have children of her own, but she loves them as if they were her own. I've been pregnant for nearly two years, so it's nice to get a bit of freedom here and there. Also, Fornau is always out looking at new projects going on in Devil's Crater. He's setting up a consulting company for city building. It seems people caught wind that he was the one to plan all of this, and other kingdoms and cities are looking for him to make aqueducts, sewage systems, and the infrastructure that's already here," Quindar said with clear pride.

"That's amazing! I know Malsour was greatly impressed with all that he did," Deia said.

Anna made a noise of agreement.

"Even powerful creatures like us get bored from time to time," Quindar said, clearly including Anna and Deia in her words.

They both nodded.

"It is good to finally have someone to talk about with these matters. Some of the young don't truly understand." Anna let out a breath.

A gong was struck, announcing the start of the war games.

Quindar snorted. "Some people like much younger company." Quindar had an amused smile as she looked to Deia and Anna.

"It is a lot of fun being with Dave. He might be a lot younger than me, and he has the endless energy. It really is refreshing. I feel like a teenager again," Deia said to the giggles of the others.

"Looks like the aerial scouts have improved on their power, now that there is a contest to show off their abilities," Anna said.

"Think she's just trying to distract us from asking about that red piece of eye candy that she's been leading around?" Quindar asked Deia.

"I think, dear niece, that she might be, even if she does have a point." Deia and Quindar smiled unabashedly at Anna, who glared at them both.

"The aerial are fast, but the ground forces are not without pre-planning," Quindar said. Their eyes moved to the ground forces that were running in a headlong sprint toward the forests.

Some were using their wings and various spells to increase their speed. All of those with similar skills were spread out over the ground forces, allowing them to pass on their skills and be available to more officers instead of under the command of a few.

The scouts were using their interfaces, talking rapidly to the flying forces that were now taking to the skies. The ground forces had a lead, but the aerial troops were quickly building up their momentum.

"The lead flyers are going to hit the rear of the soldiers on the ground before they make it into the trees. Once they get into the forest, it's going to be hard for the aerial forces to find the ground forces. They've become rather adept at hiding in built-up terrain. The scouts are good enough to find them in open terrain, but it will be a good trial to see how their skills are at deceiving the flyers and the flyers at finding the ground forces."

Deia looked at the ground forces; it truly was a fearsome sight to watch their charge. Beast Kin lowered themselves to the ground, using all of their limbs to increase their speed.

The Demons, with their strong bodies, rushed forward faster than creatures that were their level and half again. They truly were Creatures of Power.

Beast Kin who didn't have any ancestry of using their multiple legs to sprint forward were no less fast, making up for their differences, pushing themselves to the limit, unwilling to let down their comrades.

There was no division between the Beast Kin and Demons anymore. They truly were one people in the DCA.

"So, it looks like I will be having a brother or sister in a couple of weeks. Will be good if my sibling, my child, and yours could get together. They will only be a few months different in their birthdays," Deia said.

Quindar was hesitant before she nodded. "I was thinking that yours and your mother's child might not be able to handle it, but thinking of their parents and their inherent strength, it might be good for them to mingle with my children. Though, we're still keeping them restrained in their Human form. Don't need an angry six-year-old running around spouting their Dragon breath." Quindar rolled her eyes and shook her head.

Deia laughed.

Childbirth was not something that was easy, but with the magic healing abilities of Emerilia's people, Deia felt reassured that there was limited chance that she would die or that her child would. It was a great relief to any mother. It allowed her to focus on other things and be excited to see the little one she had been carrying for six months instead of scared of what might go wrong.

"I wonder what would become of Alkao and Anna's children?" Quindar mused aloud.

Anna went deep red, trying to reply but just spitting as her mind seemed unable to reply.

Deia and Quindar laughed at their friend's expression.

Anna huffed and looked back to the battlefield. The first scouts had reached the ground forces that were three-quarters of the way to the forest they sought to use as overhead cover.

The scouts paused for a bit before they moved up and closer to the ground forces. A few sent out spearheads from their hands.

They weren't allowed to use their Mana bolts and bombs, because there was too much of a chance that someone would get hurt or killed using those weapons.

Their range was too great with the two forces moving at different speeds. The spearheads got a lucky hit here and there. One or two people were whisked away by Krenua's officers as they were informed that they were now dead and thus out of the training battle.

"There's that overconfidence," Quindar said as the trio glided through the air almost lazily, their eyes picking up different things about the ground and aerial forces.

Anna shook her head, clearly unhappy as the scouts moved closer to get a better hit. "They're in range of the ground forces now, but it seems Kala's established her control. None of them are looking to even fire an arrow or destruction staff at the scouts."

"Maybe lull them into a false sense of security?" Deia looked back at the aerial forces that were now airborne, moving in groups of four as they split apart, using their speed to try to line up for a bombing run as best as they could and reach the ground forces before they entered the forest.

The scouts, bolder for not getting hit, dropped their altitude further to gain speed and close with the ground forces.

"Seems Malkur is trying to reel them in, but they've already committed themselves. They're doing something they've come up with to surprise the enemy and thinking they're much more powerful than they are." Anna sighed.

The scouts fired their spearheads—which were fake bolts—and dropped others from their stomachs. There were a number of spears in the ground and a few of the ground forces stopped as their training barriers said they were dead. With being so spread out, it was easy to get one or two, but to get more in a single run was much harder.

The leading ground forces made it into the treeline. The scouts tried to gain altitude to see over the forests.

Kala yelled out an order. Her people turned as one, pulling out their long-range weaponry or raising their hands. Their own spears launched from their hands and destruction staffs energy flashed out.

The scouts in the middle of maneuvering were caught unaware. They were cut in half in mere seconds.

Krenua's people moved through the skies, sending people to the ground. People were arguing about being dead or not.

"I think it's best we show them why they should listen to Krenua's forces," Anna said, a hint of anger in her voice, displeased with the actions of the very people she had trained.

Quindar frowned and let out a deep noise of annoyed agreement.

Anna and Quindar's aura flared to full effect, landing on those who weren't abiding the rules.

Their faces paled as they realized that they weren't totally unobserved.

Krenua's people crossed their arms as if to say "well, if you don't listen to me, you'll have to deal with them." People moved to the ground, accepting Krenua's people's words.

Their auras receded as Deia watched the ground forces with interest. She was brought on to teach people how to fight with weapons, something that she had mastered through her life. With her senses, she was able to pick up the ground forces as they started using various kinds of spells, gears, and items to mask their presence and locations and moved up into the trees of the forest.

"Looks like they're going to have a good round of tree tag." Deia smiled, remembering the days where they had ventured from Cliff-Hill to the Benvari Mountains, playing the game for hours to train and break the boredom of traveling.

"I was telling Kala about it once and she went with it. Ever since, she's had them jumping through forests and climbing all over Unity. They can traverse a city as easily as open fields. Probably even better as they can use the cover of the city to their advantage when fighting," Anna said.

"I have a feeling that patience is going to be the biggest factor in this fight," Quindar said.

"That and Endurance," Anna agreed.

Deia saw that as the ground forces got to the top of the trees, they stopped, gathering their strength and relaxing. They had made it to cover; now it seemed as though they were waiting for something.

"Seems that Kala has been paying attention to the aerial forces," Deia said with respect.

"See, I told you this would be fun." Anna smiled.

Deia grinned; it was exciting to see two groups press their strengths against one another and to sort out a victor.

The aerial forces were now losing altitude for speed, seeing the ground forces disappear into the forest. They started firing their spearheads out of their hands, peppering the ground forces and getting a few of them but it wasn't enough.

The aerial forces moved in and again Kala let them come, letting them think that the ground force's range was half or less than it actually was. Hitting a moving target while you're flying was damn hard. It was much easier to fire from a fixed position. There were ground forces being taken down, but it was handfuls.

The aerial forces came in low, angry at the loss of their forward scouts and eager to show who was the better. Their hunter instincts and the way that they had darted in, dropping their payloads in training, lulled them into the false sense of security Kala was betting on.

"Malkur is trying to remain in command, but he's micromanaging too much. While he works on the position of twenty, then fifteen other flight groups move into a position that he doesn't like. They're too confident in their abilities. We're going to have to check out the officers. It looks like the ones who are willing to take the most risks were promoted. We'll have to see if we can temper them with some forward thinking or we might have to change them out," Anna said.

"It's a shame, but this is why we needed this fight to see what is working and what is not," Quindar said, to try to lessen the blow to their pride.

It was then with just a quarter of the ground forces out in the open before the forest that nearly three-quarters of the aerial forces swooped down to try to bomb them out of the game.

What they found instead was Kala's wall.

Ground forces who had made it to the forest first had climbed up in the trees, turning around and looking the way that they had come. The scouts, thrown off-balance by losing half of their number, had pulled back, giving little to no information on the movement of the forces in the forest.

While the aerial forces were concentrated on the quarter of the remaining ground forces left out in the open, all of the ground forces were ready for them. The forces that were running turned to face the skies, arresting their motion and releasing their long-range attacks once again.

The aerial forces jeered, until their Mana barriers started to be struck.

The ground forces in the trees were hitting them with mass fire! They had stable positions in the trees and had been given the time to recover their Stamina and line up their targets. They used their bracelets, firing out their own spearheads.

The ground forces at the rear had been the ones who were the best ranged fighters. They used the bow, destruction staffs, and their bracelets.

Kala was focused on honing their natural talents, not forcing them to adjust to a different weapon that they weren't as good with.

The aerial forces had grouped together too tight. They were trying to get out of range, but the air was a chaotic mess as they had all converged in toward their targets. They had been so focused on their prey, but hadn't realized what was going on.

The aerial forces dropped to the ground in droves, with Krenua's people sending them off to the sides. It was a wanton slaughter.

The forces in the open weren't faring that well, but they were still spread out so it was hard to get multiple soldiers in one bombing run, even though there were a ton of aerial forces.

The ground forces, seeing the aerial start getting organized, sprinted for the forest, exuberant at what could only be called a win as their fellows in the forest provided cover with their long-range weaponry. They disappeared into the forest; the ground forces moved through the trees, gaining elevation and space.

The aerial forces were still getting sorted out, as Krenua's people moved through and told them they were dead.

Medics were deployed. If they could guide the observers through healing the different people, then they might recover some strength. As it was, they had lost a third of their forces in just two small engagements.

"The ground forces take risks, but they've got complete trust in one another and great coordination. We're going to have to work on that coordination with the aerial," Quindar said.

"Smart risks, versus showing off," Anna said.

"We'll have to see that they don't get too arrogant." Deia had trained a number of people in her life, from rangers to Dwarves. Ego was a big thing when they were being taught.

"Now that they've lost twice, they're trying all they can to make up for it. Knowing Kala, she's going to use this mass of emotions to her will," Anna said.

"Don't need a bunch of hotheads," Deia agreed.

The trio watched as the aerial forces moved in, trying to see through the canopy and pick out where the ground forces were.

Sometimes, they were right over a position but the ground forces would cease their movements, waiting for them to pass before moving to ambush locations. Here and there, they would appear at random, cutting down the ranks of aerial troops, further frustrating the aerial forces.

Anna and Quindar's faces would have made a grown man quiver in fear as they watched. They had got them into the sky and taught them the basics, moving onto how to bomb and how to fight in the air, but it looked as though the command structure was not strong enough and they had allowed too much freedom to the aerial forces.

Deia watched as the aerial forces started carpet bombing the forest, clearing out some of the ground forces as their "bomb" spears fell through the canopy. They got their largest amount of kills from this, but it was uncoordinated.

The ground forces were patient and calculating. They had been working on stalking one another, on patrolling and thinking on tactics and positioning. Their weapon skills might be weak in areas so they stayed their hand, fighting the battles they knew that they could win.

The battle didn't last much longer before the trio agreed that it was done. The aerial forces came back to the fields outside the forest to land and recover their energy before getting back into the air.

As the training battle ended, the aerial forces watched the ground forces appear out of the forest over the space of forty minutes; they'd been spread throughout. Their losses were just an eighth of what the aerial forces had taken.

"So, what do you think?" Anna asked.

"I think that they're going to be some good students. They've got a great foundation. With that, I can turn them into some damned impressive fighters. Bit of the elven ranger approach: work on archery and attacks at range, see what their abilities are in making traps as well as scouting. It's clear that the aerial scouts are good at picking out people in large areas, but in overhead cover it's a lot harder for them to have a good idea of what the enemy is doing. What have you got in the way of magic training?"

"Kala wanted to get the basics down and then look into working it in," Quindar said.

"She doesn't have much of a talent in magic—another reason we wanted to bring you over," Anna admitted.

"Okay, well, I can't teach all of this by myself," Deia said.

"Well, we've also got a budget from the Devil's Crater government for training our forces. You can hire people as you want to train them up, as long as you pass it through Kala," Anna said.

"Well, that makes things a lot more interesting," Deia said to herself, tapping her chin in thought.

Chapter 13: Growth

Hamdir looked out over Alephir. The city was nearly five times the size of Terra. A smile crossed his face as the corners of his eyes crinkled in joy. He sipped from his tea as he continued his appraisal of the city.

"It is good to see Alephir recovering so quickly." Shard's blue hologram flashed into existence next to Hamdir.

"Much faster than I thought possible. When we came back, I didn't think that it would be possible that we could recover so much of our strength, even with the Stone Raiders helping us out. For months, we have been simply trying to stay afloat, shutting down facilities we simply don't need because of our reduced population." Hamdir paused. "I think it's time that we started to look for more people who might be interested in joining the Aleph. We have plenty of room and work to be done. Our factories are producing goods for people all over Emerilia and we've become a major power. Even the elves and Dwarves have recognized us as an extended part of their people." Hamdir shook his head in disbelief.

"A lot has changed in the time that you were gone," Shard said, a bit of sadness in there.

Hamdir smiled sadly at Shard.

The AI had watched over their homes as they disappeared, trying his best to see that they survived until his masters came back. For all those years, he only had the Grey God to talk to, losing facilities and automatons and having to shut down himself time after time to try to keep Alephir even running.

"Frenik has been making a number of deals with the Dwarves. I was scared that the Dwarves might feel threatened with the return of the factories. It seems that they're fine with it. They're constantly swamped with requests for small items that they have to take trained smiths away from larger tasks to complete. Just the number of people looking for Dave's screws—their cost was astronomical.

We can bring the price down, take the pressure off the Dwarves and let them focus on making their items." Shard sensed Hamdir didn't want to talk about the time that the Aleph were gone anymore.

"Good! I don't want to get into any conflicts if we can help it."

"The Dragons are moving from Mithsia Mountains again, this time with all of them," Shard said.

"What are they doing?" Hamdir asked. Akatol had been around when Hamdir's father was alive and he was a young boy. He knew the stories and how ruthless Akatol was.

"I don't know, but from what they seemed to be doing last time, they were running a test," Shard said.

"What makes you think that?"

"They moved in, used their various attacks and then did it for a while, but there was a person who was outside the range of the total domain charging what looked to be a soul gem."

Hamdir's eyebrow rose. "I've never heard of the Dragons using any sort of tool to assist them in fighting. If they are starting to, it will be interesting to see what will happen."

Some people were scared of the Dragons, seeing them as all-powerful beasts without a master other than the Lady of Fire. There were great tomes filled with stories about people who killed off Dragons. Hamdir knew that few of these stories bore any truth. Someone who attacked the Dragons without provocation was swiftly dealt with. There was once a nation within the Densaou Ring of Fire. They mined the rare materials on the Ashal continent created by the heat of the volcanos and their runoff.

The Dragons were only a few decades old when the people started to attack, thinking of taming the beasts or killing them for the materials in their bodies. They were able to heavily wound a Dragon and captured it.

The Dragons had acted swiftly and effectively. In the space of a week, they cut off the people, and then turned their homes to ash. The Dragon had been freed.

The Dragons entered the cities of those around the ring of fire, decreeing that people were not allowed to come within a certain distance. Also, if they were attacked, they would return the attack tenfold. Only if the Dragon was deserving of their punishment would they not interfere.

Most thought that the Dragons would just go and kill off other nations because they angered them. But the Dragons kept to themselves and worked on building their power, and were left alone. When one of their family acted out against the people of Emerilia, they were the first to react, subduing and, in a rare few cases, eliminating those who had gone too far. They assisted those who were affected in rebuilding.

It wasn't perfect, but it worked.

"I thought that they had killed off Akatol when they fought over Ashal," Hamdir said.

"It looks like he was banished to a prison of some kind, stored as you were," Shard said.

Hamdir drank from his cup. Dark thoughts moved through his mind. The energy and vibrance that he had felt a minute ago seemed to be stopped by a wall in his mind.

Akatol was a threat to all the people of Emerilia.

"What do you think will happen with the Dragons' attack?" Hamdir asked. Shard could run hundreds of simulations in minutes.

"If they are able to siphon off one Dragon's power and transfer it to another, then I think they can crack the ice palace. As for how long it will take? That varies on their attacks and what Akatol puts into his defense." Shard tried to stay neutral as possible. "I don't have enough data on the Dragons to make an accurate prediction of the outcome."

"I thank you for your opinion, anyway," Hamdir said with a smile to Shard.

Shard bowed his head slightly at the compliment.

"What about the technology they're using? It sounds like the Stone Raiders' power-storing amulets and soul gems."

"They are extremely similar." Shard's voice became strained.

Hamdir gave Shard an odd look. "What kind of soul gems are they using?"

"Vault."

Hamdir's eyebrows rose. "How did they get vault soul gems? There aren't many factories. Dave and our own factories are the only ones in existence and we aren't even selling them off to other people. The Stone Raiders and our own soul gems are used for power storage movement. We haven't even replaced all of the other soul gems we have. Dave or someone in the Stone Raiders must have sold them one. There..." Hamdir's finger tapped on his cup in thought.

Someone in the Stone Raiders has a connection to the Dragons? How? And who? Just talking to a Dragon is something only said in legends.

Hamdir didn't notice Shard's guarded expression.

"The Dragons are splitting up. One group is staying outside of the total domain; the others are entering and beginning their attacks," Shard said.

"Could you show me?"

Shard shared a video through the interface.

They were watching through a scout that had been sent out as soon as they found out about the three creatures returning to Emerilia.

It and several dozen others had exited drop pads around Akatol's ice palace, taking up positions to wait and watch.

Hamdir watched as Dragons came howling out of the sky. Their breaths were all the colors of the Affinities. They hit with enough power to send chunks of ice out of the ice palace's walls. They landed, surrounding the palace as they continued to stream their attacks.

The ice palace lit up in color, seals trying to defend and the light of their attacks being reflected by its spectacularly reflective surface.

It was truly a show of massive power. Even if the Aleph used all of their automatons, they wouldn't have been able to do a sixth of the damage that the Dragons were putting out.

"Good luck," Hamdir said.

The mystery of how they had got a vault soul gem lay in the back of his mind, but more than that, he had hope that the Dragons might be able to deal with Akatol before he came up with some other terrible plan to increase his power.

***

Josh closed the same video feed that Hamdir and Shard had been watching.

He hoped that the Dragons had a way to defeat the creature lying in the heart of the ice palace. It seemed that they had some plan. Otherwise, he doubted that they would have appeared in front of the ice palace and fought with all of their strength.

He let out a sigh and stretched. He was sitting in his office in the Stone Raiders' main tower. "Well, enough of this crap. I'm going to get out and do something!"

In a flash, he was out of his chair and at the door into his office. He opened the door, stretching as he walked and kneading his back with his knuckles. "I know this is supposed to be as realistic as possible, but making my back hurt from sitting in a chair for so long?

There are some things that they could have done without," Josh complained.

He got to an elevator and stepped in. He looked through the clear walls. The entire building was slowly being changed from stone to soul gem. It was cool to see as the soul gem ate upward through the towers with every day.

His elevator stopped in the training areas. He stepped out to wander through the large areas. Magical coders had been working for days to add in protections and barriers in the area so that the Stone Raiders could go all out on one another in the various training areas.

They had also gathered a number of masters from across Emerilia who taught all manner of subjects. They also did lectures in the Mirror of Communication school.

The Stone Raiders, with the aid of the best tutors and training areas, had worked to refine their skills.

There were a number who were taking the time between fights to work on their fighting ability. There were many weapon masters within the Stone Raiders. The more they learned, the more they realized that there was so much more to understand.

Our strength didn't originally come from our stats. It came from us embracing Emerilia and fighting as if that was the only way to do it. I doubt there are many Player guilds that can compete with the spell casting and weapon handling abilities of our people.

Josh found Dwayne talking with a Dwarven trainer. Josh waved to Dwayne, getting a nod as Dwayne continued to talk to the trainer, deep in discussion. Josh took the time to look around the training area.

Their little guild had now grown to nearly three thousand members. Getting in was really hard as Josh didn't want to lose the identity of the Stone Raiders with all of the new recruits rushing in to fill their spots.

Lucy vetted the people with her contacts both on Earth and in Emerilia. Cassie ran the recruitment; she looked not at a person's level, but at their commitment and how they fit with the Stone Raider values.

Then it went to the different leaders; Lucy, Florence, Kim, Dwayne, and Josh had the final say. Every person who joined the Stone Raiders needed to pass this and then some tests before they were allowed to attend training classes.

Once that was complete and they had shown their ability, they were accepted. It was the longest process of any guild, but it meant that the people they had were the best.

The Stone Raiders' fame had grown in leaps and bounds. There weren't many who would challenge their position as the number-one guild in Emerilia.

Dwayne finished his talk, shaking the Dwarf's hand, and headed over to join Josh. "So, you escaped your office and decided to come bug me? You want to see the people from Gudalo coming in?"

"I didn't escape it, just quickly left before someone can come up with an issue that I need to deal with."

"Tell me about it. It feels like I'm some kind of damn warrant officer with all the damn fires I seem to be putting out," Dwayne complained, but he couldn't hide his smile.

"You said that the people from Gudalo were coming here?" Josh said, with a confused look.

"The prisoners. They should be checked into their new living quarters soon."

Josh's face took on a sour expression.

"Look, I know you don't like how close this is to slavery, but it's way better than what most people would have on Earth if they were put into prison. Here, they can learn more skills. They've still got some freedom, and through their hard work, they can get free and clear with new opportunities and skills under their belts to do something for Emerilia," Dwayne said. "I don't like it much, either, but we're not treating them bad and it's not as bad as it could be."

"I know—just, it's weird."

"Well, we can go take a tour if you want, get to check them out?" Dwayne suggested.

"It would put my mind at ease. Didn't Alkao take a whole lot of them to help out in Devil's Crater?" Josh had just been swarmed with things; he hadn't been able to keep track of it all.

"He's taking about seventy percent of them. He's got all manner of jobs. Lucy and Florence were talking to him and the Aleph. They've created a job board for the people that all three of us need. The prisoners can also apply for these different positions. Better to give them something that they enjoy and can excel at than restricting them to the same droll job that they hate." Dwayne led the way to the elevator.

"Seems I'm not the only one who has been busy." Josh smiled, happy that they weren't just going to be using the prisoners for forced hard labor.

"Hah! You think that we get anything close to a break around here!" Dwayne slapped Josh on the back. Most people would have been thrown a few feet with the power of the simple back slap.

"I know we don't! Hell, I didn't think we would be opening Terra to everyone so early. Already eighty percent of the city has been paid for. We've been hiring Aleph engineers to keep on expanding the city now that Dave is spending all his time working on different projects and lecturing within the Mirror of Communication," Josh said.

"Who would have thought that we'd get a city all to ourselves and that it would become the economic heart of Emerilia?" Dwayne shook his head as they stepped into the elevator. The

Stone Raiders inside greeted them with nods and continued their own conversations or waited until they reached their floor.

"Well, I think we should plan on going on an excursion. All this sitting is making me forget that this is a game. With everything set up, it's not going to be hard for Shard to run most things," Josh said.

"That could be fun. You want to go check out a portal?" Dwayne laughed at his friend's expression. He clearly knew that he had Josh's attention.

"Sure! It's been awhile since I've fought something from another realm. Which one are you thinking?" Josh asked.

"Well, there's one to the west of Devil's Crater. It's undiscovered right now. The DCA scouts saw that there was a heavy concentration of mobs in the area. They didn't confirm that it was a portal, but in my heart, I have a feeling."

Josh felt the conversations dim around him, all of the people in the elevator listening in. "How long would it take to reach?" Josh asked.

"About a week or two of traveling. It's past the Ashal River and near the Northwood," Dwayne said.

"Florence was saying something about getting heavenly falcons. If she can get them, then we can keep supplies coming in as we move. See if the Aleph would be interested in scouting for us. If they find a portal there, we'll give it a go. Think of the amount of people who would be going through Devil's Crater to check out a new portal? Also, if it's a good enough realm, we could put an ono down." Josh's thoughts had quickly devolved into excited ideas.

They could try to send teams out to put down the ono and file out; however, the scouting party would be under a lot of pressure from the creatures in the wilderness and their chances of making it were slim. Also, if there was an ono down, they would have to rush people through it to establish a base. If they couldn't get control of the area then they would lose an ono.

"Maybe it will connect to a realm other than the Alturarans!" Dwayne said, his own excitement building.

The two of them grinned at each other, their sense of adventure making them visibly excited.

"Scouts first and then confirm with Florence and Lucy. If so, then we can put out a guild-wide raid," Josh said, trying to be realistic, but the possibilities, they were just too exciting!

They continued through Terra, quickly sending out messages and making plans.

Within the hour, every Stone Raider heard about the possibility of a portal raid.

There were only a handful of portals open: three to the Alturaran's lands, one to the Ooinfa realm, and one to the Ikiul realm.

In no time, they were at the greenhouses.

Josh and Dwayne's tones were less excited as they entered. There were groups of people all over the place. Most wore simple clothes with a necklace and a simple bracelet. They were the prisoners from Esamael's armies.

They looked around in amazement. Even being so close to the Per'ush islands, few had even seen the islands. Most saw the lower islands, not the magical higher islands that were filled with all manner of magical devices.

When they came to Terra, they had been scared. Now, they looked around in amazement. They might not be geniuses, but Gudalo had a long history of mages who had failed to make it into the mage's college and instead stayed in Gudalo in hopes of gaining more insight into the world of magic.

The machines and items of Terra wouldn't be out of place in the higher Per'ush islands. Sure, many of them were going to be working simple jobs, but they couldn't believe the amenities within their homes: Hot water on demand, no need to have a Fire mage or a fire—just turn a knob. Also, toilets that flushed, not a simple hole dug in the ground away from camp.

Josh and Dwayne walked through. There were people being shown what their apartments could do. Others were being taken around the greenhouses to become acquainted with them. The various farmers and gardeners who had tested out the greenhouses first were now on hand to teach these prisoners how to manage them and use them to grow food throughout the year.

Josh and Dwayne left the growing towers feeling better. The prisoners didn't look to be too happy with their situation, but they seemed interested enough and it was clear that they wouldn't be treated badly.

They moved to the refinery, finding again more people being shown the different facets of the refining equipment. The same happened with those who were in charge of keeping the gardens and streets in their best conditions. Down with the miners, it was again more lessons on different types of equipment after they'd been shown their homes within Terra.

It seemed that they had been ready to accept the worst. Now, the prisoners were still hesitant, but it seemed that a ray of hope had crawled into their hearts.

Josh was surprised by a prompt that jumped into his vision.

With your accommodations and leniency toward the prisoners, their efforts will increase by 5%.

Josh looked at the interface in shock.

"I wonder if there is any way to increase that?" Josh looked over Terra. With the help of the prisoners, their allies, and the vendors they traded with, Josh felt more positive for the future.

He had been scared of it all coming apart, failing miserably. Although there still was a chance of it, he felt that the immediate pressure and stress of failure had lessened greatly.

"Well, we should probably hurry to the meeting with Lucy or else she's liable to kick our asses," Dwayne said.

"Crap, I totally forgot about that," Josh complained. He'd just escaped his office!

***

"While we're all here, I should also let you know that the first round of the onos have been placed." Lucy looked to the various Stone Raiders leaders.

"Cliff-Hill, Devil's Crater as well as Per'ush's highest island have all received one. We have also placed one in Verlun and Haugr in Gudalo. Nadorf, Asha-moor, Kufo'tel, Xen'ur and Sel'heam in Opheir and every major Dwarven mountain have also received theirs. Mostly, we've got a ton of sea-going people using them. Now that Melhoun is out, he's been causing problems. Convoys have gone missing so the onos come at a much-needed time. In Heval, So-Durn, Veloria, Cout'sah, Zol'Ord, Ber'dar, Zolari, Isefret, and Tawre have also joined the network. Ashal has the most onos distributed, with every kingdom, nation, and state having at least one ono in the same city as their normal teleport pad. It looks to me like they're going to be purchasing onos just to make an interlinking network of their own to pass through their kingdom when they're being attacked or are in times of need. However, we still have primary rights on the onos as Dave and Steve worked with Ela-Dorn to create them. We were also able to leverage some resources and money from most of the places that we put the onos. It will pay for the next fifty onos, nearly two months of production. The Aleph are stepping up another two factories to deal with the demand. I have also ordered another ten teleport pads. Right now, they're on credit, but I hope that by the time we receive them, we will be able to pay for them ourselves."

Everyone in the room looked shocked with all the progress that had been made.

"What about Markolm?" Josh asked.

"I've talked to them. They're really isolationist, so it doesn't seem that they'll be interested in the onos even if it does open up other trade routes," Lucy said.

"I think that they might come around once they realize the trade opportunities that come with the onos. Most of the port cities have joined us as they see how goods are already passing through Terra at a crazy rate. For them, they're staying alive by investing into them."

Josh tapped his finger on the table. "As you might know, there is a possible portal location near Devil's Crater. I was wondering—how viable would it be to connect an ono to the location?"

"Well, I would say that it would be worth it if we can control the portal. I know that the resources that are reported to be in the Ashal wilderness are some of the best in Emerilia. I haven't seen them and I don't know the value of them so I'm not sure how viable it would be to put an ono there." Lucy glanced to Florence.

"If there is an expedition, I can have a look over the kinds of goods that are being moved out of the area. With our own guild members getting reduced fees, I can figure out the loss for travel against what they will make selling these items through the guild. If the Ashal wilderness is as resource-rich as I've heard, then I think it might be a good plan for us to put an ono there," Florence added.

"Better than say, putting an ono next to the portal in Opheir? As long as it's next to a portal, we'll make a lot of gold back," Lucy rebutted.

"If it's in Ashal, then we would be getting gold from not only the portal but also the surrounding area. Also, Ashal is supposed to have the best of everything, so that portal has a high chance of having something incredible on the other side of it," Florence said.

Dwayne, Josh, and Kim grinned to one another at this. They were already excited for what they might find on the other side of the portal, thinking that it might have some kind of extremely powerful place on the other side of it. It made their fighting spirit rise.

"We can spare an ono for it, but only if the Ashal wilderness is as rich as it's supposed to be and the portal is something great," Lucy said, being the cold logic that the group needed.

"Very well," Josh agreed. He wasn't able to hide his excited smile. He lived to raid!

Chapter 14: A Memory of the Past

Light smiled to herself. Since Khanundra had come back, she had been filled with inner excitement. With the leader of her angels returning, it confirmed that her legions of angels would also return. They numbered in the millions and were the strongest force on Emerilia when they had been imprisoned.

She had sent out her messengers and brought the few champions she had back into the fold. Khanundra was training the champions and assuring their loyalties as well as visiting the different loyal followers of Light.

She was seeing an upsurge in the Mana pool that was created by the devotions of her supporters. Her champions were growing stronger than ever and Khanundra's contribution was also not slim.

Dark might be an idiot in most manners, but I will have to thank him for the power he showed me with his second Demon Horde.

"You called for me, my lady?" Khanundra's voice flowed through the room. It was pleasant as it was respectful toward Light as she bowed before her goddess.

"For too long, you have been away from my side. You have remained loyal throughout the years. It is time that I rewarded you for your undying loyalty." Light seemed to float from her chair, coming to stand before Khanundra's bowed figure.

Although Khanundra was nine feet tall, Light was nearly sixteen. She looked like an immortal statue, filled with beauty, every inch of her glowing perfection.

"Khanundra, will you become my champion? Will you be my sword and shield in Emerilia?" Light's voice carried through the room, her very skin radiating light, making the rest of the room seem dark.

"I will give my life to you, my lady. My sword and shield are already yours," Khanundra said, without even a quiver in her voice.

Light touched Khanundra.

Khanundra let out a slight gasp as power flowed through the room. She was raised up, gritting her teeth as her wings spread out, surrounding her in pristine glowing white light. Threads of golden light reached toward Khanundra, coming from every direction; they surrounded Khanundra, making a golden aura that slowly seeped into her body, her strength increasing rapidly.

Khanundra pulled in a cold breath and opened her eyes. They were filled with golden light, making her look like a divine warrior.

The light seemed to dim after some time. Khanundra's aura stretched out across the room, making a few quiver at its strength. It had to be said that these people lived with the Lady of Light's aura daily.

Khanundra's wings seemed to be lit with a golden glow from within. Her eyes were a bright golden color, her skin like porcelain that had been blended with a golden essence.

Khanundra came back to the ground. She tried to prostrate herself and instead left a crater in the floor as she flew through the hall. She used her wings to steady herself; the wind in the room seemed to be from a tornado with just a single flap of her wings.

"My lady, I am sorry!" Khanundra tried to show her respect but found herself being tossed about with her massive increase in strength. It had more than doubled!

"Khanundra, stop." Light smiled. *She is stronger than I had ever hoped! What will happen when I turn the rest of my angels into my champions? No one will stand in their way. They will kill everything that dares to make devotions to another god! I will pull the other gods from their seats! I will make them beg for the end, for me to end their reign!*

None of her inner maliciousness made it to the surface as she gave Khanundra a motherly smile. "Child, your strength has greatly increased. This is not a blessing that I have given easily. Take your time to see that you learn to control it."

"Yes, my lady! I will learn to command this new strength and I will use it in order to spread your teachings, words, and ways to the entirety of Emerilia!" Khanundra passionately declared.

"Good. Once your brothers and sisters arrive, we will once again be able to show the people of Emerilia the way of Light." Light smiled softly. *They'll rue the day that they ever thought to bow to another god, and forget the power that us gods have! Take their devotions from me, will they? I will bathe in their blood for their insolence!* An old and terrifying anger ran through her veins as she remembered the many insolences that the people of Emerilia had committed against her.

Chapter 15: Bringing in Some Extra Firepower

Malsour looked at the recording that Louna, his sister, had sent him. It showed several Dragons attacking the ice palace with everything they had. It was an incredible sight and the ice palace was clearly reducing in size.

It was slow work, telling of how strong Akatol's magic and abilities were, but the Dragons were driven and they were not going to be deterred.

He closed the recording and walked through the Aleph power station. It didn't take him long to access the secret laboratory hidden within the power station's structure.

He heard more than saw Dave working in one of the isolated rooms off to the side. Malsour moved closer; before, the door to the room had been closed and Dave hadn't let anyone in.

"Come on in," Dave said. The sound of a carver came from the room he was in.

"What are you doing in there?" Malsour moved to the room where Dave was.

Steve, also interested, moved toward the room, too.

Malsour's eyes went round at the sheer number of runes that littered the inside of the room. There were also soul gems in the four corners of the room. It looked like the inside of a cell where a crazy person had been staying for the last ten years. When Malsour looked closer at the runes, he saw that they were grouped together into coded pages.

The number of these pages just had to be seen to be believed. He moved to a few of them. He touched one. It gave slightly before clicking. It wasn't just a page, but a rack of them on top of one another.

"Well, it's not completed just yet, but it's a teleportation array. I've been messing around with gravitational and teleportation magic. Needed somewhere to do it and I didn't want to do it on myself.

It was over-engineered, so that I could change out different parts easily. Also, so it doesn't blow up." Dave sounded frustrated at the last part, mostly muttering to himself.

"Blow up?" Malsour asked, just as Steve made it to the room.

"This is kickass!" Steve declared as he walked into the room.

"Thanks! I haven't finished with it yet and it's still not online fully, but I can use it as an anchor point easily enough." Dave grinned.

"You were saying about something blowing up?" Malsour asked.

"Well, there were some heat transfer issues." Dave shrugged. "I tested out a much smaller design that was based off the same principles in a lab in the Mirror of Communication." Dave waved his hand as if it was a non-issue.

"You want us to use this thing that you haven't even tested out yet in reality?" Malsour asked. "Suzy was right—sometimes you're blind to reality!"

"Hey! I prefer visionary!" Dave said.

"He is right. This isn't anywhere close to finished; the runes haven't been filled in and most of those metal plates haven't been engraved," Steve said.

"When the hell did you turn into the responsible one?" Dave shook a metal sheet at Steve before he headed back into his workshop to deal with the teleportation array.

"Says just how crazy this plan is," Malsour muttered under his breath. Leaving to work on his own projects, he saw Steve head over to a table where the bags of holding and other spatial holding items were spread out.

"So, he's finally roped you into this as well?" Malsour waved to the storage items.

"Well, after learning about coding from Dave, I've been looking into it. I'm made up of magical coding so it would make sense if

I knew how everything works and try to figure out a few upgrades." Steve looked up from his work with a grin.

Malsour shook his head. Steve was already an incredibly powerful creation. Dave and Malsour had worked with the Aleph and Shard to make his body as strong as possible, to increase the amount of power he could store. "You been working on any upgrades?" Malsour asked.

"Get in there! I know you fit—I made you!" Dave could be heard yelling from inside the room that housed the teleportation array.

"I've been trying something out, but it's a surprise. You're not allowed to go into the fifth test room!" Steve said.

Malsour's eyes thinned, looking at Steve as if trying to find out what he was keeping a secret.

"All right, but I'm interested now!" Malsour said. Every inventor or builder usually wanted to keep the full scale of their projects a bit secret just to wow and impress others. Malsour knew this from his own experience. He was fine with letting Steve show off his work when he wanted to.

"What are you up to?" Malsour looked into the crazy room—as he liked to call it.

"Trying to up the power of the damn array, without alarming the Jukal. Apparently opening wormholes between planets isn't looked upon too kindly by the froggy bastards!" Dave waved a carver at Malsour before he darted a glance at a bank of coded metal sheets that were out from the wall.

"Hey! Not my fault I was born a frog! Would you rather I told you before you alerted the Jukal or after?" Bob yelled back.

"Well, a bit of warning before I did the grand reveal would have been nice!" Dave yelled back as he pulled a metal-coded sheet from a rack and placed another in its place.

"Hi Bob," Malsour said to the two Gnome feet that stuck out from under the racks of coded plates.

"Hey, Malsour. Mind giving us a hand? Damn Snow White over there put this all together but the power output is too large and the signal so easy to detect that we've got to change it all around before we can test it," Bob said over the sound of a carver at work coming from Dave as he worked on a code plate.

"Well, what are we supposed to be coding for?" Malsour took off his cloak and put it outside of the room that had coded plates strewn across the floor.

"We're seeing about creating summoning doorways," Dave said. "I had just figured out how to open a summoning doorway between Emerilia and the other realms, which are really just cages where powerful creatures have been grown by the Jukal. I was just showing Bob here and then he told me that the Jukal would have a shit fit with all the readings this thing is giving off. So, we've got to reconfigure it. Then, once we have that done, we can start testing to see if the damned runes will even work." Dave carved symbols into a plate as he talked.

"So, you're building kind of a shell to hide the emissions that the summoning array would give off, and then copying a summoning circle and directly accessing the different holding areas or realms of the Jukal. How much power is this going to take?" Malsour asked incredulously.

"Not much, actually. The biggest thing is making it seem just like a summoning, not a machine doing it. The creatures are being held in one of the moons around Emerilia anyway," Bob said.

"That makes sense. I've always thought that creatures were summoned from other planets, kind of like how the aggressive species come from different planets. Though the portals to other planets take up a ton of energy while a summoning can be done by an albeit rather powerful summoner with powerful resources who doesn't need nearly as much power." Malsour clicked his fingers together as it started to make sense.

"Well, if you could give us a hand, it would help out. We've got a lot of silver to put into these runes and a bunch of coded plates that can be cleared." Dave waved at different piles.

"Let's get started." Malsour rubbed his hands together gleefully.

***

Kala watched her soldiers train with a sense of pride. Just a week and a half ago, they had defeated the aerial troops. It was nearly a complete victory. Although her people had done well, she had seen a number of flaws and she didn't want them getting big heads about their victory.

They'd been given a half day of rest, mostly for Kala and the other officers to get to meet Deia and work on their troops' training regime.

First, Deia had integrated magic into the training. They had records of everyone's magical Affinities and their stats. From that, they were able to make different classes.

Some were designed where people worked to solely develop their magical talent, but others to use it to augment their fighting styles and another to work on fighting without magic. Everyone went through these classes. Some were better than others in different areas, but having a knowledge of them all was good to not only train, but know of when fighting different enemies.

Every week, Kala instigated fighting matches to see how people had improved. Stats and skills were good numerical ways to see someone's ability, but seeing them in action was the best way to realize their ability. Now, she was starting to see people using their magical abilities and being wary of what people might do with their magic. They were more alert and determined.

Krenua's people had also joined in on the training, seeing the value of it to develop their own skills. It only made Kala's ground forces work harder in order to prove their strength. A bit of friendly competition did wonders.

Deia floated through the ranks of people fighting. People from every race had been hired to teach the DCA. They were all masters in their field. Most kingdoms weren't able to hire people like them due to their cost.

Deia had got Suzy to work some of her magic, talking up Devil's Crater, and they had come to train the DCA cheaply. They were some of the best trainers that Kala had worked with.

Kala moved through the training area, from where people were fighting one-on-one to the range where people were firing arrows, hurling spears, trying out crossbows and their bracelets.

Deia floated over with a smile on her face. "It hasn't even been two weeks, but they're learning quickly. I can't wait to see what they're going to be like in a month."

"This progress has only been possible through your trainers and your own instruction."

"Thank you, but you gave me a good base to work from."

Kala grunted and the corners of her mouth rose ever so slightly. She was proud of what she had accomplished and the abilities of her people.

Deia paused her movement, frowning as she checked something. Myriad emotions rolled across her face. "I have to go!" Deia said suddenly.

"Something wrong?" Kala asked.

"No, nothing's wrong. My mother is having her baby!"

"Oh, oh! Well, go, get out of here! I'll cover for you!" Kala waved her hands.

"Thank you!" Deia moved away quickly and then faster and faster. It was nothing close to her proper speed, as she didn't want to go too fast and hurt her baby.

***

Dave stood up from where he had been working, changing out the different plates, adding in new racks and altering the teleportation and gravity room. It was nearing completion but it was a big undertaking.

Prompts started to fill his vision.

"Woo-hoo! Quest rewards!"

Quest Completed: Friend of the Grey God Level 6

Create transportation network across Emerilia

Rewards: Unlock Level 7 Quest

+10 to stats (stacks with previous class levels)

+600,000 EXP

Class: Friend of the Grey God

Status: Level 5

+60 to all stats

Effects: Access to hidden quests.

Access to the Imperial Carrier *Datskun*

Quest: Friend of the Grey God Level 6

Distribute "Band-Aid" across Emerilia

Rewards: Unlock Level 7 Quest

Increase to stats

Quest Completed: Bleeder Level 4

Create transportation network across Emerilia

Rewards: Unlock Level 5 Quest

+10 increase to stats (stacks with previous class levels)

+400,000 EXP

Class: Bleeder

Status: Level 4

Effects: +30 to all stats
Ability to disable Jukal Link

Quest: Bleeder Level 5

Distribute "Band-Aid" across Emerilia

Rewards: Unlock Level 6 Quest

Increase to stats

Level 232

You have reached Level 232; you have **150** stat points to use.

He quickly checked his character sheet.

Character Sheet

Name:	David Grahslagg	Gender:	Male
Level:	202	Class:	Dwarven Master Smith, Friend of the Grey God, Bleeder, Librarian, Aleph Engineer, Weapons Master, Champion Slayer, Skill Creator, Mine Manager, Master of Space and Time, Master of Gravitational Anomalies
Race:	Human/ Dwarf	Alignment:	Neutral Good
Unspent points: 150			
Health:	42,300	Regen:	22.16/s
Mana:	14,680	Regen:	51.30/s
Stamina:	4,740	Regen:	45.50/s
Vitality:	423	Endurance:	1,108
Intelligence:	1,468	Willpower:	1,026
Strength:	474	Agility:	910

"Fire is having her baby! They need a healer!" Malsour yelled.

Bob sat up so hard, he smacked the rack above him. Malsour dropped the plate he had been working on.

"I'm going to get Jules!" Dave yelled, tripping and falling over different plates and items.

"I'm coming!" Malsour yelled.

"Bob, we'll be back in a minute and then we'll need you to take us to Fire's home in Per'ush and then to Densaou!" Dave yelled, already halfway through the shop and headed for the door.

"I'll be ready!" Bob yelled to Dave and Malsour's backs.

Dave and Malsour moved with all the speed that they could put on. They were like twin air streams, moving faster than a person could see with their eyes.

They got to the ono, both of them watching anxiously for ten minutes. The teleport pad was currently connected to another location, people moving through the event horizon, leaving and entering Terra. After a few minutes, the teleport pad closed down; moments later, its runes started to move as it connected to the ono.

They ran through again, people yelling out as they sprinted through the teleport room and headed into the city. Most people had never seen anyone move as fast as them and were left in disbelief of what they had seen.

Dave and Malsour headed right for the medical center attached to the teleport pad control center.

"Where's Jules?" Dave demanded of the healer on duty.

"Over at the main healing building," they said without pause.

"Thanks!" Malsour said as the two of them ran out of the room. Dave stepped into the sky, dragging Malsour with him as they took off like bullets toward the main healing building located in the center of Terra. They came back down, landing in front of the hospital.

"Jules—where is she?" Dave yelled.

"Third floor, in her office!" someone yelled out.

Dave and Malsour went to her office, leaving blurry images, wind throwing anything that was light and not tied down. They got to the third floor at breakneck speed.

"What's up?" Jules asked, just as she finished reading the message from the first healer at the teleport pad.

"Deia's mom's having a baby, need your help!" Dave said.

"Okay, where is she?" Jules grabbed her bag of holding and a coat.

"We'll take you." Malsour picked her up in a princess carry before she knew what was happening, and ran back through the hospital and right out toward the teleport pad again.

They rushed through the still open teleport pad, heading back into the power station facility. In just a few minutes, they were right back where they started.

Bob was waiting for them, his eyes glowing silver as they stepped in close to him.

"What is this place?" Jules said, as they entered the hidden laboratory filled with different items. Steve watched them all as Bob raised his hands. Mana filled the room.

"Here we go!" Bob said.

They appeared in Fire and Mal's apartment. Fire was breathing heavily, holding Mal's hand before her features twisted and she gritted her teeth together in pain.

Jules looked around. They had somehow been teleported from that laboratory into the room. Jules didn't need to waste her time on questions; she would have time for that later. She jumped out of Malsour's arms and moved to Fire.

"Hello, my name is Jules. Seems that this little one is ready to come out. I'm just going to make sure everything is okay and guide you through this," Jules said in a calm voice. Smiling to Mal and Fire, she rubbed her hands and touched Fire's belly.

"So, looks like Deia's going to have a sibling. Do you mind if I ask what your name is?" Jules said, her voice calm as she checked on the baby and mother.

"Fire, her name's Fire. I'm Mal." Mal rubbed Fire's shoulder even as she tried to break his hand with her grip.

What sounded like a jumbo jet plummeting to the ground could be heard breaking through the sound barrier before slowing down. A wave of heat passed over the area and a rush of wind billowed outward. Deia stepped into the room, flames dying around her.

"Fire, okay, well, the baby is turned the wrong direction, but that's easily fixed. It's going to feel a bit uncomfortable though," Jules said.

"Everyone ready?" Bob asked.

Mana once again flooded the room.

In a flash, they all appeared in a large apartment cut from rock. The heat climbed in just a few seconds, but Deia and Malsour both used their power to block the heat from affecting Jules. The others all had their own ways of dealing with the heat.

Thankfully, the couch that Fire had been on came with them.

Jules didn't have time to look around much. If she did, she might have noticed that they were in a volcano and that a number of Dragons moved toward the apartment, taking on Human forms to watch as their creator brought her fourth child into the world.

"Dave, you've been my assistant before. I'm going to need you again. Get over here," Jules said.

"What do you need?" Dave asked, not one bit of hesitation in his voice.

Chapter 16: Secrets

Jules sunk her consciousness into the baby in her hands. Fear welled up in her as he failed to cry. She checked his body. He was part Elf and part Human, but his power was incredible, as if all of his body vibrated with energy. His body was strong, much stronger than even a Level 50 Player's and he was but a baby. His heart beat soundly and he was in good health.

Jules opened her eyes, finding herself looking at two twin fiery eyes.

The baby moved, awkwardly, as if already trying to crawl in the air.

Jules smiled and sent a bit of healing toward his stomach, giving him a belly button.

"You have a beautiful healthy baby boy." Jules wrapped the baby in a towel Dave held out, passing it to Mal, who then laid the boy against Fire's chest.

Sweat covered her clothes and her hair.

Jules touched Fire's foot, sending healing through her. In just a few minutes, Fire's body was as if she had never had a child. Jules even gave her a Stamina boost so she wouldn't pass out from exhaustion straight away, but get some time with her baby.

She wiped some sweat from her forehead and slowly stood up. Her knees had long ago become numb from being on the ground. She glanced around, finding a few dozen humans all watching Fire, Mal, and their baby boy with unbridled love. Deia moved to Fire, looking at her baby brother as Malsour smiled with the other humans. As Jules looked at them, she saw a marked family resemblance between them all.

She stepped backward, finding the Gnome standing there, watching with a look of happiness on his face.

Jules's eyes went wide as she saw past the people and saw the molten lava that filled the inside of the volcano they were in. "Where the hell are we?" Jules muttered.

"We're in the Densaou Ring of Fire," Dave said, still close to her. They were both still covered in the muck of Fire giving birth.

"Why don't we get cleaned up and then I can explain a few things to you," Dave said.

Jules looked to Dave and then the scene around Fire and Mal before she nodded. "Sure."

"Okay, there's a shower this way." Dave guided her to the shower. "I'm going to rinse off my hands and then I'll be with Fire and Mal. When you're done, just come out and I'll tell you what I can."

"Okay." Jules took a shower, cleaning up and taking new clothes from her bag of holding. She stepped back out, finding the people spread out across the apartment, either making food and drinks or talking to one another. Each gave the newborn and his parents some time to themselves.

Jules moved back into the room where Fire was lying with the boy perched on her chest, fast asleep. Someone had also cleaned him off. Mal looked at the boy with clear love and affection in his eyes.

Dave had his arm around Deia, who was leaning into him as she looked at her mother, father, and sibling, her own hand on her own belly.

The Gnome sat off to the side, drinking some tea. All of the people were really kind to him and treated him like some sort of powerful uncle.

Dave saw Jules returning. He said something to Deia, who smiled, disentangling herself from Dave and talking to her parents as Dave walked over.

"Let's get something to eat and drink." Dave guided Jules to the kitchen.

"Want something?" one of the people inside asked.

"A drink and something to eat, please." Dave smiled.

"Very well, Uncle." The man smiled. They moved into the group of people around the kitchen, quickly getting a plate of snacks and some drinks.

"Thanks." Dave took the food and drink, and headed through the apartment to a balcony with seats that overlooked the interior of the volcano. Deia joined them after a few minutes.

"Thank you for everything, Jules. I know that when the time comes for this little one that I'll be in safe hands." Deia hugged Jules.

"Happy to help." Jules beamed.

"Well, have a seat. We've got lots to talk over." Dave grabbed a sandwich and ate it quickly.

Jules looked out over the inside of the volcano. "What are those flying creatures?" One of them came closer, becoming the size of an airbus before transforming into a Human as it stepped into Fire's home. "Dragons?"

"This is the home of the Lady of Fire. Deia is a demigod. The woman who just gave birth is the Lady of Fire that you have heard about in Emerilia. Now that might seem like a lot, but trust me, in a few minutes it will seem like just a minor footnote." Dave and Deia shared a look before they turned to Jules, their faces serious.

Jules's face was pale as she looked around the room, sensing the auras from these people. She couldn't detect them at all! *How powerful must they be that I can't even glimpse at their power?*

***

Jules came back to Emerilia, or reality. Bob, who had introduced himself part way through their conversation, stood next to Dave and Deia.

Jules put her elbows on the table, her hands holding her forehead with what she had seen. *If anyone heard what I was thinking, they would think I lost my mind!* She wanted to ask how this was all possible, but Dave, Deia, and Bob had explained it to her.

Bob was the Grey God, Fire was *the* Lady of Fire, Deia was her daughter and thus a demigod, Malsour was a Dragon, and she was sitting in the middle of a volcano filled with Dragons.

Well, all of it seemed relatively small compared to what she had learned.

"We were grown in vats, fed a simulation and then told this was a video game when in fact it's reality. This is some crazy ass *Matrix* shit." Jules sat back, her hands going to her legs.

This is real—then the Jukal made up the fact that I lost my legs. Made it up for Dwayne as well. All of the worry I went through, trying to find a solution, a way for me to survive and make money—they created that despair so that I would play this game, just to entertain them! My whole life just to give them some years of entertainment!

She shivered, thinking about the intimate moments that the system might have recorded between her and Esa, or the private moments she had to herself. Everything was tinged, as if it was somehow dirty.

"It's hard to take in," Dave said.

"What the hell do I do, now that I know all of this? I can't tell anyone because, well, then I would seem crazy to the rest of the Players! I can't try to get away from it, because there has to be a way that the Jukal keep Players from staying around after their cycle. Even if we try to fight them, they've stacked everything in their favor!" Jules hadn't felt this kind of uselessness since she had lost her legs. She felt as if nothing she could do could ever raise her from the low that she was now experiencing.

"We can fight. We can do everything in our power to defeat whatever the Jukal send at us. We defeat these people and creatures that were imprisoned, and we start to fight back against the Jukal," Dave said.

Jules didn't say anything for a while. Slowly she smiled. "Well, at least now the mystery of how Deia got pregnant is solved. Was wondering what kind of money it would take for the developers to allow a Player to have a pregnant character."

Dave and Deia smiled as the two of them looked to each other. One Player, one POE, both of them fighting together to create a better future.

Jules's fighting spirit filled her as she sighed. "All right, well, seeing as my game is now partly ruined, what can I do to help? It's time those Jukal got a swift kick in the ass." Jules smiled.

Inside, she was still scared, confused, and it felt as if the very ground beneath her feet was shifting. But she had picked her path and she would take it to the end.

***

Boran-al was disturbed in his work when his Mirror of Communication pulsed. He moved to the mirror without hesitation, kneeling as he pressed his hand to the mirror.

He left the room that he had been working in and appeared in what looked to be an identical hall to the one that the Dark Lord lived within.

"My lord," Boran-al said to the floor.

After he had been sent to his new place of study, commanding the Alturarans that the Dark Lord had been able to bring under his command, he had come to understand the kind of power that his lord now wielded.

"Have the divine wells been completed?" the Dark Lord asked, his voice raspy and cold.

"Yes, master. I have completed two and am working on the third," Boran-al said.

"Good, that will be enough. The champions have completed their preparations and are ready," the Dark Lord said. "I will activate the secondary portal and send through the divine wells. We will let the forces trapped within the Grey God's realm escape and come to the fore. Emerilia will succumb to war, with death and destruction ruling over all. When our enemies have weakened one another, we will send forth our forces to claim victory."

"Yes, master." Boran-al shivered with excitement, his mind already thinking of the experiments he would do, the torture he would visit upon those who had turned away from the Dark Lord.

"See that the well is sent as soon as it's charged." With that, the Dark Lord disappeared from the Mirror of Communication hall.

Boran-al also left. He turned and looked at the soul gem matrix that lay in the middle of the room. Around it were complicated Magical Circuits. They followed the circuits that were created around the Dark Lord's power well.

Boran-al was the only person other than a god who had been allowed access to see a god or goddess's divine well.

He had studied and learned the Magical Circuits, as ordered by the Dark Lord. Now, he understood why. They could harvest the power of Alturara. Then Boran-al could ship the charged well to Emerilia, where it could be taken to the Dark Lord's hall and integrated with his divine well, charging it without the overseers, the rest of the Pantheon, or the people of Emerilia knowing that he had gained so much power.

The divine well was made from multiple interlinked grand soul gems. Together, they could hold the same power as thirty vault soul gems.

With the Alturarans' devotion toward their new god, the divine well was charging faster than Boran-al had been able to predict and he was working on making the third one. His biggest bottleneck was supplies. The Alturarans had a number of dark materials at their disposal and Boran-al was making soul gems from them, but he needed grand soul gems now.

With the Dark Lord opening the second portal, he would once again be able to easily get the supplies he wanted. Boran-al looked to the other end of his massive workshop. Standing there was a portal.

The first portal was still sitting in the valley filled with Alturarans. The Dark Lord didn't need them yet, but the Alturarans didn't need many resources. They moved slowly and could live for thousands of years without fail. More of them gathered by the day and simply waited.

The portal seemed to wake from its slumber. Mana gathered around it as noises came from within the metal circle that would hold the event horizon. There was a clicking noise as more and more power was fed into the portal. The clicking stopped and the building static of Mana seemed to explode.

In a flash of light, the inner area of the portal went from looking at a plain metal wall to looking into a dark cave. Dark creatures wreathed in shadows moved forward, passing through the event horizon and entering Alturara.

These people were the Dark Lord's trusted champions. They had lived for decades as fighters, assassins, and even emperors, killing hundreds of thousands. All of them were stained with darkness. They reveled in the pain and destruction of others. They would look death in the face and embrace him as an old and familiar friend.

Now they bowed to Boran-al as they saw him move toward them.

"Take this one back to our master. I will have another one shortly." Boran-al pointed to the almost full divine well.

The largest and strongest moved to obey. A skinny, emaciated-looking man moved to Boran-al. He bowed deeply. His skin looked as though it belonged on a dried-out mummy, his eyes wild and excited.

"Master said that there might be use of our talents here in making sure the rest of the Alturarans know their place." The man's voice was barely a whisper, but the cold way in which the man talked and the way his eyes flashed in joy made Boran-al smile.

"Go, find the Alturarans that have been raised up to be champions. It will be good to have more of our master's people here. I am interested in seeing how one might torture these Alturarans. It is something that I have been unable to experiment with." Boran-al's voice filled with regret.

"It would be an honor to bring back some of them for your experiments," the mummy champion said.

Boran-al's face opened in a wild and hungry smile. Anyone would feel a shudder go through their body at the bloodthirsty and twisted expressions that the two shared.

The strongest of the champions heaved together, picking up the divine well from its magical circle. The circuit was broken but the second divine well a bit away was already starting to glow as it seamlessly took over and started to collect the power that the Alturarans devoted toward their new god.

***

Dave said good-bye to Deia in Per'ush. She needed to go back through the teleport pad there. Otherwise, people might ask questions.

They arrived back in his laboratory. Malsour and Bob went off to work with the array. It was near completion now.

"I'll talk to you later. I'm going to go see Lucy. This is all a bit much to take in," Jules said.

"I understand, it's kind of crazy," Dave said with a small, reassuring smile.

"Bit of an understatement," Jules said with a dry laugh.

Dave knew that there wasn't anything he could do for her right now. Just as he, Suzy, and Lucy had come to understand Emerilia and their homes, so did Jules need the time to understand it all.

Jules waved and headed out of the laboratory.

Dave scratched his head and moved toward the array. If they could get it working, then they would be well on their way to getting some extra fighting power. Also, they could start to miniaturize it so that they could make an easier summoning hall to use, instead of the massive array they had now.

Chapter 17: From Faraway Lands

Suzy sighed and sat back in her chair in an office in the Terra smithy. She had been coordinating deals, helping out Florence and Lucy, dealing with the prisoners, the trades that the Stone Raiders were doing as well as the smithies, factories, and different patents that Dave had put out into the world.

She had been one of the driving forces behind the population boom that was happening in Terra right now, though she had barely been able to see it. She now looked out of the massive window behind her office and looked out over Terra. There were still lots of signs of construction. The mining drills were still at work, cutting out what would be the next section of Terra. People were already asking whether they could rent places there. All of Terra had been rented out. People were moving in supplies still, but the city didn't seem to stop.

People came in from all over Emerilia at all kinds of times. People came from every continent and kingdom. Terra was the land of neutrality. People had tried to fight here, exercising old rivalries, only to be thrown out. The Stone Raiders made it clear that no one was to fight in the city unless it was in the training arenas. If they started using violence or trying to force people, then their automaton police force run by Shard would deal with them.

Many gangs and black market people had been kicked out for trying to steal or force others to do their bidding.

They didn't care whether they were gangsters or kings. If they followed the rules, then the Stone Raiders would leave them alone.

Even with the lenient rules, people didn't argue that the Stone Raiders were weak. It was easy to see, looking at their achievements and this very city, that they were not someone to be taken lightly or annoyed.

There were embassies for nearly eighty percent of Emerilia's people. Some were there more symbolically than anything, showing off their power, but most were there as a show that they would stand together in the face of whatever tried to harm Emerilia.

Suzy looked at the city, seeing its hustle and bustle, people hawking wares, the vibrations under her feet of weapons being forged or repaired. People trained in arenas as goods and supplies moved through the cities and Aleph automatons patrolled.

There was a knock at her door, ending her thoughts.

"What is it?" Suzy asked with a defeated tone as the door opened to reveal a smiling redhead.

"I've come to steal you away from all of this." Induca moved into the office and closed the door. She leaned against it and looked at Suzy.

"I've got lots of work to do though, hon, as much as I would like to spend three days and nights kissing *every* curve of you," Suzy purred.

Induca pushed off the door, her hips swaying as she moved toward Suzy. "I've always liked women in power, and I've always wanted to do it in their office." Induca said her every word slowly and with care, pushing Suzy's chair back and turning it so they were facing each other.

Induca's fingers traced Suzy's jaw and her lips pressed against hers. Suzy's heart fluttered as she rubbed her legs together, releasing her control and letting Induca take over.

Induca pulled back and looked into Suzy's eyes. "Still busy?" Induca's finger that had been holding her chin now traced down Suzy's neck.

"Always got time for you." Suzy's legs moved slowly as heat spread throughout her, and she bit her lips, excited by the thought of Induca and herself in her office.

"Good." Induca slid to her knees and pulled down Suzy's pants.

***

"Where the heck have you two been?" Dave waved his hands, a carver in one and a coded plate in the other.

"Oh, we just had some catching up to do." Suzy turned slightly and blushed as she held onto Induca's hand.

"Don't ask questions you don't want answers to," Dave muttered to himself as Malsour, who had just come out of the teleportation and gravity array, scratched his head awkwardly. No brother really wanted to know when his siblings had been off with their lover.

"So, Induca wouldn't tell me what was going on. She just dragged me down here. I have a lot of work to do, you know," Suzy complained, looking to Dave as if it were his fault.

"Hey! Why do I get blamed for this? Hire more people to take over the work!" Dave whined, not at all in keeping with the heroic stature that someone might think of when hearing the name Dave Grahslagg.

"Not my fault that a lot of people are idiots! Now, what have you been playing around with?" she asked.

"Well, one thing really. Well...kind of two." Dave waved them over to the room Malsour had walked out of. Runes had been moved around and there was a smooth piece of the floor in the center about twenty meters in diameter.

"I've got the Dwarves working to make the components of one thing; Steve is helping me between working on his own project on putting it all together. Then, I've finished working on different power sources: we've got a Mana well factory at work and a small fusion reactor that I could make more of if I wanted to, but there is simply no reason to do so right now. So, I've been focusing on gravity and teleportation manipulation. I can teleport myself pretty well." Dave disappeared and reappeared two feet to the left, his face looking a bit pale from the Mana usage. "I don't want to use it much so that people would figure it out. Also, takes a bunch of energy. Though other than that, I've got this!" Dave waved at the room.

"And, what is this?" Suzy asked. Unlike the people of Emerilia, she didn't understand just how impossible teleporting was without a teleport pad or portal. The only people who could do it were the gods and goddesses of the Affinities Pantheon.

Malsour answered first, an eager smile on his face. "Well, there are multiple things at work here. One is your basic summoning circle, which we turned into code. We also made it variable, so that you can now pick and choose which creature you want to summon. There is also a barrier system, so that the creature can't escape and cause havoc. Then, there's also a suppression and simultaneous amplification system, much like how Dave made your staff. It boosts the summoner's Willpower and makes it easier for them to make a soul binding contract with the summoned creature."

Suzy looked at it all. It would basically punch holes through space and time, tearing creatures out of Jukal storage and then bring them back to one point and make it easier for the person summoning them to assert their control over them.

"You finally finished it? The summoning hall?" Suzy said, unable to hide her excitement.

"Oh, hell yeah, I did. Though, we need you to test it out. You know the most about the summoner's lifestyle and you can tell us if anything is going wrong," Dave said.

Suzy looked at the room with appreciation. She had become a summoner, knowing that she didn't want to get directly into the fight but provide her friends with close support.

She had thought about walking the path of the pure summoner, breaking open holes between realms to pull a creature to be her servant, or soul binding creatures to her like she had done with Steve. Dave had promised that he would look into summoning so that she could instead walk the path of the creation summoner, imbuing her Willpower into multiple creatures made from various materials that would serve her and boost the fighting abilities of Party Zero. They could hold off the enemy, dealing with lower-level creatures while her party dealt with the bigger threats.

Steve provided support to Suzy and they were close, though she let him roam around and do as he wished. He had a soul binding contract with her, but he was unlike any creature that a summoner might attract. Only extremely high-leveled creatures of legend would be able to communicate with their masters. Although Suzy was impressed with Steve, she wanted another soul-bound summoned creature to increase her defense and in-close abilities. With her summoned creations, they were usually at range, unable to help her.

"Okay, so where do we begin?" Suzy asked.

"Well, pick what kind of summoned creature you want." Dave smiled and shared with her a sheet filled with the various creatures that one might be able to summon.

***

Suzy looked over the sheet with wide eyes. There were nearly a hundred creatures. All of them had descriptions next to them. It was as if she were at a store or a restaurant ordering an item, not getting into a wildly complicated ritual that would give Level 100 summoners difficulty to just get some of the lower strength creatures on the list.

Her eye caught on something.

Lightning phoenix.

She clicked on the name and a box of information appeared in her sight.

Lightning Phoenix
Many have heard of the Phoenix, a bird whose very wings look like dancing flames and with them, they carry the winds of change and rebirth. Their Vitality is unrivaled and their power is enough to make Kings and Queens jealous if they reach maturity.
Lightning Phoenixes are a much rarer breed of Phoenix; their bodies are gray and black. As they pass through the skies, the skies break ahead of them, the very air scared of the master of lightning.
No Phoenixes have ever reached maturity due to their low initial level. Their link to their master means that they create a psychic link with their masters when soul bound, instead of other common summoned beasts.
They will react to emotions with more strength than commands. This can lead to their untimely demise.

Starting Level: 0	Potential Level Threshold: Unknown
Soul Binding Contract Cost: 10 Willpower	Abilities: Lightning attributes Psychic link Unknown

She let out a breath of air. She had never heard of such a creature before. It also had no upper limit. Some creatures were limited by their level or they would be summoned at a certain level. The lightning phoenix would be bound to her at a low cost to her Willpower as it would be Level 0; it meant that she would have to raise it by sharing her experience. If she was able to raise it up, then there was no limit to the strength of her summoned beast.

Suzy smiled. For her, completing a few quests or upgrading the level of her classes in order to get some experience just took time. If she was to head out on some dungeon-clearing quests, she could easily level up the creature.

"Lightning Phoenix—let's give it a try," Suzy said.

There was a noise off to the side, as if someone had a shelf of metal components come crashing down.

Steve came out of a room, complaining as he shook off metal plates and bits of soul gem.

"What? I want to see this other contracted thing!" Steve kicked some bits back into the room he'd been in. He tried to close the door, but couldn't, finding things in the way. "I should clean up some time." Steve kicked other items out of the way before he shut the door. "Okay! So let's see what this thing can do!" Steve grinned.

Malsour and Dave moved to the array. They shifted around various things, conferring with each other as they turned dials on two workstations in the walls. The runes in the room moved around, changing positions.

It took a few minutes before they all settled down.

"Okay, so, Suzy, you stand here." Dave pointed at a cleared portion of ground before the large circle in the center.

Suzy did so.

"We'll power this thing up. Should take no more than a few minutes to do, so have your soul binding contract and spell ready. You won't have to spend any energy on the summoning, so just focus on bringing that creature under your control." Dave looked to her.

"Okay." Suzy had been thinking of this moment for nearly two years. She was excited and nervous. Summoning and contracting a beast was some of the most powerful magic that a summoner knew.

"Activating summoning," Malsour said.

The runes around the room started to glow with energy, coming from four different corners where soul gems were embedded into the walls. A hum of Mana filled the air as the circle Suzy was in lit up with power. The runes between her and the summoning circle lit up; the circle started to glow with power.

Then, there was a flash of massive power. Most summoners had to use their blood to make these summoning circles because it was more accurate and the power needed was extraordinarily high.

A screech tore through the air. In one moment, there was nothing in the main circle, and then there was a small bird. It looked to be about the size of Suzy's hand. The screech had been its infant roar.

Sparks crackled along the bird's wings. It had a cute appearance, but Suzy felt that this would become an incredibly powerful beast in the future.

As it soared forward, it sounded as if lightning were chasing it, instinctively using its lightning power to increase its speed. It hit the barrier around the summoning circle. It let out an indignant squeak.

Suzy used a far sight spell to look at the lightning phoenix. It had a regal and powerful air even in its infant state. It screeched; white lightning raced from its mouth and hit the barrier. Its body looked like living lightning given phoenix form.

"Suzy!" Dave said, pulling her out of her thoughts and studying the creature.

"Got it," Suzy said, embarrassed that she had paused before casting the soul binding spell. She pulled out a dagger. Cutting her finger, she quickly drew a magical circle on her hand before she reached out toward the phoenix.

"Come here, little one. Let's have lots of adventures together and raise you to be a big, proud lightning phoenix," Suzy said in a calming voice as she cast the spell.

The phoenix lowered itself and came closer to Suzy, as if recognizing someone more powerful than it.

The phoenix bucked lightly under the pressure Suzy was putting forward. Then it stopped fighting. It looked up at Suzy with scared eyes. The lightning phoenix was a noble and great beast and yet it looked up at Suzy with the fear of an infant. It had been awoken into a strange place and Suzy was casting a seal on it.

"Don't worry, little one." Suzy smiled at the phoenix.

It looked apprehensive for a bit as the spell finished. Suzy closed her eyes, feeling something leaving her body. She let out a breath as power flew down her arm, connecting with the bloody magical circle on her hand and toward the lightning phoenix.

Prompts appeared around Suzy as she took a few breaths, trying to stabilize how she felt and the sudden loss of power.

If gaining stats was like becoming a god, losing them was like having a cold knife cut out a part of you. Losing a part of her Willpower, her very soul, momentarily disoriented Suzy.

She took her time reading the prompts.

You Have Gained A Soul Bound Creature

The Lightning Phoenix is yours to command. Unless you break your contract with the creature or allow it to die, the contract will not be broken. Controlling this creature takes 10 Willpower from your overall stats (does not affect Mana recharge).

Soul Binding Contract

You have created a soul binding contract with a Lightning Phoenix. For a portion of your Experience, you can increase this creature's level and abilities.

The Lightning Phoenix is currently Level 0 and gains 0% of your experience.

Well, I'll be changing the amount of experience she gets really soon. Suzy moved to the next prompt.

Name Your Soul Bound Creature

Your Lightning Phoenix does not have a name. Do you wish to give her one? Y/N

"Okay, so you're female and you need a name." Suzy smiled after reading the prompt. She had thought of naming Steve, only to find out that he already had a name.

"Can we drop the barriers and enchantments?" Dave asked.

"Sure." Suzy's eyes never left the little lightning phoenix that was flapping its wings, staying in a hover as it looked at Suzy. "How does Lu Lu sound?" Suzy asked.

The phoenix cocked its head to the side before it let out a chirruping noise.

"I'll take that as a yes?" Suzy asked.

It made the same noise again.

"Lu Lu, it is." Suzy smiled as the barrier dropped and the different runes in the room stopped glowing.

The phoenix approached Suzy slowly. It smelled her, circling a few times, and then it came to land on Suzy's shoulder.

Suzy tensed, expecting to get shocked by the lightning that ran over the phoenix's body. Instead, she just felt the small claws of the young phoenix holding onto her shoulder, digging through part of her shirt but not making it to her actual skin.

The phoenix was warm and her feathers were light. None of the lightning around the creature hurt Suzy.

She looked to the phoenix. She had four wings, two on either side, with a large tail. She was clearly meant to achieve great heights and then use air streams to glide to her destinations. She had a long neck that ended in a head similar to an eagle's head. Her large eyes looked to Suzy, as if trying to understand her better.

"Hello there, Lu Lu," Suzy cooed, holding out a hand to the creature.

She looked at Suzy's hand, and then Suzy's face once again. Suzy inched her hand forward and stroked the phoenix's feathers.

Lu Lu flapped her wings, getting comfortable before she let out a pleased cooing noise. Suzy gave her a light scratch. Lu Lu turned in to it, clearly pleased with the petting.

Suzy began to take her hand away, but Lu Lu let out an indignant coo, poking Suzy's hand and then pointing at her back.

Suzy laughed, petting the phoenix again. It seemed to relax, lowering itself and flapping her wings to get comfortable. Suzy turned back to the others by the door into the room.

"She's so cute! Hello, Lu Lu!" Induca moved closer.

Suzy was afraid that Lu Lu would get scared again, but Induca started to scratch Lu Lu as well.

She let out content coos at the attention.

"Looks like a weird flying kite that ran into a power line," Steve said.

"And the mood's gone." Dave sighed. "Malsour, up for a beer? Seems this thing works. After this, we can go see Ela-Dorn. See if she can help us out with making this a bit smaller."

"Sure, though before we see Ela-Dorn, I'm going to take a shower and get some sleep." Malsour looked at Lu Lu, Suzy, and Induca with a happy smile.

"You going to summon a creature as well?" Dave asked.

"Well, that murmador did interest me. I've never heard of something like it and it would look cool as hell," Malsour said.

"If you get one as well, then we can go on some quests or just go and grind some experience out to level up our beasts," Suzy said.

Lu Lu rose up, flapping her wings. It seemed she agreed as well.

"Well, I heard that Josh might be planning a raid on a portal," Induca said.

"That'd be a good chance to do some leveling up," Dave agreed.

"I'm going to get back to work," Steve said. "Nice work with the flying electrical socket."

Lu Lu hissed and Steve grinned.

"Looks like she's got some fight in her." Steve chuckled and left.

"Beer o'clock!" Dave announced.

"I think we're going to take Lu Lu back to our apartment, get her settled and see about getting her some food. Then, work out a plan to get her to level up some," Suzy said.

"You'd like that, wouldn't you, baby girl?" Induca said in her baby voice. Lu Lu seemed to approve, jumping onto Induca's shoulder. "She likes me!" Induca doubled up on Lu Lu's scratches.

"You know, most people get a cat." Dave shook his head and walked out of the room.

***

Ever since Bob had told Dave about the kill switch that was implanted in his body, he'd been thinking about it.

He had looked at various ways to stop it. He'd spent hours looking at his own body, trying to find it. He'd even looked at recordings that Bob showed him of other Players who had come to the end of the Player cycle, dropping dead by the Jukal's command.

He had been able to gain some clues.

From people's gestures, it seemed that it originated from around the clavicle. There was no great big explosion; a person would only hold their chest as if they were having a heart attack and then fall forward. Moments later, their body would start to dissipate, as it did with all other creatures that were killed and looted.

Dave had been studying himself, as well as POE's and Player's physiology.

Apparently, the POE had the same kill switch in them. He couldn't find any difference that would allow him to pick up whatever the system was.

He'd even had Bob change into Human form so that he could see what a Human without the kill switch would look like. There had been no noticeable difference to Dave.

Dave rubbed his face and let out a frustrated noise.

"Hey, Dave, I might have something." Bob walked over, watching something on his interface. He made it a larger screen and shared it with Dave so that he could see it as well.

It showed someone using a Mirror of Communication.

"This is five minutes after everyone else died," Bob said, his voice flat. Seeing so many people die had been a rather morbid experience.

Dave watched as the person left the Mirror of Communication.

They sat up before their face distorted in familiar pain. They coughed blood and collapsed back on the bed they had been using. After a few moments, they started to pixelate and dissolve.

"How is that possible?" Dave asked.

"It must have blocked the signal," Bob said. "When you go into the Mirror of Communication, it creates a kind of dampening field around the user, so that no one can try to hook up, say a mind recorder to try to figure out what they're saying to others. It was a big problem last millennia, anyway. Now, it creates a signal dampening field: the Mirror of Communication processes all incoming signals, passing it to the user, or blocking it."

"So, if we were able to create that same kind of field and block those signals, then we could stop the kill switch from activating. It's not a complete answer, but it's a Band-Aid of sorts." Dave leaned forward in his chair.

"If we can get that signal, record it and figure out what it's supposed to be doing, then we can probably find out what the kill switch is and then come up with a strategy to destroy them." Bob snapped his fingers.

"Okay, so we need a signal suppression device as well as recording abilities," Dave said. "We're going to need to make this out of soul gem constructs. This coding is too complicated for the normal coding plates."

Soul gem constructs were capable of doing much more than a coding plate was. They could have much more coded into them compared to an ebony sheet. They also removed the need to integrate a power source and were the best at distributing heat.

"Well, I can probably rip some of that suppression coding from the Mirror of Communication, then get Shard or Steve to simplify it down," Bob said.

"Then, all I need to do is make a simple recording device. However, before I can compile that information, I'm going to need some receivers to pick it all up." Dave looked to Bob.

"We can't use the infrastructure I have. The Jukal are checking up on my shit. What about the onos?"

"That could work. I can update them to make a transmission system through the soul gem constructs. With them spread across Emerilia, we can use them as relays for compiling the data," Dave said.

"Perfect. We can back up the interface systems as well. I'm not sure if the Jukal will be able to turn it off or not. They need servers to be able to connect to one another over large distances. Otherwise, people would only be able to connect to those within fifty kilometers or so."

"I can do that." Dave nodded as a sense of relief filled him.

"Now, we just have to figure out what to do with the next generation of Players."

Dave looked to Bob in shock. "What?"

"When one Player cycle is in the game, there is another Player cycle being born and trained. Right now, they'll be mature in thirty years. In the Earth simulation, a day for them is about a week on Emerilia. There are currently three Player cycles in the system, for backups. Nearly seven million people. Once they near maturity, the time dilation is turned right down so that a day for them can be a month or so for everyone on Emerilia. Right now, they're just simply brains in a vat," Bob said.

"Where are they?"

"I can show you," Bob said.

Dave opened and closed his mouth. The people who would replace him were essentially his brothers and sisters. They had been born by the same Human progenitors and born from the same place and went through experiences on Earth.

"Uh, can I?" Dave asked.

Bob snapped his fingers. The room disappeared and they reappeared in a massive complex.

Dave stood up from his chair, feeling numb as he looked over the plant.

There were several levels, further divided into sections. They were filled with pods that were about a meter tall and a half meter wide.

As Dave watched, a rack extended out of the wall. A large automated robot grabbed the container, moving it from the rack to a different machine.

Dave's Touch of the Land had unconsciously spread through the room. He knew what was in the jars, but he couldn't believe it. He squinted, using far sight to see the container. Within it, there was a brain with a cap on it. A spinal column was sheathed in metal.

"There's no need for a body. The liquid in the tanks see to the Players' needs. The cap records and sends signals, allowing the AI to figure out the best way to get people addicted to Emerilia. The metal lining on the spine manipulates the nerves, allowing people to feel the different things in the Earth simulation," Bob explained. "When people go back to the Earth simulation, many of them say that things don't feel as real as they do in Emerilia. This is because they've been conditioned. It's also because once a Player cycle is active, their brains here are uploaded to the Altar of Rebirth's and a new body is printed for them."

Dave walked along the catwalk, his boots clanging on the metal decking.

Machines were constantly moving, changing out the Player capsules' solution or adjusting the encapsulating cap and metal coverings on the brain and spine.

Bob walked behind Dave.

The facility extended on into the distance, row upon row of minds, of people who were living out their lives on Earth, thinking that it was reality.

"What safety measures have the Jukal taken here?" Dave asked.

"There's a flush system, filled with a poison that will kill the brain. The other is they will cook them with heat. The last resort are bombs that line this facility. They will explode, destroying all of the supporting systems and cutting off access to the Earth simulation servers. Even if someone's brain doesn't die from the explosions, they'll slowly run out of solution without any of their senses perceiving anything as their brain withers and dies." Bob's voice turned hard.

Dave shook his head. That way of dying would be torture; he couldn't imagine what would happen to someone if they couldn't do anything. They would have nothing but their own thoughts until they finally died.

"We're not going to let them die." Determination filled Dave as he looked at the containers.

Bob smiled and looked to Dave. "I was hoping you'd say something like that." Bob sent Dave a message filled with information.

"What is all this?" Dave looked through the various technologically advanced systems that he was seeing.

"This is the coding that I have to overwrite the machines in here. It will systematically eject everyone in here from their simulation and then send them to an Altar of Rebirth. The machines think a new Player cycle has started while the people will be pulled from their lives and thrust into Emerilia. Sure, it won't be pretty and all of them will have the kill switch, but if we can get that Band-Aid on the altars, we can get a whole lot of them out before the Jukal realize it," Bob said.

"Though, they are going to notice it, and if they do, then they just activate their fail-safes—this facility goes up and everyone who hasn't been pushed out of an altar dies," Dave said.

"I've looked into making an Altar of Rebirth myself. The tech is complicated as hell. I know how to create humans and subspecies, but even I am stumped with the Altar of Rebirth. You can't even get plans for them. And if I or someone else was to see their secrets, much like the Aleph and the portals, the Jukal will kill them off," Bob said in a serious tone.

"There has to be a way." Dave sighed as he looked at all of the people, just helpless brains in a tank.

"For now, we work on getting this Band-Aid thing to work, and we think of ways to help the people out here." Bob clapped Dave on the shoulder.

Dave sighed, but nodded. "Rome wasn't defeated in a day." Dave glanced around the facility one more time. "Let's get back to the lab; I have work I need to finish."

In a flash of light, they left the facility. It was as if they were never there as millions of containers and thousands of robots silently looked after the Players.

Chapter 18: Best Laid Plans

"So, how are we looking?" Josh asked Lucy.

"Terra, the guild, the quests we have going on, or the plans for this portal raid?" Lucy leaned back in her chair and looked at Josh with a raised eyebrow.

"Portal?" Josh said, as if he wasn't sure it was the right answer.

"The Aleph have agreed to send scouts. You need to talk to the Devil's Crater ambassador. He wants to send some of the DCA with you. Get them to experience a raid and get some insights of how to fight mobs. Also, shows that they're a fighting force and not just training all the time," Lucy said.

"Okay, I can do that." Josh nodded.

"Good. Then when you get that done, the Aleph will check out the place in three days with automaton scouts, then take say a week or two for you and the raiding party to get there. Once you secure it, put down a drop plate and we'll send in an ono," Lucy said.

"Why not put the ono down before?" Josh asked.

"We don't want to put the ono down right in front of a portal we don't know that we can get to or not. Be a waste of resources. Also, with the DCA helping you out, you can ensure their aerial forces move supplies to and from your front lines."

"See, I knew you were the right person to plan this out!" Josh smiled.

"Go, talk to the Devil's Crater ambassador!"

"Fine!" Josh left her office. "Thanks, Lucy!" he said, already halfway to the elevator.

"Having a few weeks without you will be a vacation!" Lucy yelled back, smiling as she heard Josh's chuckles.

***

"Where you off to?" Dave asked Steve as he twirled his axe around in his hands. The blade made whirring noises as it cut through the air. It landed in Steve's palm.

"Hunting! Josh and Dwayne decided to check out a new untouched portal; we're going to go and check it out, see the sights, clear out some creatures, you know—same old." Steve grinned. "You wanna come?"

Dave wanted to, but he had work to do.

"Come on, you won't even need to use magic. You can fight at the front with Lox, Gurren, and me," Steve said. "When we come back, I'll even help you figure out that coding you're working on."

"I thought that you were spending all your time on your project," Dave said.

"It's nearly done. I've got some time to spare and when we take this portal, you can test out that wonder device that you and Ela-Dorn came up with...you know, that portal controller thingy." Steve waggled his eyebrows.

Dave took a deep breath and looked at everything in front of him. The summoning hall worked; Ela-Dorn's people had the plans and were already working to make another. His armor project was all under the oversight of the Dwarves. Bob and Shard were working on the whole ship dilemma.

"Look, if you agree to go on this portal excursion, I'll tell you how to make that spatial holding bag interaction with the physical world work," Steve said.

"I've been working on it for weeks! Why can't you tell me now?" Dave complained.

"Well, I haven't totally figured it out, but if I put it through some of the old cycles, I think that I can come up with the answer," Steve said.

"Give me the answer first, then I'll agree." Dave crossed his arms.

Steve groaned like a child being denied candy by its parents. He made to complain, but seeing Dave's raised eyebrow, he let his shoulders slump, a look of "why did this happen to me" on his face.

"Fine! It's only the Aleph scouts going out right now. We've got some time before they find anything, though you've got to help me in roping in the rest of Party Zero! Oh, Anna and Deia will also be coming with a group of their aerial and ground forces, simply to observe and see how we fight and teach their people," Steve said, seeing Dave start to stand up.

Dave let out an angry breath and sat back down.

"I only know because Josh was talking to the representative from Devil's Crater," Steve said.

"You overheard them?" Dave asked.

"In a manner."

"Steve, you're not to use Terra's information tech to spy on people," Dave stated.

"But Shard does it!" Steve pointed out.

"Yeah, but he has rules and guidelines, you've...well, you're you!" Dave held out both of his open hands and gestured at Steve.

"Thanks, dude," Steve said dryly. He held up a finger, his eyes moving from side to side as if reading something. "Okay, so, you want the good news or the bad news?"

"Bad news," Dave said.

"I figured out how things inside a spatial item can interact with the physical world. Though, it means I'm going to have to code my damn core out because I can do it by weight, but to have those weight changes I'm going to need to make a gravity or weight thingy that will increase and decrease weight to create controls for the ship," Steve said.

"Huh?"

"Okay, so, as there's more weight in a spatial space, it is greatly reduced but it is still an increase. What I am proposing is a system that when someone's in a spatial space...damn, say that ten times fast! Well, anyways, someone's in there, if they do actions, then I create a machine that their actions will increase the weight of the spatial item of holding, thus sending a signal through another machine on the other side, acting as an interface. Think of it as using Morse code, but with weight increasing and decreasing and then using that to pilot armor stuffed with magical coding!" Steve sighed and sat on a laboratory desk heavily.

Dave was happy that he got Malsour to build this place from metal and stone, or else Steve's metallic ass would've broken most of the tables in the laboratory.

"Though the good news is that the Aleph scouts have reached where the portal is supposed to be and are entering it. Want to watch?" Steve's excitement had already returned, forgetting about the large project that he would have to complete.

Dave smiled and shook his head. It made sense. When you put stuff in a bag of holding, its weight increased, if only at a percentage of the original item's weight. "Fine, but you're helping me out with this damned coded armor!" Dave said.

"Sure, just add it to my to-do list." Steve rolled his eyes and sent Dave a link on his interface.

***

Deia looked up from the message she had just received from Alkao as well as the forum posts by the Stone Raiders.

"Well, looks like we're going to watch a portal raid." Deia felt excitement well up in her, but then it was tempered by the knowledge that she would be there as an advisor, making sure that the DCA ground forces learned something out of it all and to make sure that they came back with new experiences instead of dying.

Meanwhile, the fighting would fall on the Stone Raiders for the most part. They would clear the way and then clear out the portal forces so that they could take it and claim it for their own. Then a private chat request appeared from Dave; she accepted it.

"Are you going on this portal raid as well?" Deia asked.

"Who told you? Was it Steve?"

"He just said that it was going ahead!" Dave said defensively.

"Woman's intuition." Deia smiled to herself.

"Well, yes, I think I am. I've just been cooped up here and working on projects for the longest time. Think it's about time I got back out there and worked on my fighting skills again. I haven't really been able to see how strong I am with these new stats."

"And you're a show-off at heart," Deia teased.

"I heard that the DCA will be sending some people out to go and watch us and get to know the area better," Dave diverted.

"Yes, I will be watching over them and we'll be shadowing the Stone Raiders so that they get some experience in the field. Better than just training them all the time or having them on guard or assisting the Devil's Crater Guard."

"I think that we can convince the rest of Party Zero to go. Everyone's a bit restless," Dave admitted.

"Be good to blow off some steam," Deia agreed.

"Well, seeing as we might be heading out in a few days, I was wondering if you would give me the pleasure of going on a date—say, tonight?" Dave asked.

Deia smiled. Even with all of his work, he occasionally pushed it off to show romantic gestures. It made her feel butterflies all over again. "Okay, but I want to see if Quindar, Anna, and their other halfs want to come, too," Deia said.

"Okay, but I get you afterward," Dave said.

Deia knew that he would just want to sit together, the two of them talking and cuddling until they fell asleep. To her, it sounded like bliss. "I can agree to that deal." Deia's worries and fears seemed to fall away as she smiled.

"Good! I'll be over in an hour or so!" Dave said. "I love you!"

"I love you too," Deia said as the chat ended.

She felt as if everything was a little bit brighter as she moved outside of her office and floated up into the air, headed for where she could sense Quindar and Anna training their forces.

***

Dave settled back down on the ground as Deia continued to study him with her arcane sight.

"What questions are rattling around in your head?" Dave smiled.

"You're using magic to move, but I've never seen anything like it except with teleport pads and portals," Deia said.

"With my high gravity skill, I learned a bit about gravity manipulation." An orb appeared out of nowhere and landed in his hand. "I use these to manipulate the gravity around me, allowing me to fly. Better than cumbersome wings and the like. Also programmed some other things into these orbs."

"So, you have those orbs around all the time?" Deia asked.

"Yeah, they're much easier to use than trying to sort out a gravity spell formation all by myself," Dave said.

Deia smiled and shook her head as the door inset to the mountain opened. Quindar opened the glass door with a wide smile and a baby on her hip.

"Deia, Dave, please come in!" Quindar waved them in.

"Thanks for having us, Quindar." Deia hugged her.

"No problem!" Quindar smiled.

"How are you doing?" Dave held out his hand, only to get pulled into a hug.

"Much better than I was, thanks to you lot." Quindar grinned. "Now, get in here, the both of you. Fornau is making up dinner, Yoalin is putting the little ones down to sleep, but this mischievous little lady already had a sneaky little nap so she's full of energy." Quindar looked at the excited little Human toddler in her hands who looked up at them with wide eyes, pawing at her.

She had a happy expression on her face from the attention and her mother's tone.

There was the sound of flapping wings behind Dave and Deia. They turned to see Alkao's massive wings working to bring his mass to a halt while Anna touched down easily, walking to Quindar.

"Hey, Quindar, who's this little tyke?" Anna smiled at the baby in Quindar's arms.

"Viloa—she's going to be a downright troublemaker," Quindar said with a proud smile. "Come on inside. No good just sitting around outside all day!" They were ushered into Quindar's home.

It was built into the cliffs that ringed Devil's Crater. There was a hidden ridge that would allow a fully grown Dragon to fly out, then this more hidden entrance that one couldn't see if they didn't have the right magical artifact: a simple engraved piece of metal that Malsour had made.

The house was made like a modern open plan apartment with two floors. To the right of the entrance was an office; the back right was the kitchen; back left a dining room; to the left was a living room that connected directly to the dining room. Upstairs were bedrooms and living spaces.

Yoalin was just coming down the open staircase. She smiled and waved at everyone, coming down to greet them. She had the same sharp chin and features of the Dracul clan. It made her look noble, but there was a softness to her eyes and smile that made people want to become closer to her. In her current state, she looked tired but happy.

"Everyone, this is Yoalin, my aunt and the reason that I have any freedom!" Quindar said.

Everyone introduced themselves as Quindar looked after Viloa.

Fornau appeared from the kitchen. "Hi everyone! Sorry, just working on dinner!"

"Well, I'll give a hand," Dave said. He was rather proud of his cooking skills.

"Come on into the lair!" Fornau smiled and waved at everyone.

Quindar and Deia moved to the living room.

"You need anything, darling?" Dave asked Deia as she let out a content sigh, arranging cushions on the couch to support herself.

"Juice or something." Deia smiled.

"Can do. Anyone else want anything?" Dave looked around. He got the order of drinks for everyone and headed off to the kitchen, where Anna and Alkao had already walked off to.

They were talking to Fornau about different things, holding hands as they stood close to each other.

If Anna wasn't so stubborn, then they'd probably be well on their way to getting married. Well, saying that, I'm only engaged to Deia right now. Sure, we will get married sometime, but we already have a baby on the way. Dave shook his head and snorted.

"Something wrong?" Fornau asked.

"Nope, nothing. Just looking for where you keep the drinks. Need three juices," Dave said.

"Just check them out over there." Fornau pointed at a closet that had been magically coded to work as a fridge.

"Ah, modern magical coding. Nothing quite like it," Dave said to himself, opening the fridge.

Fornau cooked up a feast with Dave's help while teaching Alkao on the side. Anna, Dave, and Alkao talked about the upcoming portal raid. Anna would be running things from the aerial forces while Deia would be handling the ground forces.

Dinner was great, with everyone smiling and laughing. Viloa finally nodded off and Quindar put her to bed.

Yoalin, who was reserved at the beginning, quickly relaxed. To her, it was odd to be around people who weren't Dragons. Though, looking past their differences, she was laughing and talking with the rest of them soon enough.

Dave checked the guild's message boards. The Aleph's aerial drones had already made it to the portal's location. The automaton scouts would be there in two days.

They relaxed and celebrated. Melhoun, Akatol, and Khanundra might be out and about in the world, and there might be tens—if not hundreds—of thousands of creatures released out into Emerilia, being released in just three or four months, but in that night, they were just people sharing a meal and coming together.

Anna was roped in with Deia, Quindar, and Yoalin to look after the children as they woke up.

The men were happy to deal with the dishes instead of cleaning up the now awake and messy babies.

Once everything was cleaned up, they moved to the living room. Dave shared his interface with everyone; the Stone Raiders were live casting the drones' feeds as they entered the cave system around the possible portal location.

"Damn, that is not a big opening," Dave commented as the drone entered through a cave. Once inside, it quickly gained access to what looked like a temple of some kind.

"Damn, now that is one hell of a sight," Fornau said.

The temple was in bad condition. In places, it had fallen apart, but in other locations it was stable. The drone panned around. There was a dome around the temple with dirt and ground that had been compacted above.

"Looks like there was a Mana barrier or shield active—must have been up for a few hundred years. Something buried the temple and the rest of the forest grew over it," Fornau said.

"How do you know it was buried? Couldn't it just have all of that dumped on it?" Dave asked.

"Look at the different layers along the walls. If I was a betting man, I would say that the ground underneath the temple was moved by some Earth mages, lowering the temple and then pouring all of that on top of it. They dispersed it well; the forest is holding the covering together well even without the shield. They spread it out so there's only a small hill over the temple," Fornau said.

Dave nodded. Fornau knew more about Earth mages and what they could do than anyone else Dave knew.

"What are those things moving on the ground?" Alkao asked.

A few drones moved around the temple, looking at the earth around it and the temple's structure. Others were moving low.

The temple itself had stairs that stopped at three different landings. On either side of these landings, there were statues of the different Affinities.

The stairs reached a fourth and final landing, with three pillars on either side. They were faded, but they looked to be colored according to the six different Affinities with statues on top. Past the pillars, there was a singular walkway with six different pools that ran next to it. There was one filled with white raging wind, another with a flaming tornado, a third with golden light, a fourth with shadowy flames, a fifth with water that raged against the sides of the pool but never escaped it. The final one was a grand forest filled with rare plants.

Past these pools, there was an open gathering area that led to the domed central temple. It looked like a Roman or Greek temple. There was an overhanging roof with six pillars holding it up, connected to a domed building with wide doors leading inside.

It would have looked like a great marvel if it wasn't for the shades that drifted around the place.

Shades were souls that had been unable to find rest. Their attacks had a corrupting poison effect and they couldn't be hurt by normal steel weapons. They had to be either attacked by a magical blade or one made from silver or Mithril. Even magical effects on these creatures were only half effective. If left alone, they would drift by themselves. If someone or something walked into their territory, they would do everything they could to destroy it.

They weren't the only creatures there, but the first ones that the Stone Raiders would have to deal with.

"Is there something moving in those pools?" Dave asked, his instincts bringing him back to the six different Affinity pools.

Here and there, an odd flicker happened. Many people wouldn't notice at all, but Alkao's keen senses and Fornau's advanced knowledge allowed them to notice what Dave was talking about.

"Earth spirits." Fornau, shocked, looked at the Earth Affinity pool.

"Sprites?" Dave asked.

"No, sprites were made after the spirits. Spirits are Affinity creatures. They are formed when one kind of Affinity magic saturates an area so much that they are given form. Sprites are creatures imbued with the power of an Affinity. Spirits are made from it. They won't attack someone with a high Affinity for their element, but anyone they judge to not have a high enough Affinity, they'll tear apart. I have only heard about them from my brothers and sisters; we have a few of them in Densaou Ring of Fire. Fire is able to communicate with them and we have an amicable relationship, even the Dragons from other Affinities, as the spirits have been able to ascend to rational thought. The eldest then teach the youngest, making it so that we don't have conflict. Though these—there is a lot of them. It also looks like they haven't the strength to leave their Affinity pools by themselves. Look at the area between the pools and the temple," Fornau said.

Alkao and Dave did as Fornau said.

"They look like the shades from the first, but they have an Affinity glow to them," Alkao said.

"These must be shades that walked into the different Affinity pools. When they did so, the spirits were able to take command of them. They infused their Affinity into their bodies. They're Affinity shades now. I've heard of spirits taking over hosts, but it's usually animals. Even they would be more of a fight to control than the shades. For the Affinity spirits, it must just be like walking in the open door of a house," Fornau said.

If there were a thousand of different levels of shades in the first area, there were a few hundred different Affinity spirits, and then maybe a hundred Affinity shades. Past them, there were various creatures. These were animals that had wandered into the temple's underground ruin. They had been strong or fast enough to make it through the shades, only to fall into an Affinity pool and be overtaken by an Affinity spirit.

There was everything from bears to blessed sabre tigers. Their innate strength would put them on level with a Demon. Though they had stopped gaining levels as they were overtaken by the spirits, the spirits had been able to become more powerful. So, even if they were Level 100 creatures, their magic power was on par with a Level 300 mage. Combined, they would put up a fight against a Level 400 or 500. There were about one hundred of them hanging around the entrance to the temple.

The drone moved inside. There were blossoms of fire, singular pieces of rapidly moving wind. They seemed to have almost Human features as they moved around. Some of them conversed with one another. They stuck in their own Affinity groups, but they didn't attack one another.

"Free Affinity spirits," Fornau said, as if not believing what he was seeing.

"A description would be useful," Alkao said with a small smile on his face.

"Sorry, sorry—I've only heard of one of these creatures. They are like the leaders of all the Fire spirits in Densaou Ring of Fire. They can freely leave areas thick with Mana energy related to their Affinity. They have something similar to a consciousness, and while they can cast on instinct like the regular Affinity spirits, they can also take the time to create complex spells. Their mastery of magic is high, but they are weak to weapons from their opposing Affinity, much more so than their lower beings that have taken over the beasts or shades. These, at least, have a protection of some sort—they're pure and bare magic. I don't think that we can clear out this place," Fornau said seriously.

"Why?" Dave asked.

"The Free spirits might be affected by weapons from an opposing Affinity, but they are empowered by weapons of the same Affinity. They are able to invoke powerful spells with similar capabilities of Level 700 or 800 people. There might be about thirty of them, but they're absolute monsters and their speed is incredible. They can run away and hit their attackers with incredibly powerful spells!"

"There are five Free Affinity controlled shades past the regular Free Affinity spirits, and three more controlling powerful creatures' bodies," Alkao said.

With Fornau's declarations, Dave and Alkao felt clearing this place was becoming more and more impossible.

"Those are shades and creatures that have been overtaken by Free spirits. They're two or three times stronger than the ones outside," Fornau said.

The drone continued onward. There was an open area where the Free spirits had stood. Another set of stairs led up to a landing where the shades inhabited by Free spirits stood; then the creatures; and then finally there was a throne on a top landing. Around the throne, there were six statues depicting the gods and goddesses of the Affinities. The area around the dome was meant to allow people to look up at the gods and goddesses in praise.

A man sat on the throne. He looked to be a refined man of Asian descent; his age gave him a dignified appearance. His long black hair was pulled back into a ponytail; a section of it fell over half of his face. He held his head with one hand, a bored expression on his face, as he held a katana with his other hand, the blade pointed down at the ground. The blade was hidden by gray smoke.

Behind him lay a portal; to either side there were several large chests of loot.

The man's eyes looked to the drone. Dave's eyes stopped; his breath caught in his throat as he looked back into the man's eyes.

For a moment, Dave thought he saw a shadow of a smile before the man's eyes once again looked toward the entrance into the temple.

"Fornau, who is that?" Alkao asked.

Silence spread through the room. Only the noises of the women dealing with the children could be heard and Anna's displeased noises at dealing with "baby muck."

Alkao and Dave looked up to Fornau, whose eyes were stuck on the man on the throne inside the temple, the final boss and guard of the portal.

"I don't know. I've never seen anyone or anything like him." Fornau looked at them with a pale face.

***

A similar scene was taking place in the Stone Raiders' headquarters as everyone looked at the video feeds from the underground temple.

No one knew what it might be. Shard was looking through records to try to understand, as well as using all manner of sensing to try to get some sort of clue.

"Well, he's just sitting inside what is a sea of Affinity creatures. None of them are attacking him. He looks like he's got some kind of blade, but there's no discerning Mana to it," Dwayne said.

"Looks kind of like the Mana Dave uses," Kim said suddenly.

"What's Dave's Affinity?" Josh asked.

Everyone looked to one another.

"I don't think that he has one," Lucy said.

"Though he uses all manner of magic," Josh rebutted.

"Maybe he has all of the Affinities around the same level?" Kim asked.

"So, what, then? This person has all of the Affinities?" Josh asked.

"Spirit King Consolidation," Shard said suddenly. Everyone looked to him; he had his own seat at the conference table.

"This person is the accumulation of the spirit's energy within the temple. There are two kinds of spirit kings. One is a manifestation of every single kind of Affinity coming together. They all have to be of an extremely high level and then combine together. They can use every kind of magic with nearly instantaneous casting, though they're psychotic and usually raving mad, devouring other spirits and killing anything that enters their domain. The second king is the consolidation king. They have an extremely strong soul, but high-level spirits try to take them over.

"By comparison, the shades have a limited Willpower. They're very easy to take over. Here, the original soul residing in the body has retained control of themselves and defeated the spirits that invaded their body.

"They can have varying control over the spirits that reside within them. The more that are contained within them, the more power they have, but also the harder it is for them to maintain their sanity," Shard said.

"So, this guy has multiple high-leveled spirits trapped within his body, all of them trying to tear his Willpower apart and subdue him?" Josh said.

"Precisely. If they are united in a cause, then his power will be immense. I believe one such cause will be if we are to attack this temple, then he will be able to unleash his full power on us as the spirits are very territorial and will do everything in their power to destroy those who enter their domain," Shard said.

"How powerful is this guy going to be?" Esa asked.

"Possibly stronger than a Dragon, with the ability to use any manner of spells. He will also be highly resistant to magical attacks and will more easily disrupt spells cast at him," Shard said.

"Well, this just went from crazy hard to impossible." Lucy snorted.

"Hey, we're the Stone Raiders. We can defeat anything!" Josh declared.

"We can if we have the time and resources. Right now, we've got the resources, but we're needed to manage things here. Also, we've only got four months until we're going to be neck deep in escaped prisoners!" Lucy said.

"Shard, how powerful are these creatures in terms of levels?" Cassie asked.

"Their levels will be two-thirds to one-quarter of their actual strength once you get past the Affinity pools. Once you get to the

Free spirits, they're going to be two to three times more powerful than their displayed level until you get to the king. I don't know what his power level would be, but I would estimate from five to eight times more powerful." Shard's answers left the room in silence.

"We can get together nearly eight hundred Stone Raiders, and can probably double that number in Player guilds if we ask," Dwayne said.

"The mages guild will be interested in this and they'll send some of their more powerful figures," Kim added.

"Our allies won't go for it, but we can pool some adventurers and the DCA forces will be able to help us some with the low-leveled creatures," Lucy added begrudgingly.

"It's going to be one hell of a fight," Esa said, summarizing what everyone was thinking.

"Might take a few weeks just to get to the temple. Once we get inside it..." Lucy shook her head.

Josh sat back in his chair and looked at everyone in the room. He rested his chin on his knuckles.

"I have just a few questions." Josh paused just long enough that everyone's attention was focused on him. "Would this be fun? Sure! I know that it would be hard as hell and that we're probably going to die more often than not, but if there were no time restrictions and we didn't have Terra, would you want to back out?"

"No," Dwayne said. Everyone else seemed to agree with his words, even if they weren't too pleased with it.

"When we were clearing out the Aleph facilities, it was hard, but it was also fun as hell! Sure, we lost a few levels here and there, but would you agree that we came out of it stronger than when we went in?" Josh asked.

"Yes." Lucy was the first to agree this time.

"If we're to build a camp outside the temple, somewhere that we can defend and I will front the cost of the darned onos, will that make everyone feel a little better?" Josh looked to Jules.

"Yes." Jules nodded to Josh. Lucy and the others also agreed. The cost of an ono was still incredibly high, but the amount of wealth they had built up in-game was not inconsiderable. Josh could also sell off some of his assets on Earth to buy in-game gold. He would be fine with the money he was getting from endorsements and streams.

"My final question: what did we come together for? Was it to manage cities, to train in seclusion? Or was it to get the hell out into the middle of the damned wilderness, to do what others couldn't and engrave our names at the top of dungeon's leadership boards? To open portals that no other guild would be able to even look at? We were the first people to open a portal. We were the guild that fought at Boran-al's Citadel, the Devil's Crater Cliffs, the Aleph's cities! We have shown Emerilia and we have shown ourselves that no matter what, we can triumph. We might get hammered down at times, bite off more than we can deal with. You know what? We've only become stronger from it! So, I say, let's go raid!" Josh yelled out, his eyes dancing in excitement and his fist raised in declaration.

"Well, if you say it like that, I'm in," Dwayne said.

"I guess I have to follow this idiot." Esa grinned as the two of them bumped fists.

"Well, hell, Affinity spirits, a temple, and a portal. Sounds like a fun time." Kim smiled.

"Well, someone is going to have to put you dumbasses back together," Jules said with a small smile.

"Fine, I'll do it, but we'll need a few days to talk to the other guilds while the automaton scouts reach the temple and can check it out on foot," Lucy said finally.

Cassie and Florence shook their heads; they were just there to see the video. When it came to fighting, that was in the others' realm.

"I knew you beauties wouldn't give this up," Josh said with a wide smile. The others laughed, smiled openly or shook their heads, trying to hide their smiles.

"Feels good to be the one picking out what we're doing, not just doing quest after quest. I'm looking forward to some of those event raids!" Dwayne said.

"Dude, we just agreed to go raid a portal. Now, you want to take on the creatures from the event?" Esa slumped back in her chair with a sour expression.

Dwayne let out a hearty laugh at Esa's actions.

Josh looked at them all. They had done a lot together and come far, but through it all, they were the same people who had come together to form the Stone Raiders.

Chapter 19: Back to School

"Why don't we just make up our own collection of runes?" a student asked. It was a common question in Dave's lectures, which didn't mean that he liked to answer it that much.

"Why? Because it's already complicated as hell. If we start adding more and more symbols, then it's going to make things much more complicated. Right now, everyone is using the same kinds of symbols—just working them in different combinations and voila, you've got magical coding. If people start using their own libraries, then sure, things could work, but you're going to have to define everything all over again, would take a lot more time and then someone trying to learn your library of symbols is going to be totally confused with how they were using the other library they were using. Then, you've got say ten different libraries of symbols—you're going to lose your freaking mind from dealing with all that! Every time you work on a project, you've got to find a different library with different symbols and rules in them or—" Dave held up his finger. "We use one library of symbols that we all agree on, then we use them in a ton of different combinations, share the advances we've made and then we're all, at least, on relatively the same page."

"But this library has all been made up by you," the student said.

"Well, I did make magical coding up," Dave said.

"So, you just want to be the creator of all this, take the credit and then overcharge us for all the materials!" the student accused.

But Dave could see that they wanted nothing more than a rise out of him.

"Are you stupid or did you just get hit by a mule a dozen too many times?" Dave asked in a dry voice. "All of the libraries and symbols are in books that you can access for free. This class is free to take, as well as the testing laboratories. If I wanted to, I could charge money. I don't need to, so I don't. I'd rather see more people coming up with answers to the problems I've been seeing. I can't code everything myself and it's always better to work with others, whether by collaboration or in competition to push yourself forward. Look at Earth's coding—there were dozens of ways to do the same thing. Some of it was elegant, but some of it was downright crap. Here, we're building a repository of good and interesting coding, coming together to create something great. The library we're using is a good level ground for everyone to start with. What people come up with, that's the interesting part. And with the same library, it's possible for anyone to take apart anyone else's work and understand how it works, or build something amazing. So, this crap about me being some magical coding monopolizing prick, well, that's just some stupid ass fantasy. I welcome people to out-code me. Hell, I know that there are people out there who can out-code me on different interfaces and projects!"

"You've been hiring people right out of this class if they have good abilities in coding and stealing them from other powers!" the student said, indignant at Dave's words.

"Stealing them? I offered many of them jobs. Some of them took it; some of them didn't. I do have a number of factories and smithies out there that need magical coders. I know that there are a number of powers that are trying to recruit people out of this class to help them, and other students are striving to work by themselves," Dave said, unperturbed. A number of people had attacked him for one thing or another.

If they think they can rile me up with this crap, they should have learned a thing or two about the nut jobs who said I was going to destroy the planet or send us into another ice age for dropping refined materials into the Atlantic Ocean.

"Look, what people do is up to them. I know that I and a number of my businesses have approached people asking if they would like a job. Hell, there's a list over on the side of the classroom of people who are looking for skilled magical coders from all over Emerilia. It's a hot subject and we need more people who know it. Here, I teach the basics, the starting blocks. It's up to everyone to figure out what they want to do with it," Dave said simply.

"You use your relaxed attitude and your money to blind people to the fact that you're just using them!" the student spat. His arguments from before were now blatant attacks on Dave.

"Think what you want. I ain't your mom or dad to tell you what I think you should do." Dave shook his head and clapped his hands together.

"I bet you don't even code. You just use others for it!"

"I certainly work with a number of people who can code. I can't do everything by myself!" Dave laughed. "Now, let's get along with the lesson, shall we?"

"He's trying to deceive you, to make you his slaves to take you away from the true art of magical coding!" the man yelled out to everyone. Then, he disappeared from existence.

"Okay, well, seems someone learned Magical Circuitry, but didn't want to learn coding and had a bone to pick. Now let's get back to material usage," Dave said, talking as if nothing happened.

A few people laughed and smiled. They'd come to learn, not have someone use their class for a political speech.

"As you know, different metals have different conductivity; they also have different heating temperatures. With the magic of magic," Dave grinned at the light laughter in the room, "we can do a lot more to remove this excess heat, purify these metals to a high degree and allow us to code runes that, with Mana running through them, would overload the metal and melt it. With a proper heat sink or heat extraction," as Dave talked, an image of two different runes appeared above him, "we can increase the number of runes on a piece of metal without fear of overheating. Now! Quick question—if I'm coding something complicated, what is better: a single big sheet of coding or multiple small ones?" Dave looked out at the classroom. Someone raised their hand.

"You in the blue," Dave said.

"Multiple smaller pieces," she said.

"Why?" Dave asked.

"With more pieces, you can cool them down more. The heat won't rise from multiple different locations as complex runes heat up more; you can focus your heat draw away from the runes," she said.

"Very good! Also having it in smaller pieces makes it much easier to replace! Otherwise you've got to have someone with a high Dark Affinity come along to remove what you've done! That said, I personally prefer to work with massive sheets, carve in my code, and then cut it down into more manageable sections," Dave admitted.

Someone raised their hand.

Dave pointed to them.

"What about the complex arrays that have interchangeable coding?"

"Looks like we've got some good questions today! Well, it would all depend on what you're trying to do. There are multiple different ways to do that. One of the most simple is the circular formation. You can move the different sections of the circle, matching the coding up so that it works. This can work for an off and on switch as well as limited changes. More complicated it is, the more confusing it becomes. The second, which I like, is the slot method. You have your sheets or individual runes; then you simply have them in different racks—you can pull and place them as you need," Dave said.

"What about for more complicated circuits and codes like a teleport pad?" the same person asked.

"Well, then there are two different ways. You either have a command code set up, kind of like a computer and then you add code sheets to it, like you would traditionally code back on Earth. Or, make a highly complicated interchanging system that moves around the individual lines of code or the runes," Dave said.

A bell sounded in the auditorium.

"Okay, so that's the end of class. If you've been having your coding melt, try the different cooling methods! Also, all of my lessons are saved into the archives, so you can access them at any time. I'll see you all later!" Dave waved to them all and disappeared from the auditorium stage.

He stood up from his chair, cracking his back and yawning.

He simply had too many projects to work on. He had been able to offload different parts to the Dwarven Master Smiths or the coders he or his companies had hired.

He was still working to optimize the summoning hall. He had finished with his power sources; he needed to get started on the armor he had planned for, but the Dwarven Master Smiths weren't yet finished with their different components. He had paused in working on his more powerful weapons and although he had plans for a ship, he was again waiting on others to make the various different components. Although he wanted to get working on the ships months ago, there was little time for him to do so. Also, it wasn't as needed as other projects and the coding and tech needed was far more advanced than what Dave had. He'd offloaded most of it off onto Shard and Bob, who were taking Jukal systems, reverse engineering them and looking to use corresponding runes to code it. With Bob's knowledge and Shard's ability to translate technology into magical coding, it was moving along at an incredible rate of speed.

Dave looked around his apartment. "Okay, this sitting around and working on magical coding is all good, but sometimes you've got to take a break." Dave stood, a smile on his face. Today he wouldn't work on coding. It was about time he checked out the Dwarven tournaments.

***

Deia had been working with the DCA forces for a month and a half. She floated up to meet with Quindar and Anna. They had all been working hard with their forces to strengthen them, but now they would have another fight to see where the DCA needed to improve.

It was the ground forces' job to hold a small fort and some outposts that had been made in the forested region of the northwestern sector.

The aerial forces were to find the enemies' positions and then defeat them.

"So, what do you think will happen this time?" Quindar asked.

"Well, Malkur and Efri have stopped micromanaging so much and the chain of command pulled themselves together. I'm hoping that they lost some of their cockiness, but I don't know the results." Anna shrugged.

"How did Kala's people do?" Quindar asked.

"They did well, taking in what I was saying pretty quickly. We got them working and understanding magic a lot more. They're like friggin' sponges for information. They've become better at fighting both in close and at range. I think you'll be pleasantly surprised. That said, I'm thinking, and hoping, that they will come to a draw," Deia said.

"Oh?" Quindar said, curious as to Deia's reasoning.

"Well, if they come to a draw, then they get to see what the other group is capable of. Up to this point, they have been competing against one another. If we have them show that they're both pretty good, we can start to show them that by working together they can fight a lot more people and come out victorious. Both of them have their strengths and weaknesses. Together, they're stronger than when they're apart," Deia said.

Anna nodded slowly in agreement. "We want them to fight in small groups, but to still be able to come together, supporting one another when they need it. To do that, they need to know that they can rely on one another because they're both strong and fierce at what they do."

"You two are tricky," Quindar said.

They moved off toward the forest, while the other trainers of the different groups mingled together at the camp, having a few beers and watching the men and women they had trained fight it out on their interfaces and the large seer stones.

The training exercise started with the flyers taking to the sky. The ground forces scattered outward through the forest, making a number of scouts watch for the aerial forces, while the forces in the outposts and the fort did their best to hide their different fortifications' positions.

The flyers didn't come in fast and confident as they had with the first training exercise. Now, they floated above, looking down at possible targets. They relayed what they saw back to the flyers waiting on the ground. They continued flying, making no indication that they had seen something.

"Good. They're not reacting. Even if the forces on the ground see them, they won't know if they've been spotted or not," Deia said with approval.

"Telling the scouts to not rush in but observe was a big blow to many of them. We had to switch a few people around." Anna didn't sound pleased.

The scouts checked over the forest a few more times. Malkur and Efri sent out probing attacks. They moved over the forest, bombing different areas.

"They're dropping bombs in locations other than where they suspect the ground forces might be to make it look kind of random, making the enemy think that they just got some lucky hits in and try to hold their position," Quindar commented.

"Smart," Deia said.

The flyers kept up the bombing for a number of hours. The ground forces had to work overtime, telling the command where the multiple bombing flyers were coming from. Their height was too much to hit without a mass attack that would point out the location of the ground forces.

Slowly, the aerial forces became more and more accurate with their hits, taking out the different outposts as they were revealed.

It was clear that the ground forces were getting frustrated, but through it, Deia was smiling.

"Your people are getting hit pretty hard. What are you seeing that we aren't?" Quindar said.

"The aerial forces' defenses," Deia said with a sly smile.

Anna smacked her head as Quindar looked to the aerial forces and then swore under her breath.

"You're used to being on the offensive. Dragons don't really need to come down from the sky if they don't want to and Anna is always in the middle of the fight. While aerial forces do have great striking power, how well versed are they with close armed combat?" Deia asked.

"They're okay, but not the best. We taught them to scoot and move, get a better line of attack and come back to hit the enemy, and don't rush into airborne enemies unless you have to. The likelihood of hurting your own people accidentally or getting wounded and dropping out of the sky is too high." Quindar sighed.

"I can see your ground forces now," Anna said. "When did they leave the defendable fortifications?"

"They left as soon as it started. They moved out with the scouts in every direction. When they saw the direction that the aerial forces were coming from, they sent their people back in that direction." Deia smiled.

"Damn, should have circled around and come over the forest at an obscure direction to make it harder," Quindar said.

"Mhmm." Deia looked to her ground forces. They had moved through the forests, moving as fast as possible while also being stealthy. They had moved in groups no larger than ten and spaced out.

This is where small group tactics came to the fore. They all started coming together. They checked out the aerial forces' camp that was set up in a clearing. There were tents that held food and water for the people coming back as well as other tents with soul gems to charge their weapons and armor. Then, there were planning tents where the leadership were meeting.

The aerial forces continued to bomb the almighty hell out of the outposts and forts. The ground forces that were remaining in the structures were getting whittled down, because there was little to nothing that they could do.

Just as the aerial forces were on the cusp of victory, the ground forces struck. They didn't even leave the cover of the forest. Spearheads flashed out from the underbrush; inert grenades were thrown into the leadership, soul gem recharge, and canteen tents.

Chaos reigned through the camp as Krenua's people tapped people who were "dead" and they had to lie down, watching as spear points tore through their camp. Larger spearheads that simulated Mana bombs also landed in their midst.

"What is with the Mana bombs?" Anna asked.

"We took the Mana bomb circuit from the aerial's breastplate, took it to the Aleph, asked them to speed up how fast it shot out. They're really short range, but they're as good as your aerial forces' and not as annoying to lug around as Dwarven artillery. A Dwarf trainer came up with the idea," Deia said, proud of her people.

The aerial forces tried to retaliate, while others tried to take to the skies. It was true chaos on the ground. Nearly four thousand of the ground force soldiers had been lying around the camp. They had anywhere from an hour to ten minutes to move into the best positions.

Now, they were hitting the largest targets with precision, killing anything that tried to put up a fight. Still, they didn't charge inward but stayed back, firing everything they had into the camp.

Fifty thousand were reduced to fifteen who were able to escape.

The ground forces disappeared into the underbrush as spears rained from above, the aerial forces trying to kill them off.

"I think that we can call this one a draw," Anna said.

"Agreed," Deia said.

Both of them were proud of their people. The ground forces had learned how to think on their feet and more about fighting techniques. The aerial forces had learned coordination and to make the best of their situation.

They were much stronger than just a few months ago. Now, it was time to put the two groups together and see them work as one fighting force.

Deia's heart twisted in her chest. There was barely a month left until the first waves of creatures from Bob's prison were supposed to be released, about the same time until she was expecting her child.

She placed her hand on her stomach. Her heart felt constricted as she worried about the future.

Chapter 20: Dragon's Wrath

Akatol felt unease as more of his ice palace's defenses were being steadily eroded away. When he expected that they would run out of Mana and would have to leave, they stayed. They stayed well past what he had thought their limits would be. He thought that he had a few months to complete his preparations. Instead, he had been working with minimal sleep and rest in order to complete his designs. He was supplying his ice palace directly with some of his power to try to slow his family down more. The power drain was making it harder for him to focus, but he needed time more than anything.

He had commanded his total domain to increase. It was a large power draw, but it was showing results, tearing the waters out of everything nearby. He was draining the nearby lake, killing creatures and items across a great area. From all the power that was flowing in, he was creating blood soul gems.

Blood soul gems are made from the life-force within another creature. Akatol was not done with the bodies of those ill-fated Players who had wandered into his domain. There was barely a flicker of power left in them, but it was enough to hold them. As they were being used as mediums for Akatol's spell, the bodies had stayed around. He poured power into them, their bodies being imbued with the power of hundreds of other creatures and altered through a blood seal. They were transforming into blood soul gems.

Once they were complete, Akatol took the soul gems, crushed them up, added some of his own blood and then used them to create his powerful magical circle. It filled up the mountain.

Akatol was half crazed from the sleep deprivation and the thoughts that his family had betrayed him. He wanted them to see the light! They were the true rulers of Emerilia! They just needed to take it!

He had just started to draw out a formation with his claw as he felt something break. He looked up. His senses expanded outward, as he found a crack in his ice palace.

"No! They should have taken two more weeks!" Akatol yelled, oblivious of the fact that he had lost track of time with his work.

He poured energy into the ice palace and turned back to his work. With his recovered energy, he was able to reduce the effectiveness of the other Dragons' attacks as he burnt the energy he had taken from sacrifices he had made throughout his life.

***

Denur moved forward. Her attack intensified as she noticed a portion of the ice palace that had not simply melted but appeared to be cracking.

Induca and Malsour had wanted to be there to help in ending their father's legacy of death. Denur had fought against it. The two of them were in Terra working on increasing their strength and on various projects. They were now two of the stronger Dragons among the Dracul family.

If Denur was to fall, she knew that Induca and Malsour could rise up to become the pillars of the family. If they were to all die, then there could be a power vacuum that would leave the family with an uncertain future.

As she got close enough, she raised her body up. Her front feet dug into the ice palace, both of her claws tearing great chunks of ice from it. They seemed to glow with red light as the damage increased.

The rest of her family, sensing that victory was at hand, moved to add in their own attacks.

Those who were outside the total domain sent messages to the Dragons who were resting in the Mithsia Mountains.

Denur saw a part of the ice palace fall inward! She doubled her power output. Her breath turned to a white flame from the heat given off. Puddles fell around her as she climbed up on the ice palace. There was a surge of power from inside.

Akatol was fighting back.

No, you don't! Denur focused her attack on the weakness. She lost track of how long she was there, but she could hear the howls and roars filled the skies as her sons, daughters, grandsons, and granddaughters and five different generations announced their arrival.

They came in out of the night sky, their breaths lighting up the sky. Night seemed to have a second sun under their onslaught.

There was an almighty cracking noise as a part of the ice palace gave way.

They continued their attacks, tearing and attacking the palace in any way they could. Suddenly, a whole section of the ice palace fell away.

"Follow me! Bring in everyone! Destroy the total domain magical circle!" Denur yelled, jumping into the hole in the ice palace.

The magical circle was made in blood and bound to Akatol. Magical attacks wouldn't be even a tenth of their strength in this area. However, physical attacks could easily break up the lines of blood.

The other Dragons followed. They needed to get inside before Akatol reinforced his palace or had time to react to their entrance. The faster they could close with him, the less time he could plan and react.

Denur landed with a thud. She moved through the mountain that lay under the ice palace.

Others opened up different holes with their magical skills, heading directly to the deepest cavern of the mountain.

Denur quickly reached the bottom of the mountain. She was shocked by what she saw. Akatol was skinny from bleeding so much. Around the room, people, on stakes, were slowly being turned into blood soul gems. He was tracing down an incredibly complex magical circle in the floor. Where the soul gem lay, it turned into blood-red lines, as if they were a natural formation on the floor.

Denur let out a howl. Flames shot from her mouth and hit Akatol.

He dropped a wing as a Mana barrier formed over him. He crushed the blood soul gem in his hands.

Denur's eyes went wide as it went inside the wounds on his hands. Smoke seemed to appear around him as he rose up, his Mana barrier holding. His eyes glowed with a crazed red instead of its original blue. The red smoke was actually clouds of blood if one was to look close enough. His aura exploded outward as he let loose with his breath.

Denur had to use everything she had to stop his breath from beating hers.

Dragons appeared in the cavern, letting loose with their own attacks, trying to weaken Akatol.

He looked as though he were laughing, as if this fight was nothing to him. Akatol's breath turned from flames into a vortex.

Denur turned and ducked as the blast slammed into her Mana barrier and sent her flying.

The other Dragons continued to press their attacks.

He's using blood soul gems directly in his blood. It's tearing his body apart from the inside as he uses it, but it will give him a massive increase in Mana, enough that he's stronger than me in terms of power.

She made to stand up, spitting out blood as Akatol moved. His body was covered in a red and blue smoke as he activated his movement technique.

He tore into the ranks of Dragons. He tossed them away as if they were ragdolls. They slammed into the walls, howling out. The mountain shook with the Dragon's hits.

Akatol raised his hand to tear out a Dragon's throat as he laughed crazily.

"Die!" Louna's voice rang out through the mountain.

Akatol turned to look at Louna, a look of confusion on his face.

"No!" Denur roared out.

Louna raised a Mana barrier and shield. Akatol breathed a water stream that cut through the different layers. The other Dragons who could fight unleashed all their attacks on Akatol.

Denur rushed forward, a look of panic on her face as she unleashed her own attack.

Akatol didn't even look up as Louna's shield and then Mana barrier failed. She had been tired from taking the shift before and recovering in the Mithsia Mountains. She had rushed back to assist her family. She didn't have a necklace and no way to recover her lost Mana within Akatol's total domain.

Akatol's hand was wreathed in ice shards tainted with blood. He opened Louna's throat with a blow.

Louna coughed; her body convulsed and her eyes went wide as dark blood fell from her wounds. Denur felt as if a part of her soul had been torn away from her.

"Naughty daughter put Daddy away for a long time," Akatol tutted. "Sleep now."

He dropped Louna, his own third child, to the ground as if a doll he had grown bored of.

Denur hit him with everything she had and slammed into him.

He laughed. His tail whipped out and slammed into Denur's side.

She braced against it but she was still sent flying again. She felt something crack in her chest as she impacted the wall.

Akatol jumped forward. Ice spears, water geysers, and ice claws appeared as he targeted his and Denur's great-great-grandson Kolq. The youngling lasted for just a few moments.

Denur cried out again. Her body was broken: one of her legs at an odd angle and one of her wings crushed. Still she rose, charging Akatol once again. There had to be an end, a way to stop him!

Even as she fought onward, tears fell from her eyes, not out of physical pain, but the loss of her family members.

They had become utterly close and inseparable. They had shared trials together and come through it on the other side. They were expected to live for hundreds, if not thousands, of years. She couldn't bear watching her babies and grandbabies killed so easily. She would sacrifice anything—even her own life, her happiness, take eternal punishment—just to destroy Akatol and save them.

Eliona, Hawsan, and Petal fell under Akatol's attacks as he let out crazed laughter, throwing them aside. His own flesh and blood. He had lost any sense of sanity. He grabbed a forming blood soul gem and the giant it was forming from, gnashing them between his teeth as power flooded him. He was an unstoppable maniac.

Denur threw herself at him so many times, trying to stop him. She let out a compressed breath, everything that she had left.

It made his barriers flare up, changing from clear to a pinkish hue. Others joined in. He let out an enraged roar; ice spears raced out in every direction and crashed into shields.

"Dear wife, stop your meddling. Everything will be fine soon. I will show these creatures that we are the true rulers of Emerilia," he said in a sickly sweet voice, stalking over to her while attacks slammed into his barriers.

Dragons tried to charge in, but were hit by a vicious magical attack or thrown aside by a swipe of Akatol's tail.

Denur tried to limp away, flaring out her good wing at him to hurt him.

Ice spears nailed her wings to the ground and he stomped on them, her bones breaking like dry twigs. He systematically broke her other limbs into uselessness and then pinned her neck down with ice spears and a net.

There was nothing that she could do.

"I'll be back soon, sweetness." Akatol let out a small childish giggle that sent shivers down Denur's spine.

He moved so fast that the very air was disturbed.

Sounds of breaking bones and cries of pain rang out.

Denur continued to fight. She was in Mana fatigue; her body was broken, but this was her family. She didn't care about any of that!

There was a flash of light as a sole Human appeared in the mountain.

"Oh look, the creator has come to play!" Akatol said. Someone whimpered as they were dropped to the floor, ignored by Akatol.

"Die." The voice was cold and ruthless.

Denur wanted to tell Fire to run away, that she couldn't defeat Akatol.

The mountain seemed to explode with Mana.

"How is this possible!" Akatol yelled. "I can't die! I'm a god!"

Denur's restraints were removed. She turned her head.

Fire was wreathed in flames, a creature of pure Mana. Her eyes were merciless as fireballs, fire storms, spears, Dragon's breath, devil's inferno—all these spells and more were simultaneously being cast at the same time. Akatol's shielding was impressive, but they tore through them like a needle through paper.

"None of us are gods." Fire's words shook the very air. A sword of flames erupted from her hands and tore through Akatol.

He fell and the light went out of his eyes.

"Burn till there is nothing left," Fire spat.

White flames tore through Akatol, feeding off of his Mana, Stamina, and Health. It was a forbidden spell that would hold a creature at the threshold of death, not allowing them to pass away, but feel as their body was burned away by unstoppable flames.

Denur's body shook in pain as tears rolled down her face. She saw the broken bodies of her family strewn around the room. She had been too confident, too sure of their power.

There was nothing she could do. She was broken, useless to help them.

Nothing mattered—everything hurt. She cried, shuffling along on her broken limbs to the closest of those who had fallen. She rubbed Louna's head with hers, letting out a keening noise. Even through the tears, she tried to smile. "It's going to be all right, baby girl. Everything is going to be all right." She didn't need her senses to know that Louna's soul had already left.

Denur started singing. It was a familiar song to the Dragons. Denur had sung it for them, one and all. It was a song from their childhood, one that sung to the pride of the Dragons, how they would look after one another no matter what. Denur sung her song, a sad smile on her face as tears fell. But her voice—her voice didn't crack as she sung that song one last time for Louna, as she sent her to sleep, telling of greater days in the future, of adventures she would have.

Denur felt as if her heart would break, knowing that Louna and the others who lay unmoving in that room would never be able to once again go on their own adventures. Their journey ended here.

Denur laid her head against Louna's.

"It's okay to sleep. Mommy's here," Denur said quietly. Tears silently fell down her face.

***

Fire could only look over her children: wounded, dead, and in the throes of loss. She bit her lip as tears came to her eyes.

They didn't know when they would make it into the ice palace as Akatol continued to reinforce the ice palace and sometimes even push back the Dragons.

When it had finally collapsed, Fire had been in Per'ush in disguise, watching over the mage's college. She'd had to leave without raising suspicion and raced to her secret chambers to teleport to the ice palace. Once she arrived, she'd teleported inside; however, the battle had only lasted minutes, the Dragons moving at speeds that would leave most people in awe and fear.

Now her heart twisted in her chest as she raised her hands to call down healing spells on the wounded while she assessed wounds, finding those who were in life-threatening condition.

"No one else dies today." Fire's voice was harsh as tears left streaks on her cheeks. Her eyes turned to orbs of flame as power surged around her, spreading outward to encompass all the injured. The power needed to move Dragons was massive and it would overdraw Fire's energy. She was past the point of caring about that as she pulled the wounded through a teleportation spell, arriving in Densaou Ring of Fire.

"Healers!" Fire's voice passed through the mountain. She looked haggard as she disappeared and then reappeared in the ice palace. Once again, she spread out her senses; her face contorted in pain before she disappeared again with any remaining injured.

Without pause, she went from Densaou Ring of Fire to the ice palace, her actions automatic until all of the wounded and dead had been pulled from the ice palace.

Fire arrived back in her apartment, slumping to her knees and hanging her head. She sobbed freely, her heart torn apart as she continued to hear Denur singing to her daughter and grandchildren who had closed their eyes once again.

Mal, seeing Fire sobbing on the floor, rushed to her. He held her to his chest; she was too weak to even move her arms to hold him. Mal sat there with her crying against his chest. Pitiful howls from the Dragons echoed through the Densaou Ring of Fire.

In the past, Dragons had turned against the family and Emerilians; killing them to protect the family and Emerilia had been the hardest task that Fire and the Dragons had dealt with.

Dealing with the loss of so many of their family members was a deep shock that left them struggling to cope with the losses.

Chapter 21: Continue Down the Set Path

Event: Of Myths and Legends

3 Creatures of Power have escaped their imprisonment and have arrived back on Emerilia.

The Event: Of Myths and Legends has begun!

Kill the Creatures of Power to gain rewards and experience. If you fail to kill the creatures, then Emerilia could be forever changed.

Creatures of Power located on Emerilia: 3

Creatures Killed: 1/3

Across Emerilia, this screen covered people's vision.

Induca received a second message. Her smiling face turned almost gray as she woodenly walked over to a chair and collapsed into it.

"Induca, baby, what's wrong?" Suzy asked. The two of them had been about to go out for some lunch when they'd gotten the good news.

"Why? Why would he do that? How could he be so fucked up?" Tears streamed down Induca's face. She covered her face with her hands, her body shaking as she cried.

Suzy got on her knees, hugging Induca from the side.

"He killed them. He killed his own flesh and blood. Why? Why couldn't he have just gone and died by himself with his crazy beliefs?" Induca continued to sob incoherently, wrapping her arms around Suzy and holding her tight as she cried.

Suzy felt tears well up in her own eyes at the clear pain Induca, the woman she loved, was going through. There was nothing she could do but hold her and hope that she could support her through this.

***

Deia and Dave had been off on a date in Unity. She dropped the fork she'd been using, reading the message from her mother.

"Akatol is dead. However, he killed eight other Dragons before he could be killed. Several more are pretty heavily injured," Deia said in a private chat with Dave.

Dave's face became serious as he looked to Deia. "What should we do?"

"The family is in mourning. They're dealing with everything, but it's a big blow for them. Mother is asking that you take a look at the blood runes that Akatol made inside his ice palace. She'll be at Quindar and Fornau's home. She can teleport them to the Densaou and then us to the ice palace. Bob will meet us there," Deia said.

"Okay." Dave paid for the meal and held out a hand for Deia. With a press of his hot bar, he changed out of his formal clothes and into his armor.

Deia, too, changed into her armor. The two of them took to the air as Dave used his gravity orbs to send them flying out toward the cliff walls around Unity.

Fornau let them into the home. The excitement and happiness that had been visible just yesterday was gone. Everyone was somber. Even the children seemed quiet as their parents prepared to leave for the funeral.

With a flash of flame, Fire appeared in the main living room. Deia and Fire hugged. Fire looked as if she had aged years, her face lined with wrinkles and pain. She had only just got back her Dragons, her first children. Now, Akatol, their father, had turned and killed off eight of her family.

Quindar, Yoalin, and Fornau all hugged Fire and gathered around her with their children. Fire blinked rapidly, looking at those children.

Deia held her mother's hand. She could only guess what was going through her mind.

In a flash, they appeared in Densaou. In the next, they appeared in Opheir.

"Find out what Akatol did here," Fire said.

"We will," Dave promised.

"Mother, can I come with you?" Deia asked.

"Certainly," Fire said, with tears in her eyes and a trembling smile on her lips. She reached up and moved a piece of hair out of Deia's face.

Deia hugged her mother. As she did, the Lady Fire's resolve broke as tears fell down her cheeks and she sobbed into her daughter's shoulder.

***

As Fire was regaining her composure, Bob arrived. His lips were pressed together as his eyes seemed to want to say that he would be willing to do anything to take this pain away.

Once Fire was ready, she and Deia disappeared in flames, leaving Dave and Bob to work.

Already, the Dragons had taken their dead and wounded, headed back to Densaou. However, before they'd left, they'd created a series of barriers and enchantments so that no one could enter the mountain. The ice palace was melting at a fast rate without Akatol's Mana to support it. The ground had turned into a marsh as water once again covered the ground.

"If only I knew about Akatol's return or I was able to keep the prison shut," Bob said as he and Dave looked over the runes covering the floor.

"There was nothing that you could do, Bob," Dave said in a firm voice.

Bob made to argue, but let out a breath instead. "What do you make of this?" Bob waved at the runes.

"Killing circuit," Dave said.

"Looks like he was using the runes to make a disease of some kind. It was targeted using the blood of the sacrifices. Dragons would have been immune, though a great number of other populations would have been affected. It looks like there is a way to heal the disease. I guess Akatol was going to gift this cure to those who followed him." Bob shook his head.

Dave nodded. He specialized in mechanical coding, where Bob had a deep background in biology. After all, he had almost single-handedly created humans and their subspecies on Emerilia.

"Let's make a record of it. I can get the AI searching for this in the future so that it isn't made. Then, let's destroy it," Bob said.

"Agreed," Dave said with a grim expression. This Magical Circuit was a clear weapon, one that meant to spread death and destruction across Emerilia. It brought him to think about the weapons that he himself was making.

He focused on his work. Bob disappeared a time or two so that the members of the Pantheon wouldn't be able to locate him.

Across Emerilia, people were getting the news about the Dragons. People had been watching the mountain with long-distance spells and eyepieces. They had seen the ice palace break and the Dragons rush in. They'd heard the fighting come to an end and then seen the Dragons headed toward Densaou. This time, however, they passed over southern Opheir, using the wind stream to get back to their homes.

Because the wounded had been instantly teleported back home with the dead by Fire, the people of Emerilia assumed all who didn't leave were dead.

It was a shock that ran through Emerilia's people and Players.

After all, Dragons were the strongest existence known under the gods and goddesses themselves. Hearing that nearly twenty of them had not reappeared after attacking the ice palace was enough to scare the hardiest of adventurers.

However, some people were excited. They saw this as proof that the Dragons weren't invincible. Therefore, they had a chance to take down a Dragon, earning fame and riches.

On the other hand, others instead looked toward Densaou warily. The Dragons were known to repay those who attacked them with ruthless efficiency. They'd lost a number of their people and people wondered whether the Dragons would vent their anger out on those closest.

Bob and Dave destroyed the runes and collapsed the mountain on top of it. Bob left Dave in Unity, where he met up with the Stone Raiders who were readying themselves for the coming portal raid.

***

For two days, the Dragons nursed their injured back to their complete Health. Their Vitality was strong enough that if nothing directly killed them and they had enough food and time, they would recover to their original state.

Although their bodies were all fixed, Densaou Ring was a sad place.

The eight dead, massive Dragons lay within the largest volcano. It was as if the Dracul family had been stabbed through the heart.

Deia, Dave, Mal, and Suzy did all they could to help.

All of the Dragons had gathered in Densaou to pay their respects.

Finally, the time to say good-bye came.

Denur stood in front of the eight bodies and the gathered Dragons. Nearly sixty Dragons looked back at their matriarch. Some cried; others had stony expressions.

"Today is one of the hardest days I have had to endure in my life," Denur said. "Today, I put my daughter, three grandchildren, and four great-grandchildren to rest. It feels as if my heart has been ripped out of my chest and that I have lost the strength remaining in my body. I wish that there was something that I could do to see them smile one more time, to hear their laughter as they played games, or even just scold them for getting into trouble."

The Dragons smiled a bit and a few more had tears trail down their faces.

"But that won't happen, anymore." Denur took a deep breath. "Many of you have been talking over the last couple of days that we should hole up in Densaou, that we should let Emerilia deal with their issues. There is a war coming. We all know this, but I say we should not let our fear control us, but rather our hope. Every person who came with me to Opheir volunteered, knowing that to let Akatol upon Emerilia was to make us complicit in a genocide made in our names. Akatol was my husband at one time, until his mind became twisted by greed and power. We might keep to ourselves for the most part, but we are still people of Emerilia. This is our home. Battles will come up in the future and we will lose more of our family."

Deia could see the weight that rested on Denur's shoulders as she didn't flinch away from leading her family, even with the recent losses in her heart.

> "This is the highest price that we could ever pay. It is one that I have been thinking over these past few days, leaving my heart and soul in pain. We have great power. We are the second strongest people on Emerilia. When Demons and angels walk our lands, when beasts of the air, sea, and land return, we will be the only ones capable of helping. This family came together when we were sent to another realm. We became stronger than ever before. Now, our very bonds between one another will be tested. I will not force you to join me, but I will not rest un-

> til these threats to our family are eliminated; not until this event is finished and we are safe will I rest. Any who volunteer are welcome to join me in creating an alliance with Terra."

Deia let out a shocked breath. Saying that she was joining with Terra was saying that she would take up an ambassador position within Terra, representing the Dragons and offering their support in upcoming conflicts.

Deia glanced to Fire, seeing the pride in her eyes as she gently rocked Deia's brother, Daniel, in her arms.

She looked to Yoalin and Quindar, each of them holding a child, as Fornau held two.

Deia touched her stomach. Even as they had lost family members, life continued on.

***

Josh looked over the gathered Stone Raiders, DCA forces, mage's guild, adventurer's guild, Fellox Guild, and Portal Purge Guild. Fellox was the second rated guild in Emerilia. They had challenged the Stone Raiders for the first placed spot. Even though they had been defeated by the Stone Raiders, they maintained an amicable relationship.

In comparison, the Portal Purge was a guild that focused on finding and clearing portals and then attacking the other creatures beyond. They were the best at what they did and didn't have any animosity toward the Stone Raiders.

It had just been a couple of days since Josh had sent word out to everyone, but these forces had already gathered.

The creature in Opheir had been killed. From what people were putting together, it was clear to Josh that not even this combined force would have been able to deal with the Dragon hiding in the ice palace.

He was eager to get going, to truly see what Ashal's wilderness had to offer and clear out the portal. It was going to be one hell of a fight.

He thought of a saying he'd picked up from Kol: *It's only with the hottest fires and the greatest ambition that the best weapon can be forged.*

Josh was hoping that this portal raid could temper the Stone Raiders and the others with them so that they could be able to fight whatever came at them in the next couple of months.

The Dwarven tournament offered riches and fighting, but fighting one-on-one was nothing like the battles Josh and the Stone Raiders had been stuck in.

Each of them had some of the best gear and supplies. What they needed were powerful opponents to go up against, to increase their levels and fighting skill.

"Deia and Quindar have returned. Vrexu and Efri are ready to move," Anna said to Josh.

He nodded. The others had already returned beforehand, leaving the Dracul family in peace.

"All right! Let's go and clear out this portal!" Josh's voice rang through the general chat. People cheered, some raising their weapons up in the air as they started forward and through the western keep.

Thousands of POE and Players moved forward; wagons trundled along, carrying any supplies that they might need.

The western keep's gates opened for them, letting them exit Devil's Crater and walk forward out into the Ashal wilderness.

Josh stepped off to the side of the path.

"One hell of a sight." Lucy sat on her floating carpet.

"Untouched beauty," Josh said.

Beyond the keep, there was nearly a kilometer of rough ground before it reached a forest that covered all of Ashal. The trees here were tens of meters thick, hundreds of years old. They had an ancient and formidable aura to them.

Their massive raiding party snaked down the simple road.

DCA scouts took to the air and moved through the forest. A smile grew on Josh's face. Here, they were truly going into the unknown. They were the first to head into Ashal by themselves. There was no knowing what they would see in their travels.

Just the road to the portal would be an adventure.

A sense of excitement filled Josh as he stepped forward, headed out into the unknown, the star of his very own story.

Chapter 22: Ashal Wilderness

Party Zero moved with the rest of the Stone Raiders. The DCA were providing scouts so that they would have some warning before they ran into any large beasts.

The guilds had also sent out their own scouts, making multiple layers that should catch any possible threats.

Behind the passing raid party, a number of Earth and Dark mages raised a road along their path. It would make it easier for those who came later and for moving materials if they weren't able to fly for some reason. If they were out front, then they were more likely to step on an animal or threat in the wilderness. At the rear, they could be sure of their security, focusing on their work as their guards watched on.

In the first day, they only had small skirmishes with some Level 400 and 500 beasts. Most of them were trying to defend the territory that the raid group had walked into.

They would send out a few parties a day to deal with larger groups of creatures so that they would never reach the main group. A few made it past but never in large enough numbers to be of a real threat. Leaving them alive was inviting an ambush. They also had high quality meat and materials. Despite this logic, to Players, there was a larger driving factor: the amount of experience they gave per kill.

Deia was off watching over Vrexu's brigade while Anna watched Efri and his people.

Induca and Malsour were still with their family and were due to return by nightfall. Lox, Steve, Gurren, Dave, and Suzy were together.

Lox was in command, but was joking around with the others.

They seemed to know Dave and Suzy were down a bit and so they were giving them space while being goofs, trying to take their minds off it.

Dave cracked a smile, shaking his head at their antics as they recalled their adventure to the Dwarven tournaments, where Gurren had woken up on the roof of a brothel with no idea of how he had gotten there. It seemed he had fallen asleep early so Steve and Lox had carefully put him on the roof the night before.

Dave looked off into the distance, sensing something with his Touch of the Land. "Damn, that is one big creature." Dave tried to match what he was seeing with the creature library someone had made for Emerilia. It was like an encyclopedia of everything that walked the planet.

Even with his high Intelligence, it still took him some time before he found something similar.

"Ebony plated rhino? Well, they do look kind of similar," Dave muttered.

"Ebony plated rhino?" Lox asked in a serious tone.

"Sorry, just saw one a good distance away. Damned thing is massive." Dave shook his head.

"I'll let Josh know. Where was it?" Lox asked.

"About three miles to our front and two miles north," Dave said simply. "We shouldn't go anywhere near it."

"We might not go near it, but they're highly territorial and where there's one, there's more. They've got skin that makes it hard to use magic against them. No magical weapons or spells. Just have to go right in with physical weapons and they can hit hard enough to put a Level 400 down in one hit," Lox said.

"Ouch." Steve grimaced.

"Look out for more of them. It's probably easier if you don't look for them specifically, but things that might show something being in a place it's not supposed to. Your Touch of the Land isn't going to be too effective on these big bastards," Gurren growled.

"Will do." Dave submerged himself into his senses. With Gurren's pointers, he was able to find nearly half a dozen other ebony plated rhinos just half a mile away from where the raiding party was going to pass through.

"Well, I just found about four of them near where we will pass," Dave said.

"I've talked to Josh. He said that we should head over and get rid of them if we think they're a threat. I sent a message to Anna. She can get some of her flyers to help us out. Let the rhinos chase after the flyers; then we can take down the rhinos one by one," Lox said.

They headed out of the line of Players and POEs who were weaving through the forest. They were a bit spread out because of the forest. Even though it seemed like a nice relaxing day and people seemed to be idly chatting as if they were out on a stroll, all of them were ready to react to anything that might happen. A few of them talked among themselves as they saw Party Zero move away from the main group and head out into the forest.

These murmurs became interested mutterings as DCA aerial forces as well as Dwayne and two other parties joined up with Party Zero.

"Nothing like a little stroll through the Ashal wilderness to make a man feel alive again." Dwayne took a deep breath of the fresh air around them.

"Come to steal all our glory," Lox complained.

"Merely share it. I've heard that these ebony rhinos are rather formidable. Don't want you to break a fingernail," Dwayne said.

Lox laughed, snorting slightly. "Welcome to the hunt!" He clapped Dwayne's armor.

"Since I'm just joining in on this, what's the plan?" Dwayne asked.

"We get the flyers to hit them, take aggro and kite them. We move in, hit one at a time—it's going to take a hell of a lot to kill them. Blunt weapons are the best. We get the flyers to bring us another rhino and we do it all over again," Lox said.

"Sounds almost easy when you put it that way," Gurren complained.

"Good, because we're going to be in the front line. We've got the best defensive abilities so we can hopefully stop the rhino's charge, allowing everyone else to surround the beastie and pulp it to death," Lox said. "Dave, you see anywhere where it would be good for us to set up a defensive line so we could stop the rhino?"

"I think I have a place. There's a small hill that overlooks a creek. It's too steep on the sides for the rhinos to get up. We just need some Earth or Dark types to raise stones, have boulders at either side and then we can funnel the rhinos right into you two. Then, we get around behind it and start hitting away. It shouldn't be able to get free before we put it down."

"Let's make sure those walls are extra strong. A rhino's foot can probably kill a Level 200 pretty easily. After all, these are ebony rhinos in Ashal; assume that every attack can probably kill you. They're probably around Level 700 or 800. It's really hard for other beasts to kill them. Even though they're affected by melee attacks, they're strong as all hell," Lox warned.

The Stone Raiders nodded. A serious atmosphere surrounded them. There was a time to mess about and a time to get serious. They checked their gear and readied themselves. They moved off quickly and quietly toward where the rhinos were laying down.

"The scouts are saying that they're having trouble finding anything. The foliage is thick and their different sights aren't letting them see the creatures," Dwayne said.

Dave, leading the way, slowed his pace. For the first time, Dave felt unsure. He hadn't clearly sensed these creatures, but rather a number of signs that he felt could have been created by the ebony rhinos.

"Dave, give us a location. Once they've got it, tell them to drop a bomb on the place. That should be enough for you to pick up where they are, right?" Lox asked.

"Yeah, that would work," Dave said.

"There we go," Lox said. "First, let's fortify that rise you were talking about."

Dave guided them to the rise. He'd found it was a rock with some dirt and grass on it; the dirt around all but one of its edges had been worn away by the stream that ran along it.

The mages went to work, pulling up stones and making two large pillars that extended into a wall. They were the only way to access the rock unless someone had the Strength and Agility to directly jump onto it—like the Stone Raiders.

The ebony rhinos weighed several tons and were made to run in straight lines, not jump. There was naturally no way for them to get on top of the rock without going down the corridor.

Quicksand and other measures were added to the corridor in order to halt each rhino's progress so that it couldn't hit Lox and Gurren with its full strength.

Once everything was set up, Dave opened up his map. He placed a waypoint where he thought the creatures might be.

They waited for some time. The aerial scouts checked and rechecked that they had the right place. Even with all of their abilities, they were unable to find out where the rhinos were. They quietly moved down below the canopy of the massive trees.

These trees rose as much as two miles from the ground, making it exceptionally hard to see what lay below them with normal sight.

It was the main reason that the aerial forces spent so much of their time working on their different sight spells and skills to determine what lay beneath cover.

"Targets are confirmed. Even though I'm looking right at them, it's really hard to sense them unless they move," the scout's leader said to the party.

Dave smiled, relieved that his hunch had paid off. It was only because of his strong Touch of the Land, that combined skill of the Affinities, that he was able to sense that there was even possibly something in the area.

"We've got lowest of Level 200, young adult-looking type, to a Level 735. This thing is massive."

As the aerial scouts looked at the rhinos, the rest of the party were able to see red outlines of the creatures. They were rough because of the distance between them and were only an outline. There was no actual detail to the images.

"We'll start with the lowest-leveled ones and then move up to the strongest. There's four of them altogether," the scout leader confirmed.

Lox looked around at everyone. They looked ready.

"All right, bring on the rhino express!" Lox slammed his Dwarven shield down. The twin points stuck into the dirt and then rock underneath as Lox braced it against the left side column. Gurren grunted, slamming his shield down and doing the same with the right side column.

"Bombs away," the scout leader said.

Mana bombs exploded among the ebony rhinos.

Creatures of flight took to the skies as smaller animals ran for fear of what might come after the explosion.

The rhinos let out enraged bellows as more Mana bombs were released. They did some damage to the rhinos, but most of it was through the pressure waves of the bombs, rather than their chaotic magical energies.

The aerial scouts moved apart, different groups aggroing the creatures and pulling them in different directions.

The fighters on the ground readied themselves, standing behind Lox, Gurren, and Steve. Dave stood off to the side, ready to fight when needed, with Dwayne on the opposite side.

Mana bombs trailed off as the aerial scouts sent down Mana bolts in order to keep their target's attention. The Mana bolts were getting closer and closer as the underbrush of the forest rustled ahead of the corridor.

"Incoming!" the DCA aerial scout being trailed by the rhino yelled. Flying right down the corridor, he was followed by the rhino youth as it tore out of the underbrush, tossing its head.

Ebony Plated Rhino

Level 217

Its eyes locked onto those who were hiding at the end of the corridor. It had two forward-facing eyes under two massive horns and above a single larger horn that pointed straight forward like a spear.

"This is a youth?" someone yelled out. The creature was one meter wide, one and a half tall, and four long.

Its mouth rested beneath the shield-like face. Its skin was wrinkled, looking like an Earth rhino's, but as dark as night. Hitting the eyes was an impossibility; in fact, it had virtually no weaknesses on its front.

Its side and back were also heavily muscled and looked like slabs of armor that one might find on a tank. Cracking the skin of the rhino would be hard, but with blunt weapons, they could cause internal injuries.

The rhino entered the corridor. Gurren and Lox leaned into their shields. Steve also leaned forward.

"Quagmire!" one of the mages called out. There was no need for them to call the spell out to cast it, but they did it to inform the others.

The rhino's momentum seemed to be arrested. It hit Gurren and Lox's shields with a massive hit, bouncing back a bit only to find that its legs were stuck in a muddy quagmire. It yelled out, trying to release itself, but only sinking in further.

"Finish it off!" Lox yelled.

Dwayne and Dave left the way, jumping onto the walls while pulling out blunt weapons and hammering down on the rhino. Lu Lu's lightning attacks slowed the creature as she quickly used up her limited Mana supply. Suzy's rock and Earth golems joined in on the melee, as did the rest of the Stone Raiders.

In a matter of minutes, the rhino gave up and fell over, leaning against the walls.

Suzy flicked her fingers, directing her Air creations toward the rhino. There was a wet sucking sound as they freed the rhino from the ground before taking it out of the corridor.

Mages repaired the corridor, talking to one another about making it more effective.

Dave checked Gurren and Lox's shields. They were okay, barely a scratch on them. However, their enchantments needed recharging.

In five minutes, they were ready for their next customer.

"Number two, ebony rhino order up!" Steve yelled.

Like with the first creature, the second was stopped before it could reach Gurren and Lox.

The third hit their shields, making them grunt against the strength of the ebony rhino.

Dave was pleasantly surprised as a screen filled his vision.

Level 233

You have reached Level 233; you have **155** stat points to use.

He grinned. These rhinos were strong beasts. As such, he was actually able to get enough experience to level up.

"Damn, it feels good to gain another level!"

The other Stone Raiders grinned and cheered, working on their corridor as Suzy moved the third body off to the side.

Now, it was time for the last and strongest rhino.

It was Level 735. This kind of beast couldn't be found on any other continent. The third had only been a Level 504. A two hundred level difference was immense.

It had taken them twenty minutes just to wear down the third. They carefully examined the corridor; one mistake and the rhino would be able to tear them apart. It was nearly three times stronger than the levels of everyone there, but on a stat-for-stat basis it was only about one hundred levels stronger on average.

Dave was stronger than it stat wise, but his strengths lay with magic and outthinking his opponents.

A tree was toppled in the distance. The whole forest shuddered as it fell onto the others around it.

The aerial scout was breathing heavily, not daring to move into the corridor as the rhino shook the splinters off its body, some as big as a man's forearm.

"Steve!" Lox called out.

Steve fired out bolts from his hand, angering the rhino and taking its attention.

It turned for the corridor and started building up its momentum again.

"Suzy!" Lox said.

Around the rhino, Earth and metal creatures appeared, hitting the rhino. They would have torn any normal opponent to shreds, but now their attacks were more likely to break them than the rhino.

The rhino seemed to glow with a red light. The summoned creations were even weaker than before, as if their Mana had been suppressed.

It continued forward, picking up speed at an alarming rate.

Dave destroyed ground, trying to trip it up. It jumped over the opening. A quagmire slightly paused it before it slammed into Gurren and Lox. Dave and Dwayne braced them as they were all pushed back half a step.

They pushed forward as the rhino bucked and moved, its horns tearing the corridor apart.

"Mages, repair; everyone else—attack!" Dwayne yelled out.

This had been a simple clearing mission: take out creatures that would attack them if they sensed them. It shouldn't have been anything hard to handle.

Right now, none of them were thinking that this was anything easy. They were fighting with everything they had and the rhino's massive hit points were only slowly declining. They hit weak points, but still it was like hitting a steel wall.

Everyone's arms and limbs were getting numb from the impacts.

The mages were doing everything in their power to just maintain the walls and try to slow the rhino. It truly was a beast worthy of Ashal's infamous wilderness.

Dave thought of what would have happened if he hadn't stumbled across this creature with his Touch of the Land.

He continued to slam down on the creature with a summoned war hammer. It felt as though he were cutting a tree instead of trying to kill the creature.

One person was too slow and got hit by the rhino's horns. He was tossed; blood came from his body despite the fact he was roughly a Level 500 talent with his stats.

He downed a Health potion as everyone else continued their attacks. Even the DCA scouts joined in on the fight. This rhino was nearly two to three times the size of the original rhino youth, a seething mass of angry and armored beast.

Gurren and Lox were just able to stay on their feet even with all of the training, strength, and gear.

"Not my first rodeo!" Steve yelled, jumping up onto the wall. Using the flat of his axe, he slammed it against the rhino. Each of his blows brought the rhino's Health down in big chunks.

The Stone Raiders yelled out, hitting harder and faster. Suzy's phoenix let out a screech. Lightning moved from her mouth as if it were twin black and white snakes coiled around each other.

It hit the rhino, stunning it and dropping it to the ground. The lightning attack had stunned the creature, allowing the Stone Raiders an opening.

Although it was nearly immune to magic normally, if that magic got within its protective armor-like skin, it could kill them.

Suzy called out buffs, enhancing Strength and Stamina; the rhino went slack, its Health points drained.

Still, other than a few scratches, there were no openings in the rhino's natural black armored hide.

They slumped down where they were; if one part of their group had paused or given up for just a minute, then they would have lost one or more guild members. They thought of themselves as powerhouses, and they were since when they had started with the Stone Raiders. Though everyone was a powerhouse compared to when they started off.

"Damn, I forgot what it feels like to be truly scared of a single opponent," Dwayne admitted.

"Feels like we're always getting swarmed with lesser talents. Been awhile since I fought something that was so much stronger than me."

"Same. Gets the blood going though." Lox whistled and wiped sweat from his brow.

"You're right about that! Nothing like fighting a creature well above your level to make you feel alive." Dave laughed, his breathing quickly coming under control.

"Now, how the hell are we going to deal with these rhinos?" Suzy looked to the four massive corpses.

"Well, we'll need to skin them, then we can sell them off. They make high-class potions and their meat is divine. Cost as much as some people's monthly wages for a single meal," Lox said proudly.

"How we going to open these suckers up?" Gurren poked holes in Lox's plan.

"Well, Josh owes me a favor," Lox said.

"Okay, so what, we're going to haul these things over to the rest of the guild and then get Josh to skin them?" Dave asked. "You do know that they weigh as much as Steve!"

"Hey! I've been on a diet!" Steve complained.

"You don't even eat!"

"See—air diet." Steve winked.

"Yes, Lu Lu, you're a much cuter contracted creature—yes, you are." Suzy scratched the tired Lu Lu. Her attack on the rhino had drained most of her Mana reserves. She preened under her mother's attention, stretching outward.

"Well, looks like someone is growing up." Dave looked to Lu Lu.

"Yeah, I've been giving her a one hundred percent experience draw. I want her to level up as soon as possible so that she can be capable of defending herself," Suzy said.

Lu Lu let out a pleased *chirrup.*

Dave laughed. It seemed like the little phoenix loved the attention.

"Well, when Ela-Dorn finishes with those summoning halls, I want to see if I can get something a bit...bigger," Dwayne said.

"Not about the size, but about how you use it," Steve said.

"I saw you slapping a rhino with your axe just a few minutes ago!" Dwayne retorted.

"And sometimes, it's a really good idea to hit bigger things with a big axe!" Steve said with a brilliant smile.

"Oh, I think I just had an aneurysm. Hi, my name's George. What's your names?" Gurren held out his hand.

Lox snorted and slapped the hand away, a smile on his face.

"So, how are we moving these multi-ton rhinos?" Suzy asked.

"Oh, I have an idea or two." Lox smiled at Steve.

A few minutes later, Steve was complaining. It was easy enough to wave spatial items over the rhinos, capturing them inside. The four rhinos were held within two rings. Steve had strengthened steel links through the two rings that hung from his shoulders. "I think I just heard a gear give way!" Steve complained.

"Oh, stop complaining and watch for holes. I don't want to have to pull your ass out of a ditch again!" Dwayne said.

Steve muttered about the inequalities of a contracted beast while everyone continued on toward the raid party with high spirits. They kept out an eye for creatures that might be in the forests but few tried to approach them.

"Look at that—Myrai's root," someone called out, checking the area before moving to pull up the rare medicinal root.

Ashal's wilderness was like an entirely different world than the rest of Emerilia. Everywhere one went, there were rare and aged resources that could support a family for a year in Gudalo.

That said, with all of the dangers, everyone checked the area before gathering materials.

"It might be worth setting up an ono when we get to the portal just for all the riches we're gathering," Dwayne said.

"I heard that the mage's guild is interested in studying the creatures that are defending the portal. They don't have anything recorded that's like these creatures and no more than two types of Affinity spirits in a single area," Suzy said.

"Yeah, they're going nuts about that Human-looking character who's sitting on the throne. The Aleph, even with all of their records, haven't been able to shed any light on it," Dwayne said.

There was a loud noise behind Dave.

"Man down," Steve said, his voice muffled as his face was stuck in the ground.

"Fer the love of Mithril! How in the bloody mountains did you do that?" Lox yelled, his fists on his hips, looking at the helpless Steve.

"Hey! Give a man a hand. I can't move my hands to get these friggin' rings off!" Steve tried to pull himself upward with his legs but only served to shake himself around.

"I would ask how many brain cells do you have left in there, but I know there's nothing," Gurren complained.

Dave sighed. He used a spell that reduced gravity, allowing Steve to right himself.

"That gravity magic is some good stuff. Might have to look into it for adding onto my weapons," Steve said.

"Just try not to stick your head into any other small hills we come across?" Lox asked.

"No promises!" Steve said in a semi-serious tone.

Gurren and a number of the other Stone Raiders moaned in complaint.

The DCA scouts looked to one another as if wondering how the Stone Raiders were able to do anything. It seemed that they were having more trouble just moving their loot than actually fighting a herd of ebony rhinos.

"I've heard about how resource-rich Ashal is, but since I've been here, it's been incredible the types of things we've found. Just going from Devil's Crater to the portal, others would be interested in just gathering the resources along the way. Also, it could be the start of an adventuring road. I heard that there have been a number of dungeons and lairs found in the area," Suzy said, ignoring Steve's accident.

"All of the dungeons we've marked seem to be of the highest quality; being left to themselves, their creatures and resources have increased in ability by a large margin," Dwayne agreed as they continued onward.

"I can also tell you that opening a few mines in the nearby area would be a good idea. I know that Grahslagg Corporation would be interested in dropping off a few automated mining drills in the area," Dave said.

"Ashal truly is a wilderness that rewards the brave or foolish," Lox said.

"If one can get past the dangers that lurk around," Gurren said.

"Well, we should hurry up if we want to get back to the rest of the raiding party before night falls," Dwayne said.

***

Josh heard screams, followed by gurgling noises. Parties that were on standby rushed to where the scouts were.

"Air snakes!" someone called out on the information channel.

Air snakes were ethereal-looking creatures. They were see-through to most people; they could be sensed by using arcane sight but otherwise only when they were moving erratically could one see them.

They flew through the air. Their main attacks were a powerful Air spear and a poison that could take out anything below Level 1,000, paralyzing them.

Their poison went for fifteen grand soul gems for just a tincture of it. However, getting that poison was not only difficult, but led to many deaths.

Summoned Air creatures cut out toward where the Air snakes were.

After ten minutes, the fighting was over.

"If I was allowed to go then I would have been able to finish off those things in seconds," one of the Portal Purge Guild members said.

"Yeah, it's just the guildmasters playing favorites. The Stone Raiders and the DCA are getting all of the action. So what if they have higher levels—we're better at fighting!" another said.

"They are the top ranked guild. The DCA is the highest rated POE fighting force right now, below the Dwarves. I wouldn't want to be fighting against a Dwarven warclan," another opined.

Josh pulled out some jerky and bit into it. They weren't part of his guild and he didn't overly care what they said. He was secure in his knowledge that no matter what the Stone Raiders were ranked out of the guilds on Emerilia, to him it was the best.

Lucy floated over on her carpet as summoned creations and the fighters who had gone out to support the scouts came back carrying wounded.

"Three DCA died, one Fellox Player," Lucy said, seeing where Josh was looking.

Josh let out a sigh. "It might be good training for the DCA but I can't help but feel upset when we lose even one of them. Emerilia's AI is just so advanced that I can't think of them as just NPCs. Why the hell would a game want to have such developed characters?"

Josh didn't see the complicated look on Lucy's face as he took another bite of his jerky.

"Well, shows that you're Human. I think if we just started treating the POE like expendable resources that we'd lose a little bit of our humanity," Lucy said.

Josh looked to Lucy. "That was deep, and call me soft, but I agree."

"Three more days and we'll reach the portal," Lucy said.

"So, thoughts on putting an ono there?"

"I think it might be a good idea. The people who have gone off to kill off creatures have come back with some good loot. The group that killed off the ebony rhinos two days ago—the meat by itself is worth three common soul gems per kilo. The hide, it's some of the strongest I've ever seen. They're holding onto it to give it to Florence; she's looking for a leather worker who might be able to turn it into light armor. There's a lot of beasts out here, all of them powerful and with valuable resources. Also, Suzy came to me asking if they put some money forward, whether Grahslagg Corporation could get a lower rate for moving materials from here. They want to set up a mine," Lucy said.

"Damn, I've got to see about going out and fighting some of these creatures. Can you see if Florence could contact me if she does find someone to make armor out of that rhino hide? I'd definitely be interested," Josh said.

"Send her a message yourself, you lazy ass!" Lucy complained.

"But you're faster than me!" Josh complained.

"You annoying Lucy again?" Cassie appeared from where she'd been checking on the newest Stone Raiders who were coming out for the first time. She had wanted to make sure that she had picked well, talking to Esa about the newbies.

The better the recruits she could get, the stronger the Stone Raiders would be. With their limited spots, it was key to get not only the strongest but the ones that best fit with the guild.

"Yes." Lucy flicked her hair back.

Josh rolled his eyes. "Fine, I'll send the message myself." Josh pouted as he opened up his interface and sent a private message to Florence.

There was a yell from behind the raid party.

"Wood nymphs are attacking the engineers and mages making the road. The people back there are dealing with it," Lucy said calmly.

"Looks like the Ashal wilderness is living up to its reputation." There was a deep rumbling from the rear before all noises of fighting died down.

"Looks like Malsour dealt with it," Lucy said, a trace of worry in her voice.

"Something the matter?" Josh asked.

"It's just...you know that Malsour and Induca lost someone they were close with?" Lucy asked.

"I didn't but they've been kind of withdrawn since they came back," Josh said, clearly sad for the brother and sister duo.

"Yeah, well, now you know why," Lucy said.

"They say time heals all wounds. Hopefully they'll be able to get past it. Losing a loved one is never easy." Cassie's hand unconsciously found Josh's and squeezed.

Malsour and Induca might be POEs but they were good friends with Josh, Lucy, and Cassie. When talking and interacting with them, it was hard to think of them as just programs made up to entertain them.

Chapter 23: The Sound of Progress

Kol's hands pressed into the materials in front of him. The temperatures were strong enough to melt down to a person's bones.

In Kol's hands, the rounded length of metal was smoothed out, like clay in the hands of a master. A blade formed and then a series of runes. Even though Kol was just using his hands, he left behind perfect lines that looked as if they had come from an Aleph factory.

He reintroduced the metal to the furnace once again as it had cooled too much for him to be able to easily manipulate it with his smithing art.

He opened his eyes, looking around the upper floor smithy. Here and there were a half-dozen Master Smiths, either working on their own projects, Dave's projects, repair jobs, or teaching others. There was a group of forty or so Dwarven smith hopefuls. Their background varied as much as their races.

There were just a few Dwarves in the group. Many of them were working on different weapons and using different materials to get a better understanding. Others had Master Smiths looking over their shoulder to show them something. Others were planning out what they wanted to do.

They were the next generation of Master Smith hopefuls. Only one in ten thousand had what they needed to make it not only to the level of Master Smith in knowledge of materials but also realize their smithing art.

There might be one in a thousand that could pass all of the other requirements but never come to understand their smithing art.

Then there was one in one hundred of those who found their smithing art who had a strong enough Willpower to use Mithril and truly be called a Dwarven Master Smith.

A small smile crossed Kol's features as he looked at all of the masters and talent displayed in his smithy.

Cliff-Hill smithy was the largest smithy under Grahslagg Corporation. Many people started off working there, taking refined materials from the Aleph and Dwarves, creating various items, working on their coding skills and abilities. The smithy in Devil's Crater made more complex Magical Circuitry or coded items. They were also capable of repairing any level of weapon, up to and including Weapons of Power. They also did custom weaponry and armor from the materials that were supplied by different adventurers and customers.

Terra smithy was on a whole different level compared to the other smithies.

Here they hired magical coders right out of the Mirror of Communication classes. If someone had the skill and temperament for it, they could come to work at Terra's smithy, their food and accommodation paid for. They would work with other Magical Circuit geniuses and there was a chance that they might meet with Dave Grahslagg himself.

Dwarven Master Smiths also flocked to the smithy, working alongside other geniuses and able to gain resources for working on set projects.

Terra was the leading innovator of smithing and magical coding techniques. It was the first ever tower made completely from a soul gem base. It empowered and revitalized the people working there as well as increased the strength of their works.

Terra was vaunted as one of the highest quality smithies around. The Dwarven mountains that had been around the longest had tools that had been imbued with the strength of millions of weapons, absorbing Mana from every Affinity to become stronger over centuries.

The difference between Terra smithy and these other smithies was that it was easier to gain access to. For set prices or materials, the various smiths and coders within the smithy would be happy to look at different projects.

Every day, new ideas were being tested out.

"Master Kol, Frenik has arrived in Terra. You are scheduled to go and meet with him," Shard said through a private chat.

Kol sighed and looked at the metal that was quickly becoming cherry-red in the furnace. "Tell him to come up and meet me. I'll be finished with this in a few minutes."

***

Frenik looked around in wonder. He had lived in Aleph cities for most of his life, though he hadn't ever seen them as busy as he saw inside Terra. The streets were packed with people of every race, from POE to Player and hundreds of guilds and kingdoms.

Walking through Terra was like walking around Emerilia.

He attracted some attention as his group of centurion automatons moved around him, protecting him from any type of attack.

Restaurants were doing a bustling business; smells invited Frenik to come and enjoy the delicacies available.

A behemoth was carrying a drunk person spouting nonsense off to the side.

Frenik's eyebrows rose as he saw indentured prisoners walking around freely. They wore collars that wouldn't allow them to attack people or escape their service. Although they didn't seem to be overjoyed, they were going about the day with no one batting an eye. No one tried to harass them as they continued on their way.

Stores were filled with fighters, monks, adventurers, and mages. For every kind of profession, there seemed to be a store.

Roaming automatons reminded people that although they were free to visit Terra, they should watch their behavior.

Buildings were no longer just simple box-like affairs. People had added their own flair; they came in all manner of colors. Most of them looked more modern, with clean lines, silvers and whites with clear glass, or in some rare cases, soul gem windows to show off the goods inside.

Towers rose up into the sky. Transports moved from one location to another, moving goods and people. The skies were filled with traffic. Walkways extended over the roads, people moving through them.

Parks and growing towers were artfully placed so that the cities didn't just seem to be lifeless constructs. Greenery curled up walls or was carefully maintained in parks that lay off from the main thoroughfares.

There were more discreet businesses away from the main roads, allowing someone to get a beer in a quiet location or to have a meal in peace after a long, hard quest.

Terra had a revitalizing energy; it truly was a place where anyone might be able to find what they wanted. The streets became busier the farther one went.

Frenik stared at the refinery that was overhead on the opposite side of the city's ring. It never stopped; the massive facility was in constant motion with materials moving in and out of it.

He continued on his path, shaking his head at the marvels that were happening in Terra.

He wasn't tall enough to see it, but the second section of Terra was already in development and would be complete in just a few short months, ready to take on more people and businesses.

He made his way to the Terra smithy. People were moving in and out with all manner of materials, weapons, and wealth.

Terra could serve any person's needs, though there were a limited number of smiths, so some of the work was sent off to Devil's Crater or Cliff-Hill.

Frenik walked into the smithy.

"Who the hell does he think he is just because he's got a few automatons?" someone complained.

Automatons were rarely seen. Before a few months ago, they had just been legendary machines, but it seemed that Emerilians got used to change rather quickly.

"Master Frenik, Kol has asked that you meet him up on the top floor. He's currently working on something. He's sorry for the delay," one of the smiths working the front table said. They waved to an elevator.

"Thanks." Frenik smiled, and his automatons moved with him into the elevator. After a short ride, he was up in the top floor of the smithy.

Frenik stepped out of the elevator and stopped moving. His eyes roved around the room, trying to find Kol across the large floor. Instead, they fell on the different items that were being made.

Excitement filled Frenik as he looked from weapons to armor, to powerful rings and necklaces. Each and every item that came from this floor was worthy of being called the best in all of Emerilia. Although there were a few Weapons of Power, mostly those being repaired, these items were as strong as the weakest Weapons of Power.

Frenik looked over racks of spears, swords, shields, axes, morning stars. There was no end to the types of weapons; there were even magical staffs and different ranged mechanical weapons. Frenik looked over these items with a reverence. They were weapons of war but the craftsmanship, the detail in each and every one of them...

Frenik touched them, sinking his senses into them. They were powerful and elegant, with the kind of quality that his forges could only come close to.

His factories made great mass-produced weapons, but without the individual detail that these smiths could bring, they were inferior. When compared to the highest strength weapons here, his weapons were like comparing a stick figure to a beautiful landscape painting.

They were both paintings and works of art that only a true master could make; the other was presented well but it didn't have any special depth to it.

He slowly reached where Kol stood in his workspace.

People's conversations stopped as they walked past, looking in to see as Kol worked.

Frenik tried to be as quiet as possible, looking at Kol. In his hands, he held a cherry-red sword. Already it had a faint design in the blade and its edge looked as though it could cut through a tree as if it were butter. It was a short sword that belled out slightly before coming into its final point. Kol's hands moved over the blade; silver that had been resting on the top of the blade sunk into it, disappearing from sight.

He's probably laying down magical coding on the inside so only someone who comes into contact with the blade can tell what its abilities are.

Frenik tugged on his beard, watching as Kol's hands moved over the metal. Kol tossed in a few different materials from his belt, and then he heated it up again.

The metal sparked but was again cherry-red in just a few moments in the powerful soul gem-powered furnace.

Kol ran his fingers over the sword, his eyes closed. He changed it slightly before running his fingers along the edge. The edge became firmer as the heat started to be rapidly pulled from it. By the time Kol was at the end of the sword, it looked like dirty steel.

Kol flicked the blade; ash fell from the blade, showing a weapon that looked as if it had been polished for days, not a single mark on it.

There was almost a chill in the air with the metal as Kol turned it in his hand. The blade easily cut through the air with a slight humming noise. Kol put the blade down on the workbench with a sort of reverence.

"Oh, hey Frenik, sorry about that," Kol said, noticing Frenik as he looked up from his work.

"No matter. It was a pleasure to see you work. You still good for that talk about incorporating more Aleph items into the smithies' supply chain?" Frenik asked.

"That I am. Come, we'll take this to my office." Kol led the way through the shop.

Frenik followed him into an office. Two automatons followed him in, and the others stayed outside.

***

Kol looked to Frenik, sizing the man up. As Dave had made his workshop, he had brought Kol in on just who Bob really was, the creation of Emerilia, and the Jukal Empire.

He'd also brought him in on all the plans he had for the projects that the Dwarven Master Smiths were working on.

It had been a lot to take in but Kol had always thought that Dave was thinking in the long term and he'd had his suspicions of what the projects that Dave was handing out were meant for. He also had magical coders from all over Emerilia working to solve issues to coding problems that he'd had.

Now Frenik was another part of this massive puzzle.

Kol opened a private chat with Frenik. He didn't want any part of this conversation getting out. He already knew that Terra's protection was great but the private chat system was nearly infallible.

"I didn't think discussing the number of factories we can have working on cutting down materials to specifications to make them easier to forge would need a private chat," Frenik said.

"They don't. What I have to ask of you is something that no one else can do and something that we're going to have to keep a secret." Kol gave Frenik a serious look. He waited for that to settle in before he continued. "Dave has brought me in on a project. Simply put, I have never heard of something the kind of scale he's thinking. Also, most of it is in the developmental stages and we only have a rough idea of what we're going to need. However, from that, we're going to need a lot of different components and all of them need to be identical. Having this with master crafters is just not a possibility, but your factories have proved time and time again that they can make things to a high grade repeatedly. We need that."

"What are these components going to be needed for?" Frenik asked, curious.

"For that, I don't know if I can tell you or not yet. What I can do is give you a bunch of plans and ask if you can complete them in a certain period so that they will function and that I can get them in the quantities I need."

"I can let you know, but I'm going to need to see them. If you want, I'll make an oath," Frenik said.

"As much as I trust you, it would be best, just because of the pressure it would exert on you to warn you if you're close to revealing something."

"Understood and no worries," Frenik said with a disarming smile. He knew that Kol wouldn't take these measures unless he absolutely felt the need to.

"Frenik, will you swear that you will not tell anyone what the purposes of these plans are? You will not hint at it and do everything in your power to make sure that people don't come to understand what they would create?" Kol asked.

A prompt appeared in front of Frenik, the box repeating what Kol had asked.

"I agree," Frenik said.

Now Kol would be warned if he broke this oath.

"Thank you," Kol said, breathing a little easier. "Now, there are three main projects. One is a missile. Basically, think of it as a seeking Mana bolt attack but with a grand working bomb and harder to hit. Another is a self-contained ship to fly around Emerilia. There's going to be tons of components but we've got the basic ideas figured out. Then the third is called a Band-Aid—Dave hasn't come up with a better name, and he hasn't finished it—but essentially, once this thing is worn by a Player, they won't mysteriously die at the end of their Player cycle."

"He has something that could actually be capable of doing that?" Frenik said in excited tones, leaning forward.

"Well, he has the idea and the plans, but we simply don't know if it will work or not." Kol sighed.

Frenik sat back in his chair. *A ship that could fly through the air—it could remove roads altogether. And missiles—it sounded as if they would be capable of destroying cities and would be extremely hard to fight against!*

"Okay, what components are we looking at and how many?" Frenik pushed down on his excitement.

"Have a look." Kol sent over complete blueprints on the projects. The ship was a list of parts. Dave had created a mock-up but they simply didn't know how big everything was going to be, so relying on the exterior mock-up wasn't the best. The Band-Aid was a complex series of thin coded plates. Making them so small would be hard, but possible.

Frenik slowly looked through them, muttering to himself and making notes on his interface. "I'm going to need some help on some of this stuff, but I think we can get it done. Once I know how things would work out, I can give you a time estimate. I can do this by myself in a few days or I can get Shard to do it in a few minutes."

"You can use Shard. No one's getting into his Magical Circuitry—Dave and Bob checked," Kol said.

"Good to know that he's secure. Who's this Bob?"

"Grey God," Kol said.

Frenik's eyes widened. He thought that he couldn't be shocked anymore.

"Trust me, I know—the more I learn, the more I find out I don't know anything. It's a bit overwhelming at first." Kol shrugged.

"Well, thank you for trusting me." Frenik sent off the information to Shard.

Shard asked to join the private chat; Kol allowed him.

"We can complete these projects within eight months. We might need more time with any later components you make due to other people taking up factory lines," Shard said.

"Perfect. Then I'll leave that to you," Kol said.

"Thank you." Frenik stood. Kol did so as well, and they shook hands. Both of them felt that their actions would have far-reaching effects, but right now, there were too many questions and not enough answers. So, what that effect might be, neither of them could fully imagine.

***

Ela-Dorn slid in the last coded plate. She pushed the rack into the large arch of the machine she'd been working on for the last couple of weeks.

It was supported on a stage. Above the stage, two arches came together to create a domed open space. Looking directly at the arches, there was a circle under the arches and another that extended out between two of these curved pillars.

Underneath the circles, there were magically coded sheets that looked much like a server might. The ones under the small circle were simple, while the ones under the arches were complicated.

There were also coded blocks that moved around the outside of these coded plates.

"One summoning hall complete," Ela-Dorn said to herself, letting out a satisfied sigh as she moved to the command console that was back behind the small circle.

Ela-Dorn waited a second, looking to her helpers. They were professors and various students from the Aleph college, as well as Aleph engineers and machinists.

She pressed a button on the console. The soul gem within the open console glowed; power surged through Mana channels to the small circle.

If someone was to look under the stage, they would see the coded plates start to light up. As light seemed to pass down the stacks of coded plates, runes engraved into the circle started to light up from the outside rings into the center. As the runes finished lighting up, the coded stacks below lit with Mana; a Mana stream spread from the small circle, touching the circle that the arches lay upon.

The stacks underneath started to glow with energy. Four soul gems that lay under the arches lit up, and runes on the pillars started to light up, reaching toward where they intersected as the runes on the circle below lit up and made their way to the center.

The runes on the circle and those where the pillars met lit up at the same time. A Mana barrier appeared between the arches. The room seemed thick with Mana.

"Okay, well, it starts up pretty easily," Ela-Dorn said with a shaky voice, nervous about the next part. "Everyone check your personal Mana barriers!"

She checked her interface against the buttons and pressed a few of them on the console. A whirring noise came from underneath the arched circle. The coded pieces underneath moved into a new position, new areas of coded plates activating.

When the portal had activated, it had made a field that would mask its signature, making it appear as if it were a summoning ritual, not a machine made to summon creatures from other realms. It also activated a Mana barrier that would protect those summoning the creature and enhance the powers of the person standing within the circle in front of the summoning arches.

The last coded plate slid into place off its circular system.

Power thrummed through the area as all of the runes grew a little bit brighter for a moment. There was a flash of light as within the arches a small pup appeared.

It unfurled itself, as if waking up from a long sleep. It stood up and looked around the arches and the people beyond before locking eyes with Ela-Dorn. It let out a confused bark as Ela-Dorn felt her heart melt at the cute little creature.

It had some wolf heritage but it was already a third the size of a grown bear in puppy form. Its fur was an odd mixture of white grey and black, making it appear smoky. Its head was completely black, as were its eyes. But instead of being scary, they were cute as the little pup scratched at the Mana barrier.

Ela-Dorn moved toward the little pup that was eagerly scratching at the Mana barrier, his little tail wagging ferociously. Ela-Dorn stepped into the small pad. She quickly opened up her hand, creating a bloody seal on her palm before she held it out toward the little puppy.

There was hardly any resistance as she felt her Willpower stretch out toward the little puppy.

He pawed at his nose, as if there was something annoying him slightly.

Prompts appeared in front of Ela-Dorn.

You Have Gained A Soul Bound Creature
The Shadow Wolf is yours to command. Unless you break your contract with the creature or allow it to die, the contract will not be broken. Controlling this creature takes 5 Willpower from your overall stats (does not affect Mana recharge).

Soul Binding Contract
You have created a soul binding contract with a Shadow Wolf. For a portion of your Experience, you can increase this creature's level and abilities.
The Shadow Wolf is currently Level 0, gains 0% of your experience.

Name Your Soul Bound Creature
Your Shadow Wolf does not have a name. Do you wish to give him one? Y/N

With such a weak creature that would not be as powerful as Lu Lu or Steve, the requirement to dominate the creature was cut in half.

"Kelo," Ela-Dorn said.

Kelo looked up at Ela-Dorn, his tail wagging as his tongue stuck out the side of his mouth.

Ela-Dorn could only laugh at the excited puppy.

He let out a shrill *yelp.*

Ela-Dorn moved to the console and pressed a button.

The barrier closed and the runes lost their glow as the power from the summoning hall was cut off. The blocks that had been placed before were now pulled back into their start-up positions, ready for the next summoning.

Kelo raced forward with happy yips and yaps. He jumped on Ela-Dorn's leg. His tail wagged so fiercely that it shook his rear legs as he tried to lick Ela-Dorn.

She laughed and picked the little guy up, being rewarded with kisses as he tried to squirm out of her hands and get closer to her face.

"Well, I think that we can call this one a success," Ela-Dorn said, besieged by dog kisses.

The tension in the room had evaporated, turning into cheers and laughter. They'd spent long hours working to take Dave's plans and turn it into an entirely enclosed and efficient machine.

Now, all of their work had paid off, as was made clear with the yapping and excited Kelo.

Chapter 24: Halfway Point

"Welcome to Ashal River, ladies and gents," Josh said over the guild-wide chat. The trees gave way to reveal a calm-looking river that cut through the middle of Ashal's wilderness.

Vrexu had his forces pushed outward, looking for threats on the ground. Efri had his forces looking for ones in the air. Scouts were looking into the waters, seeing just what lay down there.

A scout flying above the waters let out a scream.

A creature that must have been a hundred meters long and twenty wide, jumped out of the water.

An Air blade slammed into the beast. A thin line of blood was seen. The creature wasn't heavily wounded, but it was enough to throw off its direction. It dove back into the water; the blood mingled with the water, as the calm waters turned into a turbulent froth as other predators sensing or tasting the blood now in the river went into a frenzy.

A battle was happening under the surface of the river, churning it up. After about twenty minutes, the fighting seemed to taper off.

A half-dozen creatures had come out to fight. The creature that had tried to eat the scout wasn't able to defend against the others and was torn apart.

Others even fought one another, seeing that they were distracted.

"Well, I sure as hell don't want to be taking a boat across that," Dave said.

The Stone Raiders had moved ahead of everyone else. They were the fastest group on foot. The DCA had just barely been able to keep up with their innate physical abilities and stats.

When looking at the map, it was clear that they were going to have to cross over the Ashal River somehow, or else take a detour of nearly two weeks around it.

"Looks like we won't be sleeping much tonight," Malsour added, giving Dave a weak smile. His losses were still too recent for him to move past just yet.

Dave slapped Malsour's shoulder. "All right! Dark mages on me! We've got a bridge to build!" Dave said over the guild chat.

"The rest of you make camp and be on the lookout for creatures," Josh said.

Over the last couple of days, they had been losing people here and there. A number of Players had even fallen victim to Ashal wilderness.

They were cocky. Even if they died, they would come back. It made Josh want to be around the POE more because they were always vigilant.

He didn't want to lose too many people before they even got to the temple. They hadn't gotten into any massive battles, but they had walked into different creatures' territories, where half of the raiding party had been stuck in the fighting.

Dave and Malsour moved closer to the water's edge, pushing out their senses, figuring out what materials they had to work with.

"What are you thinking?" Malsour asked.

"Simple arching bridge over. Magical code the thing so that it will resist impacts from the creatures below," Dave said.

"Maybe an electrical enchantment, something that will hurt them when they hit it. Train them to not hit the pillars," Malsour said.

After another fifteen or twenty minutes of talking, they figured out a plan and passed it on to the other mages who were standing around, ready to help.

First Malsour and the Dark mages infused their Mana into the bedrock below the river. It was the most secure foundation one could find. They rose great stone pillars, all the way up from the bedrock to the edge of the water.

Then, they worked with the Earth mages and those creating the road, who cleared out the area closest to the pillars. The Dark mages created rock and metal that grew from the pillars back toward the shore, seamlessly connecting with the section of road that the engineers had made. The bridge would be fifty meters tall so that the creatures in the lake below couldn't jump up and kill the people walking over it. It would extend nearly seven hundred meters to allow for a gradual rise and also keep people away from the banks of the river.

Pillars rose out of the water like deep sea beasts, stopping once they had reached their highest peak. Rock grew out from them, connecting in the middle, creating a brace as well as the road that flowed down to connect to the other pillars that had been grown directly out of the bedrock below.

A few creatures, seeing the rising pillars, slammed into them, thinking them as other beasts trying to impose on their territory.

Ranged attackers and mages fired at these creatures. A good wound was enough to make the other creatures turn and attack them.

As the bridge extended, the Dark mages started to move onto it. With less distance between them and what they were working on, it was easier for them to manipulate the Dark Affinity materials.

The simple flat road grew walls. Metal extruded out of the stone to create a superstructure of a roof. Stones grew across this as if they were vines climbing up a wall.

Glass was formed, creating skylights. There were even a few protrusions off the side of the bridge, in case anyone wanted to look down at the river or try to hunt the beasts below. Everything in Ashal was of great value. Who knew if there might be rare creatures lurking in the river to be fished out?

The Dark mages continued forward. The river was nearly eight hundred meters wide and they had started to raise up the bridge two hundred meters from the edge of the water so that the incline wasn't too steep for wagons and people, and it was high enough to deter the massive creatures hiding under the waters.

Dark mages behind the first ones worked on the finer details. Mages added in Mana lights and created places for soul gems to be placed in order to power the bridge. Gates were also added. They didn't want some kind of creature making the bridge their home while it wasn't in use.

Dave and other coders helped to carve in the magical coding. Dark mages who were also well versed in magical coding added protections to the pillars, following the basic code that Dave and Malsour had come up with.

The base of the pillars illuminated with lightning. The surrounding water smoked now and then as creatures found the defensive measures that had been put in place to deter the water creatures from attacking the bridge.

There were a few skirmishes with different creatures, but none of them were major.

The covered bridge reached its apex as night started to fall and the moons came out. The Dark mages switched off, not wanting to become fatigued in the Ashal wilderness.

Still, pillars continued to grow, passing over the river.

There was no need to stop building because most people had an incredibly high Endurance and could go a few days without sleeping. They also had great night vision. Through the night, the bridge continued onward. Pillars rose out and then grew into part of the bridge. Steel moved from old sections toward the new like snakes, fusing with one another before the stone was extruded out upon this superstructure.

As night fell, the rest of the raiding party appeared.

Everyone moved onto the bridge, closing the gates behind them as they were able to get some proper rest.

The DCA continued to patrol and some of the guild members went off to look for resources or kill some powerful beasts for experience.

It wasn't until the next morning that the bridge started to once again lower down toward the other bank.

River creatures had attacked the pillars all night. These pillars, rooted in bedrock, with a metal superstructure and magical coding, didn't even budge with the impacts from creatures up to Level 1,500.

Dave felt a cool sweat just thinking about the behemoth that had risen up to smack into the pillar. It was three times the size of the first beast that had tried to kill the scout and moved through the water like an arrow through the air. It made the bridge shudder a bit. The electrical discharge from the bridge had been enough to wake everyone up.

The stunned beast quickly recovered its senses and sped away from the bridge.

In the space of a night, they had built a bridge that would have taken people back on Earth nearly a year to finish. It was also incredibly strong and had heavy defenses. It was more of a castle over the top of the water than a bridge.

Dave handed Malsour a cup of warm Xer. They both took a deep drink from their mugs and looked over the bridge.

"Well, now onto the temple," Dave said.

They'd scheduled for the crossing over the river to take a day. Now they were ahead of schedule. Dave was excited to see what other wonders Ashal had and see this portal location for himself.

"Two more days and we should be at the portal," Dave said.

Malsour made a noise of agreement.

A creature looking like a massive boar but with a horn on its head suddenly appeared at the edge of the bank. It let out a battle cry.

This attack was supposed to slow a person's ability to react and their movement speed.

Dave felt his speed decrease even as he conjured a spear of water, sending it through the air, guessing the creature had an Air Affinity.

"Blood hog! Earth Affinity!" Lucy called out.

DCA aerial forces stayed away from the creature as earth and wood started to rise from the ground around it, forming into Earth spears.

The aerial forces fired out their Mana bolts as Dave's attack landed. It hit the hog, making it shake its head slightly. It let out a snort as it fired its own spears at the bridge.

As Malsour raised his hand, a wall of stone appeared, covering all of those on the mouth of the growing bridge.

The stone cracked in places as the spears hit.

Dave could still see what was going on with his senses.

The DCA were hitting the hog at range with their Mana bolts. The hog was tough and shrugged off most of the damage, but with so many attackers, the smaller wounds were piling up.

Malsour raised his fist violently. He had been working with the bedrock of this area for an entire night. He had come to understand it to a high degree.

A bedrock spear jutted out of the ground, slamming up and into the hog's chin and into its brain. The bedrock then exploded outward.

The hog collapsed, dust rising around it.

Malsour let out a deep breath. He'd had a long night and the power he'd used wasn't inconsiderable. Thankfully, most creatures weren't able to make Mana barriers and relied on just their physical toughness. If the hog had been able to manifest one, then Malsour's spear would have broken off on the Mana barrier.

"Looks like things are much more interesting on this side," Malsour said. The stone wall he had made was removed in a flash, once again revealing the outside world.

Dave drank some more Xer. Malsour did the same. They looked to each other, grinning slightly.

Dave looked out on the vista again, seeing the Northwood that they would pass within a few miles of as they headed directly for the portal.

Although the wilderness they were in was impressive, the Northwood had trees that dwarfed the simple wilderness they were traveling to. There were few records of the creatures in the Northwood. These areas had simply not been touched since the start of Emerilia. There were a great number of treasures to be found, though the risk was also incredibly high.

Dave only had to think of the Level 1,500 creature that had smacked the bridge last night. *There could even be Level 2,000 beasts in there. There really are no limits in Emerilia.*

Chapter 25: Leaving Your Mark

The two days passed by quickly. Guilds and parties went off to get resources and find creatures; there were some really strong creatures that had appeared out of the forest as they moved.

Party Zero went out, mostly gathering resources. They were also called upon by the DCA, providing impromptu training.

The DCA soldiers could see the difference in their own strengths compared to those of the guilds' and were eager to become stronger.

Dave caught a ride every so often with the wagons, taking the time to continue his lessons on coding. It continued to bear fruit.

He smiled as he disconnected from the Mirror of Communication.

Quest Completed: Skill Creator Level 10

Personally teach 3,200 people your Skill (2,894/3,200). Or help your students reach the level of Apprentice (193/200). Or help your students reach the level of Journeyman (0/1)

Rewards: Unlock Level 11 Quest

+20 Intelligence (Stacks with previous class levels)

+20 Endurance (Stacks with previous class levels)

+20 Willpower (Stacks with previous class levels)

+1,000,000 EXP

Quest: Skill Creator Level 11

Personally teach 6,400 people your Skill (2,894/6,400). Or help your students reach the level of Apprentice (193/400). Or help your students reach the level of Journeyman (7/10)

Rewards: Unlock Level 12 Quest

Increase to stats

Level 234

You have reached Level 234; you have **95** stat points to use.

"Always feels good to get a few extra stat points!"

He checked his character sheet.

Character Sheet

Name:	David Grahslagg	Gender:	Male
Level:	214	Class:	Dwarven Master Smith, Friend of the Grey God, Bleeder, Librarian, Aleph Engineer, Weapons Master, Champion Slayer, Skill Creator, Mine Manager, Master of Space and Time, Master of Gravitational Anomalies
Race:	Human/ Dwarf	Alignment:	Chaotic Neutral
Unspent points: 95			
Health:	42,300	Regen:	22.56/s
Mana:	14,880	Regen:	52.30/s
Stamina:	4,740	Regen:	45.50/s
Vitality:	423	Endurance:	1,128
Intelligence:	1,488	Willpower:	1,046
Strength:	474	Agility:	910

His stats had shot up over the last couple of days as he realized that holding onto his stat points out here was a bad idea. He might be a powerful being but Ashal had quickly reduced his ego.

It now was nearly two million experience for him to level up a single level.

He moved toward Party Zero. Everyone was together—even Anna and Deia had been able to get away from their duties—as they were finally approaching the last kilometer before the temple and the portal hidden within.

"Well, this is creepy," Steve said.

Dave stretched out his senses. A few creatures were around the temple and none of them made any noise. As if scared that they might attract the attention of a nearby predator.

The Aleph scouts had thoroughly checked the area around the temple. There was only one entrance to the earthen mound that held the temple.

They trekked around the outside of the dome.

A crack rose up twenty meters along the dome. It was framed on either side by rocks. Although the rest of the earthen dome looked like a natural hill, here it was easy to see that it was actually a manufactured construct. The crack was about ten meters wide at the bottom, reaching up and coming together.

"All right, let's set up camp!" Josh called out.

The mages who had been making the road expanded their efforts out, all of them working to raise a smooth rock square, complete with drains and sewers. Earth mages unleashed their power; trees groaned as they used their roots to push themselves out of the ground and out of their path according to the Earth mages' commands. The ground shook as steel and stone with roots in the bedrock rose upward. Stairs and different levels appeared; thick steel wound through the massive fortifications.

Arrow slits were made as the walls continued to grow. It took all of the Dark mages to work as one to create the walls. One section of the wall—forty meters wide—was finished so fast that it was visible to those protecting the mages, looking for animals that might charge them and watching the crack as well.

The wall was four meters thick and fifty meters high. At their peak, the walls had crenelations with mages' balconies every ten meters. An enclosed balcony overlooking the walls was equipped with spikes and razor-sharp steel. As the first was finished, a second twenty-meter section of wall rose from the ground.

As the walls went up, the forest was moved back. It was slow work. To see was to believe; the power of these mages when working together was enough to fell trees and remove underbrush for ten kilometers around the growing outpost.

Trees walked closer; their roots dug through the ground before they delivered themselves to where summoned creations were quickly cutting them into uniform planks and timber supports. The trees blocked off their sight lines so they needed to be removed. With them being so massive only a few dozen of the massive trees needed to be felled.

As the different trees and undergrowth were moving to be sorted out by the summoned creatures, the Earth mages started to level out the ten kilometer wide area.

Where different plants had been removed, dirt and rocks were rolled in to fill these craters. Then the grade of the ground was changed, sloping steadily down and away from the outpost. Not only would someone attacking them be seen ten kilometers off, but they would be down a slope, allowing those in the outpost to easily deal with them.

It was slow work and the different natural fauna was still moving itself. These trees were nearly two hundred meters thick and eight hundred tall. The summoned creatures numbered in the thousands but it would still take them days to deal with all of the trees and different plants that had uprooted themselves and marched to their work area along the side of the earthen dome covering the temple.

Earth resources that they had found would literally come out of the ground and walk into their bags of holding.

Dave checked over the walls. There were now two sections up and the third was rising from the ground. This one was different as it had a ten-meter wide and fifteen-meter tall gate and faced the crack that led into the temple.

There was just a hole where the gate should be. A metal or stone door might sound like a good idea, but if anything hit it then it would have the elasticity of wood.

The wall grew. It was now eight meters thick and took nearly twice the time it did for the other walls. With that done, the mages moved to the next wall.

The outpost would be two hundred meters long, facing the crack. The walls on either side would extend outwards six hundred meters before being closed off.

The mages and engineers who had been working on the road had greatly refined their abilities over the four-day journey. They'd become faster as they were the slowest part of the entire raid party. Making roads was easy to them now. Engineers moved about, checking the area. Earth mages made it flat and changed the composition of the ground so that it would support the road. Dark mages created gravel so that the roads wouldn't shift once placed, as well as a massive sewer system and a drainage area that was many miles deep.

Only when these things had been completed was stone and metal created over the top. It came out in gray sections, the rough scaffolding underneath filling in and then being covered over by massive rock blocks.

Here and there, engineers marked out different spots. Dave and a group of those trained with soul gem construction came behind. They placed down soul gems in the center of some of these basements or open areas that had been marked off.

Once placed, the soul gems were activated. They unfurled, growing to meet the different lines that the engineers had lined out. They had planned this outpost down to the inch so everything flowed easily.

These soul gem constructs grew into their spaces, sinking into the ground and securing themselves to the supports that were rooted in the bedrock. The soul gem constructs slowed their pace as their power reserves were depleted.

Vault soul gems and other charged soul gems were connected to the power grid that the Dark mages had engraved into the rock pad that was growing through the outpost.

The soul gem constructs took this power in, continuing to grow. They didn't grow too tall, needing metal and stone supports that the Dark mages could provide in order to reinforce the soul gem construct buildings.

Within an hour, a quarter of the walls were up; four kilometers around the outpost had been cleared and graded. The rock pad that was the basis of the outpost was half done. Soul gem constructs were rising from the ground like jewels in contrast with the black and silver walls.

A roar sounded out from the forest. One of the moving trees seemed to have stepped on a sleeping jungle tiger. The creature attacked the massive moving tree, its black claws cutting deep into the bark of the centuries-old tree. The tiger was massive, fifteen meters tall and thirty long. It looked like a tiger from back on Earth but with two tails that ended in spikes and it was green and brown with black teeth and claws.

"Why the hell is everything in the damn forest looking like moss!" Dave complained to himself.

The natural camouflage did make it incredibly difficult to spot these powerful beasts. Dave could easily pick out creatures with his Touch of the Land and others had similar spells but their range wasn't too big. They would only be able to give a minute or two warning if a creature charged toward the outpost undetected by the scouts.

The aerial forces took to the skies, gaining altitude. Scouts spread out, looking for other threats that might be attracted by the tiger's growls. DCA ground forces checked their simple Mana bomb mortars. Mages revolved Mana around their bodies, ready to fight in a moment. Shields and weapons were brandished, the excited atmosphere of just moments ago shattered.

The engineers and Dark and Earth mages continued what they were doing without stopping. The faster they could finish off the outpost, the sooner they could have some cover from the creatures that were banging on their front door.

All of the forces checked in that they were as ready as they could be. The aerial forces were buffed by the support mages and their attack started.

Dave saw as the DCA and the other flyers moved in formations where the tiger was tearing the five-hundred-year-old tree to shreds.

They released their attacks: Mana bombs, arrows, spells, Mana bolts, and Mana grenades. It looked as if a miniature sun had risen with all of that power focused on just one beast.

The tiger let out an angered shout and turned to face the aerial forces. It lunged at them, reaching nearly thirty meters in the air. Its fur was burnt in places but it looked more pissed off than hurt.

Dave took a running leap. His orbs pushed him into the air as gravity stopped to affect him. He concentrated on a soul gem in his hands.

He pulled out a torch to heat the soul gem up, making it malleable and entirely unstable. Dave conjured a Mithril mitt on his left hand; he sunk his consciousness into the orb.

He reached seventy-five meters high before he came down on one of the complete walls. He didn't move as he landed, entirely focused on the soul gem.

The tiger continued to try to attack the aerial forces. Its Health whittled down as the different air units hit the tiger and then rushed away before it could do more than swipe at where they had been. It wasn't like the ebony rhino; Mana attacks would most definitely hurt and wound it.

Josh held the ground forces at bay. If they could beat the beast from the air, then it was worth it. A good melee fighter knew when to take aggro and when to let others do it.

The ground forces watched, silently cheering on their aerial allies as they took the tiger down to half of its massive Health.

It dropped to the ground; the impact shook the ground as it shook its head in anger. Five Mana bombs exploded next to it, making it turn away from the blast. It let out an angry yell, as it now found itself no longer in the cover of the forest, but rather looking at the growing outpost filled with mages and ground fighters. It started moving forward, letting out an angered shout.

"Ranged!" Josh yelled out. Mages and anyone who could hit the tiger at four kilometers let loose their attacks.

The aerial forces continued to harry the tiger but it paid no attention to them. Most basic beasts would just turn and attack whatever was aggroing it. This beast was a Level 957. It wasn't sentient by any means but it was incredibly smart. Although it knew it couldn't fight off the aerial forces, it was the king of ground battles.

It crossed a kilometer in bare seconds. Spells and attacks rained down on it as it moved from side to side to throw off the attacks.

"Mana shield!" Dwayne called out. The tiger's speed and strength was not something that could be simply stopped by the melee fighters' strength alone. Maybe if it was just the top Stone Raiders with their best gear, but there was four other guilds as well as the DCA ground forces.

Mortars released, their Mana bombs adding to the damage. The tiger was down to just a third of its Health.

"Is everything in this wilderness a boss-classed beast!?" Fellox's leader Gimel barked.

Magically coded blocks were thrown out and connected to soul gems' power output. A shield of blue, so thick that it looked like glass, connected between these blocks, covering the front of the raid party.

The tiger leaped, as if taking down an elephant. Its claws slammed into the shield, making some of the thick layers shatter. The tiger bounced off and cried out in pain.

"Attack!" Josh yelled out on the general chat.

"Melee, take aggro. Ranged, light the bastard up!" Dwayne called out over the Stone Raider chat.

"Support buffs!" Lucy called out over the support channel.

"Mages—stop it from getting up," Kim yelled to her mages.

There wasn't enough room for everyone to get in on the action. Half of the Stone Raiders, Portal Purge, mage's and adventurer's guild as well as Fellox and the DCA forces stayed back so that everyone wasn't falling on top of one another.

Dave came out of his working. He'd been barely able to keep the soul gem stable as he used his smithing art to alter and imprint new coding into it. He was about to throw it on the ground, thus activating it, when he saw that he wasn't needed.

Ragged cheers came from the Stone Raiders who had finished off the tiger. It slumped to the side.

The others relaxed, a few jealous that they hadn't been able to directly fight the tiger, but knowing that too many people would have made it incredibly difficult.

Dave smiled, letting out a breath as his guts started to uncoil from the fear he'd felt. His hands shook from unreleased adrenaline and his breath coiled as his head cleared from the pressures of creating a high-grade magical code within the greater soul gem in his hand.

A roar ripped through the forest, not ten kilometers away. Another and another roar took up this call.

Shit. Well, at least tigers on Earth live alone most of the time. I hope this one wasn't part of a group? Dave looked to the walls. The wall facing the crack had been completed. There were also two walls twenty meters wide that extended back from it.

They would need another twenty-eight sections per side and then another five to close in the area. The Dark mages were burning their Mana at a crazy rate, pulling on their vault soul gems and their linked amulets. Dave could see support people handing out these amulets like candy to those who weren't in the Stone Raiders or DCA.

Walls rose up one every five minutes. Even at that pace, it would take five to six hours! Dave didn't think that they could keep this pace up so it would most likely be closer to eight or nine hours.

"Dark mages—with me!" Malsour called out.

They stopped working on their half-made walls and moved with Malsour.

He stopped where the left wall would meet with the wall that intersected with the road. Walls started to rise here, creating a corner and a strong point.

The guilds moved so that they were between these corner walls and the walls that had been already made. Dark mages ran down the line in front of the raiding party, quickly raising the walls a few meters, just to give some kind of cover.

People were moving everywhere. They created formations that stood where wall sections hadn't been built yet, creating a wall of bodies.

Malsour and his mages worked together to raise four walls, creating a strong point and corner for these formations to butt up against.

Now Malsour and his mass of Dark mages ran to the other side of the outpost's planned walls. In a matter of minutes, they raised another four wall sections.

Mages and ranged forces rushed into these walls that jutted out like towers while the Dark mages ran between the raised walls.

They worked together, rushing to put up more walls.

They only made them a few stories tall, but having something instead of just a simple rise and people hiding behind it would greatly increase their fighting ability.

Dave had his senses spread out. He wanted to join those on the front line but he had taken on a support role. If he was to join the battle, then his abilities were bound to draw attention from spectators and gain him more interest from the Jukal Empire.

He bit his lip as he felt ten different creatures racing toward the outpost. He gripped the working in his hand tightly. He jumped from the wall he stood on and moved to a soul gem building.

***

Josh's ears were filled with the noises of people moving. The Dark mages were overtaxing themselves to the limit. All construction had stopped inside the outpost as everyone who could help out with building the massive walls moved to that task.

They had all been on alert for threats, but now that one had appeared and was stronger than they had expected, they needed to get the walls up faster.

People rushed into the completed corner sections. As the walls grew, melee forces ran up the stairs, pulling their ranged weapons.

All of the summoned creatures had been pulled back. Now they were either hidden over the open ground or they stood, waiting for the tiger's pride to attack.

"We've spotted them! Nine in total! Levels 749, 815, 954, 367, 412, 384, 579, 721 and 987!" a scout called out to all of the forces waiting in the outpost.

It was as if a breath of cold air had fallen over everyone.

"Ah, well, looks like we should be getting some good experience and materials," Dwayne said to Josh over the general chat.

"I've always wanted a tiger pelt," Josh said thoughtfully.

"Gross, dude. I'm much more interested in how they taste! I've heard that sometimes high quality beast meat can return not only Mana and Stamina but both. We'll be eating better than kings tonight!" Dwayne laughed.

Dwayne and Josh might be a little apprehensive about going up against such powerful creatures, but they couldn't show it.

Gamers naturally challenged one another, even if they were in the same team or guild. Having better weapons and gear was all good, but the person who did the most damage, or showed just how awesome their abilities were—that was what true gamers lived for. They aimed to be number one; if they were number fifteen or sixteen, they would do everything in their power the next time to be better.

Dwayne and Josh's words ignited the Players' fighting spirit as they pulled out their best weapons and gear that they had been holding onto until they entered the temple. Many of these weapons weren't soul bound and thus could be lost if they died.

But the gauntlet had been thrown down! No gamer would let such a blatant challenge go! They were the best in Emerilia and they were going to show the rest of the world!

"You Players are crazy," Vrexu said to Josh on a private chat.

"Ah, we're just competitive." Josh grinned.

The scared expressions had turned into eager smiles and grins. Sure, they could die here and lose some stat points—so what? This was the biggest raid EVER! They had gone deeper into Ashal wilderness than any other group. Running away might be the smart idea, but these tigers offered the type of challenge that they had come to Ashal for.

Guilds and teams checked with their people, making sure that they were ready, making sure everyone knew their role. With just a few words, they could coordinate with one another. In this battle, seconds would count.

"Three west side, five east, two south!" a scout called out.

Josh saw as the tigers left the cleared area around the outpost.

They were massive. Three were actually bigger than the first tiger they had run into.

"Aerial moving in to attack. Mortars, you are free to fire as needed," Efri said over general chat.

"Understood," Vrexu said. The two DCA forces had become much closer as they had fought through the wilderness. The separation created by fighting one another in Anna's war games in Devil's Crater had been repaired as they were forced to work together.

They'd come to rely on and work with one another. As the aerial forces dropped their Mana bombs onto the oncoming tigers, the ground forces fired their Mana bomb mortars. It took incredible trust and coordination for this to work. If the aerial forces dropped, then they could be hit by the mortars' Mana bombs.

The tigers roared. The younger ones tried to attack those in the sky, falling behind the older and more powerful tigers that surged toward the outpost.

Under their skin, Josh could see the powerful muscles stretching and pulling. They were magnificent and powerful beasts but today they'd learn why you shouldn't fight the people and Players of Emerilia.

"Ranged, release!" Gimel yelled. Spells and ranged attacks carved through the air.

"Fire as targets come into range!" Vrexu said. Spearheads shot out like arrows, exploding as they came into contact with the ground or the tigers.

The ground jumped up, creating a barrier for the attacks as the tigers plowed forward, losing Health here and there. But it wasn't enough to slow them.

The Level 989 let out a roar that seemed to shake Josh's very soul.

A green light fell over all of the tigers.

"It's some kind of buff!" a scout said as the tigers continued forward, their Health bars covered by a green light, showing that they had additional protection.

As they reached one kilometer, they were within range of all the ranged weaponry.

The Level 384 from the east had its green protection drop off from its Health bar. The Stone Raiders were on average around Level 300 when not including the more veteran units that had been with them since the beginning. As the tiger's protection dropped, it took less than ten seconds before the tiger's Health hit zero and it collapsed to the ground.

No one cheered as they moved to their next target.

The Level 589 from the west was the second to go, followed shortly by the 367 from the east and the 412 from the south.

The tigers had been reduced to six fighters, all of them above 650.

"Mana shield!" Dwayne yelled out.

Mana shields, unlike Mana barriers, made a solid wall of Mana. Any attacks from either side would be blocked, including physical attacks.

Fights along the open sections of wall stopped as Mana shields rose.

The southern Level 954 hit first. The entire shield shook with the impact. It bounced off a few feet of the shield, losing half of its Health in that one blow.

The east shield took multiple hits, one from the Level 987 and one from the 721 tiger.

They were thrown back; the mages and ranged on the complete walls fought with everything they had.

The Level 653 hit the shield, their momentum stopped but they weren't thrown back; the shield was the one to give way.

Aerial forces concentrated on the east side. Melee fighters closest to the Level 600 that had made it in were covered in buffs as they rushed in, aggroing the tiger. Thankfully this one wasn't as smart as the higher levels and the tanks could offset their attacks, pulling the tiger in different directions.

The melee fighters were as big as the tiger's paw but still they stepped up, lashing out with their attacks to take aggro off one another before protecting themselves from the tiger's attacks. They could only take a few hits before they would lose their footing or be injured, so their coordination had to be amazing.

"I've got him! Come here!"

"Need Health!"

"Buffs incoming!"

"Nice sneak attack!"

"Someone else aggro!"

"I've got aggro!"

"Watch out—big boys are coming in!"

Josh listened to the controlled voices of the Players and POEs.

There was only slight panic when calling out for heals. Even that was quickly fixed as people chain healed together, getting people back on their feet in a few seconds, making them almost invulnerable for a few moments with the healing over time spells.

Josh pulled out his daggers. The fight had devolved into party fighting. There were too many enemies for them to focus their efforts like they had with the first tiger. "Dwayne, Kim, Lucy, Esa—let's go cause some trouble. I want that Level 900!"

Dwayne and Esa let out roars. It was a skill that emboldened others and increased their fighting abilities. They charged forward. The Level 721 was occupied and the melee fighters were getting slapped around by the Level 900.

Josh slinked away out of the Level 900's vision, picking up speed as he did.

Dwayne and Esa landed their hits. Lucy threw out buffs that increased their speed and Stamina recharge, decreased their cooldown, and gave them a layer of protection.

Kim unleashed Mana bolts from her hands and threw out poisoned darts. These darts decreased defense and would make the tiger sluggish.

The tiger let out a pained yowl at the hits. Each of the Stone Raider lieutenants was equal to a Level 800. The difference between them and the Level 900 tiger was massive, but working together they'd taken down a fifth of its Health bar in just a few seconds.

"I've got aggro!" Esa yelled, defending as the tiger laid into her.

Josh took his chance to attack. His body seemed to turn into a shadowy dart as his senses locked onto the weaknesses of the tiger. He dodged past the wildly moving tails, as the tiger moved its entire body suddenly to land a massive attack on Esa.

Esa went flying. Josh felt power flood through his weapons as he locked onto an artery that ran between the tiger's neck and shoulder blade. He passed in a bloody streak. His blades dug in deep, cutting through the tiger's tough hide and digging deep into the muscle and sinew of the tiger's neck.

Josh dropped to the ground, rolling and taking off. None of the blood had even touched his clothes as blood pumped out of the tiger's neck vigorously. Josh looked at the side of his screen as Dwayne let out a roar, beating his shield, to draw attention away from Josh, who once again turned into a phantom blur. Josh circled around.

Esa was back in the fight but her armor was dented and dried blood colored her lips and ran down from the corner of her mouth. She took aggro from Dwayne, who was getting heavily beaten.

Kim and Lucy were supporting but they were overwhelmed.

Josh looked at the deep wound he'd left. The tiger's pelt now had a bloody red coloring it as it moved around, slightly sluggish. But before Josh's eyes, the wound knit back together.

Josh once again turned, moving out of the creature's peripheral vision when the very ground seemed to erupt under the tiger. The air seemed to shimmer in anger as the tiger was hit from multiple directions.

He watched as summoned creations attacked from every side, pulling the tiger's Health downward.

Induca appeared, like a goddess of war, as she unleashed a continuous stream of fire onto the tiger. It let out a pained yell, trying to get away from the attack as Steve appeared from the midst of their fight with the Level 700 tiger.

"Put me down!" Gurren yelled, at odds with Steve's war cry.

An angry Dwarf was thrown through the air. "I'm going to kill you, Steve!"

"Fuck, I'm not a Dwarven dart!" Lox barked, following Gurren as they flew.

Look more like baseballs than darts, Josh thought as the fire disappeared. Gurren and Lox's swords dug into the tiger as they flew over the beast.

It lurched forward with a pained growl. Its back caved downward in reflex as twin red grooves were left in its pelt.

Gurren and Lox hit the ground, tumbling for a few meters.

The tiger turned to attack them as Induca's flames once again slammed into it.

"Home run!" Steve yelled, planting his foot and swinging his axe with all of his strength.

The tiger had been turning its head away from the flames; now its eyes went wide as it saw an axe as big as a man being swung like a baseball bat from the opposite direction. It didn't have any time to react before Steve's axe slammed into its skull.

The tiger's head snapped back from the impact. A great bloody line appeared on its head as it fell backward.

Steve nearly fell over, getting himself together as the tiger turned back to face him.

It let out a roar that shook the ground. Grass and plants grew in seconds, covering Steve as well as all of those within ten meters of the tiger.

Its tails lashed out, hitting Gurren and Lox as its paw hit Dwayne, making him spit blood, unable to defend or move from his green prison.

Josh came in from the side of the tiger. As he passed, the grass moved as if a light breeze had just passed over them. Josh's daggers cut through the tough hide and punctured the tiger's heart. The time between Josh stabbing the tiger and the blade coming out on the other side of it was less than a second. It seemed as if he had teleported to the other side of the tiger. Fresh blood dripped from his blades.

The tiger let out a pained yell as its Health dropped down to a sixth of its health pool. Its body healed the massive wound Josh had inflicted upon it. Its hold on the Earth prisons relaxed.

Steve tore himself free, pulling Dwayne out as if he were a carrot.

The tiger looked to Josh with red glowing eyes. The others had injured it heavily but two of the biggest hits had come from Josh. It leaped toward Josh.

Josh evaded as the tiger was thrown to the side by a powerful fireball. Lightning arced down from the sky, taking the tiger to a seventh of its Health. It wasn't deterred as it chased Josh.

Josh had spent an incredible amount of Mana and Stamina on the last hit; moving that fast burned his Stamina at nearly ten times his normal rate.

The tiger, although massive, was not slow. Josh had to dodge constantly, burning up more of his Stamina with his high speed movements. He drank a Stamina potion as Dwayne freed Esa. Healing light fell over him as he then ran toward the tiger.

Steve had freed Gurren and Lox, and the trio moved over to the tiger.

Josh was smacked by a paw. Blood rose up in him as he hit the ground and rolled. He spat blood; his armor had taken a lot of the impact but his Vitality wasn't all that high.

He jumped to his feet, burning Stamina as he pulled out a high-grade Health potion. He downed it. He'd had so many Stamina potions that they were nearing twenty percent efficiency.

Steve, Lox, Gurren, Esa, and Dwayne were covered in boosts. Lucy panted from the Mana she'd spent as the five melee fighters let out their yells. The tiger's tails lashed out, hitting Steve so hard his upper body dented as he was sent back twenty feet, creating a groove in the ground.

The other four made it into range! Their weapons lashed out, the pain making the tiger look behind it.

Lightning and fire came together, exploding just above the tiger. It was like a hammer of the gods had rained down on it, breaking its back and slamming it into the ground.

Even Josh was tossed by the force of the combined spell.

Summoned Air creatures that had pulled back with the magical spells now launched themselves forward, cutting at the tiger and whittling away at the less than ten percent Health that was remaining.

Josh got his feet under himself, seeing the tiger raising its neck to let out a roar.

The ground under Josh's feet exploded outward as he rushed forward. He held his blades out, burning his Stamina. He barely felt the blades sink into the tiger's neck as he came to the other side, stumbling as he lost all power in his body. His breath came in heaving pants as the tiger's life blood colored the torn-up ground.

Its head fell forward, its eyes lifeless from the last hit.

The remaining tigers let out a roar that shook the ground. Their Health recovered, bringing them back to one hundred percent Health!

The Level 700 at the east wall tore into the guilds and DCA alike.

Josh couldn't even move as it tore through its encirclement, a red hue around its Health bar as its tails lashed out, sending the melee types flying.

Its paw broke Josh's Mana barrier, and its claws dug through his armor and into his chest.

Josh's Health bar dropped in seconds as he spat blood. He used the last of his strength to lay a powerful curse on the tiger that killed him. His vision turned white as he found himself in a blank-looking room.

You have died in Emerilia

You have been returned home.

You have 5:59 hours (game time) until you can respawn at (Alephir)

Or

1:59 hours in real life

Would you like to play a different game while you wait?

"That fucking tiger!" Josh yelled into the room, going through his interface and accessing the shared guild room within. "We're putting an ono down there now! There is no bloody way I'm missing out on this raid!"

Chapter 26: You or Me

There was just three tigers left.

Dave couldn't do anything but sense as the Level 700 tiger went on a killing spree. His consciousness was infused into the soul gem building he was working.

He had connected to every amulet that the Stone Raiders and their allies were wearing to draw power from the soul gems to fuel their spells. Using that as a homing beacon, he created a magical code.

Dave linked the magical code up with the rest of the soul gem constructs. Power flared out from the buildings. It passed to the DCA, the Stone Raiders, and everyone else wearing the amulet.

A second sun filled the skies.

The tigers yelled out, disoriented by the hasty flashbang spell Dave had created, powered by several vault soul gems and other lower-classed soul gems.

Dave let out a breath and held his head, clearing it after a few seconds as he looked around. He stood in the middle of an unfinished floor. Only about a foot of the floor had grown; superstructure extended all around him and upward.

His heart seemed to stop as his eye found Malsour.

Dave had seen Malsour fight many times. He was the type of fighter to save his strength, use the minimal amount of force to alter the balance in his direction. That was completely in contrast to the war Demon riding a steel surfboard with great billowing clouds of darkness following behind him.

Deia was wreathed in flames to his left, and Anna to his right in white ribbons of air that howled to be released.

The Level 700 tiger was pawing at its head, unable to hear or see anything in the passing of the flashbang spell. Flame spears seemed to appear in its hide. Lightning poured from Kim's hands as other mages unleashed their spells.

The tiger shivered, lowering itself in deference, but the time for giving up was gone.

Induca floated in the air, hurling spear after spear, so fast that their pressure waves tore up the ground as they passed overhead. The tiger was thrown back as they impacted.

The mages and ranged fighters added in their attacks. The tiger couldn't do anything to fight back; it was off-balance. It couldn't even try to run away. The tiger had come to kill these supposed weaker creatures, but had instead found a hidden Dragon lurking in their midst.

The Level 954 at the south entrance wasn't as badly stunned as the Level 700; still, it never saw Anna, Malsour, and Deia's attack coming.

A spear of solid metal formed, runes engraved down its length as it tore through the sky.

Anna unleashed an attack that cut through the air, turning a small region into a vacuum as air was forced out of the path of the spear. A focused explosion ignited behind the spear.

It had howled as Malsour released it. Now it passed in silence, a silver streak that sent shivers down Dave's spine as he was unable to look away.

It smacked into the tiger, throwing it back and leaving a bloody hole in its side. Still the tiger was alive, speaking of its natural toughness. It had barely gotten to its feet when three more spears seemed to materialize in its side.

The tiger moved for a second before going limp.

Silence seemed to fall over the outpost.

In seconds, the battles had finished. Everyone was in shock. Most eyes turned to the members of Party Zero hovering in the air.

Dave looked out over the outpost. The recently graded ground was now filled with signs of battle as well as the bodies of the eleven tigers.

"Healers, get to work! Dark mages and engineers—hurry up with those walls as fast as possible and make them seventy-five meters high!" Lucy called out over the general chat, taking command as Josh was dead.

People downed Health potions as healing lights appeared.

Dave bit his cheek, angrily grabbing his twin conjuring rods. He had the strength, he had the damn abilities, but he'd stayed his hand, running around and applying a buff to everyone.

Sitting back is much harder than charging in. "All this and we haven't even made it into the temple yet." Dave shook his head.

***

Deia felt arms twine around her as a familiar and comforting smell filled her nose. She leaned back into the embrace, smiling as she looked up at Dave.

"I'm not happy with you getting into the middle of the fight, but I understand why you did it," Dave said, his voice gruff.

Deia stroked the side of his face and kissed his cheek. His face was hard, as if it could have been cut from rock. Deia knew that was just his way to hide his fear from her.

She felt a pang of regret for her actions but she still felt that she had done the right thing.

"How are the DCA?" Dave asked.

The two of them stood on one of the completed walls near the crack. Night had finally descended. The soul gem constructs lit up the area as Dark mages continued to work. People were sleeping in tents as well as in the soul gem constructs and completed walls.

"They're a bit shaken up, but it seems like us telling them that if they work together they can be more powerful has finally sunk in." Deia looked to the corners of the outpost. Here DCA aerial forces were launching off, changing patrols. They would continue to watch over the now eight-kilometer-wide open area around the outpost as well as survey the surrounding forest so that nothing could sneak up on them.

"Good. They're decent fighters and I know that the battle we had isn't the kind of battle they would like to be fighting but they did well," Dave said with approval.

"They took quite a few casualties but with their medical training, potions, and moving the wounded back, they've got about two hundred wounded and no fatalities," Deia said.

Dave nodded and his features relaxed.

"How are Lox and Gurren?" Deia asked.

"They're in the medical tent. They got hit pretty good. Thankfully, Steve was able to dose them up with healing potions and ran to the medical tent with them both. They're not in critical condition and they should make a full recovery in a few days," Dave said. "We can go and see them if you want?"

"Yeah, let's do that." Deia held Dave's hand. Just as she was about to use her flames to slowly descend down the side of the wall, it seemed as if they were picked up in a ball of force, heading over the wall and toward the healer tents.

All of the walls were now fifteen meters tall; having something was better than nothing, the engineers agreed.

Still, even as night was coming, the Dark and Earth mages were at work, clearing the area outside the outpost, working on the area inside and raising the massive walls that would keep them safe.

Malsour was going to raise all of the walls to fifty meters high, and then he'd go back and raise them to seventy-five meters as Lucy ordered. However, it would mean that the walls would be six meters thick instead of four. These kinds of modifications had to be done with care so that the walls' stability wasn't compromised.

"Who would have thought that we could build something on this scale when we first met?" Dave looked to the growing outpost, soul gem constructs reaching ever higher into the sky.

Deia just smiled, squeezing his hand as they slowly came down near one of the busier towers in the outpost.

It was the largest and had been turned into a hospital. Healers moved around, administering poultices and checking on their patients.

Although there had been a great number of people hurt, as long as someone got to the healers and they were alive, chances were high that they would be healed up within a few days. People who had lost limbs took longer to heal because the spells ran off the patient's own Mana and Stamina within their bodies to get stronger.

They drank Stamina potions and bland concoctions that would give them everything they needed to regrow their limbs. A number of them had already been released, told to come back if they had an issue, or for check-ups.

Others who had been opened up or punctured by the tiger's claws had been sealed back up and were walking around.

Healing magic was truly in a realm of miracles. Combined with the medical knowledge that Jules had thrown in, healers had become powerhouses at pulling people back from the brink. In a day or two, all of the injured would be ready to raid the temple.

Dave and Deia found out where Lox and Gurren were. They headed through the tower, moving to the third floor.

Lox and Gurren were lying in beds, another three people in between their beds.

"I raise by one lesser soul gem," one of the three said.

"Looks like it's getting a bit pricey," Gurren said.

"Dave, Deia, come to join poker night?" Lox asked from his bed.

"Heyyy!" Gurren turned over to smile at them, holding his cards to his chest so no one could see them.

"Well, looks like you two are doing okay," Dave said in a gruff voice.

Deia had an amused smile on her face.

"Tell that to the healers. They want to keep us in here for the next day!" Gurren complained. Lox grunted, tossing two lesser soul gems into the pot of soul gems that lay between the five poker Players.

"I'd prefer not to. Don't you like a bit of rest?" Deia said.

"Who can rest when the temple is right there?" Gurren said.

"Thankfully we've at least got cards to pass the time," Lox said. The person next to him folded so Gurren pulled a card from the deck, putting it face up with three others.

"You seen Steve around?" Lox asked.

"No, why?" Dave asked.

"Well, his armor was really dented in, and he might be blaming himself for putting us in this condition," Gurren said.

Deia frowned and pressed her lips together. Thoughts rushed through her head. If there was any enmity with her party, then it could lead to them not working as well together.

"We don't blame him. We know that he was just helping us to get into the fight—wasn't his fault that the damn thing was a pain in the ass. Also, he did save our lives with that massive hit he landed on the tiger," Lox said, as if reading Deia's thoughts. The man to his right knocked on the table.

"Wish I could have smoked that tiger like he did. Dude gets crazy worked up when one of us is in danger." Gurren tapped his hand against the table.

"It was meant to be a surprise, but I've been working on something for you two," Dave said.

Gurren and Lox looked over with clear interest.

It was well known that Dave's creations had been changing Emerilia by degrees. They had also seen the blades he'd forged for the Devil's Crater generals and Anna, and they understood the power of the Abscondita armor that he wore.

"Oh?" Lox said, ignoring the table. Even those who were playing were only half paying attention, listening in.

"I've got most of the components. I should have the others in a week or two and then it's just a matter of pulling it together." Dave smiled.

Deia looked at Dave with a thoughtful expression. She knew the project he was talking about; she was just surprised he'd been able to complete it so fast.

Dave smiled proudly. "Sometimes you just need some help from your friends."

Gurren and Lox looked to each other.

"What is it? A shield?" Gurren asked.

"Or a sword?" Lox asked.

"Just have to wait and find out, though it should make it possible for you to meet Steve in terms of power," Dave said mysteriously.

Lox and Gurren looked to Deia.

"Don't look to me. I might have an idea of what it is but he loves his mysteries." She gave Dave a wry smile.

He was openly smiling, happily hiding his project.

***

Malsour, Induca, and Suzy sat on the completed sections of wall extending out from the crack. They drank warm cider, making idle talk.

"You really should take a break at some time, big brother," Induca said.

"I will once the wall is finished." Malsour gave Induca a smile.

"He says that but I know as soon as this wall is finished, he'll find some other project to bury himself in!" Induca huffed.

Suzy chuckled and hugged Induca, who was sitting in her lap.

Malsour smiled into his cup, taking another deep drink.

"I heard that once the walls are finished, they're going to be putting an ono in so that the people who died can use the teleport pads in Terra to reach here and we can offload our goods and prepare for the raid." Suzy's eyes shined in excitement.

"Told you that you'd enjoy going on this little adventure," Induca teased Suzy.

"Hey! I know how to have fun! Just get wrapped up in work is all." Suzy murmured the last part into her cup.

Malsour chuckled at the two's bickering and looked out over the outpost. He didn't really see it as emotion surfaced.

After the deaths of so many of his family members, he'd been angry. When he'd seen his fellow guild mates and the people who had made up the raid party getting injured and killed by the tigers, he'd allowed his anger to take over.

Now, after all that tension and fighting, he felt calm, as if he had once again found himself. He took a deep breath and let it out.

He was sad at having lost his family members, but even he understood life was fleeting and short; he couldn't be too scared to fight, to go forward and do what he wanted. Even a Dragon could die. They might live for centuries but they were still mortal. He had researched and read about the world, tried to understand its mysteries and locked himself away.

He had become more powerful in the time he had been with the Stone Raiders than he had in the last two decades before it. He'd made friends, gone on adventures, fought countless enemies, and come close to falling himself.

And for all of that, I'm incredibly lucky. I have a family who loves me, friends who would go to the ends of Emerilia for me. If I take one lesson from those who died, it's that I need to do what I love and enjoy, to take risks.

Malsour smiled sadly to himself. A wave of emotion flowed through him as he laughed to himself. The stars above blurred as he thought of those he had lost. He didn't think about their loss. Instead, he remembered the moments he had spent with them, moments that brought a smile to his face, where he had laughed and lived life with them. When he and Louna had flown for the first time, two young Dragonlings, free in the sky, racing ahead of their other brothers and sisters. Denur lightly chiding them as they raced through the skies, twisting, turning, and diving. The world was full of mysteries and potential; they had no fears or regrets as they lived in that moment.

Malsour closed his eyes and smiled to himself. When he opened his eyes, he looked at the cup of cider in his hands.

It was these moments he would cherish and think of. He wished in his soul that he could bring them back, but he was infinitely grateful that he had been a part of their life and they had been a part of his.

Induca and Suzy were giggling, the two of them talking nonsense to each other.

Malsour looked over to them, seeing the love that they shared.

He took a deep breath. As he let it out and looked to the skies once again, he felt at peace. Death might come for him at any time, but he was going to live every moment as if it was his last!

That was his promise he made to those who had passed away. He would fight with his friends; he would fight for Emerilia and if he was to fall, he would do it happily, knowing he lived a great life with great friends.

What more could someone ask for in their lives?

Chapter 27: A New Destination

Dave left Deia to get some sleep as he went searching for Steve. With his Touch of the Land, it wasn't hard to find the massive metal man. Dave found him in the building that crafters were using to work on gear. It was the loudest place in the outpost and thus far away from all of the other buildings.

Even in the dark of night, hammers could be heard at work. There was a small smithy located within the building for repairs.

Dave walked in, greeting a few people with a smile and a wave before he reached the smithy around the back of the building where Steve was.

Steve's right leg was damaged and he had deep scratches on his right shoulder. His Mithril-covered core was exposed.

With a glance, Dave could see that it had been worked on. The bonds were stronger and less spread out, having being broken by a Dwarven Master Smith, thus allowing them to come together in a new formation that strengthened it.

Steve was working on the outer shell that covered his torso.

Dave looked at it. There was a large dent in the front of it from getting smacked by the tiger's paw.

Steve worked the heated metal, hammering it back into shape. He used a pair of tongs to grab the armor and put it under a blowtorch, heating the affected area.

"Looks like someone has been helping you out with your Mithril covering." Dave leaned against one of the supports to the outdoors smithy.

"Yeah, I've been helping them understand magical coding a bit better—they've helped fix up my Mithril covering, made it a lot stronger." Steve forced a smile.

"How is your chest plate?" Dave looked at it under the blowtorch.

"Caved in like a sonvabitch. Would have gone in more if the Mithril inside didn't stop it." Steve watched the blowtorch.

"Gurren and Lox are going to be back out in a few days," Dave said.

"Good." Steve sounded relieved.

"You know it's not your fault that they got hurt, right?" Dave moved into the smithy.

"Dave, I threw them into the battle. I put them in the position they were." Steve's eyes met Dave's.

He might have been made by two AIs but Dave saw the guilt that lay behind his eyes.

"Sure, it wasn't the way that I would have gone about it, throwing them like baseballs, but it allowed you to encircle the tiger, attack from all directions and divert its attention. It was just unlucky that it used one of its legendary abilities, trapping everyone in weeds and grass and smoked them with its tails. If it wasn't for you running them to the healers, they would be in much worse condition," Dave said.

"But Dave..."

"Look, listen here, yah tin dumbass, you made a decision out there. It was the best one at the time. You act like a goof, most of the time, but I know that inside that core of yours, you're a smart dude. You made a decision, shit happened—that is life. Now here are the facts. Gurren and Lox were injured, yes; you got them aid, and now they're up in their room playing poker. Well, let's be serious—they're probably trying to escape the place right now! They knew the risks joining the Stone Raiders. They can die at any time—poof and gone. They made it through because of you. You're one of their best friends. They're thankful you helped them, so when you're done pounding the almighty dent out of your breastplate, go and see them!" Dave's eyes blazed in anger as Steve tried to blame himself. Stopping it before it could affect Steve, or his relationship with anyone, was the best thing to do.

"But..." Steve started, still not swayed.

"Don't make me ask Suzy to force you to." Dave's anger rose as he gritted his teeth together.

Steve looked away from Dave's eyes.

Dave's anger wasn't directed at Steve; he was angry at how Steve was dealing with his irrational guilt.

"I'll go see them tomorrow," Steve promised.

"Good." Dave nodded. His anger quickly dissipated as he let out a heavy breath. "I've had a long day. I'm going to get some sleep. I'll see you tomorrow, and you best bring Gurren and Lox some beer—I think the healers took it all away from them." Dave smiled.

"They wouldn't like that." Steve chuckled, thinking of his two best friends.

Dave laughed and turned around. "Night, Steve." He headed for Deia and his tent.

"Night, Dave." Steve sounded much better than when Dave had arrived.

***

Lucy watched as the walls grew around the outpost. It was almost midday before the last wall reached a height of fifty meters. There was an area of nearly ten kilometers cleared around the outpost.

Big pits burned everything that wasn't useful and had been cleared away.

Timber lay off to the side; creatures under the power of others were still working to cut up the massive trees and add to these timber piles. All the timber that could be had been stored in spatial chests and stored on the traveling wagons.

"The walls are all fifty meters tall now. We'll start work on growing them to seventy-five meters in a few hours," Malsour reported to Lucy.

"Well, then it's about time we got that ono in place," Lucy said.

Malsour nodded. They stood in the middle of the outpost. Many had gathered around as Lucy pulled out steel plates. She and Malsour placed them together, creating a drop pad. Lucy stepped back and sent a private message to Josh.

Around them, walls now protected the ono as well as defended against anything that might come through it. Even though it was only connected to Terra, being paranoid had helped out the Stone Raiders in the past.

A light flashed into existence. Lucy shielded her eyes. As fast as the light had appeared, it disappeared.

There was now a larger pad where the drop pad had been. There was also a terminal off to the side. This was a counter that would accept soul gems and open a connection up with Terra.

The ono's runes lit up as it powered up. Through the ono's event horizon, there was one of the many teleport control rooms in Terra visible.

"Well damn, you are a sorry lot to look at." Josh walked through, appearing in the outpost.

Those around the ono laughed and cheered. They now had a connection to Terra and wouldn't have to travel through the Ashal wilderness with their loot.

"Now who has my gear!" Josh demanded. He'd lost his armor as well as some of his enchanted rings and jewelry.

Behind him, other Players who had died walked out of Terra and into the outpost; with them came people from the trader's guild as well as the Exdar's.

"Hey, Florence, we've got quite the haul for you." Lucy waved to the wagons that were filled with chests and bags of holding, ready to return to Terra with their goods.

"Bring them on through!" Florence said with a happy smile.

The wagons went in through the opposite side that people were arriving.

Wagons and their teams came through the teleport pad. Including Aleph automaton carts carrying multiple vault soul gems. Dave talked to the one commanding them as the Aleph carts moved away from the ono and toward the soul gem constructs.

People headed into Terra to relax. Today they would relax; tomorrow they'd venture into the dome to see the Six Affinity Temple for themselves.

The soul gem constructs that had slowed their progress were now growing up toward the skies once again.

Engineers as well as sightseers came through the teleport pad. The area around the ono got rather crowded really fast.

Lucy and the Stone Raiders' leadership moved away from the ono. They had plans to make. The Fellox and Portal Purge also followed.

Efri and Vrexu were seeing to their forces as well as coordinating with their people back in Devil's Crater.

***

"Okay, so Vrexu and Efri will be moving their forces through Terra and back to Devil's Crater. Kala and Malkur will be bringing ten thousand of their people here. Their aim is to work on practical skills, scouting the area around the outpost as well as hunting down creatures in the area to build up experience," Anna said as she and Deia stood atop one of the walls, overlooking the DCA forces. There were so many of them that they'd filled half of the towers, most of the ground and the walls when sleeping. There just wasn't enough room for one hundred thousand soldiers.

"Makes sense. Where are we needed?" Deia asked.

"Well, we can either stay here training those who come through. Alkao wants to rotate people through on a weekly schedule. We've got four weeks until the Dwarven tournament ends. Then, anytime from a week to four after that, the event is going to start. The other option is we go back and train people back in Devil's Crater. If we leave here, then they're going to bring their strongest people to watch over them. We're basically here to watch over and protect," Anna said.

"What about the trainers in Devil's Crater?" Deia asked.

"They're going to continue training anyone and everyone who comes to them," Anna said.

Deia tapped her lip in thought. "I'm fine with staying here. There's not much I can teach that the other trainers can't. Also, I'd like to see what happens within the temple." Deia smiled.

"I thought you might say something like that." Anna grinned. "I agree. We'll stay here for this rotation. Then, for next week, we can decide to stay here or return to train the others in Devil's Crater."

Chapter 28: Six Affinity Temple

Josh looked to Gimel, the Fellox guildmaster and Portal Purge's guildmaster, Kim Soon-Ok. For the last day, they had been gathering their strength, readying their guilds for the raid ahead. The Stone Raiders had brought seven hundred guild members, Fellox four hundred and Portal Purge brought five hundred.

It was the largest group ever pulled together to raid a portal location.

"Well, let's get started, shall we?" Josh asked.

Gimel and Soon-Ok smiled in agreement.

A great gate made from cut down trees and banded with metal swung open ahead of them, revealing the crack in the earthen dome. It seemed as if the crack led to another dimension in the afternoon sun; it was hard to see anything in the darkness beyond.

The three guildmasters stepped forward. All of the guilds had been organized according to their abilities under the combined command of the guild leaders.

In the first area, they would fight in their parties but as they moved farther up the different levels of the temple, they would start to group together, allowing for things like chain heals, buffs, and to bounce mobs between multiple tanks instead of just relying on one. These formations were best for fighting creatures much more powerful than the guild members.

They moved through the crack. Josh had to blink, his eyes adjusting to the low light conditions. Magical lights illuminated the Six Affinity Temple. Some of the rocks in the dome's walls lit with magical light. With Josh's high night vision skill, it was easy to see within the dome.

Shades randomly wandered around, moaning as they moved.

They didn't show any interest toward those who had walked into their domain. Lucy had pulled up information and videos on shades; as soon as something alive made it within range of the shade's senses, they'd attack.

"Time to get started," Josh said. Even though he'd lost fifteen levels, he was eager to get started. The best way to gain levels was from defeating hard enemies. It wasn't his first time losing levels and he doubted it would be his last. He wasn't going to let his death stop him from having fun!

"Shades are Level 200 to 400," a scout reported. With the scout skills, everyone was able to see the levels of the shades.

Parties spread out along the edge of the area. Everyone moved quietly, as if talking too loud would alert the shades.

The first shade let out a pained howl. Its random meanderings turned into a full-on charge as someone came too close to it. It raced toward a party.

"I've got it!" The tank of the group stomped his feet and made noise. The shade altered its course and raced for the tank.

He held his war hammer with his two hands across his chest. The shade's ethereal hand turned into a claw as it struck. There was a screech of metal on metal as the shade let out a pained yell.

The fight had started. Those who were outside of the crack quickly moved inside the dome.

More shades sensed or were tripped by the nearby members of the raid party. Howls filled the air as people pressed forward, getting into the fight.

Josh and the guildmasters spread out through the raiding party. They would lead them forward, but if one of them went down then the others would take up command. If they stopped in the middle of the fight and there was confusion, then they could lose their momentum and fall back. Here they couldn't slow until they cleared each level of creatures completely.

Worries of the upcoming event and thoughts of the future were put to the side; here there was nothing more but working with your guild mates and the raiding party to move forward.

People talked into their party chats as Health bars fell.

Buffs, curses, spells, and special attacks brought new light to the earthern dome. To a gamer, it was a sight that raised their fighting spirit. This is what they lived for.

There were tense moments as people were heavily wounded by getting mobbed with shades. Other moments where people moved through the shades as if they were nothing. People showed off their skills, all of them enjoying themselves, tense with the knowledge that they could fail, but excited to push past their limits.

Shades were looted and people moved forward; parties would break it all down at the end of the battle. For now, they advanced.

As they pushed away from the walls on either side of the crack, more and more shades ran toward them. Parties grouped together to deal with the shades' larger numbers.

They celebrated their kills and would defend one another so that they could get done with their cooldowns and heal up.

There was a sense of belonging and trust that came with the gamers. They might talk to one another with just a few words, and have never met before, but for five minutes they would work together as if they had known one another for years. All focused on defeating their enemy and keeping their other teammates alive.

Josh was in the midst of it, talking to his different parties as they moved forward. Spells crashed through shades as weapons shaved Health points from the shades' Health bars.

Like this, they were able to kill off the shades around the Six Affinity Temple.

"All right, everyone get yourself back up to one hundred percent. We've got the Affinity spirits next," Josh said to the raid party.

Healing spells were cast as people drank Stamina and Health potions, restoring their various bars. Others changed out weapons.

People broke down into six groups, one for each Affinity. Going forward, they would be split into these groups to deal with the different Affinity mobs that they ran into.

If someone was a Light party and ran into a Fire Affinity, they would call over a Water party to deal with them.

"These Affinity creatures are going to be a pain," Kim said, next to Josh.

"We've got to make sure that they don't fight same Affinity type parties," Lucy said.

"I've never heard of a creature that can actually get stronger by getting hit with a weapon or attack with the same Affinity." Josh shook his head and snorted. "Going to test how coordinated we are."

Lucy and Kim made noises of agreement.

"Everyone is ready to continue," Dwayne said over the leadership party chat.

"Dave and Malsour have found something in their search," Lucy said.

"Let's go and see what they've got!" Josh said.

***

Party Zero were a Fire Affinity party, so they were going to be focused on fighting the Water spirits.

Dave and Malsour could make their weapons have Fire-attributed magical coding on them. They had also modified Steve, Gurren, and Lox's weapons and armor with conjured and created metal sheets. Suzy's Air creations would provide support to Induca, and Lu Lu was perched on her shoulder, eager to meet their next foe.

The little lightning phoenix was now as big as a dog. As she gained more experience through her bond with Suzy and her own attacks, she grew not only in power but stature. However, she didn't weigh that much with her hollow bones and Suzy was strong enough to hold the still young phoenix.

Dave and Malsour had been using their senses to try to see whether there were more mysteries to be found with the Six Affinity Temple. With all of the Mana within the earthen dome, it created a sort of fog for their magical senses. It was only after some time of searching that they were able to pick up on the magical coding that ran under the first level of the temple.

They advanced up to the last set of steps before the Affinity pools. Now that they were much closer, they could clearly sense and understand where the coding was. They still couldn't understand what the magical coding was, but knowing where it was was a great help.

Malsour and Dave created metal and items within the coding.

The pools flared to life. The Fire one actually exploded before its flames were cut off.

The energy that had been fueled into the different pools was cut off. Affinity spirits that had been moving through the different focused energies of the pool were now out in the open.

People excitedly talked to one another about the various rare resources that they now saw where the pools had been. Over the years, different attributed plants had grown in these pools, becoming rare treasures.

The Affinity spirits, now without their Affinity pools, seemed to lock onto the raiding party. They didn't scream or make any noises—they unleashed spells.

Shields and Mana barriers blocked the attacks.

"Take them out!" Josh yelled.

The raiding party didn't need to be told twice. Excited from their recent wins and seeing all of the materials strewn throughout the pools, in their minds, there was no way that they could lose.

Although they had been able to turn off the Magical Circuits built into the pools, the Water pool was actually a pool. So although it had lost the magical coding that gathered pure Water Mana into one place, the Water Affinity spirits were still able to stay in their water.

The entire mass of water seemed to be like the back end of an octopus. The spirits freely used the water like multiple limbs, striking at anyone nearby.

Suzy's Air creations cut off the limbs that tried to come down and hit Steve, Lox, and Gurren from above.

The trio blunted the impact of the other limbs.

Malsour unleashed coded spears that exploded when they hit the water, throwing it everywhere, giving the spirits less to work with.

Induca poured her power into the pools, heating them up and making them boil.

Dave pulled out pre-made grenades. These ones were a bit more advanced than the ones he had used when fighting Lord Esamael. These ones could switch between different Affinities.

He picked Fire, and tossed them into the water. They went off like thermite grenades, increasing the water's temperature. The water frothed with the spirits' actions and all of the heat being put into it.

The first Water spirit charged outward, rushing Steve, Lox, and Gurren. It clawed at their shields and a sword appeared in its hand. The sword was made of incredibly fast-moving water.

With each hit, it left behind deep cuts in the surface of Party Zero's defenses.

Suzy attacked it with her Air creations, trying to wound it.

"Isolate them and get them to use their magic. Their magic is their life-force. If they lose it all, they'll die!" Lox yelled.

In a second, a metal casing appeared around the spirit.

More and more stone and metal appeared around the original casing as it started to show cracks, with water rushing through.

Malsour lost the race as the Water spirit broke through the casings.

It was at half of its previous Health. Its reactions were slower as the three tanks swung their weapons at once.

The Water spirit was able to avoid Steve's hit by turning into a liquid and dodging.

Lox and Gurren's blades sunk into the creature.

Dave channeled power into the blades, increasing the potency of the magical coding on their weapons. It was like listening to rain falling on an active volcano.

The spirit launched its two hands forward, turning into twin water cannons that had the force to cut through a steel plate, aimed right at Lox and Gurren.

Steve threw himself forward awkwardly, taking the twin streams on his body. He took one hit on his right leg, the other directly in the face.

Lu Lu let out a shriek as Steve rolled away. Light turned into a stream as lightning poured out from Lu Lu's beak. The Fire Spirit's Health dropped by the second as Malsour launched several coded spears.

Sections started dropping from the Water spirit, not returning as it didn't have the strength anymore to restore its body.

Dave conjured a crossbow and let loose the bolt at the spirit.

It rolled with the attacks.

Lox and Gurren roared as Steve took wounds intended for them, their swords flashing in the light as they attacked.

The Water spirit fell to the ground. Its water-created body disappeared, leaving behind a Mana core.

"Attack the pool—there's two more of them hiding in there!" Lox said.

"I've got Steve." Dave moved to the big man, who was having trouble getting up. "Your right leg is messed up—stability control got shot to hell." Dave looked at Steve's face. His head looked as if someone had fired a high-powered rifle into it at point-blank range.

"Do I leruk purdee?" Steve said. The gears and coding in his head were clearly visible as his grin turned into something out of a horror movie.

"You really are an airhead." Dave shook his head as Steve pulled a replacement leg out of his ring of holding. With his core in his chest, there was no worry that his busted head was going to do anything other than give Dave nightmares.

Malsour kept hurling spears into the water pool. Lox and Gurren were on the lookout to make sure nothing crept up on them. Induca turned the pool into a steam bath, with water evaporating every second.

Suzy supported her with her Air creations spinning around so fast as to make a whirlpool that pulled water and steam and threw it out of the pool.

The weaker spirits escaped the pool, but all of the Fire parties around the pool had dealt with the first three spirits. Their attacks destroyed the Water spirits after only landing one hit.

Steve checked his leg movement, putting the broken one into his ring of holding before he got to his feet. He didn't need to replace his face to be able to fight again, and left that for later.

Dave went back to tossing thermite grenades into the pool.

Finally, the last spirit surfaced from the pool.

Its power was on another level from the first couple of spirits. It was close to being able to sustain itself and be a Free Affinity spirit. It rose on a plume of water.

Fire prisons overlapped one another. The spirit that had meant to scare them with its power was now being cooked. It unleashed its power, cracking through the fire prisons.

Dave pulled out an orb from his pocket. It floated above his hand for a second before taking off. It slammed into the Water spirit, stopping in its center and staying there, attaching to the Mana core that sustained the Water spirit.

Its movements were arrested as it couldn't find any way to move.

Dave's orb was a prototype that came from his work and knowledge of teleport pads and portals. The orb created a sphere of influence where it would hold everything in that area at a fixed point.

He'd just nailed a Water spirit within the space-time continuum. There was no escape till the power ran out.

Now the Water spirit had nowhere to go, and the attacks rained in. They hit it until there was nothing but Dave's orb and the Water Mana core.

Dave recalled his metal orb as it towed the Mana core back to him.

He looked around. The other Affinity creatures that had been in the magically coded Affinity pools had been destroyed.

Those that were within the Earth Affinity pool were having the worst time. There was a small forest filled with valuable materials and resources that they didn't want to break, even as the spirits were using these same resources to attack them.

Already other parties had gone to help them.

"Okay, you got a spare head? 'Cause that is fucking scary." Lox looked to Steve.

"Yeah, I got one in here somewhere." Steve rummaged around in his spatial ring before pulling one out.

Dave shook his head and got to work, pulling away the old head and putting on the second.

"Thanks for that save there." Gurren held up his fist.

"Couldn't leave you hanging and I can always get more parts." Steve grinned. A gear gave way and fell down inside his head as he hit Gurren's fist with his own.

"Stop using your face! Damn thing's a mess already—damn gears are all messed up and falling apart," Dave complained.

"I'll give you a hand," Malsour said, helping Dave out.

If they were to look up, they would see the fifty Affinity animals that were roving between the Affinity pools and the overhang of the temple that the Affinity shades patrolled.

Three people had been killed in the attacks, all of them Players. Their gear was collected as they waited out their respawn time. Most of them would rush back to the temple as soon as they respawned.

Josh called for a rest for everyone to get their stats sorted out. Also, there were a number of people who weren't E-heads. They'd spent nearly two hours in the temple already, nearly forty-five minutes in the real world. Some needed to grab something to eat or deal with some real-life issues.

They left their bodies in zombie mode as the E-heads looked over the different creatures ahead and harvested the different loot within the pools as well as the cores.

The guildmasters broke it down per guild. They would hold onto it. Anyone from any of the guilds could buy the items from one another with no tax. This was something that would go on for just the raid. Only two days after the items were looted would the guilds start taxing these transactions between the guilds involved. Anyone who was buying the items from outside of the guilds would have to pay taxes on it.

With just the Mana cores, they'd made at least five grand soul gems apiece.

Mana cores were drops that usually came from creatures. They allowed someone to restore their power. They were mostly used by powerful countries in order to power things like their sewer systems, or to make their crops grow faster and more plentiful.

The higher class the core, the more power they could release. It was also based on the type of creature. With Affinity spirits, their cores were naturally much more pure than say, a hog's. Meaning that they could last much longer than another core, thus driving their price up. Also, Mana core crystals could be used to naturally enhance weapons and armor. If integrated into the smelting of metals, they could create naturally attributed items.

Dave hadn't played around with it much because of the incredible cost for the purest of cores and the fact that having a material naturally inclined toward an Affinity would make it weaker to others.

His weapons and armors were made to be adaptable between situations.

Deia and Anna, who had been minding the different groups of DCA soldiers who had been training out in Ashal's wilderness, came back from their patrols and joined up with Party Zero.

Deia was going to hang back and watch, though with her around, Lox could give up his command and pass it to her.

"So, any idea of how this place came to be?" Dave asked Anna as Deia sat between his legs, leaning against him as he leaned against what remained of a pillar.

Anna laughed to herself before she shook her head. "This was the first Affinities Pantheon."

Everyone looked at her with interested eyes.

"Well, you know when Devil's Crater sent out their scouts? I might have given them a spell that would allow them to detect this place as well as roughly this area where I thought that this place might be." Anna shrugged.

"Like father, like daughter," Malsour said, eating some jerky.

Anna scratched her head awkwardly. "Well, it was more for interest than anything. When they picked up the portal here, I thought it might be the temple but I wasn't sure. I didn't think that Josh would turn this into a thing and come to try to take the portal here."

"So, Affinities Pantheon...the place where the different gods and goddesses of the Affinities came?" Suzy asked.

"Yes. At first, it had been a place on Emerilia—people could see it from every direction for miles around. It was meant to be a symbol of power—you know, have people interact with the gods. Come for their blessings. It became clear that having the gods together was a bit problematic."

"What made you think that? Was it the fact that they're fighting one another for more power all the time?" Lox asked.

"Well, that was part of it, smart ass. Also, Dark started trying to directly siphon power out from their divine wells. After just twenty years of living here, the Affinities Pantheon was split up. They traveled to other parts of Emerilia and set up their own halls and their divine wells. Then they would meet in the new Affinities Pantheon that orbits Emerilia," Anna said.

Dave cut his Jukal link, pushing its field around everyone in the party.

"Okay, so the gods, who are actually humans who have been conditioned to think that they're all-powerful beings, lived here? So, like Fire, they live on Emerilia? I thought that they might live on the moons or something," Dave said.

"Nope, they all live in Emerilia. Light lives somewhere in Markolm. Dark lives in Ashal—well, supposedly. He does move around a lot. Air lives in Heval, kind of. Her hall actually moves around and has the best stealth abilities, so finding it is nearly impossible, even if you had the Jukal orbital sensors. Earth lives in the southern reaches of Gudalo. Though so deep underground that it would take a teleport pad to get there. Water lives with the merpeople in their main underwater city between Ashal and Gudalo," Anna said.

"What are these divine wells?" Dave asked.

"They're massive power collectors. When people give 'devotions' to the gods, they're giving them Mana and power. This power is siphoned off and fed into the divine wells. These divine wells are the basis of the gods' and goddesses' power. They don't need to pull from their own Mana pool, but can pull from this instead. They're like the vault-classed soul gems but on a massive scale. Also, when they use these power sources, there's no Mana blowback unlike when we use power from the soul gems to supplement our own. Their interfaces have AIs that will cast the spells for them. They think of something, the AI draws from the divine well and poof! It's a reality. That's how you give people the power of gods," Anna said.

"So, there's a way to cast spells from an external power source and not get blowback on ourselves?" Dave's mind opened with possibilities. *What would happen if, with the power of the power facilities or the reactors, we could manipulate them at will without any blowback?*

Dave took in a sharp breath. The gods already showed that it was possible; now Dave wanted to find out how.

"Yes, but it requires changing the implants that lay within your body. The Jukal interface that we're all using is the most basic. The one that they have is comparable to the system used by planetary governors," Anna said.

"So, would the emperor have a stronger interface?" Suzy asked.

"Undoubtedly, though there is no way to know how much processing power it has as he always communicates through aides and secondaries," Anna said.

They fell into silence. The closer they came to learning more about the Jukal and Emerilia, the more complicated and vast it seemed.

"So, what do you think these spirit beasts are going to be like?" Gurren asked while Dave once again allowed the Jukal link to be established.

"Tough," Lox said.

"They've got all of their natural attributes and their bodies have the power of the spirit within them. As the spirit feeds off the animal, the animal feeds off the spirit. The spirit is in control and is by no means smart; for that it would need to be a Free spirit or above. They're going to have a lot of magical power, and most of the spirits will have taken on creatures that are more inclined toward their Affinity. They might rank as the same level as the Affinity spirits that were in the pools, but they're going to be at least two or three times the difficulty," Steve said.

"Also, you've got to remember, they do lose their life-force as they cast spells, but by being inside the other creatures they won't dissipate when they've used all their Mana. And their Mana regeneration speed is going to be impressive," Anna added.

"Plus, they've got numbers," Gurren said.

"Easy to get caught up and surrounded," Suzy said, as they all looked at their next opponents that were moving around.

"Well, the good thing is that the mobs in the first two areas haven't respawned," Induca said.

"Yeah, having to fight them again and again would be a pain between moving up higher levels," Dave agreed.

"It might be the kind of situation that when we leave that the mobs start to respawn," Malsour said.

"Have you also noticed the different limiting runes laid down everywhere?" Dave asked.

"Yes. They seem to increase the density of the air above ten meters. I would think this is so that people can't race ahead, though I don't see why someone might want to race toward the center. There's just much more powerful creatures and the man with the Free spirits inside him," Malsour said, a curious light to his eyes as he tapped his chin in thought.

"I wonder what his story is," Deia said.

"He's got to be powerful to be at the top of those stairs. Nearly every different group of creatures I've seen is two, nearly three levels more powerful than the ones before and all of them have some impressive abilities that would be hell to deal with," Lox said.

"All right, everyone group up. We're moving to deal with the Affinity shades!" Josh said to the raiding party.

Everyone rose to their feet, excited for the experience, loot, and the possibility to put their name at the top of this portal raid's leaderboard.

Chapter 29: Progress

Traveling back to the Deq'ual system was a lot faster than when Captain Adams had headed for Emerilia.

As she came out of warp, she flashed her identification codes. She had floated, waiting for anything that might have followed her. After a few days, it was clear that nothing had.

Her crew breathed a sigh of relief. They had done everything they could come up with to make sure no one could follow them. Even though there was no sign that anyone had. It was a big risk to go and see Emerilia. Since the Deq'ual system had been settled, they had only moved to other systems to make sure that they were truly alone, setting up supply caches if they needed to run away again as well as checking out other systems that they might hide in once again.

"We have an incoming channel from Commander Sato," Quinn said.

"Put him on screen." Adams tugged on her jacket. It was the cleanest uniform; after spending so long on the ship, everything was getting a bit ripe.

"Captain Adams, welcome home. You are cleared to connect to asteroid bay three, dock fourteen," Sato said.

"Yes, sir," Adams said. *Asteroid bay three? We only have two docking bays, each of them with less than five slips to fit ships. What the hell is going on?*

"See you shortly. Your and your crew's friends and family will be there to greet you. We'll leave the political mess till later, Admiral." A smile crept onto Sato's face.

Adams paused, even after hearing it from Sato before she didn't truly believe she was an Admiral. She quickly closed her mouth before replying. "Thank you, sir. It's good to be home."

Sato's face disappeared from the main screen.

"I've got the new route," Quinn said.

"Take us in, Anders," Adams said.

"Yes, Captain," Anders said.

Over the weeks, they had become more comfortable with one another, but as they came back home, all of their military etiquette came back. Even if there was no one to see it, they wanted to show that they were the best of the Deq'ual forces.

They moved through the system, heading into the vast asteroid belts that circled the simple red star in the middle of Deq'ual.

An asteroid opened up for the ship. Even with the opening ahead of them, their sensors could hardly pick up the hollowed-out asteroid.

"It looks like someone has been upgrading the stealth technology while we've been gone," Quinn said. "Bringing up visual."

The screen changed from the spacescape to the inside of the asteroid.

Even Adams's eyes went wide at the sight.

There had to be twenty different berths within the asteroid. In these berths, there were ships being built. Each was nearly two hundred meters long and fifty meters wide. These were not scouts but true battleships.

The design was similar to what Adams had read out of her historical textbooks. Everywhere she looked, there were ships moving materials and parts, and people working massive robots or working on the ships themselves.

The ships weren't far along in their build; most were just superstructures with the main systems attached.

She knew that the Deq'ual system was going to look into making ships with the completion of her own test-bed. There had even been the beginnings of different docking slips and refineries, though it was all theoretical at that time.

She never expected that she would come back to having a fleet being made. Or the fact that they hadn't more docking slips, but in fact added in a whole new bay, complete with shipyard abilities.

Anders carefully and expertly brought them into their dock.

They ran through their docking checks, making sure everything was secured, switching from internal power to the asteroid's.

The doors leading into the asteroid had already been closed.

Adams stepped off the ship first. She came out, seeing a small gathering. She brought herself to attention, saluting Earth's flag, turned and faced Sato, who was off to the side, and saluted him.

He rose up to his full height, saluting her back.

She felt pride in what she had done and at the level of respect that Sato seemed to direct toward her.

The rest of the crew filed off the vessel, which was now the smallest in the asteroid by far.

Adams smiled and greeted people here and there. She met with her friends, noticing Sato leaving.

If she was an admiral now, she'd find out just what had happened while she was gone!

***

Two days later, Adams slumped into the couch opposite Sato. Edwards was talking to someone over his interface as Sato sat opposite her.

"Well, remind me to never leave on a maiden voyage ever again! I'm pretty sure my arm got disconnected from all of that handshaking," Adams complained.

Sato grinned at her annoyance. "Welcome to the higher ranks." Sato had seen her for a bit at these functions, including when he had pinned the admiral rank to her collar.

It had been four hundred years since there had been an admiral. Naming her as an admiral was the same as announcing that they were once again walking down the path to war with the Jukal.

"Thanks," Adams said dryly, rolling her eyes. "Now, I'm an admiral—what have you lot been up to? I've seen a lot's changed."

Thankfully there was no need for Sato to be debriefed; after all, with the Mirror of Communication, they had been able to "meet" nearly every other day.

"That's a bit of an understatement." Sato smiled and looked to Edwards. "Get off that interface!"

Edwards didn't seem to hear.

Sato took a pen out and threw it at Edwards.

He flinched. Seeing the look in Sato and Adams's eyes, he quickly finished off the call.

"I swear, he's the reason I don't have any pens left," Sato complained.

"Sorry about that. Was talking about the new sensors we're integrating." Edwards looked a bit shamefaced.

"Since you left, we've been working with the plans from Dave. He sent us complete designs on fusion power reactors, factories, automated miners, as well as refineries, weapons, armor, and what he calls a Mana well. Now, some people were able to take that and make up rough mock-ups for different systems. We also devoted some resources and time to building these things. The automated mining drills were better than we hoped, so we let some of them start to work on increasing habitat size, as well as hollowing out asteroids for materials and cutting out the foundations we would need for these various facilities that Dave passed information on."

"When you confirmed that Emerilia was real, we were able to push a lot of projects through. We already had the basics sorted out. With less testing needed, we were able to pull together systems at an incredible rate. We had all of the knowledge—everything was ready; we just had to put the things together. We ramped everything up. Five massive refineries in a few weeks, coded and good to go. Separating out all manner of materials. Dave had been giving us *everything* he had plans for. The man must not sleep! With it, we were able to take the mock-ups, things that people had been fantasizing about, and turn them into reality," Edwards said excitedly, interrupting Sato.

Sato gave him a dark look, making Edwards shrink a bit.

"Our original forty settlements are now closer to forty-five. We've got an extra shipyard, with two more planned. We've got seven refineries working all the time. The first ships should be completed in a week, with one being completed every couple of weeks. The degree of automation has been incredible. Recruitment is up across the board. People want to explore and fight the Jukal. It's not too much of a stretch to say that militarily, we are ten times stronger than before, and gaining more strength every day." Excitement filled Sato's eyes.

For too long they had been extremely careful about expanding and increasing their production of different items. This was due to it being sensed by the random Jukal patrol ships that moved through the Deq'ual system and how they might be able to sense them. The bigger they were, the easier it was to lose their biggest advantage—being undetected.

Now with the runes that had proved themselves time and time again, entire asteroids could be coded, hiding what was going on inside them.

The people of Deq'ual had not been sitting on their hands these last few centuries. In fact, they'd needed to innovate and create solutions to problems nearly every day. There wasn't a person among them who didn't have knowledge of basic engineering. Being in space made it necessary.

"With our background knowledge in coding as well as the power of our artificial intelligence banks, it was simple for people to learn how to magically code. We developed our own version of the Jukal interface that is completely isolated from the Jukal network. Added with the nanite boosters like those on Emerilia get, one person is equal to ten in terms of building. Need a superstructure? Get a big block of refined materials and a few Dark mages—they can get in there and build you a structure in days instead of months! Dave also gave us access to the magical school that is running through the Mirror of Communication. People are learning so much faster! We're generating our own coded items as well as magical spells!" Edwards said in excited tones.

"Have we had the same thing happening with pilots and ship crews?" Adams asked.

"In a way," Sato said. "We've got everyone in the military training in fighting classes within the Mirror of Communication. Right now, we're using all of this technology, but we're putting it together into the old battleship design that humanity was using—was the easiest way to do things. We've been able to reduce crew numbers considerably and we think that's only going to increase. Honestly, that's something we really need. We've got a population of nearly seventy million and two million in the military. Sure, it sounds like a lot, but the Jukal have tens of billions." Sato shook his head.

"So, what's the plan going forward?"

"Well, that's a bit complicated. There are two plans really." Sato frowned a bit and even Edwards's prior excitement seemed to dim.

"The first plan is that we wait until we've got enough strength to take down the Jukal and their controls, leading to chaos that we can use to establish colonies and a navy to defend ourselves."

"What about Emerilia?" Adams asked.

Edwards looked to Sato, whose eyes slowly came to meet Adams's.

"The second plan is that we and they come up with a plan that will allow us to act earlier. However, the plan has to be okayed by us and the council. They aren't going to let us go ahead on anything that they're not one hundred percent sure of succeeding," Sato said.

"So, basically, unless they come up with an impossible plan, we're going to sit here, build up our fighting capabilities and watch the Players of Emerilia and people continue to die for the Jukal's entertainment." Adams shook her head in disbelief, crossing her arms.

"There isn't anything we can do directly to assist them. We know that it's real and from the imagery we have from the sensor buoys you deployed, we can tell that what Dave has been telling us is indeed correct—as much as it sounds ridiculous. Though we can't sacrifice Deq'ual if we don't know that we'll succeed. If Emerilia can somehow stir up enough trouble and show that they have a plan to deal with the Jukal that we can participate in, then we will think about taking them up on that proposal." Sato didn't look as though he was happy with what he was saying but like Adams, he was subservient to the politicians of Deq'ual.

Adams let out a breath, sighing at the unfairness of it all. "Okay, so what is the plan moving forward?"

"Take the technology and knowledge we have as well as that from Emerilia. We combine it together and try to get every advantage we can with dealing with the Jukal. Also, we see if we can be of any help to Dave without giving away information that would come back on Deq'ual," Sato said.

Edwards also nodded in agreement. Without all that Dave had given them, there was no way that they would have been able to reach this level in a decade.

"We still have twenty-three years until the current Player cycle ends," Adams said.

"From what I have been talking about with Shard and Bob, it looks like it's very likely that Emerilia will be destroyed within the next year," Sato said.

"What?" Adams said, stunned.

"This is from after you left." Sato pulled out a pad and after pressing a few things, an image appeared: a massive Dragon, and then one of an ice globe in a desolate area of ground, as well as a person in comparison to the size of the area. Then there were several Dragons, all of them breathing different-colored fire onto the ice globe.

"These are Dragons. One of the first creatures to be released was called Akatol. He was the father of the Dragons—went on a genocide rampage and was locked up. He is more powerful than your scout ship in terms of defense and with his spells, we estimate that he's as strong as your first battleship's prototype weapons. He was just the first. There are hundreds of thousands—if not millions—of other creatures that were locked away that are going to be returning to Emerilia in just a few months. When they do, then the people on Emerilia are going to be in for a massive brawl. Dave has shown already how smart he is. If he and the people he cares for are threatened, what do you think he's going to do?" Sato asked.

"Fight." Adams had seen the recordings of Dave and it was easy to see that he was passionate about Emerilia and the people within it.

"Yes, he's going to fight. The man who broke Emerilia made all of this happen. He gave us designs to a stable power source that will give off unending power for centuries like it was a cookie. He gave us a stable and cheap fusion reactor! He's given us a lot of information and ideas, but what has he been keeping to himself?" Sato asked. There was no need for Adams to answer.

"Dave already told us of how the Jukal can detect him. He's got some ways to get away from their observation, but sometime he might slip up. Or he might use something that sets the AI off and they won't need much before they find out the kind of things that Dave has been working on," Edwards said. "Creating a nuke is a lot easier than creating a fusion reactor."

Edwards's words hung in the air.

"Well, then, what are the aims of the fleet?" Adams said, breaking the silence, trying to not think about what Edwards was implying.

"That still needs to be decided. I think gathering intelligence, training in the simulators as much as possible. We also have possible locations of where other Human settlements might be. Worth checking out or seeing if we can find anything there," Sato said.

Adams nodded, the rest of them getting into talking about the future of Deq'ual. With Emerilia, it seemed as if its fate was already decided.

***

Kol woke with a start. He blinked sleep away from his eyes as he looked at his interface. A message filled it.

"Sometimes I forget who trained who," Kol complained, getting up from his bed, a wry smile on his face as he stretched.

While Dave was off on the raid, he had left Kol to manage all of his affairs. Suzy's assistants were a great help in dealing with the paperwork and orders, leaving the smiths to work on the different projects. However, some of the items couldn't be given off to people Dave didn't trust completely.

Kol quickly showered and changed and headed out of his apartment. He greeted and waved to people as he moved. Kol's position was one of the highest within Terra. He was the manager of the Grahslagg smithy there. Under his command, the Dwarven Master Smiths listened. Just having them listen to what he was saying was more power than some kings and queens had.

Kol re-read the message. It simply told him to go to a room within Dave's secret laboratory.

Kol moved through Terra, reaching the teleport pad that connected to the power station facility.

People moved through the room from all over Emerilia as Kol waited for the window to get to the power station. He quickly stepped through when it was his turn and moved toward the laboratory. Stepping inside was like going into another universe.

Magical artifacts littered the room that emperors, kings, and queens wouldn't be able to find or purchase through their people. These items couldn't be sold between people of Emerilia, but with Dave's various contacts with Players and people of Emerilia, he had been able to pool these items together, or make them.

Kol pulled out a magical badge from his bag of holding. He pricked his finger and put blood on it.

The badge flashed with light. This badge would allow him to move through the room without the security measures going off. He moved deeper in the room, moving to the room that the message said.

Someone without the right clearance wouldn't see anything inside the room, but to Kol it was filled with interface screens of different projects.

The one on the far right was blinking angrily, demanding Kol's attention. He slumped into a chair and grabbed warm Xer from what Dave called a coffee maker. He'd made it to satisfy Suzy's love for the "black ambrosia," as she called it.

He raised his hand up and clicked on the project, checking the description.

Project: Ark (Shipyard)
Location: A1, A4-A10
Stage:

Mining
Power plants
Refinery
Secondary systems
Growing towers
Soul gem constructs
Defensive capabilities
Movement systems

Kol looked at the list with interest.

Dave hadn't told him about this project. Though, if the system was alerting him, then he should check it out. Dave would be interested in a report.

Kol sipped on his Xer and checked the other project screens.

Project: Devastator Armor
Location: Unknown
Stage:

Mock-up
System creation (4/8 items complete)
Systems integration
Prototype
Testing
Final product

Project: Avenger Fighter
Location: A2
Stage:

Mock-up
System creation (5/39 items complete)
Systems integration
Prototype
Testing
Final product

Project: Band-Aid
Location: Aleph Factory
Stage:

Mock-up
System creation
Prototype
Testing
Final product
Mass production
Issued to Players

Project: SSM (Surface-to-Space Missile)
Location: A3 / Aleph Factory
Stage:

Mock-up
System creation
Prototype
Final product
Part creation
Part integration
Launch platforms

Project: Ono (One location teleport pad)
Location: Aleph Factory
Stage:

Mock-up
System creation
Prototype
Final product
Part creation
Part integration
Upgrades:
Shield protection
Mana well power source
Soul gem construct support system
Emplacement around Emerilia (30% complete)

Kol looked at these different windows. Dave had explained a bit about them, so he understood what most of them were, but being told about what they can do and actually seeing them in action were two very different things.

Kol took his Xer and moved to the teleportation room.

It was over-engineered to the extreme to allow Dave the ability to test out all kinds of ideas and theories that he had. It had allowed him to prototype the summoning hall that had been pulled down from the projects wall now that it was completed.

It had also allowed him to make the hexagonal prism of orbs that formed a gravitational prison inside, the same prison Dave had used to contain the powerful Water spirit in the Six Affinity Temple in one place.

The other function it provided was making a teleport pad that ran on slightly different principles to the ones than the Aleph used and with the Jukal portals. With Kol's senses, he was able to easily sense the soul gem that was growing around this teleport pad.

He glanced over to the reactor that was placed in a corner of the laboratory. There was so much power being generated by the inconspicuous-looking device that all of the laboratory was able to sustain itself, even with its own long-distance teleport pad.

It was, in fact, supplying power to the power station as well, adding in its stream of energy so that the soul gem that was storing up its power didn't grow too fast and alert the Jukal.

Kol opened up a panel on the wall and pressed a few different buttons. The different coding plates and the runes in the floor, walls, and roof moved to the new configuration. It took a few minutes before the room settled down.

Power thrummed through the room as a portal opened in the center of the room.

Kol walked through, finding himself on a massive catwalk.

To one side there was an automated cart. Lights started to come online, revealing a corridor that extended for nearly a mile in either direction.

Kol frowned. He hadn't known about such a large facility.

His senses spread out, finding the massive magical coding working that had been made around the entire complex. Not even his own senses were capable of reaching out to encompass it all.

He sat down on the cart. "A-1," he said. The cart took off down the corridor.

Kol was about to take a sip from his Xer, his cup paused in front of his lips, as he passed a doorway that seemed to lead into darkness. The sounds of miners at work could be clearly heard.

"What?" Kol said to himself in a breathless whisper, unable to truly understand what he had sensed through that doorway.

In just a few minutes, he made it to A-1, his face a confused frown.

The cart turned and moved through the doorway. Lights started turning on in the darkness that he sensed beyond the doorway that had the two symbols A-1 carved above it.

Kol's cup fell from his numb hands.

Facing him there was a cigar-shaped vessel. It had been carved out from the very rock surrounding it. Metal supports held up the area around the ship. It was five hundred meters long and one hundred meters wide.

Kol might have not seen anything like it before, but he knew that this was a vessel for war. There were protrusions along the side of the ship that looked like Dwarven artillery, but by their size, they were as big—if not bigger—than the artillery cannons that were built into Dwarven mountains.

The entire vessel hummed with quiet power. As he got closer, Kol could sense the power within the ship. It was similar to that reactor in Dave's laboratory. Except these were much larger and hidden deep within the vessel.

Automaton repair bots moved around in a flurry, moving all manner of materials from carts that were arriving every minute and ferrying different items into the massive dock.

The scale of what he was seeing—there was simply nothing else he could compare it to. The cart came down next to an office that lay off to the side of the vessel, overlooking it from the side.

Kol numbly walked off as he started to see interface screens showing the progress of the vessel.

It was called the "Ark." Much like how Terra and the Aleph cities were formed, it had been cut from the rock. Miners then carved out different levels within the vessel and added in a power plant and refinery.

Materials were being poured into the refinery of the ship, pumping out refined materials that were passed to the complete line of factories that supplied the needs of not only this vessel but six others and the large-scale projects that Dave was handling in this yard.

Once the refinery was put in, the abilities of the yard had increased tremendously.

"Looks like A-1 is the first to get its refinery online. The other vessels are scheduled to get their refineries online as soon as possible. The amount of materials this must take..." Kol shook his head. "I was wondering where he was putting all of those resources that he had gotten from Bob. Seems that with the Jukal, he's been keeping things a bit close to the chest."

"Hello, Kol," a familiar voice said in the office.

"Jeeves?" Kol asked in a confused voice.

Jeeves was the artificial intelligence that Dave had introduced to the Dwarven Master Smiths. Jeeves was a wealth of information on all things from Earth. He had been the backing of more than one Dwarven Master Smith's discovery in the last couple of years.

"That is correct. Though in this form, I am but a fragment of my complete self. This is due to security reasons," Jeeves said.

"Understandable." Kol nodded. "So, what can you tell me about all of this? I got an alert telling me to come and check out this project."

"This is the Ark-classed ship. It is meant to hold some ten thousand people if needed, but it can operate with nearly a thousand. It is meant to defend Emerilia and protect the people who are here. Currently it has been hollowed out; its three large-scale reactors and five medium-grade reactors have been brought online and a refinery has been grown within the ship. This is meant to supplement the ship with materials. All of the other ships are in the process of being hollowed out or mined into shape; then, they too will have soul gem constructed refineries placed within them to grow into fully functioning refineries.

"As this is ongoing, then the soul gem constructs will also grow with their power of the reactors, supplying them to make various areas like living quarters, internal factories, the command lines such as water pipes, as well as gravity drives and connections to the weapon emplacements."

"So, basically, you hollowed out a bunch of rock, formed it into this Ark, then hollowed it out again, filled it with soul gem constructs and fed them power so that they grow within the vessel, creating everything inside?" Kol worked and lived in soul gem constructs, but he had never thought of using them on such a massive and complicated scale.

"That is correct. However, although the soul gem constructs can fill most of the area within the Ark, there are many sub-systems that need development before they can be created and placed within the vessel," Jeeves said.

"They're part of the project list that Dave has issued to all magical coders and the Dwarven Master Smiths. He's spread the information out over so much area and through the Mirror of Communication that no one has been able to piece it together." Kol whistled in new understanding of just how devious and smart Dave's actions were.

He stood there, looking at the "ship" in front of him. It was an undertaking that not even a dozen Dwarven mountains could undertake!

Kol's chuckles turned into a room-shaking laugh. He calmed down after some time, a big smile on his lips as he wiped tears that had formed at the corners of his eyes.

When Dave and Bob had brought Kol in on the realities of the Jukal, he had been upset by it all but he had also felt helpless—what was there that he could do? This was an empire the likes of which he just couldn't comprehend. They were thousands of times more powerful than Emerilia.

Dave, with his tenacious attitude and his unwavering focus, had pushed forward.

"Seems that the student is teaching this old master some new tricks." Kol smiled to himself.

Chapter 30: Possessed Creatures

Steve's axe hit the charging boar with so much power that the very wind was disturbed by its passing.

The boar continued its charge, barely slowed by the blow as its body was covered in dark metals, its twin tusks sharpening into points.

Suzy's creations lay broken behind it as Induca unleashed Fire attacks from above, turning the dark metal covering to cherry-red in a few moments. Anna unleashed her Air blade technique, leaving deep grooves in the boar's protective covering. Malsour placed hexes on the Affinity boar while simultaneously boosting Party Zero.

The boar had been taken over by a Dark Affinity spirit, turning the Level 400 creature into a powerhouse. Its defense was already incredible, but with that Affinity spirit, it was nearly as strong as an ebony plated rhino of the same level.

The one difference being that the boar was affected by magical spells.

"Watch the ground!" Dave said. With his high Intelligence, he was able to see the spell that the Affinity spirit released.

Steve jumped to the side, rolling out of the way of the spell's area of effect.

The others tried to do the same; Suzy used her remaining Air creations to move them to safety.

Dave held up his hands and unleashed Mana bolts from his bracelets. The air crackled, with Mana bolts landing on the boar's hide.

The boar ran on, even as its Health dropped.

Dave jumped upward, assisted by his orbs; he was able to escape the boar's charge.

The boar, now seeing none of its original targets in its path, turned in a wide circle, lining up for another charge at the group.

"This boar doesn't know how to quit!" Steve said.

The raid party had been expecting a lot of resistance to take the portal. What they weren't expecting was that the difficulty from the Affinity spirits to the animals possessed by Affinity spirits would be so much stronger than their counterparts.

These Ashal creatures weren't weak and they still retained their natural traits and abilities with the addition of the spirits. It wasn't as if they were fighting one opponent but two that complemented each other completely!

"Time to get serious." Dave looked to Malsour, Induca, and Anna.

"I've got it." Anna slowly moved down to the ground. All of them had been holding back their more powerful skills.

They might have a ranking of around two hundred—Malsour actually at three hundred and fifteen—but their actual strength was many times their stated level.

The air around Anna seemed to go still as the boar charged once again.

Anna held her blade within her two hands, her face calm and impassive and her eyes closed as she adjusted her stance slightly and bent low.

The boar fired spears of metal from its tusks.

Blades of wind sliced out from Anna almost lazily, breaking the spears with contemptuous ease. Many more followed after the first two. A semi-sphere of whistling white blades of air cut down anything that tried to reach Anna as she opened her eyes.

The boar was just twenty meters away, breaking through her Air blade shield.

One moment, she was standing still; then, in a burst of motion, so fast it looked as if she had teleported, she was past the boar.

Its eyes rolled back as its legs collapsed beneath it and dropped to the ground, lifelessly.

Dave had seen it all. She had rushed forward, passing the boar and reaching its blind spot behind its massive shoulders; she had struck out with her blade, piercing through an opening in the boar's enchanted hide to pierce its lungs and heart as she released an Air attack from the end of her blade.

It had raged through the boar, killing the Dark Affinity spirit before it could react.

Everyone in Party Zero grouped together by reflex, looking for another threat.

"The fighting is winding down. It looks like we'll be resting here for some time," Deia, who was commanding them from afar, said.

There might have been a spell that made it so that people would find it increasingly difficult to pass ten meters above the temple's grounds, but for Deia, the daughter of Fire, breaking this spell with sheer power was simple.

Dave looked around. Parties had come together, excited from their victory with the Affinity spirits. They had thought that the Affinity spirit animals would be hard but they would persevere. What they had found was just how strong these creatures were; it was a smart move to take their levels and increase them by three or four times what one could observe.

Party Zero, detecting the auras of these creatures, had been incredibly careful in dealing with them. They were one of the few parties that could handle one of the creatures by themselves. They had rescued two other parties that had been fighting the boar, taking it on themselves. The boar had been one of the strongest and most difficult to deal with.

People had retreated back down the steps and into the open area around the temple, pulling the animals with them to get more room to deal with the creatures.

The fighting had been spread all over. POEs of a certain level had been ordered to pull back. This kind of order made sense as no one was willing to lose the support of these high-level characters.

Forty people had died to the animals; another hundred and fifty had been hurt enough to need direct healing by Jules' people. Luckily, none of the people who had died had been people of Emerilia. Losing them was a big blow.

Nearly four hundred had needed to take some kind of Health potion or supporting heal from their party.

The last of the fighting ended as people relaxed. The supporting people moved around, making sure that everyone's gear was good and that they were all healed up. Others moved in, gathering up all of the scattered resources. They would be able to clean out the animals so that they could be sold to various restaurants that would go crazy for this premium meat.

"Okay, so third group of creatures down," Dave said, looking to everyone.

"I don't think there's a way in hell that we're going to get past the Affinity shades without considerable casualties," Anna said seriously. The others agreed.

The Affinity animals had been powerful but ultimately dumb in their attacks. The shades had shown that they were smart and the Affinity spirits were great and dramatically increased the power of whatever they were attached to.

***

Josh and the other guild leaders were having the same conversation.

Barabas, the leader of the mage's guild who came on the raid, raised his hand. At Level 600, he was one of the strongest POEs on the raid. Although he might look old, there was a vibrant vitality that seemed to come from his eyes. As if his age was just a cover for the excited child within.

Josh indicated for the elderly mage's guild representative to go on.

"I thank you for the great opportunity that we have been given here to study the Affinity spirits. Truly, these creatures are amazing. My people and I have been able to make a number of notes that will turn the mage's college on its head," the older man said with a kind smile to the other guild leaders. "We will support you with these next opponents but at the sign of too much trouble or creatures overrunning you, I will have to pull back my people to safety. I have brought mostly juniors and while I am able to protect them through Ashal after fighting the Affinity spirit animals, it is clear that these creatures are on another level. However, I will pass word back to the mage's college and guild. I am sure there will be those interested in assisting you in here."

"Thank you for all of the aid that you have given us already. I know that the outpost will welcome the mage's college and guild setting up within its walls." Josh nodded to the man with an open smile.

"Great! This really is the time of discoveries and knowledge. I will pass on your words immediately!" the old mage said with an excited smile.

Josh's smile widened at the old man's excitement.

The older-looking gentleman who led the adventurer's guild POEs cleared his throat and uncrossed his massive scarred arms. His armor made him look like an armored Orc tank. "We will also look to support you in this next fight. Only when we have a feeling of the true strength for these creatures will we decide to stay in support or remove ourselves." The adventurers were a proud bunch; to say that they might have met their match took guts and foresight. Glory could be earned later as long as one was alive.

"I understand. I again offer a place in the outpost to the adventurer's guild. I know there are many dangers as well as events, creatures, dungeons, and resources to come across. I don't think that the guilds here or Devil's Crater forces can harvest it all by ourselves." Josh smiled.

"Thank you." The Orc's voice was deep and guttural as he bowed his head in respect.

Josh looked to Gimel and Kim.

"We're going to be ordering any of our POEs to the rear, just in case," Gimel said. Kim, the leader of the Portal Purge Guild didn't say anything, her guild only had players in their ranks.

"Okay." Josh took in a deep breath. "It's clear that the Affinity spirits, when in control of another's body, are much stronger. These shades are going to be difficult. There are fifty of them. I want to pull them one by one, not rush in like we did with the animal shades. We were overconfident and we nearly got slapped for it."

He looked around. Everyone was focused on his words. Their haul already had been incredible. Josh had even gained back four of the fifteen levels he had lost.

The risk of continuing was great, but the rewards they had gained already had entranced everyone. The mage's college representatives were already talking to the different larger guilds to try to buy the different resources off them. The materials they might get from the Affinity shades, as well as the experience, was alluring.

Gaming was a lot like gambling. Here they had to bet that their skills were good enough to clear out the Affinity shades in order to get the rewards afterward. They were just four groups of enemies away from those loot chests that were positioned around the portal.

"We'll group together, pin them in place and take them out. If there is more than one, we have one of the faster parties kite them away from the main groups—take it on a tour or deliver it to a group that isn't fighting," Josh said.

It was a simple plan, but it was tried and tested by thousands of gamers.

"Sounds good. I have a bunch of people who had to go off and deal with things; they should be back for the most part in twenty minutes. If we can have their bots tag along with the POE guild members, they can get out of here if things go south," Kim said.

"Works." Josh nodded.

***

Twenty minutes later, everyone was back on their feet and readying themselves.

Josh personally led those who would pull back ten different shades for the ten main groups to deal with.

"Okay, so, we're agreed to use our more powerful abilities?" Deia looked to everyone in Party Zero.

They nodded. They didn't want to show off their trump cards as they knew that they would be fighting more powerful opponents in the future. Though the matter of the fact was that here they could test out these moves; when they were fighting in the event, the chances they would get to use their full abilities would be greatly reduced.

Gurren and Lox pulled out their armor as the others pulled on different jewelry that enhanced their abilities or had Dave remove the blocks he had placed on their armor. Now they would be able to use their full strength.

Dave pulled out his twin rods. Unlike when Kol had given them to him, they now had a series of runed rings along their lengths.

Moving these pieces would allow someone to change between weapons. This would mean that Dave didn't need to use them as anchors for his conjurations, storing up his Mana and keeping him from Mana fatigue.

Suzy, Anna, and Malsour wore a pendant each carved from fine metals and rings. These items had been made by either Dave, Malsour, or Dwarven Master Smiths. Their value was hard to determine.

Suzy pulled out her strongest creations. These ones were juggernauts compared to her usual creations. They were much more powerful, with their creation cores bristling with Mana.

Steve pulled off his limbs and attached his more powerful versions. He had personally worked on the stronger limbs using his knowledge of magical coding and drafted the help of Dwarven Master Smiths to make their forms as he traded his knowledge of coding. He stood back up, storing his axe within his spatial ring, and pulled out a much larger one. He let its head drop to the ground, leaving a crater underneath.

"Is that a Weapon of Power?" Dave looked at the exquisite axe in Steve's hands. His senses probed the weapon.

"Ye-up. Custom built by Edmur," Steve said with a pleased smile.

The material cost for the massive weapon must have been massive. It was made from Mithril, silver, and ebony. The runes along its length glowed with power as Steve stepped toward Suzy.

"Uh, Suzy, would you mind soul binding this to you?" Steve held out the weapon. Because Steve didn't have blood, he couldn't activate a soul bond with a weapon.

"Of course." Suzy smiled. Even though he was her contracted creature, their relationship was that of friends. She cut her finger and a drop of blood landed on the axe. A screen appeared before her before she dismissed it.

People looked over to Party Zero. Those with a high enough aura detection were able to feel the fluctuations of power coming from them as their power increased with the stat increasing weapons and items.

"Finally get to use everything." Gurren smiled, eager to push himself to the limit.

"Only act if you have to. We're some of the strongest within the guild. If we get stuck up in small fights just for fun, then others might fall." There was no room for argument in Deia's tone.

Party Zero all nodded unconsciously. When they were fighting, Deia's words were commandments. She had led them to many victories and their trust in her was complete.

Josh started to pull the Affinity shades. They were all wandering underneath the covered open area that was supported by pillars before the actual temple. In keeping with the style of the Six Affinity Temple, this area was massive. It was about fifty meters long and two hundred wide, standing just three hundred meters from the Affinity pools.

They pulled a half-dozen of the shades. There were only fifty of these creatures, but once they found a target, the power they displayed as their auras seemed to ignite from a stupor into action was enough to make the weaker people in the raid group turn pale.

As they came closer, people shook.

"They're more powerful than I thought they would be," Dave said.

The others in Party Zero all had grim looks on their faces as they stood back from the ten main fighting groups with the supporting raid members and the POEs and the mages of the mage's guild who were readying their spells.

The raid parties' auras were unleashed, reducing the impact on those who were weaker. Tanks started their taunts as those who had pulled the creatures raced toward them.

Others went on long and wide paths, pulling creatures with them and away from the ten different groups so that they didn't overwhelm them with Affinity shades.

The Affinity shades, unlike the Affinity animals, didn't just empower their bodies and their natural skills. They called down spells on the raid party members.

Those who were pulling the creatures yelled out what type of Affinity the creature they had following them was.

People changed their weapons, moving around so that those with weapons that were stronger in dealing with the Affinity were at the front. Hitting these creatures with the same Affinity weapons or spells would serve to make them stronger.

The first shade unleashed light from its hands. People hunkered down behind Mana shields. The stream of light hit like a truck along its length. The terrifying beam shed motes of light that danced lazily around as it ate through powerful Mana barriers with ease.

The shade erupted into light, even though the shade was a Dark-attributed creature. The Light Affinity that dwelled within it had changed its composition, making it almost invulnerable to Light attacks. Although its magic was weaker than it could have been, the shade's largest weakness, Light-attributed weapons and armor, was now removed.

Darklings, curses, Dark Affinity Mana bolts: all of these hit the shade. Even if someone had a weak Dark spell, they slammed into the shade. Still, it moved forward with great speed. It was stopped by a sword-wielding Orc. With a flash of its fingers, it cut through the Orc with ease. The shade's speed was greatly increased with the blessing that the Light Affinity spirit placed on it.

A golden Mana barrier surrounded it, stopping the magical attacks that had brought its Health down by a third.

The creature tore through the weaker of the opponents. It had the presence of mind to direct its attacks to those who were weaker than it.

The stronger moved to intercept and push it back. They weren't able to save the first five victims. The shade moved much faster than anything else that they had fought.

As it unleashed its lance of light, these stronger fighters were able to resist it as the mages and ranged fighters poured in their attacks.

The golden shield continued to last.

"Damn spirit is supporting the shield with its own power." Lox moved the sword in his hand. They waited for Deia's word. The Light shade was by no means the worst of the Affinity spirit shades.

In all of the ten groups, the different fighters were giving all they had and were still being thrown back. POEs drew back, moving away from the front lines to support. They were only mortal.

"These shades are at least as strong as a Level 900 creature," Suzy said.

Everyone had a grim expression on their face as they watched. In three minutes, they had lost more people than they had over the last five hours since the beginning of the raid.

Most of the veteran Stone Raiders were around Level 700 in their overall strength if someone was to look at just their stats.

Most of the highest-leveled people in the other guilds were around Level 800 by comparison.

The better of the Stone Raider veterans were around Level 900. They could fight the shades toe-to-toe, though a number of them were mages, or ranged, meaning that they couldn't take the pressure off the melee fighters.

Josh and the guild leaders of the Stone Raiders, as well as the strongest of the guild, were around Level 1,000.

Kim, with some supporting mages, glowed with magical power as she called down a lightning strike on the Light Affinity spirit. Its speed slowed dramatically as its golden Mana barrier shuddered.

Even though the Level 700s were well below the strength of the spirits, they threw themselves forward, just getting in a few hits before they pulled back.

The 800 and 900 levels were leading this battle, with everyone else supporting them and the higher-leveled people dropping massive attacks to stagger the Affinity shades.

In Party Zero, with all of their gear and weapons, Suzy, Gurren, and Lox were nearly Level 800. Steve was close to a 1,000. Dave was almost 1,100. Induca and Malsour were 1,200, with Deia and Anna standing at 1,300 or 1,400.

Dave was seen as the biggest hitter because with his gadgets, he could use all of his strength in just a few moves and still have massive Mana reserves left over.

One of the people pulling a Fire Affinity shade let out a cry. The shade was gaining on them and they weren't near anyone else. If that shade killed them, its attention would turn back on the fight. If it got behind the fighting lines of the different groups that were fighting, they'd fall apart.

"Go," Deia said.

Party Zero moved with speed that had to be seen to be believed. They rushed forward, their melee fighters out front with Water creations, which looked like scaled-up versions of Water Affinity spirits, complete with a core in their center to stabilize them.

Other creations moved to Suzy, entering her spatial ring as other Water creations fell out, replacing them and ready to fight.

Anna was the first to reach the spirit.

The slim elven woman who had been pulling the Fire Affinity shade looked up to them with glee.

Seeing the grim looks on Party Zero's faces, Anna felt a calm pass through her. She looked back to the shades with a smirk on her face.

I might be some small fry, but I'm a Stone Raider and there are many stronger members than me!

Anna came down, her hands flashing with her massive sword. A dome of rapidly moving air formed around the Fire spirit and a hundred meters in every direction.

"I used vacuum dome! All the air in the area is being pulled out. I've blessed you so that the dome will not affect you." Anna's blade continuously moved to adjust the sphere's influence. If she was to attack the Fire Affinity spirit with her Air Affinity attacks, it would become weaker, but its attacks would be more powerful with the additional oxygen in the air.

Steve pulled up his arm and transformed it into a bolt thrower.

Dave focused, creating a thin sheath of coded metal that formed over the bolts.

Metal and runes formed over everyone's weapons and armor; even Deia's arrows gained a coded layer.

Dave twisted the different rings on his rods into the right positions. He placed the rods on top of one another; they seemed to combine to create a longbow. He drew and released. Deia, who floated above, hit with her own arrows.

From Anna's attack to Dave's arrow hitting the creature, only the time it took for one to breathe had passed.

Malsour unleashed Mana draining curse, with Induca layering them on the spirit.

Lox and Gurren let out their war cries as Dave, Deia, and Steve fired their bolts and arrows as they ran.

Suzy's fourteen Water creations surged ahead. They moved like a constantly surging tide. As they reached the Fire Affinity shade, they turned into humanoid forms holding tridents. From the waist down, they were formless water.

The Fire Affinity spirit let out a shrill shriek, focusing on the Water creations and unleashing spells on them. Its attacks were weakened by forty percent with Anna's dome.

The Water creations let out their own shrieks, sounding like tortured souls that had been held under the pressures of the deep sea for centuries. Their hands flashed forward with weapons. Although spells needing heat were weakened, the water moved easily.

Cutting streams flew from the Water creations, hitting the Fire Affinity shade from every direction.

It turned into a fiery tornado, pushing back the attacks. When it reached the Water creations, they tried to pull back, but five of them weren't fast enough and fell to the tornado.

Steve's arm changed back to normal as he raised his axe to attack.

Induca let loose a spell. It struck the tornado and ripped apart the fabric of the spell.

The Fire shade shrieked in anger and pain as it held its head at having its spell destroyed and the spell's power backlash onto it.

Malsour held his ground with Induca to one side, Suzy to the other, and Dave beside her as he released arrow after arrow into the Fire spirit.

It was down to fifty percent of its Health.

The Fire shade hit Gurren with a fireball, sending him flying back five meters. Though it wasn't fast enough to stop Steve and Lox.

The Water creations also charged forward in support. They used their bodies as shields, taking hits that would have landed on Lox and Steve, allowing the two to land hits that took large chunks of Health away from the shade.

An angry red sphere revolved around the Fire shade, pushing out to encompass Steve, Lox, and the Water creations.

Sweat fell from Induca and Deia's brows. At almost the same time, they opened their eyes. Although they couldn't attack the Fire shade directly, lest they give it power, they knew the Fire Affinity intimately. Their knowledge allowed them to tear apart the spell formation as it left the Fire shade's personal domain.

Lox was covered with sweat and Steve's armor was red-hot. They were being supplied air while in the dome, but the heat in the vacuum dissipated slowly.

Anna's movements with her sword changed. Air rushed in, pulling heat out from within her vacuum sphere.

The Fire shade was down to just twenty percent of its Health. All of the Water creations had been killed off with the last attack, their cores lying on the ground, dim without power.

A sword covered in frost appeared in the center of the Fire shade's stomach and tore upward.

The Fire shade let out a shriek, trying to fight and heal itself at the same time, but the damage was too great.

In Emerilia, it wasn't always depleting someone's Health bar that led to their death; hitting their vitals was a quick and easy way to finish them off. It was how assassins could take out targets many times stronger than them.

Gurren's sword came out of the Fire shade. It fell to the ground, its Health bar shooting downward.

Gurren breathed heavily, blood down the side of his face. His breastplate was scorched where the fireball had impacted.

The dome around the battle fell away as Anna rested her sword on the ground.

"Check yourselves over." Deia sent a healing spell to Gurren.

"Thanks." Relief filled Gurren's voice. "That fireball stung a bit."

In just a few moments, Party Zero recovered from their fight. Deia already had their next target picked out.

"Attack from range. Bring it to us and we'll wear it down. Malsour, you're on defense," Deia said, highlighting a Dark spirit that was chasing another runner.

"Anna, could you get their attention?" Deia asked, a faint smile on her lips. Here they could finally present their strength.

Anna's whistle made people's ears ring. The runner saw the members of Party Zero and Anna waving them over.

They put on more speed. The Dark shade was one of the slower creatures but from its aura, the runner's clothes were wet with cold sweat. If they fell back at all, they knew that the Dark shade would tear them apart.

The air cracked around the runner as arrows passed, making their clothes flutter.

Deia floated in the air, wreathed in flames as she fired arrows. Even as her arms moved in a blur, every arrow hit the shade, her face a picture of calm.

Dave's face glowed beneath his hood. Runes across his weapons and armor glowed, though his arrows were slower than Deia's but no less accurate.

Steve, Lox, and Gurren faced the runner, a space between Gurren and Steve so that the runner could make it past.

Malsour rose up on a stone pillar. Black smoke surrounded him as he watched the Dark shade.

Anna and Induca were on the back side from the three tanks but out to the side, ready for the incoming Dark shade, but holding off on their spells that might hit the runner.

Orbs of light appeared around Suzy, lighting up the temple's grounds. They arranged themselves around Suzy in an arch. She rose up into the sky, an Air creation holding her in the air.

The seven orbs of light fired their beams at the Dark shade. The air distorted where the beams met; an Air and Water creation focused and directed the power from beams as big as a person's head to the size of a fist.

The Dark shades Mana barrier flashed into existence as the light stream hit it. The shade roared, turning to run directly at Party Zero.

Dave and Deia's arrows made it flinch. Its body rocked from side to side with the impacts. Like some juggernaut from the bowels of hell, it continued on.

Its Mana barrier failed.

Suzy's Light creations paused their attack, needing to cool down and gather their Mana once again.

Anna twirled around. The wind gathered around her; the debris around her was thrown by the tornado that seemed to gather around her. Her sword sung, the vibrations speeding up the tornado.

Induca, floating in mid-air, raised her hands as if some war goddess deciding the fate of those in front of her. Her face was emotionless as the flames that framed her moved wildly. A red flame formed in her hand, rapidly condensing into a blue flame, then a white flame and then it seemed as if the flame had disappeared altogether. Around her hand, a series of rotating flames and a tube made of flames appeared.

This was Deia and Induca's self-made spell, Plasma Cannon.

The cannons erupted. The air in the area exploded outward and cracks formed in the stone flooring. Steve, Lox, and Gurren braced themselves against the raging wind as the invisible and highly condensed flame whistled through the temple grounds. It slammed in to the Dark shade.

The Dark shade's ethereal form was as hard as steel. The impact sounded like a thunderclap through the temple as waves of force turned the temple floor around the Dark shade into a crater. The Dark shade was thrown back ten meters.

In one hit, the creature had dropped forty percent of its Health. It roared forward. Darklings appeared around it, running forward to attack Party Zero.

Suzy's Light creations once again created their light array with the Air and Water creations. The darklings were cut down within seconds under the power of their combined spell.

Malsour sent out a surge of power. The darklings slowed down as Anna unleashed her attack. The tornado she had built howled through the temple and her hair waved in the wind like some kind of warrior goddess. Her eyes glowed with white power as she stepped forward, her sword thrust out.

The ten-meter tall tornado's power condensed and flowed down around Anna's arm, using the sword to direct it.

As it moved to Anna's sword, it rotated faster and faster, condensing into a white lance of power. The debris that had been caught up within the tornado was ground down into particles as the condensed lance of air shot out like a bullet.

All of this happened faster than the blink of an eye.

The Dark shade had recovered from Induca's attack and raced forward again.

Anna's attack landed. The spinning vortex lance of air tore through two darklings as if they were paper before it slammed into its chest.

The pressure from the attack threw the ranger who had been pulling the creature toward them, even as they were just reaching Gurren and Steve. Metal and stone reached up from the ground to catch the ranger gently, getting them back on their feet.

Shaken, the runner looked behind her.

The Dark shade looked blankly at Party Zero. The darklings around it came apart like dust in the wind, a giant hole through the center of the shade.

The shade's form collapsed the dark shadows that filled it, falling away and turning into a pile of ectoplasm with a dark Mana core resting in it. A tombstone hovered above it.

The runner shook their head, not believing what they had seen. Party Zero checked over their gear. Dave and Deia's heads snapped up, and they released arrows at almost the same time.

An Earth shade had just critically wounded a mid-level 300 who had been barely holding it off. As it went to land its attack to finish off the wounded tank, two arrows drilled into it, pushing it off-balance.

"Get me over there!" Lox yelled to Steve.

"You sure?" Steve asked.

"I ain't gonna say it again!" Lox shouted, furious at the holdup.

Steve grabbed Lox and hurled him toward the Earth shade.

The metal on his sword and shield changed its form, Dave adjusting the enchantments to make him more powerful against the creature.

Lox's shield took the Earth shade in the face. All of the force that Steve had imparted went right into the Earth shade, stunning it.

Lox let out a yell. His sword flashed with a cold light and he moved with a quickness that belied his bulky stature. Even as he moved faster than most could follow, arrows landed around him, impacting the shade.

Steve let out a yell and charged forward. With each step, the ground shook around him, leaving imprints in the ground as he picked up speed.

Gurren was quickly getting outpaced. Air rotated around him as Anna rushed past. He straightened out, Anna pulling him through the air.

Dave shot forward. The air shimmered around him—Induca on one side, Suzy on the other and Malsour below them on his metal surfboard. Deia flew behind them at a sedate pace, releasing her arrows.

The group that had been attacking the Earth shade pulled out their wounded and doubled their efforts now that they had the space to think, not panicking that they would fall to the Earth spirit.

The strongest among them landed their attacks. Combined with Lox's attacks, the Earth shade quickly fell.

A globe of air fell around Lox, pulling him into the sky as they raced off through the battlegrounds toward another runner fleeing a Water shade. The runner who had been pulling it was covered in cuts but still they kept running and trying to get the creature far away from the raid party.

The runner was expecting to die, but the farther it could get the Water shade, the more time the other members of the raid party would have to react and ready themselves for the angered shade.

***

Barabas looked at Party Zero with wide eyes.

He had been with the mage's college since his youth. He'd gone on many adventures all across Emerilia. He was one of the most renowned members of the mage's guild, taking many of his students and others out into the wilds to search for new and exciting magical phenomena. He had seen battles between the hidden masters of nations and seen them fight creatures of lore.

The Six Affinity Temple was a jewel the likes of which he had never thought to see in his later years.

He had eagerly applied to come on the trip.

Only when fighting these creatures did Barabas figure out that although he was a decent match for the animals that were controlled by Affinity spirits, he was not a match for the shades controlled by Affinity spirits.

He was a Level 600, a presence the likes of which made kings and queens bow to him. He had seen many Players through his life and their strength had always astounded him. Though he had kept away from them, they were violent and temperamental creatures. They could turn on someone easily, as if not caring for life but the achievements and materials they might gain.

The Stone Raiders had shown themselves to be different; around them, miracles seemed to happen. Now he was watching another.

Party Zero was a group that had gained the attention of the mage's college and guild. They were favored by Archmage Jelanos and Alamos, who ran these two institutions.

Barabas had always been a skeptical man, not believing in things until he saw it with his own eyes. It had served him well in his path to gain a higher knowledge of magic.

Now he couldn't even believe his own eyes.

Party Zero's highest-leveled member appeared to be Level 354. Yet they were fighting creatures that Barabas scaled as Level 700 or 800.

They weren't fighting them one-on-one but it was clear that while they were using some of their most powerful moves, the shades didn't last more than ten minutes under their attacks.

Barabas had been ready to take his mage's guild associates from the Six Affinity Temple. The raid party was getting torn apart. They didn't have many people who were able to hold off the shades.

Now with Party Zero rushing in to help the raid parties, with their eyes clear and their egos thrown aside, they fought with everything they had, not willing to be defeated.

This was the power of the Players. They did this for fun, but when they focused on a task they pushed everything else to the side.

Before, they had wanted to get the most hits to try to get some more experience. Now they were only attacking when it was the most opportune time. Chaining their attacks together for the maximum power. When enough of Level 300s worked together, they could rock a Level 500's world. Here they weren't doing much damage, but slowly they were draining the shades of their Health.

People fell out of the different fighting groups. The support people hurried there to heal them and get them back on their feet. As soon as their bars were full and they were in top condition, they ran forward again.

Barabas's eyes caught the eyes of the adventurer's guild's leader. They shared a look of astonishment before turning back to the battle.

These Players were strong. Both of the POE party leaders were surprised with their abilities. As time went on, the raid party firmed up their lines and responsibilities.

Here and there Players were cut down; it was inevitable. The others did everything they could to try to rescue them, but still over a hundred had died. Many more were injured, though still not a single POE had fallen to the Affinity shades.

The guilds had pushed them all back. This was something that Barabas had not seen very often. Most times, he was used to the Players using the POEs as cannon fodder to weaken the enemy before they moved in.

After a few hours, the fighting started to lessen and the Affinity shades' numbers dried up.

One group and then another found that they no longer had any more Affinity shades to fight. They moved to assist the other groups that were dealing with an Affinity shade.

Barabas and his mages relaxed, letting their Mana regenerate naturally instead of using potions. It was much slower but it would mean that the chances of them getting Mana fatigue were much lower.

The last shade fell.

The raid party let out excited whoops, yells, and cheers, even though they were tired. They had gone up against enemies that were much stronger and persevered.

The Mana cores and loot were gathered and sorted. People relaxed, excitedly talking.

Barabas was used to this type of reaction from Players, even though a hefty number of them had died, three hundred of them—nearly a third of their force. As long as they won, they didn't care about the losses.

It would be some time until those who died were able to come back. None of the POEs had died; the guilds had figured out a way to keep them safe while still having them contribute.

Those who had died had their gear collected by their friends, holding onto it for their return.

There was a tired excitement around the Six Affinity Temple.

Party Zero were greeted like reigning champions and the higher-level Players who had been able to hold off the creatures were the center of attention as people talked about their exploits.

The other Players were jealous of their abilities but they started to go through everyone's stats, skills, and gear, looking to find whether there was any way to augment themselves to be stronger in the future.

A guild leader meeting was called.

Barabas joined, looking at everyone in the circle.

"Well, as much as that was one hell of a fight," Josh grinned and the others smiled happily, "I don't think that we should go any farther with the groups we have. These things were Level 700 or 800. There are only a few people who can handle them. If we're to move forward, I think that we're going to have to get Level 700s at least to deal with them."

"What about Party Zero?" Kim looked unhappy. Her guild members had skills on par with someone who was a Level 600.

"They're our trump card and while I'm still awed by their abilities, I don't think we can rely on them. They were running around trying to save as many people as possible." Josh had more to say but it was clear he didn't want to say it as he felt he might offend someone.

"With low-leveled people around, there's just more distractions. Having someone go down means it takes two people out of the fight: the person who is down and the one who is healing them," Gimel said. "If we have Level 700s in here, then there is not only less people around to worry about, but they can all look after themselves."

Josh nodded. Kim's face looked darker at the two guild leaders' words.

Gimel's Fellox Guild only had a handful of Level 700s.

"That said, I think we should pull everyone back to the crack. We've been fighting all day. We'll get a few of our scouts to look ahead to try to check the levels and get a read on the Free Affinity spirits. If they get spotted, they can book it out of here and into the outpost. Once everyone's back, we can go rest some, split up all of the loot, and watch how long it takes for the mobs to respawn in here. I propose that we just farm the first three or four levels for a couple of days. Get some loot, experience. This place is great for gaining some levels and testing out our abilities," Josh said with a happier tone.

"I agree," Barabas said. The adventurer's guild leader also let out a grunt of agreement.

"I'm looking forward to taking a bath and getting some food." Gimel smiled.

Kim sighed. "Yeah, we'll pick this up again tomorrow," she agreed.

"Well, let's pass the word. I need a bloody shower!" Josh slapped his legs and stood up.

"I could tell you that for free—think you burnt away my sense of smell with your rank." Gimel smiled.

Josh laughed heartily and shook his head.

***

In the center of the Six Affinity Temple, a single person sat. Their eyes flicked upward toward those it sensed beyond the temple's walls. His gray eyes glowed with power. Around him, the air seemed to shimmer like heatwaves from a rocket's engine.

This man's name was Jung Lee.

He cocked his head to the side. His senses had become incredibly acute over the years. He had needed them. As he had grown stronger, so had the powerful Free spirits that were within his body. They had become smarter in their attacks and probes, meaning that he had to also increase his abilities to stop them from invading his mind and taking over.

All six Affinities fought within him, clashing with him as much as they did with one another.

He unconsciously fended off a fight from the Dark Affinity spirit that tried to worm through the spell formation he created. The Dark spirit recoiled under the pressure that he was able to display.

Jung Lee looked out at the area beyond the temple. He had noticed the odd creations that had moved through his prison. He remembered hearing something like them from the exiled races that made up the Aleph society.

With his senses, he could see through his prison, finding a massive group of people from Emerilia and Players.

Jung Lee's heart started to beat faster. He had not seen anyone in centuries. He had been a recluse before, an alchemist who wandered Ashal to create different miracle medicines and improve his abilities.

It had been his downfall. He had become trapped, with no one to rely on to come looking for him, to save him from his imprisonment and constant battle with the Free Affinity spirits that had invaded his body.

His heart seemed to suddenly stop as he realized that they were moving away from the temple; only a single group stayed behind. Jung Lee tested their auras, easily getting past their aura suppression.

"Good talent," Jung Lee said to himself, looking at the group. "They were able to clear the way to the temple."

Jung Lee turned thoughtful as he looked at these people who were now headed out of the earthen dome that covered the temple and its grounds. Jung Lee sent out a spell. Reaching beyond the walls, he was able to find the massive outpost that had been created beyond his prison.

Hope started to fill Jung Lee. With just a person's help, he might be able to free himself of the daily fights that kept him stuck within the Six Affinity Temple.

The Earth spirit attacked Jung Lee's psyche.

Jung Lee fiercely fought down the Earth spirit, burning his own power to attack the Earth spirit. It backed off in fear, the other spirits quieting their attacks and probes.

They were used to Jung Lee fighting them off. To see him show any emotion, to go beyond what was totally necessary—they knew something was wrong.

The large group reached the crack as the much smaller group moved forward. There was a woman in flames, a man of shadows, another with wind circling around them, and a fourth just floating in the air without any clear sign of what magic he was using.

The rest of their party had headed for the entrance with the rest of the group. Including the odd man made of metal.

Jung Lee focused on these four as they cautiously approached the pillars that supported the overhanging roof in front of the temple proper. They continued forward under the overhanging roof and toward the large open doorway that could fit two carts through it.

Jung Lee stopped using his spells; instead, he looked down from his seat at the temple doorway.

The four people stood at the doorway, none of them making a sound as they looked around.

Jung Lee studied them, using his far sight to focus on them. He locked eyes with the woman who was covered in air. His heart seemed to stop as he gave her a kind smile and a tear fell from his cheek.

Seeing another person filled him with joy and hope.

He had been tempted to just give in, to stop fighting the true Affinity spirits. Now new resolve filled him.

He used all of the magic he could use before being dangerously underpowered to deal with the true spirits' attacks to write two words.

***

Anna looked to her feet as two simple words appeared. She read them out in a hushed tone as the other party members also looked at the characters on the ground.

"Help me."

All of them suddenly looked up at Jung Lee. Their hearts went cold as they looked at the refined man with a sad and lonely look on his face. However, his tears were those of joy. The scene made them all take deep and heavy breaths.

A screen filled their vision.

Quest: Possessed by Spirits

Jung Lee was once a great alchemist and fighter. He searched across Ashal for new ingredients to make different potions to enhance his abilities and solve maladies people had. He stumbled into the Six Affinity Temple when he was injured. Free Affinity Spirits entered Jung Lee's body in his wounded state, fighting one another and Jung Lee for control of his body.

After suffering for centuries, Jung Lee wishes to end his suffering.

Failure: Do not complete this quest within 1 month

Rewards:

Gain 5 stat points to use at your discretion

(???)

Anna's eyes went wide. Finding quests that would allow those to complete it to gain stat points were incredibly rare. She had never seen a quest give five whole stat points. The difficulty of the task could be imagined.

She dismissed the screen and looked up at Jung Lee again.

His eyes went red for a moment as the air around him shuddered. A low growl came through the temple as his eyes switched to white, and then gold. His fingers clamped around the sword in his hand, which flashed with different colors.

"We'll be back," Anna promised, looking to the rest before they all turned and left.

Chapter 31: Welcome to the Cause

After leaving the Six Affinity Temple, Party Zero and most of the people who were in the outpost headed for the ono and through to Terra.

Anna had requested a meeting with the rest of the Stone Raiders leadership and Party Zero.

Josh granted it, all of them meeting in the Stone Raiders tower in the meeting room where the guild's leadership discussed the future.

The four who had stayed behind to try to gather information all had dark looks as everyone took their seats. Dave looked deep in thought, leaning against a wall, with too much energy to sit down at the table.

"Okay, so what's so important that we can't go and clean up?" Josh asked in a light tone. His smile faltered at the looks from the four who had looked into the temple.

"When we were looking into the temple, we caught the eyes of the man who is sitting in front of the portal. With what we were able to observe, his name is Jung Lee. As we saw him, it seemed that he noticed us." Anna sighed and shook her head.

"Did he try to attack?" Dwayne asked in an alarmed tone.

"No. Instead, he wrote a message on the ground in front of us, just two words." Malsour looked to the others. "Help me."

Others in the room had a variety of emotions when hearing this.

"Maybe a subquest?" Kim asked.

"What are we helping him with? It could be a trap," Cassie said.

"Free Affinity Spirits are powerful creatures with strong wills and abilities. They can enhance someone's ability by a great margin. Though they overtake the person or creature that they are within. They might have a modicum of intelligence but it isn't great enough to be called sentient. Here Jung Lee was able to write out a message. I sensed all of the Affinities within him. All of them Free Affinity spirits," Anna said.

"We've talked among ourselves. What we think is that Jung Lee somehow had all of the Affinity spirits gain access to his body at one time. He is still in there, but he's been fighting off the spirits within his body the entire time he's been in the Six Affinity Temple. After he wrote the message in the stone, his eyes changed color, as did the Affinity that ran along his sword. It was as if he was fighting all of the Affinities that were within his body," Induca said.

"So, what? There's a man in there who can't do anything because of all the Affinities that are fighting for control of his body?" Dwayne asked.

"Essentially," Malsour said.

Kim shook her head. All of the Party Zero faces were serious.

"Okay, so is there anything we can do? Is it worth doing anything?" Josh asked.

"In the coming war, we're going to need strong people. If we can help out Jung Lee, he might be the kind of person that will help us greatly." Dave pushed off the wall, his eyes hooded.

"Bit serious, are we?" Dwayne said with a slight smile.

Dave calmly put his hands on the desk and looked at the people around the table—all of Party Zero, Cassie, Dwayne, Josh, Esa, Jules, and Lucy.

Anna felt her heart tighten with the look in those eyes. *So, the time has come,* she thought, scared, but understanding of Dave's actions.

It felt as if the air in the room became a little more thick as Dave cut the Jukal link to the room. Already it was hard to pick up a signal in the heavily warded conference room but now nothing was getting in or out.

If someone was to try to use their interface, they would have been met with difficulties.

"I think at this time everyone knows that on Earth my name is Austin Zane, CEO of Rock Breakers," Dave said, his voice calm.

Cassie's eyebrows rose. As she looked to the others, they didn't show any shock but rather nods of confirmation. She looked back to Dave as if seeing him in a whole new light.

"You might also be wondering how the hell I have so much time to play this game and be an E-head." Dave smiled. "The simple way of putting it is I'm not an E-head."

"You've got some kind of remote tech?" Esa asked.

"No, I'm not using any tech at all. My avatar of Austin Zane is being run by AIs so that Earth's economy doesn't just collapse. Everything that you think was your life on Earth is a lie, a simulation to make you want to play video games, to play Emerilia and fight for a race that nearly exterminated humanity and now uses us for entertainment and to deal with the races that threaten them," Dave said.

Dwayne snorted and shook his head.

"Bit farfetched to troll me." Dwayne looked to the other faces in the room. A sliver of doubt crossed his eyes as he saw not only did Party Zero look as though they accepted this fact, but Jules's and Lucy's eyes were also steady, looking at the four others.

A Gnome appeared in the room with a flash of light.

"Dave?" Bob asked.

"I think it's time that these four finally learned the truth," Dave said, a sad smile on his face as he looked to the four looks of disbelief.

"I have one question. If you were to log off, then why would you be greeted by a Gnome that is supposed to only be in the game?" Dave asked.

***

An hour later, the four disbelieving faces were ashen as they looked at the others in the room.

Josh's hand shook as he ran it through his hair and let out a nervous laugh.

Bob had visited each and every one of them on Earth; he had even brought them together and dropped them off in their houses. There was no interface—nothing to indicate they were in a simulation. Yet it shouldn't have been possible.

Their beliefs were shaken as they returned to Emerilia.

Party Zero, as well as Jules and Lucy, told them the story of the Jukal, of the Human race. It had left them shaken in more ways than one.

"How?" Josh said.

"The people of Emerilia are real." Dwayne looked as if his whole world was coming down. "I was never actually disabled in combat—that was a situation that they made up so that I would come to video games to get away from it all."

"Precisely," Dave said, a note of sadness in his voice but also understanding.

"This is massive. And as much as I understand that you telling us shows that you trust us a whole hell of a lot, why would you?" Cassie asked.

"With this war, a lot of things are going to change. If we survive it—hell, even if we do well—we could become some of the most powerful people on Emerilia. Strong enough that we could rally others to us," Dave said.

"We might be able to rally them to us, but the Jukal have to have a way to deal with us," Dwayne said.

"Yes, each and every Player has a kill switch in them—it's part of our bodies. There are also orbital satellites that can drop missiles and kinetic warheads on us. Then there is also the moon base that is filled with automated robots and weapons that could wipe us out many times over," Lucy said.

"There are also the ships that are always orbiting Emerilia. While we should be able to not worry about the *Datskun* carrier, the others have more than enough power to sit above us and drop rocks on the different continents, dropping us into an ice age," Dave reminded her.

"So, what the hell are we going to do? Even with all this info, we don't have ships. We don't have weapons that can fight them!" Kim said.

Dave tapped his fingers on the desk. "Well, that isn't necessarily true."

Now everyone except Malsour and Steve's eyes were fixed on Dave.

"Dave, what have you been working on?" Deia asked, as if learning about another one of his creations that he seemed to come up with on the fly.

"Insurance. Basically, if we win this war and we can fight everything off, then we don't know how the Jukal are going to react. If we have to employ weapons that should not be on Emerilia, then things are going to get dicey and we'll have to strike out. If not, then we can bide our time, grow our strength more and then move on them first. To do that, we need resources and items that can fight them in space or allow us to survive on Emerilia. Terra is one of those projects. So are my other ideas," Dave said.

"What about Terra?" Josh asked.

"Well, it's more than just a city. It's meant to be a shelter in case anything goes wrong and we need to hide from the surface of Emerilia, which we shouldn't need to as I've looked into protecting it. Basically, I've been working on the defenses of Emerilia as well as tools that will allow us to strike out at them," Dave said.

"What's your plan?" Dwayne's playful tone from just a few minutes ago was gone. Instead, they were seeing the side of Dwayne that had been hardened in the flames of war and asked to go back into it time and time again.

"Plan? I don't have one for what the hell we're going to do, though, I do have resources and tech that we can use that will allow us an advantage," Dave said.

"What is the point of bringing this to us?" Josh asked.

"For a couple of reasons. One, because if you know now, then you can plan for what is going to come. Also, you can start to understand that while you like POEs, that they truly are real," Dave said.

"Deia, you're really pregnant?" Cassie asked suddenly, cutting off Dave.

"Yes." Deia smiled and rested her hand on her large belly as she looked from Cassie to Dave. The two of them smiled at each other before Dave looked back to Josh.

"Also, it can give you a kick in the pants to push everyone forward. The event has been a great motivator for people. Having this nestled in the back of your mind, how hard are you going to push people to train and do better?" Dave asked.

Silence filled the room.

"Okay, so what resources do we have?" Dwayne asked again.

"Showing is better than telling." Dave looked upward. "Shard, could you cover for us?"

"Anti-detection protocols in effect," Shard said in a serious tone from above.

"You might want to stand," Dave said.

"What's going on?" Josh asked.

"Trust me." Dave smiled.

Josh sighed. "You and your bloody riddles." Even as he complained, he stood up from his chair and everyone else followed suit.

Orbs appeared around Dave, flashing out in eight different directions. A spell formation flashed between the orbs as Dave closed his eyes. With a surge of power, they disappeared from the conference room. In their absence, Shard started running a program that he, Dave, Malsour, Bob, and Steve had come up with to fool any possible sensors the Jukal were using to get inside Terra.

Already the city was covered in complicated sensor- and transmission-killing runes, but Dave was an overly cautious man and he had only become more paranoid with the Jukal.

They appeared within the secret laboratory's gravitational and teleport room. The runes on Dave's orbs dimmed as the spell formation between them collapsed. They returned to their master and disappeared.

"This is where we've been working on our different projects, though I think you'll be more interested in seeing the main yard." Dave checked the different settings on the command console to the side of the room.

"You mastered teleportation magic?" Anna asked.

"Well, kind of." Dave waved his hand side to side.

"When moving a lot of people, he still needs a grounding point to go to and from. This is his own custom one. Only he and Bob can teleport to here; anyone else would find themselves stuck in the ground around us," Malsour said.

"Looks like Kol is already down there." Dave pressed a command. The room lit up with power, and the runes lit up in sequence before a portal appeared within the middle of the room.

On the other side, there were carts waiting.

Dave stepped through; the others followed, finding themselves in a large hallway. After everyone had come through, the portal closed.

"Welcome to Facility One, or as I like to call it, Black Hole," Dave said.

Around him, lights all started to come online, showing a massive hallway. Automated carts moved up and down it with storage chests in their beds.

"That doesn't sound ominous at all," Dwayne commented as Dave sat on the cart and waved for the others to join him.

"Well, I needed some way to refer to it if we're talking about it somewhere less secure. In here, the runes and coding have the same strength as the ones in the lab," Dave said as everyone got on the waiting carts and they took off.

"How large is this place?" Josh asked in wonder.

"About ten times the size of the current Terra," Dave said.

"How the hell did you make it?" Lucy asked. It was also her first time finding out about this place.

"Well, after building the miner drill factory, I made a few extra, provided them with materials and power, then sent them on their way. I supplied the place with power through the teleportation array that we just came through, as well as materials that I gained from Bob. I got the first bay cut out and started up a refinery in the belly of the first Ark prototype. Then I had the repair bots work on making fusion reactors. After that, this place became pretty much self-sufficient."

Behind them, the teleportation array flashed as automated carts of materials came through the portal.

"Where are those materials coming from?" Lucy asked.

"Well, I think that should be the first shipment of parts from Frenik," Dave said.

"For what?" Dwayne asked.

"Not one for surprises, are you?" Dave grinned. "Frenik has been making the components we'll need for the missile systems that are in bay three. He is also working on items called Band-Aids. Essentially these are devices that strengthen a person's aura so that the Jukal kill switch won't work. However, they aren't a permanent solution. We're hoping that with the Band-Aids we can get enough information on the kill switches so that we can come up with a way to destroy or remove them. He's also making components for the varying systems that are part of the Arks. The Arks are space-based warships, or at least they will be if I can get all of the small issues dealt with." Dave frowned.

"You're building missiles and warships?" Josh asked, a little shocked by everything.

"Yep, missiles to take out the orbitals and anything else that tries to hit us from the skies. Then warships so that we can take the fight to whoever wants to screw with us," Dave said.

"However, right now, the fighters and warships aren't much more than shells. As Dave said, their main systems aren't all ready so we're waiting for other people to solve the issues that we've found with them," Malsour said.

"How?" Kim asked.

"Mirror of Communication coding school, through the smithies, the factories, the Dwarven Master Smiths. I had Shard and Steve break up the different components and systems we would need, based off the information Anna, Bob, and Jeeves have on the ships that make up the Jukal fleets and the Human warships of the past," Dave said.

"As you said, it's been centuries since the Jukal fought humanity. How is using the old Human warship designs going to help us?" Dwayne asked.

"The Jukal aren't all that inventive. They have a craftsman economy. They make things to last, not to be innovative. They've only integrated a few things into their ships. Updating their ships would mean that they would have to completely change the design from the ground up and ships can take from five to fifty years to complete. Most of the ships that are flying right now have been around for centuries, only getting slight changes to their build and infrastructure every few decades," Anna said.

"Who is this Jeeves?" Kim asked.

"I am Jeeves, Lo'kal's personal AI, adapted for use to assist the Dwarven Master Smiths. My current personality module that you are now conversing with is a split off of my main system. This has been done to maintain security of this site," a monotone voice said from around them.

"Damn, so you've got an AI down here?" Suzy shook her head.

"Jeeves runs the entire place, making sure that everything runs while I'm not here. It's best if he does it as there's less people to find out what's going on," Dave said.

They came to a stop outside a doorway marked A-3. Lights turned on as Dave stepped off of the cart and onto a catwalk beyond the doorway. The catwalk circled the entire massive area. Below it lay all manner of machines working away. It was a massive assembly line.

Thin metal shells moved along belts as sheets covered in runed magical coding were slotted in, as well as soul gems. There were three main sections: the body, tail fins, and nose cone.

"Meet our surface-to-space missiles." Dave waved to the munitions factory.

"We reverse engineered the seeking systems from the Human and Jukal systems. The main body contains the soul gem, which acts as a power source and the payload. Basically, we took the same system that the Devil's Crater aerial flyers have on their chest. Though in this case instead of just making Mana bombs, all of the power that is stored within the soul gem on impact will be instantaneously converted into rampant Mana. As for the engine—well, Dave came up with that," Steve said.

"I came up with the idea and put together the theories behind it," Dave said.

"They're basically gravitational engines—one hell of a lot of thrust, really fast. Anyway, we took that information, processed it through a few hundred thousand simulations to find out the best models and we got these." Steve waved at the end of the line, where the one-and-a-half-meter-long missiles were being stored in racks before being placed into storage crates on the back of an automated cart.

"If someone was to have a shield that was tuned to any of the Affinities, these would work against it," Malsour said.

"Over here, we have bay A-2, which is where we're carving out the basics of the fighters." Dave walked along the catwalk through another door.

"While we have an idea of what they will become, everything is conjecture. We've put a halt to this program, focusing on the ships instead," Malsour said.

"It's much easier to work on something that's larger than something small and miniaturized like these fighters," Steve said.

"So, what are we going to use to fight them in space other than the missiles?" Josh asked.

"Well, that's where A-1 comes in." Dave walked out to the corridor again and jumped on the carts that had been following them.

"What's in bay A-1?" Induca asked.

"The Ark. It can use the missiles you just saw. It also has the strongest Mana barrier and shields that we've ever made. Seven different fusion reactors to keep it producing energy and Mana constantly. Dwarven artillery pieces are built into the hull as secondary weapons, though these have been modified to use grand working rounds."

"Grand working rounds—like those grand workings that Esamael's people were using?" Dwayne asked.

"One and the same. We simplified it a little bit. We created a magical coding matrix, grew a soul gem around it and powered it up. We took the Dwarven artillery piece, coded it so that it could dissipate the heat build-up better, and now it can fire nearly three rounds per second on target. And with the grand working round, it doesn't need to wait for a soul gem to charge it up—the power will be right there, ready to be used." Steve grinned.

"Right now, it's in its first stages," Dave said as the carts turned to enter bay A-1. Inside, the lights were all on, showing off the warships berthed there. "As you can see, its exterior was cut out from rock. The interior is a complete soul gem construct; eventually it will eat up the stone that makes up the basic hull and also turn it into a soul gem construct. It will have everything encoded into the soul gem, from shields to control runes for the weapons. They'll be sectioned off to do different things, but even if this thing gets badly wounded then the fusion plants can fuel the soul gems and make them regrow the armored plating that will cover it. That's actually how the ship will be armored. It will grow it itself." Dave smiled.

"So it's going to be a soul gem created ship." Anna looked down on the warship as they floated over to the two-story office that overlooked the ship. The carts used air runes to move across the space.

"Exactly. It will be able to store twenty times the power that Terra can; it will generate three times the power of our power station and it will be fast. We used same coded gravity drives that we made for the missiles and we are working on teleportation coding. As long as there is a point to go to, we can teleport to it. Though doing it blind wouldn't be the best bet seeing as we could accidentally teleport inside a planet, take a chunk out of it and kill ourselves in the process." Dave shrugged.

They came to a stop at the office. Kol stood there, waiting for them.

"Dave, I knew that you would do great things, but this—I never thought that you'd come up with this." Kol waved at the warship.

"It was a combined effort. Why do you think I have you handing out so many projects to all of the Dwarven smiths?" Dave laughed.

Kol rolled his eyes as they fell on Gurren. "You okay there, lad?" Kol asked, his worry clear.

"I'm fine, Gramps," Gurren said with a smile, waving away his worry.

Kol's hand landed on Gurren, squeezing him a bit. "Good to have you back."

Gurren smiled at his grandfather as everyone spread out in the office, looking at the warship.

"So, you built a warship." Cassie looked at it beyond the glass windows.

"I knew that you weren't just playing around in your workshop all the time," Deia said, standing next to Dave.

He kissed the top of her head and his arm circled around her back.

"We kind of built a warship," Malsour said.

Kol snorted in the background and shook his head. The others averted their eyes to look at the ships.

"Sure, it looks mighty impressive—the defensive coding is some of the best and the weapons work, as well as the drive. Though there's a lot more needed on a space-going vessel. Right now we don't have any way to compensate for the higher gravitational forces that we'll be put under when using the ship," Malsour said.

"It's about forty percent done from a planning point of view," Steve said. "As for not turning into mush when flying the thing. That, well, that's a problem. Though we have an idea of how to fix it. Jeeves and I are both running computer cycles to figure out how to have the gravity code move us forward, while having another gravity spell on the inside of the ship, making sure that everyone isn't being thrown about. So, yes, it looks damn amazing, but its systems aren't complete. We can get the shell ready and together in a month or two but we're going to have to go back and insert new coding into the soul gem construct."

"To think that you were building all of this right under our noses." Josh let out a short laugh.

"Well, you didn't know about everything else that was going on," Dave said.

Silence descended on the room. Kol, Steve, Malsour, and Dave looked to one another, the others in their own thoughts as they looked on the warship or thought on what they had learned in the past couple of hours.

Dave was nervous. The more people who knew, the more people who could give away their secret. He trusted these people but there was always a faint chance. If they were to win they needed to trust one another, but they couldn't let the secret out before it was needed.

"So, how the hell are we going to get the ships out of here? Teleport them?" Dwayne asked.

"Uh, well, we have a solution, but it's kind of ambitious," Dave said.

The people in the room focused on him.

"As you may or may not know, we have created something called a summoning hall. It will allow you to gain a soul-bound companion that you can select, for a soul gem cost. What we haven't said is that the *realm* that these creatures come from is actually a holding center within one of the moons. With the three moons, two of them are being used by the Jukal. The summoning hall is meant to mimic what a summoner does and connect to these realms, basically open a one-way portal to pull creatures from this storage facility to Emerilia. What I want to do is open a way to enter this facility. Once we can, then we can start building a teleport array there to start work there," Dave said.

Everyone looked at him.

"Seems that not even we have the full picture," Malsour said dryly, looking to Steve.

"Well, I wanted to see if it worked in the first place. Now that Ela-Dorn has done it with the one that she has made, we can be sure that the security on this facility is not that strong or else the Jukal would have reacted.

"The facility really is meant as a storage area, much as with the facilities in the north and south pole where Players are made—they create varying creatures then hold them in different areas that the summoners lock onto when they do their rituals," Dave said.

"What? Players are made?" Josh asked.

Dave's face turned grave with Josh's words. He opened his interface and his secret files that he only opened when he had cut his Jukal link. Although the Jukal saw what he saw, they weren't able to directly hack his interface to read all of his saved files.

Dave pulled up a video of when Bob had taken him into the Player storage facility and sent it to everyone.

They watched it. Some covered their mouths in horror. Others' faces became darker in anger. Others seemed in disbelief.

"What you're watching is the inside of one of the Player creation facilities in the north of Emerilia. Under the massive ice caps, there are facilities in the north and south that create Players. During the years when they're being matured for Emerilia, they're held in these places. It's more cost effective to hold us in this state than to give us bodies. It's only when we first play Emerilia that we're able to gain our true bodies, complete with Jukal link watching through our eyes and a kill switch in our bodies," Dave said in a cold tone.

"Is there anything that we can do?" Kim's voice was hollow.

"We've got Shard, Jeeves, and Steve all working on trying to take whatever information we have on the Altar of Rebirths, so that we can create bodies for everyone who is stored in the facilities. Though it's hard. The Jukal's protocols that look after the portals are weaker than with the Altar of Rebirths. Each altar has an AI watching over it, with enough alarms and tripwires that the Jukal would know if you're doing anything but casually glancing over an altar." Dave shook his head.

"Why can't we just use the altars?" Lucy asked.

Dave pursed his lips together to retort but instead frowned, looking to Malsour, Steve, and Kol.

"We might be able to save a bunch that way, but they're all going to have the kill switch in them," Dave finally said.

"Give them Band-Aids as they come out?" Suzy said.

"Feasible." Malsour looked to his conspirators.

"Have to ask Bob—he'll know if he can recode it or something. Though the thing is that if we do this, then the Jukal are going to know. When we start to fight back, we need to know that we're ready," Dave said.

"To get back on track, how are we getting these ships out of here?" Dwayne asked.

"We make a connection to the summoned-creature moon. Then we create a teleport array there and start moving machines through. We stealth code it up and then we create a massive portal. We fit each of the bays here with a short-range portal. They go through here and exit right out into space. If we're fighting through the atmosphere to get into space, then the Jukal can shoot the hell out of us," Dave said.

"Well, this is a lot to take in." Josh shook his head. He was at a loss of how to express the confusion he felt.

"It is, though you need to know. The Stone Raiders are the strongest guild in all of Emerilia. We can't be fighting for just the best rewards—we need to fight to survive," Dave said.

As Dave looked at the people in the room, goose bumps formed across his scalp and neck. It was as if he were looking at a group of wolves. These intelligent hunters were focused on Dave. They had become E-heads to get away from Earth. Now, knowing that the conditions that many of them had to suffer under in order to be forced into this game world or how they were cajoled, they were annoyed. But knowing that there were others like them out there who were stuck in vats, never knowing what was real or not, lit a fire in them.

He saw their determination, their anger, and their drive in those eyes.

This group of people had changed Emerilia more than any other group in centuries. If they were to work together toward their goals, Dave didn't think that anything was impossible.

"So, we've got the tools. Now it's time we made a plan," Josh said.

Chapter 32: Prison Break

They had been able to come up with some rough plans within bay A-1's office. Though it was a rough outline, it was something. Everyone had been too disturbed from what they had learned that day to focus all their energy in planning for their future.

One thing became clear: knowing that Jung Lee was actually a person who had been captured for an unknown period of time, the decision was made to try to rescue him. To do this, Dave was going to have to go into the Six Affinity Temple and confront him himself. Once he did that, he could learn the condition of Jung Lee and figure out a way to free him.

The allure of the raid had somewhat dimmed for them all.

They organized for people to venture into the Six Affinity Temple and go no farther than the Affinity spirits.

The shades and Affinity spirits were a high enough level that everyone could gain some good experience and loot. The mobs would respawn after just forty minutes. They were weaker than the creatures that the first raid party had fought by about half, meaning that a few could fight the Affinity spirit-controlled animals.

The outpost was already expanding. Terra was a burgeoning metropolis and was set to double its size in just a month. The miners were cutting out the third section that would be added onto Terra; that would make it three kilometers long.

Instead of the mix of stone, metal, and soul gem constructs of the first section of Terra, the second and third would be largely made from soul gem constructs. Mana wells had been placed around the second section as well as a few secret fusion reactors. The rest of the power would be supplied by the large power station.

As the second section had been the test-bed for the soul gem constructs within the cylindrical city, the third section was naturally progressing a lot faster.

Already people were asking about rent and lease rates. People knew that the event coming along would be no simple affair. The biggest merchant houses and nobles were trying to get their place within the safe haven that was Terra.

Lucy was very careful in how she accepted people for the city. She didn't want it to be a bunch of nobles looking out for themselves but rather those interested in Terra and the people there. Her networks were being stretched to their limit as they sifted through applications.

However, all of that was far away for Dave, who sat with Lox, Gurren, Steve, Malsour, and Induca.

"Okay, so I'm going to need to teleport in to get to Jung Lee. I don't want to give away that I have this ability, so we're going to need to put up some kind of interference so that the Jukal don't notice me. Also going to need to be close so that I can use my Touch of the Land to get in there and not appear in the ground," Dave said.

"I have an idea for creating interference. I'll need a bit of time to work on it," Malsour said.

"Once I'm in there, we need to get a recording of Jung Lee to see just what the hell is going on with him," Dave continued.

"I can draft up a coded sensor box that uses all manner of different sensing skills like I do," Steve said.

"Once that's done, we can pull back, see what the hell's going on with him and then try to figure out a plan to help him out," Dave said.

"Let us know how we can help and we'll be there," Kol said. Gurren and Induca nodded.

"Well, I do have something I'm working on that I need your opinion on." Dave smiled.

Steve chuckled while Malsour wore a knowing grin.

"I'll get started on the interference devices," Malsour said.

"Same," Steve said. The two of them moved to different workstations as Dave waved for Induca, Gurren, and Lox to follow him.

He took them into a room with all manner of different parts lined up in different spots. To one side there were two large humanoid-looking creatures. They were made from black armor, with their faces angled forward.

"Trying to make another Steve?" Gurren looked at the ten-foot-tall black creations.

"Not quite," Dave said. There were missing parts within the armor and it was clear that they weren't yet complete. "This is the Devastator armor. It's meant for melee type fighters. It can greatly increase one's melee abilities," Dave said proudly as he knocked on one of the armored suit's legs.

"Dave, you do know that there ain't no room in the thing for someone to fit into it?" Lox said dryly.

"I know. The user is actually held within a spatial dimension. When you're in there, every action you make, the armor follows. To you, it won't feel like you're wearing armor, but that you've just got a bit bigger and a whole lot stronger," Dave said.

Gurren whistled and circled the armor as he inspected it closely.

"Now, the Devastator armor is not just a straight boost. The stronger its user, the stronger it will become. Just linking all the different components from the Dwarven Master Smiths was a fucking pain in the ass." Dave laughed and leaned against the wall.

Induca smiled as Gurren and Lox admired the massive suits of armor.

"Now, all I need is for you two to decide if you want any extras," Dave said.

Gurren and Lox's actions stopped as if time had broken. Slowly they looked toward Dave.

After a few moments, Dave and Induca burst out laughing at their shocked faces and slack jaws.

"Ah shit! Dammit, Malsour, I owe you ten gold," Steve complained, leaving the doorway where he'd been hiding.

"Told you they wouldn't know what to say." Malsour's voice drifted through the laboratory.

Lox and Gurren quickly recovered.

"These are for us?" Gurren asked quickly.

"Yes. There are a few bits and pieces I'm waiting for someone to figure out for me to complete this, but I can change things to a certain degree so that they're better suited for you. Once I have all of the parts together and your changes, I'll forge all of these parts together and infuse my Willpower into them to create my first true Weapons of Power." Dave smiled.

Lox and Gurren's faces took on a pale color as they looked from Dave to the armor.

Weapons of Power were only made by Dwarven Master Smiths and even then, they didn't make too many. These weapons could be called their life's work. Each of them would take a part of their Willpower, making them stronger while also guaranteeing that the weapon's strength wouldn't be used by anyone with intentions that went against the creator's moral code.

To Dwarves, Weapons of Power were holy relics. For Dave to be gifting them both Weapons of Power was an incredible gift.

Then, like a dam had broken, the two of them started to ask questions and talked over each other in a fervor.

***

Malsour wiped sweat from his brow as he looked at the two dozen massive needles that he had spent the last two days working on.

He stored them in his spatial ring before he kicked the base of Dave's foot. He had fallen asleep on top of his workspace. He hadn't slept since they left Devil's Crater for the Six Affinity Temple.

With Malsour's kick, he woke up immediately. He'd been working on the different things that Gurren and Lox had asked for.

The two Dwarves, after giving their suggestions and talking to Dave for hours, had then returned to the Six Affinity Temple. If the armor increased their own abilities, then they were going to get in on as many raids as possible to clear out the first layers of the temple's defenses.

Induca had gone to find Suzy.

Dave looked at Malsour with blurry eyes.

"They're done." Malsour tapped his ring.

"Steve!" Dave yelled, getting up and stretching, cracking his back as he did so.

"Box is done!" Steve yelled from his private lab.

"You stroke it more than once and you're playing!" Dave yelled before he turned to Malsour. "I wonder what he's working on in there."

"You and me both. That said, I don't think he keeps the biggest secrets around here." Malsour looked to Dave.

"What? I didn't know that half of my plans were going to work out. Thought it was best to keep them a bit close to the chest in case they didn't really work out," Dave complained.

"It definitely wasn't because you wanted to seem like some evil overlord with a secret hidden base," Malsour said.

Dave let out a dry laugh and scratched his head awkwardly. "Well, I guess that we should be going."

Steve appeared from his lab, opening and closing the door so that no one could see what was going on within.

"Not even Dragons keep as many secrets as you lot," Malsour chided.

***

Dave stepped out of the ono and into the outpost located outside of the Six Affinity Temple.

Lox, Gurren, and Induca had met up with them within the outpost. Suzy was dealing with managing all of Grahslagg Corporation while Deia and Anna were off training the Devil's Crater Army within Devil's Crater once again.

They attracted a few people's stares as they moved out of the outpost.

Focusing on his Touch of the Land spell, Dave took a few moments to check that the area within the Six Affinity Temple was clear before he looked to everyone in the party. They nodded and spread out, using their movement abilities as they took off, surrounding the earth dome that covered the Six Affinity Temple.

They pulled out the meter-long spikes that Malsour had made and stabbed them into the ground at different markers Dave had put down.

They met up on top of the dome. Malsour activated a runed disk; the different spikes lit up as their runes activated.

"The field's active. For a few minutes, no one will be able to see us," Malsour said.

Dave pulled out a large box with a strap on it and pressed a button on the front of it. "See you in a bit." Dave closed his eyes, focusing his Touch of the Land once again. He could sense everything within the Six Affinity Temple.

He disappeared from on top of the dome.

***

Jung Lee felt his perception dim slightly. He had been watching the different groups coming into the earthen dome, attacking the lowest creatures for loot and then retreating after they reached the Affinity spirit-controlled animals.

He frowned, remembering the people who had put odd spikes around the perimeter of the earthen dome. With his senses, nothing that happened around the Six Affinity Temple escaped his notice. Although he couldn't see outside of the dome, inside he knew everything that happened.

His Intelligence was so high that his memory was almost photographic. He compared the different builds and Mana signatures of the people who had ventured to the mouth of his temple with these people who were running around. Three of them were the same!

When someone appeared in mid-air above him, he looked to where the Half-Dwarf with gray eyes and runes covering his face looked at him.

"Hello, Jung Lee." The man smiled.

"Sorry about this. When they all work together, I can't control them! Dodge!" Jung Lee jumped upward. Gray wings extended from his back as his sword cut at the man, his weapon leaving a rippling gray light that howled through the sky.

The man disappeared from one spot to another.

The gray blade of force left a solid line in the temple's roof.

"So, you have all of the Affinity spirits in you?" the man asked.

"Correct!" Jung Lee flipped in the air as he punched out with his sword. A vortex of gray energy in the shape of a drill lashed out at Dave.

A hole appeared in the wall behind Dave, killing a number of the different mobs standing on the stairs. Again, he disappeared and moved to another location.

"Do you know what you need to take back control?" Dave didn't sound the least perturbed as he reappeared again.

"Soul binding contract! Though I'm not strong enough to do it by myself! Cutting net!" Jung Lee called out the move that the Affinity spirits performed.

His blades slashed through the air, creating a gray net that chilled those who were watching it. As if a cold knife had been unsheathed in the middle of a fight.

Dave again changed positions.

The net hit the floor, cutting it, creating perfect squares where the sections of the net had hit.

"How do you weaken them?" Dave asked.

"Need someone to help suppress the other Affinities one by one for me to take control," Jung Lee said through gritted teeth. Finding a way to limit the strength of the Free Affinity spirits would be incredibly difficult. Although someone might be able to suppress five of the spirits, through their actions they would increase the power of the Affinity spirit that they resonated with.

Pressure pulled at Jung Lee, as if it were pulling him apart. His wings changed into a rainbow of colors as vibrant Mana lashed out of his body.

Orbs appeared around Jung Lee.

"Sorry about this—bit of a pain in the ass fighting all over the place. My name's Dave." Dave smiled.

Jung Lee looked at the orbs out of the corner of his eyes. A smile appeared on his face, his hope like an inferno within him.

"My friends and I are working on a way to free you and let you regain control. It's going to be a bit hard, but we're not ones to do the easy thing. It will take us some time but we should be able to help you," Dave said.

Jung Lee grunted, the forces pulling at him too strong for him to fight.

"Good. You're strong as hell. Nearly out of power on my prison. Well, I'll be seeing you soon, hopefully. If you find yourself somewhere strange, don't worry about it," Dave said.

With that, he disappeared from Jung Lee's vision and the orbs around Jung Lee disappeared with him.

Now that there was no threat in the area, the Free Affinity spirits in his body once again started to fight one another and Jung Lee as they forced him to walk back to his chair.

However, they found that Jung Lee's crumbling resolve was suddenly much stronger, not letting in anything.

***

"Does it seem that we're in here more often than not?" Malsour asked.

"You might be right on that one." Dave smiled to Malsour as they worked inside the teleportation array within Pandora's box.

Malsour snorted, eating his sandwich, and looked at the new addition to the room.

It looked like the skeleton of a box with pillars on every side.

"Okay, so, we've got the gravity clamps in place so that we can hold him down." Dave pointed to the large metal sections in every corner of the box. "And then we've got the magical suppressors." Dave pointed to the different pillars that rested along the faces of the box. He looked over the runes and structure. "Well, I think we're ready to give it a try."

Malsour moved to the command console at the side of the room, looking to Dave in the center. "Powering up the magical suppressors."

Dave stayed in the center of the square. Having all of the Affinities, he was the best test subject.

Runes lit up along the different supports before the pillars started to glow and rotate into position as runes activated on their surfaces.

Dave felt as if he had aged decades in just a moment. His entire body was weak as his Willpower and Mana was suppressed.

"Yeah, that sucks." Dave checked how strong his different spells were. Where he could have immersed himself in the different Man-as before, now he could only summon a wisp of it on his finger. Barely a thousandth of his power and even then, the toll from casting these spells rapidly brought him to Mana fatigue.

"Shut it down," Dave said.

Malsour cut the power. It felt as if Dave's strength flooded back into him. The difference was heaven and earth.

"So?" Malsour asked.

"Yeah, it's really damn effective," Dave said, happy to have his power back. As he closed his fist, gray smoke appeared around it for a few seconds.

"Okay, so Suzy has that soul binding contract that will allow Jung Lee to control the Free Affinity spirits," Malsour said.

"I think we're almost ready to free him," Dave said.

"Never thought that I would be doing something like saving a man from being possessed by Free Affinity spirits." Malsour shook his head.

Dave made a noise of agreement. *What freaks me out the most is that from the quest screen, if we were to kill him, we would still win it. I don't think that there would be many or anyone else who would have thought to try to help him gain control over the spirits that are raging through his body.*

It was an outrageous plan. Most people would go for the easiest solution; what Dave and Malsour had created circumvented having to eliminate Jung Lee. It came with a lot more risk, but the rewards could be imagined.

"Okay, one last check." Dave slapped a metal disk to his chest and stepped out of the teleport array.

"Ready?" Malsour looked at the console.

"Ready," Dave agreed.

Malsour pressed a button and the teleport array activated. Using the metal disk, the teleport array was able to lock onto Dave with ease, using it as a beacon much like the teleport pads used the drop pads in being placed.

Dave flashed into existence within the square he had been standing in moments ago.

"Okay, looks like all the preparations are complete." Dave pulled off the metal disk as the glowing runes of the teleport array faded away.

"Now we just have to hope it all goes according to plan," Malsour said.

***

Jung Lee was once again sitting in his chair. Instead of an impassive look, he had a smile on his face. His face had taken on a healthier glow, looking like a person instead of an empty husk.

The disrupting field around the earthen dome switched on again.

Jung Lee's heart beat quicker as he looked up.

"Hey, Jung Lee!" Dave's voice came through the temple. "Time we got you out of here!"

Jung Lee's body was already turning when a massive force was brought down on him. He was forced to the ground as he couldn't move.

"Sorry about that," Dave said from behind Jung Lee now.

He felt something attach to his back and then there was a flash. The weight on him disappeared for a split second before he was looking at a different floor. Beneath him there was a runed pillar.

He was suspended in mid-air but the pressure on him didn't allow him to move. Even with the great gravitational force upon his body, he felt as if he was being suppressed.

The Free Affinity spirits within him were greatly weakened, allowing his mind the kind of freedom he had not known for centuries. Where his mind had been automatically fighting off the Free spirits, it was only now that he realized what pressure he had been under every day since he had been possessed.

The gravity changed, moving his body so that he was no longer kneeling in mid-air.

He looked at the five different people in the room with him.

A High Elf held out six different contracts with runes on the back of them.

"Hello, Jung Lee. My name is Suzy. I am a summoner. I've made up these contracts so that you can gain control over the Free Affinity spirits within your body," she said without pause. "Now, the process of soul binding a creature to your command is not easy. First, you will initiate the contract. By this, I mean I will present you with these contracts. You need to agree to them. Once you do so, then the different creatures will fight you in a battle of will. With the magical suppression on you, it should be a lot easier to gain control of the different spirits within you. Once you defeat one, then the contract will be completed. You will lose part of your Willpower to bring them under your command. Then we move onto the following spirit. You should get better at suppressing them with your power, but as you will lose some Willpower each time, you're going to need to do it faster and faster as your Endurance will decrease in large fights of Willpower."

Jung Lee took all of this in. He couldn't even blink he was so suppressed.

"All right, well, let's get started." Suzy held up a contract.

Suzy had made these contracts herself; usually one could make a contract within their heart, their interface translating it into a contract for the person to accept. Here, Suzy had simplified it. She'd written up the contract so that there was no need to mess around with the details that would be held within a contract mediated by their interface.

Malsour had also worked with her to make the contract stronger. If it was agreed to, the power of the contract's seal on the creature would be many times stronger than that of a contract made through one's interface.

Jung Lee read the contract and accepted it.

Runes that had been painted onto the contract glowed, their power so great that they turned the contract to ashes.

Jung Lee fought with the first Free spirit, Light. He unleashed his pent-up anger and rage. Under this century-old anger, the Light spirit was quelled.

It didn't have the ability to even fight back.

Jung Lee took control of the creature. A golden light fell over him as his aura increased in power. The raging Free Light Affinity spirit was suppressed, turning from a raging beast into a calming and docile power.

As the glow finished, Suzy held up another contract.

As he accepted it, once again it was burnt to ashes.

He took control of the Dark Affinity spirit. It fought him like a dog unwilling to give up its meal.

Jung Lee's aura was oppressive, making the others in the room break into a cold sweat as a dark light surrounded Jung Lee for a moment.

Although the fight felt as if it had lasted minutes, it had been hours.

Everyone was tense, their weapons out and their Mana circulating in case something went wrong.

The fights started to get harder and longer. Even as Jung Lee was exhausted as he suppressed Fire and Water, he continued onward.

His drive to gain control over himself once again surpassed the limits of his Endurance.

Another contract was burnt as Jung Lee started to fight with the Free Air Affinity spirit.

The Air spirit was elusive, dodging his attempts to hold it down and overpower it with his strength. Even when he felt he had it cornered, the spirit would escape his grasp, exhausting him and his strength.

His anger ignited and new slivers of power started to fill him. He paused in shock, realizing that this power was coming from the now soul-bound creatures. Feeling their master's need, they supplied him with power. Instead of being controlled by the power, he could direct and use it.

He was shocked by it so much that the Air spirit nearly hit him with an attack that would have made the contract fail.

The other spirits defended him, beating the Air spirit back as Jung Lee pounced on it.

The Air spirit quivered, unable to stop all of the other spirits that were as strong as it, as well as Jung Lee.

Working together, the fifth spirit was contained.

The last contract was held up in front of Jung Lee; he accepted it.

The Earth spirit located in his feet trembled as it felt Jung Lee focus on it. It didn't even try to fight as it accepted the contract.

Jung Lee didn't have time to celebrate his victory as unconsciousness overtook him, a slight smile on his lips.

Chapter 33: New Partnerships

Deia, Anna, and Quindar floated in the air, watching the Devil's Crater Army. Now, the aerial and ground forces were working together in two teams to defeat one another.

Vrexu and Efri's brigades had come together after fighting side-by-side on the way to the Six Affinity Temple.

Now that they were working together, they had been able to increase how effective they were. Instead of just having the aerial fighting the ground forces, they were working together to defeat other mixed groups.

Kala, Alkao, and Malkur's forces rotated through the outpost, learning new skills from the trainers there as well as some real world experience. If they weren't at the outpost then they were providing security in Unity or the keeps.

The changes that the DCA had undergone under the three women's instruction had been incredible.

As they watched the two forces fighting in the forests to the northeast of Unity, they had somber looks.

The event was fast approaching and the DCA would be heavily involved in the fighting. Many of the people they had taught might not make it through. However, they knew that with their training, they had a much better chance than before.

They just hoped that it would be enough.

"They're much more cautious, sending out probes instead of just stand up fighting," Anna said with approval.

"It's about time that they started fighting that way. Their whole tactics are built around small groups and squads. Finding out where the enemy's supply areas are, where they're positioned and then hitting them in lightning raids—that's how they can use their skills to the max," Quindar said.

"They've certainly come a long way," Anna said.

The trio once again fell into silence. Left with their own thoughts, they looked down at the ongoing battle. Unlike the fights before, this one looked as though it wouldn't be decided in a matter of hours but a few days.

***

Sola looked at the few dozen people who stood in front of her. These people had competed within the Dwarven tournament and lost or they were people whose reputation had been so great that the Council of Anvil and Fire as well as the war council had heard of them.

They looked to Dwarven Master Smith Sola, their faces filled with respect. A number of them were of a higher level than Sola.

Though she had crafted some of the finest weapons and armor in Emerilia, a warrior knew that to keep a smith like Sola in their good graces was a smart idea. With her position, she was more powerful than most kings and queens.

They all waited as she studied each and every one of them.

"Many of you are wondering why you have been asked to come here, why you have been allowed entrance into a Dwarven mountain, and then brought into this secure location," Sola said, her words passing over all of them.

"The event Of Myths and Legends will begin shortly. This kind of event has never been seen before on Emerilia. As you know, we Dwarven Master Smiths pride ourselves on the weapons and armor that we make. None more than our Weapons of Power."

The room seemed to still. Each and every person held their breath, as if the faintest movement would break the hopes that swelled up within them.

"We have protected and held onto Weapons of Power for centuries. These items are so powerful that they would be able to topple kingdoms and allow people to fight the strongest creatures of

Emerilia. The war council, as well as the Council of Anvil and Fire, has determined that we will allow you entrance to our vaults. Weapons of Power are not like normal weapons. They hold a part of the soul of their creators. They cannot be used by just anyone, but only by someone who is compatible with the soul that is within the weapon. Binding yourself to the weapon will not only take your blood but a part of your Willpower. If you accept these terms, please step forward."

Everyone in the room took a step forward without hesitation. Their faces were grim. For the Dwarves to go this far, they were starting to realize just how different this event was going to be compared to the other events they had lived through.

Sola nodded and looked to the Dwarven guards who looked after the Weapons of Power vault.

These Level 1,500s bowed to Sola before they cut their hands and pressed them against the wall.

A shimmering light fell over them for a few moments. There was the sound of ancient gears moving and locking mechanisms releasing from the massive metal door that the two guards stood in front of.

Finally, the last lock was released. The door opened and ancient air flowed out. The warriors standing in the hall felt their hairs stand on edge as a wave of focused Mana passed outward.

Sola moved into the room and led them in.

Their breaths were fast and short as they looked over the massive vault that was filled with Weapons of Power.

There were all manner of weapons, armors, and items. Each of them gave off an ancient and powerful feeling. These were weapons that had a historied past, being held in the hands of heroes who had overturned battles. Had defeated the most powerful beasts on Emerilia.

To a warrior, this room was the Holy Grail.

"Find your calling," Sola said.

The warriors looked confused but then they started to notice that there was a pull on their souls. They followed where they were being pulled.

The Weapons of Power exerted their power, finding those who met their requirements. The warriors spread out, neither fast nor slow as they took everything in.

They touched weapons, their eyes closing as the weapon tested them. If they passed, they were able to pick up the weapon. If they didn't, they frowned and moved on, another Weapon of Power calling them.

Some received the first weapon that called to them. Others took a half-dozen tries.

Sola watched them in silence. Across Emerilia, other vaults were being opened as warriors were allowed in to once again take up these Weapons of Power. She took a shaky breath, smiling as she looked at the room. She looked upon her own Weapons of Power that were stored within.

The Dwarves had truly opened up their holy places to outsiders. It showed not only their trust in others, but their drive to work toward a future together with their allies.

***

Dave hammered a red-hot piece of metal into position before using his smithing art. The two metals seemed to fuse together, greatly increasing their strength.

Kol passed him a blowtorch. Dave heated up another piece of metal, ready to join the new components together.

Dwarven Master Smiths glanced over in interest as their apprentices stopped their work to admire Dave's work.

In front of him, on a series of chains, was a set of Devastator armor. All of the components that Dave had fit together had been pulled out of their slots.

Knowing that it all fit together, he was now working with a blowtorch to connect each component individually. It was a complicated and a time-intensive pursuit. He had finished the legs on the armor over the space of six hours. Grime and sweat covered Dave as he put in the last component located in the legs.

He turned off the blowtorch and handed it to Kol as he sheathed his hammer.

He opened his character sheet. Now was as good a time as any to increase his stats.

Character Sheet

Name:	David Grahslagg	Gender:	Male
Level:	214	Class:	Dwarven Master Smith, Friend of the Grey God, Bleeder, Librarian, Aleph Engineer, Weapons Master, Champion Slayer, Skill Creator, Mine Manager, Master of Space and Time, Master of Gravitational Anomalies
Race:	Human/ Dwarf	Alignment:	Neutral Good
Unspent points: 100			
Health:	42,300	Regen:	22.56/s
Mana:	14,880	Regen:	52.30/s
Stamina:	4,740	Regen:	45.50/s
Vitality:	423	Endurance:	1,128
Intelligence:	1,488	Willpower:	1,046
Strength:	474	Agility:	910

After these stat points from increasing my level are gone, it's probably all going to be up to the classes I have to increase my base stats.

He'd had so many stat points saved up that now it was coming to an end, he felt a bit of nostalgia.

With a small smile, he placed twenty stat points into Agility and another forty into Willpower. He was going to need it soon enough.

He confirmed the stat placement and watched his character sheet change.

Character Sheet

Name:	David Grahslagg	Gender:	Male
Level:	226	Class:	Dwarven Master Smith, Friend of the Grey God, Bleeder, Librarian, Aleph Engineer, Weapons Master, Champion Slayer, Skill Creator, Mine Manager, Master of Space and Time, Master of Gravitational Anomalies
Race:	Human/ Dwarf	Alignment:	Neutral Good
Unspent points: 40			
Health:	42,300	Regen:	22.56/s
Mana:	14,880	Regen:	54.30/s
Stamina:	4,740	Regen:	46.50/s
Vitality:	423	Endurance:	1,128
Intelligence:	1,488	Willpower:	1,086
Strength:	474	Agility:	930

He squatted down and grabbed the legs, lifting them with a grunt. They were almost entirely metal. He put them within a massive furnace.

His own Abscondita armor glowed, dissipated the heat slightly so that he could put his hands inside the furnace.

Prepared Mithril inserts were placed within the legs. Dave used his smithing art to wrap the Mithril sheet over the components. His consciousness moved within the metal, smoothing out weaknesses in the metal and checked the components again.

Satisfied, he took the armored leg sections of steel and placed them over the Mithril layer.

He once again pulled out his hammer. The sound of hammer blows rang out as Dave formed the rough sections closer to the legs. He first made sections for the thigh and calf; he took more time with the feet sections.

Once that was completed, he turned to the hip, knee, and ankle joints.

Dave didn't notice the others watching. With his high Affinity for the different magics and his high Mana pool, the magical world seemed to bend to his will. Air was pulled in from the surrounding area, creating white streams that led into the furnace. The flames became a deeper, richer color as they moved like living snakes to heat the different areas of the armor as Dave wished.

The other Dwarven Master Smiths also stopped what they were doing to watch Dave work.

He hammered the last sections of armor into place, imbuing his body with strength-enhancing Earth magic. He turned the legs over in the furnace.

He took more prepared sections of steel armor, hammering them into shape and connecting them to the sections that covered the front of the legs. With each hammer blow, the air around the furnace was disturbed.

Every person who saw Dave's work felt their heart quiver in excitement and awe. They were all smiths of the highest caliber, but here they were reminded that there was always someone better, always a new way to push themselves. Instead of jealousy, it ignited the creative fires within those watching.

Dave roughly formed the sections to the leg. Once again, he sheathed his hammer as the air turned into a torrent and the flames poured forth with more energy.

Kol raised his hand and stepped backward, increasing the distance between him and the furnace as its heat reached crazy levels.

Dave stood in front of this raging inferno without flinching. Metal formed on his hands as he adjusted his barrier and heat dispersion of his armor.

His hands rested on both of the legs. Dave pushed out his senses into the metal. The roughly formed metal smoothed out and grew, connecting the front and back sections into solid parts.

The intricate hip, knee, and ankle joints became smoother and stronger. The metal took on a sheen as his Dark Affinity worked with his smithing art to remove weaknesses from the legs.

Dave moved through section by section, checking the most minute details. Pleased with what he had found, a deeper, much more powerful strength seemed to pass from Dave to the armor.

People took in a sharp breath. The Dwarven Master Smiths' eyes shined as they noticed the signs of a person making a Weapon of Power.

Those who weren't Dwarven Master Smiths didn't know all that was going on, but through the reactions of the Master Smiths they could make conclusions.

Dave opened up his eyes, his breathing a bit faster as he looked extremely tired.

He picked up the legs. The furnace calmed down as Dave hauled them out of the furnace. With his magic, he cooled the legs as he carried them to the rack he had in the side of his workshop.

He put the legs down and looked at them for a moment. The black steel legs seemed to exude power. Dave wiped the sweat from his forehead. Grabbing a waterskin, he drank deeply.

He pulled out a Mana and Stamina potion. Energy once again filled him as his eyes moved from the legs to the chest section.

Dave put the potion bottles and waterskin away. "Okay, chest section next."

Kol passed him a component from those lined up on the side of the rack and the magical blowtorch.

Dave gave him a nod of thanks and used the blowtorch on the armor shell and the component. He passed it back and unhooked his hammer. Once again, the sounds of metal being beaten into submission rang out in the workshop. After the hammer hits stopped, Dave closed his eyes, his smithing art once again fusing the components further to the armor.

The more he did with his hammer, the less he had to do with his Willpower and Intelligence intensive soul smith smithing art.

Piece by piece, the different coded components were added into the chest cavity.

The outside world bore no interest to Dave as he threw himself into his work. He only stopped to eat, drink, and use the restroom. With his high Endurance, he was able to stay awake for four days as he worked unceasingly.

Through the night, if someone were to go near the smithy, they would hear a hammer ringing out in the darkness.

Kol stayed with Dave, making sure that he looked after himself while also supplying him with materials and aid.

On the morning of the fifth day, the entire upper floor of the smithy was silent as everyone stood around Dave's workshop, watching.

He had commanded the soul gem furnace to grow just to fit his project.

In the furnace laid a ten-foot-tall set of black armor.

Even as the flames danced over it, its sharp angles seemed to reflect the flames' light. There were no seams on the outside except for where the joints lay. Even these joints were thick and strong, with protective armored caps.

Dave used his gravity manipulation to move the head into place while his hands were on the armor's chest. With his soul smithing, he easily made the final connections between the head and the rest of the armor.

With the final piece connected, the armor seemed to thrum with energy.

Once again, the dense energy of Dave's soul was released. This time, instead of returning to Dave, it seemed to link the other energies that Dave had deposited into the different sections.

The armor seemed to exude an aura of power and strength, marking it as a Weapon of Power. No other weapons would give off such an aura.

Dave used his gravity magic to pull the armor out, the furnace's flames returning to normal.

Heat shimmered off the armor but it didn't even show a red spot. It was as hot as a normal furnace.

Dave quickly used his abilities with fire to pull the heat from the armor while still retaining the strength of the armor. Dave locked it into the rack it had been assembled on part by part for four days.

Everyone looked at the armor with respect in their eyes.

"Well, I think I need a shower before I work on the next one." Dave looked haggard.

"You and me both." Kol coughed slightly.

They were covered in a layer of black soot. They looked like a mess, with only their eyes seeming to glow within their dirty appearance.

***

The fifth day after Jung Lee had been teleported into the laboratory, he woke up. He found that his magic was greatly suppressed still, but the gravity that kept him locked in place had been removed.

He was still within the odd box with glowing runes and pillars along each face.

Though he was no longer in the teleportation array.

His senses sunk within him as he searched out for the Free Affinity spirits.

Instead of raging through his body, they seemed to be waiting, like guard dogs. They preened under his attention, acting like soft puppies, but Jung Lee felt the power behind them. Their force ready to be used against anyone who attacked their master.

Jung Lee was stunned. For centuries, he had fought these Affinities, but now they waited for his command, eager to work for him. Jung Lee felt his strength was much greater than it had ever been. He opened and closed his hand before forming a fist. Silent tears fell down his face. He was free!

A door into the cell opened. He used his analysis skill. The man was called Malsour.

"Looks like you got those spirits under control. If you'd like, I can turn off the suppressors. I've never heard of someone with tamed Free Affinity spirits within their body but I think you'll feel one hell of a lot stronger once I remove the restraints. Might be best to take things slow and get used to them." Malsour smiled.

"Thank you." Jung Lee rotated on the floor, kowtowing to Malsour.

"Don't worry about it," Malsour said, quickly trying to diffuse Jung Lee's thanks.

Jung Lee looked up at Malsour with tears in his eyes and a smile that lit up the room.

Malsour coughed slightly; the pure and open emotions on Jung Lee's face made his heart twist for the man in front of him. He gave Jung Lee a smile and then cancelled the magical suppression field.

Jung Lee let out a sigh. Immediately the room was filled with a powerful and dominating aura.

Malsour had a stunned look on his face. He had only felt a similar aura in strength from his mother Denur.

If Jung Lee had wished him ill will, he could have easily stunned him with his aura. Instead, Malsour felt the genuine thanks and relief within the aura, making his body relax as he took a deep breath.

Six colored orbs rotated around Jung Lee. They became bigger and bigger, spreading out until they were in a circle around Jung Lee. In a flash, they stopped moving and transformed into the six Affinity spirits.

These eight-foot-tall creatures made from pure energy kneeled as they faced Jung Lee, as if warriors waiting for their commander's orders. Ready to carry out whatever he asked.

"You're able to make the spirits materialize outside of your body?" Malsour murmured to himself.

"It does seem so." Jung Lee stood slowly. Every motion he took seemed to be pre-planned, as if making the most of every single motion.

For a man who had not been able to move except to fight those that made it into his vicinity, regaining the ability to move freely was a luxury all in itself.

His movements also showed the strength that lay within him. As if he were a tiger, constantly stalking his prey.

The Affinities turned to streaks of light and entered Jung Lee once again. He called out flames, streams of water, enhanced his body with Earth and Dark Affinity magics. Each and every spell was simple as it was powerful. None of the Mana leaked out, neither raising the temperature of the room, nor its humidity.

Every spell was completely contained to the point that although Malsour could feel they were terrifyingly strong, he couldn't truly gauge the amount of Mana that was placed within each of these spells.

"I will indeed need some time to get used to these changes," Jung Lee said.

"Well, first, let's get you some food and a shower. Then we can talk about what has been happening the last couple of centuries." Malsour smiled.

"I wonder if the history books would be able to recount all that I have missed," Jung Lee said with a short laugh.

"Well, I'm actually a bit older than you and while I, too, was out of the loop for quite a while, I was able to figure out most of what happened in the time we were locked away." Malsour smiled.

Jung Lee was a powerful force, but with his mannerisms and actions, Malsour trusted him. He didn't want to have to lie to the man as soon as he had regained his freedom. Doing that would only make the path toward friendship that much harder.

"Oh, you are also another ancient person?" Jung Lee looked at Malsour closely.

"You could say that." Malsour's eyes changed to have slits within them as his arm extended into a scaled claw.

Jung Lee's eyes went wide. "You're a Dragon?"

"Your observation skills are pretty impressive." Malsour laughed. Few knew that Dragons could take on Human appearance. Even seeing different limbs that belonged on a Dragon, most people couldn't put it together. Yet, Jung Lee had been able to do it within moments.

"I sense you are of the Dark Affinity. Malsour, you are one of the first born Dragons," Jung Lee said, piecing together what he knew with what he remembered from lifetimes ago.

"At your service." Malsour smiled and gave a small bow.

"It seems that Emerilia has become a much more interesting place while I have been gone," Jung Lee said with a sad smile.

Malsour smiled back. Jung Lee had been a Human; with the Affinity spirits, his life had been greatly extended. Nearly everyone and everything that he remembered had been destroyed or changed with the passage of time. Dwarves and elves back then had been very insular, so it would be rare for him to know anyone in those groups who were still living.

Malsour guided him out of the room and into the lab as the two of them talked. Malsour gave a quick history of Emerilia, as well as informing him about the Jukal. Jung Lee asked pointed questions. It went on for some time as Jung Lee took it all in.

"And so now the Jukal are starting up that event in a few more weeks. When they do, all the creatures from the past that were sealed away will once again be unleashed onto Emerilia," Malsour finished.

Jung Lee sat back in his seat, the tips of his fingers pressed together. "Much has changed since I've been gone," Jung Lee said, a sad light to his eye but also understanding. "I thank you for all that you have done. I still do not understand this new world much but I have always been one to enjoy an adventure." Jung Lee's eyes crinkled as he smiled.

"Well, instead of sitting down here like a bunch of old fossils, let's go and get some food and I can show you Terra," Malsour said.

"Food." Jung's stomach shifted. He had not needed to eat as the Affinity spirits had kept his body alive. That was not to say that he did not desire food.

"Lead on, please." Jung smiled.

"Certainly. Do you have any dishes you would be interested in?" Malsour stood and guided Jung Lee out of the lab as a screen appeared.

***

Quest Completed: Possessed by Spirits

You have released Jung Lee from his prison and assisted him in regaining control over his body by suppressing the Free Affinity Spirits within his body.

Rewards:

Gained 5 stat points to use at your discretion

Gained Jung Lee's friendship

3,000,000 EXP

You Have Created a Weapon of Power

You have unleashed a weapon that can change fates and alter the path of Emerilia's future.

Quest: Dwarven Master Smith Level 5

You have created a weapon of greater quality than the quest, completing this class quest.

Rewards: Unlock Level 6 quest

+10 to all stats (stacks with previous class rewards)

500,000 Experience

Quest: Dwarven Master Smith Level 6

You have created a weapon of greater quality than the quest, completing this class quest.

Rewards: Unlock Level 7 quest

+10 to all stats (stacks with previous class rewards)

600,000 Experience

Quest: Dwarven Master Smith Level 7

You have created a weapon of greater quality than the quest, completing this class quest.

Rewards: Unlock Level 8 quest

+10 to all stats (stacks with previous class rewards)

700,000 Experience

Quest: Dwarven Master Smith Level 8

You must craft 3 Weapons of Power, 20 weapons of SS quality, or 150 of S Quality with your Smithing Art (Currently 2/3, 0/20, 0/150)

Rewards: Unlock Level 9 quest

Increase to stats

Class: Dwarven Master Smith

Status: Level 7

Effects:
Allowed access to all Dwarven Mountains and smithies.
Allowed to take on smithing apprentices.
+70 to all stats
Access to special quests.

Level 236

You have reached Level 237; you have **55** stat points to use.

Dave sighed. After saving up his stats for so long, naturally raising his different abilities, he was coming to the end of the large reserve that he'd built up.

Dave smiled, thinking on those first days when he'd been tempted to raise his stats immediately. It had been frustrating to see all of those stat points yet not dare to place them within his stats as he played the long-term game.

It had paid off, allowing his level to not reflect his actual ability. He had gained a good number of classes, many more than most had.

After these stat points were gone, it would be incredibly hard for him to gain levels. Already it took nearly two million experience for him to gain a level.

He would have to rely on his classes to boost his abilities and his own machinations and creations that would allow him to compete with those stronger than him and suppress those weaker.

Dave grinned to himself as he once again added stat points to his character sheet.

He placed twenty into Intelligence and eight stat points into all of the other attributes. He didn't know when he'd be able to put more stat points into his character sheet.

He smiled and looked at his character sheet.

Character Sheet

Name:	David Grahslagg	Gender:	Male
Level:	237	Class:	Dwarven Master Smith, Friend of the Grey God, Bleeder, Librarian, Aleph Engineer, Weapons Master, Champion Slayer, Skill Creator, Mine Manager, Master of Space and Time, Master of Gravitational Anomalies
Race:	Human/ Dwarf	Alignment:	Chaotic Neutral

Unspent points-0

Health:	46,100	Regen:	23.32/s
Mana:	15,380	Regen:	56.20/s
Stamina:	5,120	Regen:	48.40/s
Vitality:	461	Endurance:	1,166
Intelligence:	1,538	Willpower:	1,124
Strength:	512	Agility:	968

For a while, Dave looked at his character sheet before he rose from his bed and dismissed the screen.

"Damn, so only need to make one more Weapon of Power and I'll get another class increase—easy." Dave rolled his eyes, his fatigue from earlier falling away. Distributing the stats and not just dumping them all into his attributes made him feel full of energy, but not that god-like state that he'd had when dumping stat points into his character sheet.

He used his hot bar; clothes appeared on him as his hand rested on the hammer in his belt. "Lox's set is complete. Now it's time to finish Gurren's," he said to himself, a determined fire in his eyes as he stepped toward the apartment door.

***

Lox, Gurren, and Steve had been fighting within the Six Affinity Temple, allowing them to get stronger. They'd received a hasty message from Kol and raced back to Terra.

Even with their bulky physiques, they quickly and easily crossed Terra, headed in a straight line for Dave's smithy. When they got to the front of the smithy, an assistant guided them to an elevator and took them up to the top floor.

What is going on? Gurren saw the Terra smithy's elite smiths had abandoned their work to look into a single workshop.

Gurren, Lox, and Steve went over. Their mouths opened in shock at what they saw within the workshop.

Dave sat back in a chair, drinking from a canteen as he panted slightly. He was covered in soot and looked as if he hadn't slept in days. Still, his eyes shined brightly as he looked at the two massive sets of armor that hung on racks in the middle of the workshop.

The metal surface was mixed ebony and steel with a titanium mesh.

Just looking at it, Lox and Gurren felt as though they had been punched in the gut.

After a few minutes, Dave looked away from the armor, his eyes falling on Gurren and Lox. "Well, you want to give them a try?"

Dave's throat was raw and his eyes red from working in front of the furnace for so long and lack of sleep.

Lox and Gurren continued to look at him blankly. The armor exuded strength and power. Demanding respect and giving rise to a sense of formidable strength from those who looked upon it.

Steve pushed the two of them, making them stumble and recover from their shock.

They looked angrily at the smiling Steve before they moved. Without being told, they stepped forward, both of them feeling an Affinity with one set of the armor more than the other.

Gurren pressed a hand on the armor. Although it looked like some ageless statue, he could feel the power within. The hairs on his neck rose as the armor moved slightly, its face looking down on him. He felt as if he were being examined by the armor.

Gurren's mind went blank. He knew that this armor was great, and he had felt an undeniable energy coming from it, but now that he was just feet away from it, his barely restrained hopes were confirmed.

It's a Weapon of Power! This thought rang through Gurren's heart.

He took a cool breath of air and looked up at the armor's faceless helmet. Being the grandson of a Dwarven Master Smith, he naturally knew that to gain the control over a Weapon of Power, he would first need to be judged by it.

As his hand touched the armor, images, memories, and thoughts seemed to roll through his mind. He closed his eyes. Faint traces of emotions whistled by. Gurren's face turned from pale fear to red anger, as well as every emotion in between.

The flashing images stopped. Gurren opened his eyes to look at the armor; he felt a thread of Mana from the armor, as if extending out a hand to finalize an agreement.

Gurren extended his own Mana toward the armor.

The link was established. The armor in front of him no longer seemed domineering, but rather relaxing to look upon.

Gurren unsheathed his sword, slightly cutting his thumb and pressing the blood against the armor.

The blood seemed to disappear as a screen appeared.

You Have Soul Bound a Weapon of Power to Yourself

Weapons of Power contain a part of the consciousness of the Smith who made it. The Weapon of Power now sees you as its master. However, if you are to carry out actions that go against the soul thread left behind by the creator, this weapon might search out a new master.

You have created a contract with: Devastator Armor

Devastator Armor

Forged by Dave Grahslagg, this item has been made for his good friend Gurren. This armor is not only meant to protect, but to strike fear into all who face it.

Quality: Weapon of Power

Abilities:

Able to cast spells/use skills with a 20% increase in ability

All Stats are increased by 5%

Grows in power through use

Can summon:

Sword

Shield

Bolt thrower

Safe Escape

Charge: 1,000,000/1,000,000

Durability: 392,158/392,158

Gurren let out a shaky breath. The work that had gone into this armor—Gurren only needed to look at Dave's smiling face.

It gave rise to a smile on Gurren's face.

Another screen filled his vision.

Devastator Armor
Would you like to enter the Devastator Armor?
Y/N
(Can change settings for entering/exiting armor within Devastator settings menu)

"Yes," Gurren said. In a flash of light, he disappeared from everyone's vision.

Gurren felt his power soar. To him, it didn't seem that he had entered the armor but had instead just grown to fit its size. The Devastator felt like a second skin.

He rose his fists and looked at them as he opened and closed his hands. Claws appeared over his hands. Gurren looked on in shock.

He noticed a new hot bar at the bottom of his screen and he activated one of the buttons. A sword as black as night appeared, with black flames covering it. With the sword, a wheel appeared in Gurren's vision. He changed the wheel; the black flames turned red and then green.

"Holy shit, it can change Affinities by itself!" Gurren said.

With another click on his interface, a bolt thrower materialized out of gray mist that surrounded his arm. Again, a color-coded Affinity wheel appeared.

Another touch and a shield appeared in his hand.

Others looked at the armor in awe. The different Master Smiths muttered to one another, an excited tone here and there.

"Dave, did you use our projects to make this armor?" Jesal stared at the armor. It was impossible for her to not notice her own creations as Gurren and Lox, lost in their own worlds, started testing out the armor.

Dave gave her a cool smile. "Well, I couldn't have coded the damn thing all by myself!" He burst into laughter.

The other Dwarves, instead of feeling sour that their work had been used to make these incredible Weapons of Power, were instead happy to have been part of the project. Their eyes were once again opened by the Dwarf Halfling Dave Grahslagg.

Chapter 34: Party Zero and the Six Affinity Temple

Deia felt awkward as Alkao gave a deep bow to Anna, Quindar, and herself.

Today, the Devil's Crater brigades had finished their training exercise against one another. The battle had been intense, both sides having to push themselves past their previous limits.

Alkao had personally overseen the battle. With his position as the leader of Devil's Crater, he didn't directly lead a brigade. Instead, he was the head of Krenua's forces.

The mysterious group who had absorbed the teachings of the various trainers were on a different level when compared to the normal soldiers of the DCA. Few were able to pass the tests to get into the Black Hands' ranks. Those who did were tenacious fighters and trainees.

"Thank you for all that you have done for my Devil's Crater Army," Alkao said, before slowly raising his body up again.

The three ladies smiled at Alkao, accepting his gracious thanks.

"We must be going. We are needed back at the Six Affinity Temple." Deia looked to Anna, who nodded.

Alkao's serious face turned into a grin. "Well, don't let me keep you. Have fun and look after yourselves."

"Thank you." Deia smiled.

"Make sure you keep up with your training. Once I come back from the temple, we'll have to see if you've been lazing around these past couple of months," Anna said.

Alkao's grin deepened into a smile. "I'll be ready for you," he declared.

"You really are an odd couple. Well, I am going to see the children and find out what my errant husband has been up to. If you ever need me, you know where to find me," Quindar said.

After they said their good-byes, they went their separate directions.

Deia left first, allowing Anna to talk to Alkao for a bit in privacy. Deia flew slowly. The baby within her stomach kicked, as if they, too, were excited for the raid on the Six Affinity Temple.

***

Suzy looked at Party Zero gathered in the outpost that faced the crack into the Six Affinity Temple.

Over the last two weeks, a great weight had been lifted from their shoulders. The secrets of the Jukal had been revealed to the leaders of the Stone Raiders. The impact of that information was still creating waves within these figures. Yet, there was still a sense of relief. They trusted the leadership of the Stone Raiders. Even with a matter as great as this.

She looked over her party. Dave and Deia were off to the side, talking to each other in light tones, their eyes clear and bright as they smiled. Dave hugged her from behind as Deia held his hands over her large stomach. They were a picture of reserved happiness.

Steve and Gurren were having an arm wrestling contest, Steve's massive metal hand clamped within Gurren's black armored hand.

Malsour maintained the table beneath them as Lox officiated the contest.

Anna and Induca stood off to the side, shaking their heads at the others' antics, clearly amused.

Suzy let out a sigh, the stresses of the last week easing away as she walked forward.

Party Zero noticed her, greeting her as Steve and Gurren continued to fight on.

"All right, it's a draw, you two metal heads!" Deia admonished, rolling her eyes at Gurren and Steve's contest.

"I'll get you next time!" Gurren said. The two of them relaxed their hands as Malsour commanded the table to once again descend into the ground.

"Come on, let's get going or else we'll miss the next raid group heading into the temple," Deia said.

Everyone checked their gear as Suzy moved with the group.

"So, looks like that armor worked out." Suzy walked next to Dave and Deia as Induca stood on her other side, her fingers entwined with hers.

Anna walked with Malsour, the two of them talking quietly.

"I don't think I ever want to get out of it," Gurren declared.

Lox chuckled, but it was clear that he agreed with Gurren. They had been the two weakest members of Party Zero, but now, with their armor, their abilities and strength made them as strong as Steve.

They moved with a new confidence, as if stepping forward into their roles fully.

"As far as I know, they haven't got out of it since they stepped into it," Dave said, a self-deprecating smile on his face.

"Well, best to get used to it—needs lots of training." Lox's hand balled into a fist.

"And the Six Affinity Temple is perfect for it!" Gurren said.

"While we are here to blow off steam, this is also a good time for us to make sure that we are all ready for the upcoming event. We haven't fought much since beating off Esamael's army—need to make sure cobwebs haven't sprouted up." Deia's tone was light, but it had the undeniable weight of a leader.

As they passed through the outpost, people made way. Quiet mutterings were issued by those who saw Party Zero.

They truly were the hidden talent within the Stone Raiders. Even their name, Party Zero, had been a joke by the Stone Raiders' guildmaster. He thought that the members of the party would wish to change the name of their party, but with time it had grown on them, becoming a phrase that garnered interested glances and praise.

The members of Party Zero weren't the strongest within Emerilia, but they had the tenacious attitude of all Stone Raiders. They wouldn't give up; no matter the obstacles in front of them, they would endure and fight onward.

"Those suits of armor are actually Weapons of Power," one person said. The others around her had wide eyes as they stared at the twin metal giants that were as large as Steve.

"Weapons of Power? Who would be able to make entire armor suits into Weapons of Power?" someone said, refusing to believe that two people had been gifted with such grand Weapons of Power.

"Dave Grahslagg himself. Heard he spent nearly two weeks straight just putting the pieces together. Getting the materials and parts made—some people said it must've taken months," the first woman said.

"It looks like Gurren and Lox are in that armor," another person said, seeing that the two Dwarves who made up the defensive melee fighters within Party Zero weren't present.

"The power of that armor..." another person said, unable to finish their sentence, disbelief in their eyes.

"I hope that someone streams the fight from within the temple," another said.

Suzy heard this all, and smiled to herself.

They reached the gate that led to the crack.

Guards opened the gate with a respectful look in their eyes.

Party Zero smiled and nodded to them, their conversations slowing down as they checked their gear and weapons were conjured or drawn. Suzy pulled out her staff as her more advanced creations appeared from the bag of holding on her hip with a wave of her hand.

Their auras started to envelop the area as excitement filled them. Today they would be able to go all out, to test their limits and prepare for the oncoming event.

The sound of fighting could be heard within the Six Affinity Temple.

The early morning light disappeared and was replaced by the glow of roots that covered the earthen dome over the Six Affinity Temple. In the large open area around the temple, multiple groups of Players and POEs were fighting the various shades. This wasn't a raid group, but rather people looking to grind out experience and decent loot to increase their levels and abilities.

Party Zero circulated their Mana, raising their Mana barriers as well as calling out faint buffs.

"Everyone knows what they're doing. Suzy, could you pull us a shade? Let's get warmed up and make sure we're good to go, then we can work to fight some harder creatures," Deia said.

Steve stood with Lox and Gurren on either side. He no longer had his bolt thrower, but a silver band around his wrist showed runes like those found in the DCA Mana bolt throwers. Lox and Gurren likewise raised their hands, similar bands on their wrists as well.

Anna and Induca rose into the air, above and back from the three tanks. They were covered in air and flames respectively.

Malsour rose on a pillar of stone next to Dave and behind the tanks.

Suzy and Deia floated back from them. Even though Deia was covered in flames, none of the heat leaked out, showing her control over her magic.

Suzy sent out an Air creation. It sent an Air blade into a nearby shade, getting its attention before leading it back to Party Zero.

"Gurren, Lox, you have this one," Deia called out.

The others waited their turn patiently, interested in seeing what the two could do with their new armor. All of them were relaxed but were ready to intervene at any moment if they were needed.

The shade's wails came closer as Lox and Gurren fired out Mana bolts. These bolts threw the shade back a few meters as the sound of rumbling thunder from the first impacts was followed up by a dozen more.

The shade didn't make it within fifteen meters of Party Zero.

"Two more please, Suzy," Deia said.

"Coming up," Suzy said. From her bag, more Air creations poured out. These raced off, attacking shades and then leading them on a chase. It would mean that they wouldn't need to wait too much time before Suzy could pull another shade to Party Zero.

Two more shades were pulled toward the party.

Lox and Gurren took one each; it took more time for them to kill the shade.

At five shades, Steve started to help out. At nine, they drew their weapons.

Shields, identical to those that the Dwarven warclans used, appeared in their hands. They looked like massive steel doors but they were used by Gurren and Lox as if they had trained with them all their lives, the weight not bearing down on them in the slightest.

Blades appeared in their hands; thick gray fog turned into swords wreathed in gray flames.

This was the seventh setting of Affinity for the weapons: a combination of them all that only Dave had been able to figure out due to his ability to manipulate all Affinities.

Steve's axe easily cleaved apart shades while Lox and Gurren's swords flashed outward, their shields appearing before the oncoming attacks. The shades' ethereal claws, which would have left deep scratches in Lox and Gurren's personal shields, left only slim white scratches.

This was the undeniable strength from a Weapon of Power!

The rest of Party Zero watched on. This was so that Lox and Gurren could get acquainted with their armor in battle. Letting them figure out how to accommodate for the Devastator armor would make them much more effective later on.

It was like a new Player figuring out the strength of a new spell or weapon.

They started to move faster and faster as the number of attackers reached up to fifteen. Still, they were able to keep off the shades.

With each blow, a shade was killed; again, they started to move faster and faster. Lox, Gurren, and Steve started to become hard to watch, their actions blurring as they moved between targets. Lox jumped up and smashed into the ground, using one of his fighting skills. He hadn't dared to use it before, scared that it wouldn't be powerful enough to kill off the shades before he recovered from the movement.

As he landed and slammed his shield down, the rocks around him exploded under the pressure. Everything within five meters was killed; anything in ten was heavily injured. Up to twenty meters, shades were thrown away violently.

A glow covered Gurren's armor as he, too, used one of his skills. His speed increased sharply as he completely blurred, leaving behind him a path of destruction.

Steve easily dispatched a few remaining shades as Lox and Gurren defeated anything within reach.

Lox and Gurren returned to their positions.

"Can we fit a shower in here?" Gurren asked.

Lox laughed. "This Devastator armor really lives up to its name. I don't want to leave either," Lox admitted.

"Well, looks like you two are officially some badass motherfuckers." Steve laughed and slapped their armored shoulders.

Suzy winced at the ringing.

"Well, seeing as it's not too difficult on this floor, want to just separate out and fight individually?" Deia asked.

Suzy felt a grin rise on her face. Fighting together was necessary when facing powerful targets, but being able to defeat enemies by yourself—one could gain a lot more experience and the competition for who could kill the most rose Suzy's fighting spirit.

"Pair up and head out," Deia said.

Induca and Malsour went together. Gurren, Anna, and Steve also went off. Dave and Lox stuck together while Suzy and Deia continued to float together.

Suzy felt a faint frown on her face. She wanted to get out and do some killing. Deia, who was pushed to the back due to her being pregnant, would be a hindrance.

"Don't look so sad. I can still kill at range," Deia said, her eyes hungry.

Suzy's frown turned into a smile, excitement filling her once again.

"Let's see if we can't kill some more shades!" Deia said.

"Lead the way." Suzy laughed. The two of them flew away. Suzy's Air creations created a cloud around her; as they moved, the Air creations grouped up on the shades, cutting them apart.

Deia used her fire ball and pillar spell, concentrated blue flames cutting through the skies to tear the shades apart with ease.

They might be Level 300 shades, but Deia was over a Level 1,000 in just her stat points. The strain on her body could be considered extremely light as she destroyed shades with ease.

***

Gurren and Lox high-fived each other after ten minutes of fighting. Anna grinned but shook her head, trying to hide her own pride.

Their group had killed the most shades and were basking in the glory. The other parties in the Six Affinity Temple looked at them with myriad expressions, from envy and anger to respect and admiration.

Some were muttering about them kill stealing. Steve was getting a lot of heat from that. He couldn't resist ending someone who was wounded and near him.

His smile took on an embarrassed tilt as they progressed up the stairs. Ahead of them there were the Affinity pools. Already the sounds of battle rang out as people were attacking the different Affinity pools. The Magical Circuits that powered the Affinity pools had been turned off, though the Affinity spirit mobs continued to respawn.

"Shall we split, one half fight the Water Affinity spirits, the other half fight Earth Affinity spirits?" Deia asked. Having them all attack just the Water spirits would mean that some of them couldn't use their full abilities. However, many of them were able to fight different Affinity creatures.

"Sounds good to me," Malsour said. The others agreed.

"Very well. Malsour, Induca, Suzy, Gurren, and I can fight the Water Affinity spirits. Anna, Dave, Lox, and Steve, do you want to fight the Earth Affinity spirits?" Deia asked.

"Sounds good to me," Lox said, taking command of the second group.

"Okay, let's go." Deia and Induca floated side-by-side, skirting around the Affinity pools so that none of the Affinity spirits within attacked them. Gurren trudged forward while Malsour floated a little back from him.

They reached the water pool where Water Affinity spirits were hiding. The water that had been boiled off had once again returned with the portal area being refreshed.

Malsour laid down area effect curses outside of the Affinity pool. Gurren's armor and weapons took on a red sheen as he activated his Fire Affinity. Induca and Deia calmly floated in the air behind and to the side of Gurren.

"You ready?" Deia looked to Malsour, who seemed to have finished his curses.

"Yep, good to go," Malsour said.

Deia used her senses to isolate a Water Affinity spirit. Her hand flashed outward and a bolt of blue flame hit the surface of the water, bringing it to an immediate boil.

A Water Affinity spirit burst from the water, charging the half-party that stood outside. It stepped across the curse's area of effect. Black runes faintly appeared in the area, focused on the creature.

Induca unleashed a controlled pillar of flame from her hands as Deia unleashed wisps of white flame. None of the power leaked from these wisps of flame as they tore through the air. They hit the creature with explosive force, tearing holes in the Water Mana that formed its body.

It lost half of its Health before it reached Gurren.

As it reached Gurren, it was coldly rebuffed by his shield, actually being thrown back a few meters. Gurren, not letting this break in momentum go to waste, lurched forward. His sword blurred as it stabbed outward with a mechanical grace that could only be achieved by someone who had repeated the same move so many times it was engraved upon his very soul.

Holes appeared in the Water Affinity spirit. It tried to evade, only to be greeted by a wall of blades.

The Water spirit's Mana surged to protect itself, filling in the holes. It lashed out with attacks but Gurren's shield was there like a wall. The difference between the two was too great for the Water Affinity spirit to overcome.

Deia and Induca held back their attacks, seeing that Gurren had already been determined the winner of this fight.

With a wail, the Water Affinity spirit's Health hit zero. A Mana core dropped to the ground, the sound of glass tapping on the floor with a crisp, clean ring.

Gurren's hand extended and the core disappeared into a spatial ring. He had become so close to the water's edge that another Water Affinity spirit had sensed him and leaped free.

Gurren jumped backward in one massive leap.

Fighting so close to the Affinity pool was a bad idea. Malsour's curses slowed the Water Affinity spirit and did damage over time as Induca and Suzy fired spells into the creature. Steam rose from the creature. Deia and Induca had been testing their power before; now they poured it in.

Gurren, seeing that they were holding the creature back with their magic, held up his sword hand. A bolt thrower appeared; a faint red light surrounded it as a bolt was released. It impacted the spirit with a terrible force, violently combusting into Fire Mana. Steam obscured everyone's view. They used their arcane sight without conscious thought, the scene in front of them becoming instantly clear.

Deia lazily brought her knife hand across her body. A wave of force that shimmered in the low light crossed the space in a split second. Where this thin force landed, it cut through the Water Affinity spirit. Its Health dropped to zero, water splashing down as a Mana core was once again revealed.

"How is everyone?" Deia asked as the steam slowly dissipated.

"Good to go." Gurren's bolt thrower faded away as a sword appeared in his hand again. Thin white scratches that had been on the surface of the shield had already faded away as it automatically repaired itself.

"Barely used any Mana," Malsour said.

"Same," Induca said. "Shall we increase the number that comes out?"

Deia thought on it for a moment. "I'm good to use some more power. If you're all confident in facing them, we should be good to continue."

Smiles appeared on Malsour and Induca's faces, revealing their competitiveness.

"It would be pretty sweet if we were able to kill off all of these creatures faster than the other group," Gurren said, luring her to agree.

Deia snorted and smiled. "There's no way that they could beat us in speed." Deia's own competitive spirit came to the surface. "Ready yourselves!" Deia tossed out two more white flames that ran toward the Water Affinity pool before diving in. The water where they had entered exploded outward into vapor in a second.

***

Steve cocked his head to the side. His senses detected the three Water Affinity spirits that the other half of the party was fighting off. "Looks like the other group is pulling more of the Water Affinity spirits than our own Earth Affinity spirits. Looks like they want to have a competition!"

"Well, we should naturally oblige them!" Lox's attacks sped up as his sword darted forward like a serpent, its aim true and unwavering as it hit the Mana core within the Earth Affinity spirit.

Hitting the Mana core was similar to cutting a creature's head off. Without the Mana core firmly connected, the body died; without the body, the head died.

The Earth Affinity spirit turned into a loamy composition, falling to the ground with a deep green Mana core on top of it.

Lox didn't even pause as he let out a roar. Green lines appeared around his body as he used a special taunting skill.

The Earth Affinity spirits that had been drifting through their Affinity pool now turned their heads as one. Sensing someone dared to enter their territory, they rushed forward like bloodhounds.

Steve's laughter rang through the forest.

Anna's wind blades tore down into the Affinity pools, thinning out the numbers.

Dave hovered next to Steve, a spear in his hand. The spear lashed outward, keeping the creatures at bay as he danced across the ground as if he were a piece of grass swaying in the wind. His spear reached out to pierce the Earth Affinity spirits. Where the tip of his spear landed, air seemed to be violently compressed and released, leaving invisible wounds within the Earth Affinity spirits.

Steve's attacks cleaved through many; they repaired themselves, launching attacks at Steve and sending out Earth spears. Two worked together—an Earth prison spread outward, encompassing Steve within moments. Their magical power was too incredible!

Steve's eyes narrowed, seemingly becoming serious for a moment. The ground under his feet exploded as if a bomb had gone off. His axe cut outward; the axe cut through the walls. A wave of pressure blew out the bars that were meant to hold him.

His foot touched the ground. He used his forward momentum, spinning so that his axe turned into a blur, the air behind it showing ripples of force as it passed. The axe crashed into the twin Earth Affinity spirits that had created the prison.

His right foot crashed down, his head whipping to the side as his axe rested along his extended leg. With another explosive step, he once again charged toward the nearly fifteen Earth Affinity spirits that were now pushing out of the Earth Affinity pool.

Suzy looked down on the fighting with a calm and collected manner. She leveled her hand at a group of Earth Affinity spirits. Her clothes shook as a forceful rush of air raced past her.

With their speed, the fourteen advanced Air creations rushed to their master's bidding. Their bodies were revealed to all, their sword-like edges now showing. White air rushed past as they moved. They looked like crabs with limbs made of Air blades.

Lu Lu let out an angered cry. The lightning phoenix raised her imperial eyes at her master's enemies. Her eyes flashed as she opened her beak lazily. A stream of lightning easily passed the Air creation's hitting before the creations attacks did.

The Earth Affinity spirits summoned Mana barriers.

The lightning hit the Mana barriers and broke into different strands of white arcing light.

The shields supported by the Earth Affinity spirits' own Mana was equivalent to their life-force. They trembled slightly with this attack, not allowing them to make another attack as the Air creations were upon them. Their limbs seemed to meld into the wind before leaving behind thin and condensed lines of air.

These lines struck out at the Mana barriers of the Earth Affinity spirits. Where Lu Lu's attack had merely slowed them, now they poured their life-force into their barriers. They lurched forward; angered groans that sounded like boulders smashing together came from their bodies as they unleashed their attacks on the Air creations.

Suzy seemed to be a mountain in the eye of a storm, her hair faintly drifting behind her as she looked over the battle. In fact, her own consciousness was managing the fight with the Earth creations. Her attack was to pin them in place so they didn't overwhelm the others.

Still, her creations were not the weak, barely animated things of before. These were elegant and graceful, their strength equal to someone around Level 600 or 700 in strength. Normally a summoner could only make creatures that were half of their overall level. Suzy, using her Staff of Hecate and the cores that Dave had made himself, could surpass these limitations.

Her stalling action turned into a true fight.

As one creation fell, she quickly tossed out another. Suzy's control was so precise that her creations could fight alongside others without fear of them hitting the summoner's allies.

The Air creations' blades slowly whittled down the Earth shades as Anna entered the fray. Anna dropped from her high position, coming level with the Earth Affinity spirits.

The air around her sped up as she raced forward. Her short hair was erratic with her speed, her tail not moving as she closed in with her prey. She jabbed forth with her sword, revealing her hidden strength.

A vortex of wind appeared like a lance, moving as fast as Lu Lu's lightning. It pierced a dense Earth Affinity spirit and a hole appeared in its chest. At the center of the hole, one could see the glint of a Mana core before the Earth Affinity spirit dropped to the ground.

Anna's speed increased as she seemed to race through the Earth Affinity spirits. Her blade howled; wind blades cut outward in a storm, her blade blurring into a silver light.

In the time it took someone to breathe, she carried out all these attacks and was past the Earth Affinity spirits. As if time had now caught up with these spirits.

They howled out as they were attacked by Anna's Air Affinity Mana. Air, the absolute opposite of Earth, was much more potent than other Affinities.

These Earth Affinity spirits turned savage, making to follow Anna.

The Air creations descended on them, cutting many down as a massive axe and sword came in from both sides.

The remaining Earth spirits found it hard to move as runes over Dave's face and hands glowed. His eyes looked down coldly at the Earth Affinity spirits as the area that held the spirits turned into a slaughterhouse.

With Dave suppressing their ability to move as Lox, Steve, and Suzy's Air creations grinded away the shades' Health points, the pace and advantages of the battle switched from the shades to Party Zero.

The last of the Earth Affinity spirits were destroyed, their Mana core dropping to the ground.

No one rested; instead, they prepared themselves to fight again.

"We're good for some rest," Dave said. With his Touch of the Land, he was able to sense whether there was any more Affinity spirits eager to attack them.

"Dammit! They beat us," Steve pouted, hitting the dirt floor aimlessly with his axe.

Everyone had sour expressions on their faces as they looked at the other half of the party that seemed to be relaxing beside the Water Affinity pool.

"Great day for a swim!" Gurren yelled over.

Steve continued to poke the ground with his axe.

Suzy shook her head. The weapon in his hands was an undeniable treasure, yet he treated it as if it was nothing more than a stick to play in the dirt with.

Dave snorted as Lox laughed.

"We'll have to beat them next time," Lox commiserated with Steve.

"Well, that was a lot better than the first time." Anna sheathed her sword.

"The creatures are much weaker than the ones that we first fought. Seems that with all the time they grew in strength, making the first raid have to fight a lot harder," Dave said.

"Also, now we've already fought them once, it's only natural that we figure out how to deal with them faster," Suzy said.

"Plus, we're stronger since then." Lox's sword and shield seemed to dissolve into nothingness.

"What do you think about the Affinity spirit-possessed animals?" Dave looked to the next group of creatures they would have to deal with. The other parties that had come into the Six Affinity Temple were all fighting the different Affinity spirits within their Affinity pools.

Seeing as they might be sour from the kill stealing with the shades and they didn't look to be in a dire situation, none of Party Zero moved to kill these Affinity spirits.

"Their numbers are going to be annoying. I think that we might be able to fight them in these same groups, but it'd be best that we group together to fight them." Lox took on a serious tone. He might have gained a Weapon of Power, but relying on just it and diving into every situation was a quick way for someone to end up dead and lose a Weapon of Power.

There were many people who, after gaining a Weapon of Power, would then jump into some dire situation and end up the one dying. It was a tool that had to be carefully and accurately used by its master to its full potential.

"Well, let's go and see the others at the Water Affinity pool," Suzy said.

They walked over. Gurren sat on the ground with his legs in front of him. Seeing the massive Devastator armor in such a relaxed position was a rather comical scene.

Suzy looked over to Dave, who snorted at the sight.

"Heya! Want to go for a dip in the pool?" Gurren asked as if he sat on a beach, pointing at the Water Affinity pool.

"Ah!" Gurren yelled as he dropped into the pool.

Steve admired his fingers, standing behind Gurren. He looked over to everyone's stares as Gurren dropped to the bottom of the pool.

"What? You can't say you wouldn't have done it!"

No one said anything as Gurren climbed out of the water.

"Have a nice bath?" Steve grinned.

"Now I've got to clean all my armor to make sure that it doesn't rust!" Gurren used heat to evaporate the water as he studied his armor closely.

"All we need is a few water balloons and they'd be happy for days," Suzy muttered to Dave, who chuckled.

***

It only took about another ten minutes before the other Players and POEs defeated the remaining Affinity spirits.

They came and gathered around Party Zero. Having come this far, those around saw that the others indeed had qualifications and abilities that meant they wouldn't have to carry them.

Loot breakdown was talked over as people deferred to Lox and Deia. They were famous people and were good leaders.

As they made plans, a large group of Players entered the crack, walking through the cleared area around the Six Affinity Temple.

They all had the same guild badge on them.

"Look—just sitting around. No wonder they couldn't get farther than the Free Affinity shades," one of them said, their voice carrying.

"At least they took care of the simple creatures. Really is boring dealing with the low-leveled beasts." Another member of the group looked down on the various Players and POEs who were talking next to the Water Affinity pool.

"Freeloaders," one of the people around the pool said, shaking their head as the forty-person group bypassed the Affinity pools and went straight toward the Free Affinity-possessed animals.

As the first group recovered to peak condition and started to get a battle plan together, the new guild that had arrived started to lazily get into a formation, continuing to throw insults that the others could hear as they moved toward the animals confidently.

Suzy shook her head at their actions.

Making fun of other Players was common, but within Ashal it was much more natural for people to work together if they knew the dangers. This guild that had just arrived through the ono underestimated the dangers and were treating their upcoming fight as if it were a simple matter.

Deia and Lox divided everyone up. As people talked, those who had fought past the Affinity spirits were happy to share their knowledge with those who hadn't. It showed their ability and it also meant that they might move ahead further if the new fighters knew a bit more.

In the distance, animal roars could be heard, as well as the noise of weapons hitting animal hide.

Suzy looked over to see that the newly arrived guild was fighting off the creature. They were able to keep it at bay but it was clear that they had just read the level displayed by the creature and did not take into account the additional power of the Affinity spirit within.

They were facing a silver gorilla. This creature had great strength and had a lightning attack and armor that could stun its enemy or negate magical attacks. The silver gorilla was possessed by a Water Affinity spirit; as it roared, water shot out from around it.

The electrical currents over its body charged the water. As the water blasts pushed people back or made them dodge, those who were covered in water were hit by the electrical charge that passed through the water.

Five of their number were numb as the gorilla reached them. It smacked those stunned few with its massive hands and sent them flying. Armor was crumpled under its hands.

Arrows were fired at it. The gorilla, with the Water Affinity's natural enhancements, dodged in a way that was completely unnatural for the gorilla.

Spears of water rushed out to meet the ranged attackers, suppressing them as the gorilla charged the melee fighters who were taunting the creature.

The water lances changed targets, focusing on the melee fighters. Electricity sparked all over it as it charged; it slammed into the shields, passing on its lightning effect to the defenders.

The soaked defenders would have been fine if they met the gorilla straight on. Together they were stronger than the creature and their clothes stopped the electricity passing from their shields to them. With the water covering them, this all changed.

The lightning was so strong that the Players couldn't even cry out as they fell down in pain, smoke faintly rising from their clothes.

The gorilla was a creature of nature; it had no sympathy. Its fists slammed down on those on the ground, cracking and denting their armor.

The ranged attackers backed up.

"Watch out!" one of the Players within the Affinity pools called out, their tone slightly mocking.

It was too late—they had accidentally walked into the detection range of other roaming mobs.

Five more creatures piled in, attacking them.

"Get ready. If they run back here, we can kill off those creatures," Deia said.

People with grim expressions stood and checked their weapons. Getting attacked by these spirit-controlled creatures while they were discussing their next move would not be pretty.

The mages and rangers were letting loose with their weapons, trying to pull out their friends as they pulled back. Their expressions sour and panicked, the melee fighters were trying to defend them as they pulled back.

One of them started running, not wanting to die and lose their gear, and then another and another. None of them cared what the others thought; right now, they just wanted to keep their gear and levels. Some tried circling around to get their friends but instead only drew the attention of more creatures.

They ran for the stairs and the creatures followed them.

Suzy sighed, dusting off her pants as she stood.

Dave pulled out his twin rods. Gray smoke moved over them and a simple bow appeared. An arrow appeared; he pulled back the string and aimed at the silver gorilla.

The gorilla was marked by Deia.

"Only use attacks that don't contain Water Mana." Deia's voice was neither loud nor quiet but everyone heard her.

Dave let his arrow loose. Those with ranged attacks added in their attacks.

The gorilla was staggered by the attacks. Red and black marks appeared on its fur. Its Health declined rapidly under the concentrated attacks.

There was a yellow-striped serpent; the Earth-attribute creature made to dive into the ground. Malsour gestured with his hands and the ground forced the serpent out. The Fire Affinity spirit unleashed Fire attacks at Malsour.

It might be a Fire Affinity spirit but compared to Deia and Induca, it was barely a weak flickering candle. None of the Fire attacks made it within ten meters of the people standing around the Affinity pools.

The fleeing Players raced past them.

None of those around the Affinity pools spared them a glance. If they had wanted to work together, they might have cared. With their comments and attitude, those around the Affinity pools didn't care. Their eyes were cold and uncaring as they watched Players die on the ground. They were arrogant assholes, but now at least they would get some extra loot from these dead idiots.

Gurren, Lox, and Steve were the center of the defensive wall. The tanks lined up off them as their weapons appeared in their hands.

Dave slowed the creatures down with gravity. Malsour cast curses over the area and onto the creatures, draining their Health and Mana quickly.

Deia quickly organized people to fight the different creatures so that opposite Affinities would be matched to have a greater effect on the incoming beasts.

Three of the seven creatures that the cocky guild had disturbed made it to their position. Steve squared off with the silver gorilla as it smashed against his axe.

Steve was covered in arcs of lightning. "Oh, tickles." Steve used his immense strength to toss the massive gorilla backward.

Malsour formed steel around the gorilla, pinning it to the ground. It fought against the restraints just like its deceased companion. This one carried the Water Affinity spirit. The spirit started to use high-pressured water to cut through the steel manacles that kept it pinned to the ground.

Steve didn't even pause; his axe came down on the gorilla repeatedly. Water spears fired at Steve. He hit them away with his axe as mages from the Players and POEs called attacks down on the gorilla.

The water spears weakened, allowing Steve the opening he needed. He brought his axe down again, this time with all of his strength.

Around the gorilla, the ground cracked with the impact, the gorilla now in the center of a shallow crater. A flaming pillar dropped on the gorilla, its Health bar reaching zero.

Lox and Gurren had also taken on their own creatures. Their swords blazed with Affinity flames. The Affinity spirits didn't have any chance to win against their polar opposites. Gurren and Lox's hits were powerful and quick, leaving afterimages in their wake as their blades whizzed through the air.

When the creatures lashed out, the massive Devastator easily moved across the ground, its speed and agility defying its bulky appearance.

Silence descended as the last creature dropped to the ground, a loot icon above the creature.

The guild members who had run away now looked over the people they had insulted before. Embarrassed looks were on their faces.

Talking a big game was good, but if you couldn't back it up, then gamers would call you out on it.

The guild members silently moved to take back their fellows' gear. Those at the Affinity pools let them, checking their own gear and healing any wounds that they might have gained while also restoring any spent stats.

"Hey, get your hands off that." Steve pointed out that one of the guild members was trying to loot one of the creatures that had been killed by the people who were already in the Six Affinity Temple's grounds.

The person quickly took the loot into their bag, sneering at those who stared at him. "What you going to do?" the Player spat. The rest of his guild mates rushed to grab Mana cores.

Dave increased the gravity on all of them, sending them to the ground. "Malsour?" Dave asked.

Metal spikes tore through the ground and the guild members.

Silence descended as everyone looked at the dead guild members.

"Well, they were a bunch of pricks anyway," one of the Players with Party Zero said.

The Players and POEs shrugged and started making their way to recover the guild's loot and their Mana cores.

Deia frowned but only sighed lightly.

"Hopefully they'll learn from losing their loot and being idiots," Suzy said.

"Hopefully," Deia said. "All right, we'll divide the loot up, see if there are any good weapons or items we can use. Then we'll start to deal with the rest of the possessed animals."

The quickly formed raid party made motions of agreement, a number of them with large smiles. A decent guild member could have quite the loot on them.

The POEs' eyes lit up as they went through the various bags of holding and gear that was on the dead guild members.

Dave and the rest of Party Zero took some of their charged soul gems, the potions, food, clothing weapons and gold went to the others with them. They didn't need any of it but the others wouldn't allow them to go on empty handed.

Chapter 35: Gateway

All of the Stone Raider leaders were present as Ela-Dorn and a number of Aleph professors came through the teleport pad. Behind them were various components being hauled by automated carts.

Josh's face turned pensive as he looked at the different carts. His usual joking manner was cold and serious. After Dave had shown him the reality of Earth and Emerilia, his core thoughts and beliefs had been shaken.

He seemed to have aged a lot in just a few short weeks. He devoted more time to prepare for the future, to look at new possible members for the Stone Raiders as well as make alliances with the various powers on Emerilia.

His thoughts were a confusing mess. All he knew was that he cared for the people he'd interacted with in Emerilia and he would protect his fellow Stone Raiders with everything he had.

Right now, he could only look at those carts with cold and calculating eyes. These parts would make up a summoning hall that the Stone Raiders could use to contract beasts.

People were muttering and talking to themselves in excited tones, trying to guess what was within the crates that were going by while also staring at and studying the large groups of Aleph. There were a number of Aleph who came to do business in Terra, though seeing so many of them with such a large protection detail was indeed exciting.

Ela-Dorn moved over to the Stone Raiders leadership, a smile on her face. "It's good to see you all again." Ela-Dorn rarely came out of her college to do business; even for the Aleph council meetings she would only go if she was absolutely needed. However, Dave seemed to be capable of luring her out.

"You, too, Ela-Dorn." Josh smiled and relaxed a bit as he shook her hand in greeting.

With his people gaining contracted beasts, their strength would have a large increase without having to vet and recruit more people.

"Shall we go somewhere a bit more quiet?" Lucy suggested.

"Certainly," Ela-Dorn said.

Lucy and Florence talked to Ela-Dorn in excited tones as they walked through Terra, showing off its full brilliance.

People, seeing the Stone Raiders Guild leaders, moved out of their way, watching them go with respectful and in some cases worship-filled gazes.

It wasn't long until they reached the Stone Raiders' tower and made themselves comfortable within the conference room.

"How long will it take to set up the summoning hall?" Josh asked.

"It will take two, maybe three days," Ela-Dorn said.

"How many times a day can we use it?" Dwayne, too, had a serious edge to him as he had found out about the Jukal.

"It might need a few minutes to calm down between summonings, though it really depends on how quickly the person doing the summoning can win over the creature," Ela-Dorn said.

Josh, Dwayne, and Kim looked to one another. They led the main fighting groups of the Stone Raiders.

Josh nodded. "Very well. As soon as it's set up, then we can start letting people summon creatures. Now, with the ono network—how is that coming along?"

"We will be able to fill your complete order within the month. The extra components that Dave and Malsour added in have been retrofitted to the units that didn't have them before." Ela-Dorn referred to the Mana well and the soul gem construct that would absorb the excess power from it.

"What about Dave's different items?" Dwayne asked.

Ela-Dorn's face turned pensive. She had been brought in to help Frenik and Kol when they were organizing the contract for the various items.

"We've stepped up production for the Band-Aid suppression device. We are ready to push them through all of our sales channels at ten gold," Ela-Dorn said, well aware of the methods that the Jukal were willing to use in order to get rid of problems. The Aleph had once been considered a problem.

She had a good number of friends within the Players and she didn't want to see them die.

"Good. Florence, we will also sell them at the same price and try to push them out across Emerilia," Josh said.

"Okay." Florence nodded her head even though a confused look passed over her eyes.

These Band-Aids would allow a person greater protection against spells within their personal area. They were an item that could be sold for three hundred gold and not seem too extravagant.

However, she didn't want to bring this up in front of Ela-Dorn; she might be a friend, but business was business.

"You might also be interested to learn that we have figured out the defensive measures that Dave had us working on," Ela-Dorn said.

Josh's eyebrow rose in question.

"We made these clamps that can fit over a portal. They would allow us to connect to different portals. We have been working on making an attachment that would allow us to block that portal. Basically, it would create a Mana shield around the event horizon of the portal. Anything that comes through hits the shield. Being unable to pass through the currents within the portal would tear the person apart."

"That guy really does like to think ahead," Lucy said.

The corners of Josh's mouth twitched. Having a way to stop things from coming through the portals was a good idea. Most of the portals that had been opened had creatures on the other side, but they hadn't been strong enough to defeat the people fighting them and make it into Emerilia. There had only been a few breakthroughs but the events that came with the breakthroughs and the rewards meant that people rushed to put them down and once again enter the portals to take back more land from the creatures on the other side.

With the completion of these projects, they would be able to control the flow of the creatures leaving the portals.

I wonder what the Jukal will do if we start using that on their portals?

***

Edwards rushed into Sato's office, his face alternating between red and white as he held up his work pad. "I just— How can— He gave us this! It's just—well, I..." Edwards said in broken sentences, unable to formulate anything like a normal sentence.

"What is it? Where did you get it from and what does it do?" Sato asked.

"Portal tech! Dave. We can create gates to move instantaneously across systems!" Edwards said in choppy sentences, a look of disbelief on his face as his arms shook, holding the pad as if it was some kind of holy object.

Sato sat up in his chair in alarm. "Start from the beginning."

"So, I was going through the information that we were given, went on a search for items that Dave himself had worked on. Within them was all of his information on portals, teleport pads, and what he calls onos." Edwards shook his head as if he didn't believe the words he was saying.

"Portals—as in the long-distance creations that only the inner systems of the Jukal Empire use?"

"Precisely. The teleport pads look to be much shorter range items that can cross around a planet-sized area, though they have the ability to change the location that they will connect to. Onos are basically just anchors. The teleport pads can punch a wormhole to these points; the ono stabilizes it and you can go between them. The onos, however, only go to one teleport pad. They're much less power intensive and simple, but again only connecting to one place. Basically, they're just really scaled-down portals," Edwards said.

Sato let out a hiss as he shook his head. "We've never been able to get any information on the Jukal's teleportation tech. It's been one of their most closely guarded secrets."

The Jukal might not be a massive race but they still maintained an iron control over their empire due to their ability to control the economic factors within it. As well as their ability to quickly and swiftly deal with any threat they had from within their empire.

Each planet had a small group of Jukal on it, monitoring the situation there. They also had portals within hardened installations, some where the Jukal's consulate was, and others in orbit. There were always several Jukal fleets that were ready to move at a moment's notice.

If a planet rebelled, then soldiers could walk through a portal, immediately reinforcing the consulate while a fleet of warships passed through the portals within the systems. In just minutes, any single system within the Jukal Empire could have a fully armed and prepared Jukal fleet and armed forces breathing down their neck.

Thus, the Jukal retained control of their empire quickly and efficiently.

Only the Jukal created portals. This allowed them to keep control of the tech. Anyone found trying to learn about the portals was killed.

It was the reason that the Aleph were killed off. The tech in the teleport pads was much more unstable compared to the portal, so they allowed the portal facilities to continue working as they took the teleport pads and seeded them across their home systems.

Onos were new tech. They were short-range but they were much more refined than the teleport pads.

Sato and Edwards sank into silence.

Having that portal technology, they might be able to use it themselves. To move an entire fleet across star systems in less than a second.

When the Jukal came for humanity, they seeded these portals behind them, moving up their resupply line. For them, it was just a second to move from the front lines to the rear to repair and rearm. In weeks, they could have a ship back on the line while humanity's supply lines were cut and they had to fight to the bitter end with only what they had on hand.

Sato's hand curled into a fist. His shocked face turned into a cold, indifferent mask as he thought of the possibilities that this would give his forces. "When can you start testing this out?" Sato asked, a fire in his eyes.

"I will need some more resources in order to work on this." Edwards grimaced.

"Done," Sato said without a moment of hesitation. Being able to move his forces across such vast distances was a massive advantage. If he could remove the advantage that the Jukal had, then it would be a matter of putting his ships up against those from the Jukal. He wasn't yet confident in his ships' numbers, but on a one-for-one basis, he felt his battleships were stronger than the Jukal's version. He had seen the simulations of the different battles and it showed that his battleships had a clear advantage.

However, the Jukal had deep forces. They not only had battleships, but carriers and all manner of warships to contend with anything Sato sent at them.

Edwards paused, tapping his chair.

"What's on your mind?" Sato asked.

"Dave has given us a wealth of information—he's even sharing his plans for his warships and his weapons. However, we haven't given him anything in return. He's updating his personal notes to share. I don't think it's by accident. It not only allows me to see how certain things work and are made but I've also picked up on a number of different problems he's been encountering.

"He's trying to make facilities to regrow limbs and people. A kind of alternative Altar of Rebirth. He's also got a number of systems on his warship that he hasn't been able to complete. I was thinking—if I could send him some pointers..." Edwards said.

Sato took a deep breath, letting it out slowly.

Their debt to Dave was indeed great. However, there was also security to think about.

"I'm not saying we give him plans to systems, just that we send him some vague notes to put him on the right path," Edwards said.

Sato's finger tapped on his desk, his face unreadable. "Very well. Make sure it's vague and, as for the healing and regrowing tech, the Jukal are already much more advanced than us. Being a bit more specific with it—I don't think it would have much impact if it was to fall into Jukal hands."

Edwards nodded, a smile on his face.

***

Fire, Water, and Bob were sitting within Water's domain.

"Seems that Air wasn't kidding around." Water stroked his beard, a pensive look on his face.

"She is a rather complicated person to figure out." Fire drank from her tea cup, a small smile on her lips.

Across Ashal, nations and groups that had held enmity toward one another for generations were making peace. To many, they thought that it was in the light of the oncoming event.

That might have been a factor in it all, but Bob, Fire, and Water had been around for a long time. As long as they had been on Emerilia, so had the goddess Air. They knew the ways in which she worked. Although few would recognize her methods or the traces she left behind, these three could clearly see her hand at work.

"Seems that she's uniting the Ashal continent. She already got the Gudalo continent to pull themselves together," Bob said, faint praise in his words.

"Just wish that she wasn't so all over the place. Would be nice to know if she's someone we can come to rely on." Water sighed.

"Do we know what is going to happen with the event?" Fire's voice carried a cutting tone.

"I thought I knew." Bob pursed his lips together. He felt that he bore some responsibility for Fire's Dragons dying. He could see that Fire was also saddened by the loss of these Creatures of Power that she regarded as her own children.

"What's supposed to happen is that notifications will start appearing at different points within Emerilia. If someone is in the location, then they will get a notification telling them that in less than three days something will be arriving at that point. There will be no indication of what it will be—whether a swarm of nether rats, or some Xelur Demon Lord that massacred hundreds of POEs to raise his strength. I don't even know where these places are going to be or in what order," Bob said angrily. "Seems that the emperor himself has taken interest in the ongoing event."

Fire and Water looked at Bob, their faces becoming harder with the word "emperor."

Fire sighed and put her cup down. "Our preparations have been mostly complete. Denur is sending representatives to meet with the Stone Raiders."

"I have also sent my champion Welaj to meet them and create an alliance," Water said.

"There might come a time when we will need to use our own strength," Bob said. "Are you ready for that?"

"These creatures are welcome to test my strength." Fire's eyes flashed in anger.

Due to the Jukal, she had lost many granddaughters and grandsons. And she was holding onto that personal grudge.

Water also bowed his head. "I, too, will fight with my strength," Water said. Although he was a creator of the merpeople, his position was more one of respected elder who watched over them, offering guidance through turbulent times.

Although Fire was a motherly figure among her Dragons, she was much more connected to them than Water was to any singular merperson after a few generations. When Akatol had attacked her family, her anger had been ignited.

"In that case, I believe it is time that we go to Per'ush together. There are a number of different spells and skills that you might develop that could increase your power," Fire said.

Water's tea cup paused in mid-air as he sent Fire a look. She might be the weakest of all the Pantheon because her divine well was nearly always dry. Though her personal skills were something that shouldn't be underestimated. She had been building up her strength over hundreds of years. With her mage's college and guild, she had access and knowledge of different skills and spells that not even the rest of the Pantheon knew of.

Her offer showed that they were not only allies in their fight, but that she trusted him.

"Thank you, Fire." Water gave a deep bow of his head; by his expression, he was clearly relieved and deeply thankful for her offer.

"I'm off to get back to work with those growing chambers." Bob sighed and rubbed his face.

Fire and Water looked to him.

"Dave wants to revive all of the Players who are currently in the Earth simulation. With my knowledge of Human biology, after growing and creating all the races on Emerilia, I have to look at what systems I can make that could possibly allow the Players to escape their simulated prison," Bob said, his face firm.

"Good luck." Fire's tone softened. She knew that although she thought of Dragons as her children, Bob was attached to the people of Emerilia. He had, after all, made the planet and the people on it. He wasn't impressed with the decisions they made sometimes but they were still here because of him.

Water bowed his head to Bob, acknowledging the large task that was ahead of the Grey God.

"I'll be seeing you." Light surrounded Bob as he disappeared from sight.

"So, are you ready to visit Per'ush?" Fire asked.

The gods could go anywhere they wanted. Except Per'ush. On the islands, there was an integrated rune system that would cut off any god or goddess from their divine well. Also, Fire would sense them immediately.

"Whenever you are ready," Water said without any hesitation. Per'ush was a place of Fire's power; by going there, he would be completely at her mercy.

A flash of light enveloped them as they disappeared from the merpeople's city.

Light poured in through windows as they appeared to be in a large office overlooking the Per'ush islands. The room was clean but it looked as though it hadn't been used in a long time.

Fire didn't change into her disguise as she walked out of the office. Mages who were guarding the upper floor looked to Fire with alarm. They had the presence of mind to scan her first, remembering their teachings; they knew the signs that their teachers had taught them. It had been ingrained into their souls, to check for the signs of the Lady Fire.

The proud mages took a knee in front of Fire.

"Tell Alamos and Jelanos I wish to see them. Bring me instructor Kujo of the Water mages," Fire said to the guards.

They opened their interfaces and sent out her orders.

"I will be in Jelanos's office." Fire moved past the guards and down the tower to where Jelanos's office was located.

People looked at her with interest as she passed, but few were able to sense that she was the goddess Fire. Some of the older generations who had seen her before bowed their heads respectfully.

Fire greeted them with a smile and nod as she continued on her path.

"Who is that?" one person asked.

"I don't know, but the older generation is respectful to her," another said.

"Seems that things are about to heat back up now the goddess has returned," one of the older generation mages said, an excited look in their eyes as a smile passed over their face, talking to their peers.

Fire smiled slightly, seeing the younger generation's confused looks.

She arrived at the office. The secretary, who had already got a message from the guards on the higher floor, bowed deeply before Fire.

"He's waiting in his room," the secretary said in a respectful tone.

"Thank you," Fire said.

Water looked over everything with interest, inspecting the walls, the people, their clothes and studied the way that they held themselves. To him, everything was new. He had gotten reports from his people who were staying within the mage's college or working with the mage's guild. Still, this was his first time ever seeing Per'ush islands from the inside.

Fire walked into the office without pausing; Water followed. The door closed behind them with a wave from Fire.

Jelanos made to take a deep bow as Fire snorted.

"You can stop with that crap. Jelanos, meet Water. Water, this is the archmage of the mage's college, and my friend, Jelanos." Fire waved to the man and flopped down in a seat.

Jelanos's face broke from its rigid lines into a smile as he came around his desk. "Water! As in the god! Damn, usually she just comes around to bug me! Always good to meet Fire's friends," Jelanos said, his composure completely different from the grave man from before.

Water couldn't keep the corners of his mouth from twitching up into a smile at Jelanos's attitude.

"I have heard much about you from my people," Water said, his words slow and melodic.

"I have to say that there were some issues in the beginning with people being a bunch of stereotypical idiots." Jelanos's face took on a dark color before he once again smiled. "But we got that sorted! They're really studious, soak up information like no tomorrow! Even found out that a few of them have a higher Affinity to magics other than Water."

Jelanos's excitement was infectious. Anyone could see the pride and eagerness in him when talking about his students. He lived to teach the younger generation.

There was a knock at the door.

Jelanos took a few moments to compose himself. "Come in," he said, his voice imperious and powerful instead of the quicker, excited tones of before.

Another man entered and shut the door behind him.

"Alamos, this is Water. We have come into an agreement with each other," Fire said.

Alamos nodded. His official-looking mask fell but he still looked at Water with a careful eye as he extended his hand.

As they greeted each other, Fire continued talking. "Water is coming here to access our records and vaults. I have already asked that the guards summon Professor Kujo."

"Kujo is indeed the most versed in Water Mana techniques," Jelanos said.

"Water does not have much time to waste. Anything he wants is to be given to him. Think of him as my honored guest," Fire said.

"It will be done," Jelanos said solemnly.

"If you desire, you can bring some champions to the island for your protection and to also gain knowledge from the libraries. I will allow no more than fifteen. If they will be here in secret or as your guards is your decision," Fire said.

"Thank you, Fire." Water bowed his head. To give not only him access, but his strongest champions also—although it might not directly increase their levels, it would increase their abilities and strengths.

The two gods who had fought each other for centuries looked at each other. The history between them was a rocky one. But as they looked at each other, they knew that they had stepped through another threshold—from allies in name to the path of friends.

A rare smile appeared on Water's face. He had never thought that a moment like this would occur in his lifetime.

Chapter 36: Of Spirits and Beasts

The loot had been broken down and everyone was ready for the next level of the raid area.

Deia and Lox led them all forward, deeper into the Six Affinity Temple.

People gripped their weapons tightly as they readied themselves for the oncoming fight.

Induca looked at them all. She had been nervous herself when she had first come to the Six Affinity Temple. Now, after having fought the creatures and finding them weaker than the ones she had fought before, a sliver of confidence instead of nervous anticipation filled her. She might not need money or resources, but still loot held an interest for her.

The groups fanned out slightly, far enough that they wouldn't lose the beasts pulled to them to another group, but close enough that they could support one another if they needed.

Suzy's creations went off to pull in the beasts. There were rangers in the group, but after the recordings from the Stone Raiders-led raiding party, few wanted to run around with an Affinity spirit-controlled beast chasing after them.

The first beasts started to draw closer.

Those with good observation skills called out the different Affinity of the beasts, as Suzy guided them to the different groups that were specialized in attacking with one kind of Affinity.

The mages and ranged attackers unleashed their spells and attacks, violent light filling the room.

Induca, like Deia, used her concentrated Fire wisps. These white flames tore through the air in the blink of an eye, slamming into Water Affinity spirit beasts that approached their own formation.

The beasts weren't able to make it into range before they collapsed.

A Light spirit within a saber lion unleashed a stream of light from the lion's mouth at Malsour and his group.

A Water Affinity mage created a mirror, reflecting the light away as Malsour called down a tornado of shadows. The ground around the creature distorted, becoming part of the tornado as the creature was lifted off the ground. Rocks and debris slammed into it as the Dark tornado tore at the lion and the spirit within.

Malsour's power was too strong, ripping the lion apart.

With a wave of his hand, his tornado sought out more Light Affinity spirits and their possessed beasts.

Dave and Suzy were next to each other. Suzy pulled the creatures with her Air creations while Dave looked over the field of battle.

Induca felt the currents of power that moved around Dave before Fire Affinity creatures were dropped to the ground. The gravity where the beasts were located increased, making it harder for them to attack and have to use an incredible amount of Stamina.

Dave's role was to slow down the attackers so that the raiding group wasn't overwhelmed.

Steve, Lox, and Gurren were each fighting in their own groups. Steve's axe, with its glowing runes, threw the creatures back as Gurren and Lox's bodies with different-colored auras suppressed the beast's attacks.

Anna floated in the sky. Much like how none of the Water Affinity beasts ever made it within ten meters of the formation filled with Fire-attribute attackers, none of the Earth Affinity beasts made it to Anna's Air Affinity formation. She stood in the air, unleashing powerful attacks. None of the beasts lasted more than three hits from Anna.

The air vibrated with power. All but Suzy and Dave were unleashing their power. In their faces, the fight was rather simple.

Focusing their attacks on one target, it was much easier to finish them off.

Their actions were not rushed nor hurried, instead making sure that everyone was in peak condition before they fought another creature. Within the Six Affinity Temple, fighting recklessly was just asking to fail.

In an hour, all of the spirit-controlled animals had been killed off.

Everyone let out a ragged cheer as loot was collected and people slumped down to rest.

"Still haven't been able to unleash all of our power," Induca said to Deia as they descended slightly.

"I don't think that we could unless we were fighting a massive boss. If Jung Lee was still here, then we might be able to go all out. Even then some of us still have secrets." Deia gave Induca a deep look.

Induca smiled. Her Human form directly correlated with the power of her Dragon form. When she was in Human form, she was pretty powerful, but once she threw off the shackles of her Human form, her power could surge upward until it was ten times her Human form's strength. The creatures she'd killed with two or three hits would barely stand up to a wave of her hand.

Some of the Players exchanged friend requests with one another so that they could meet up later. A few of them logged off, their bodies turning into motes of light and dispersing or they commanded their body in zombie mode to return to the outpost.

Induca saw Dave frowning at the Players who turned into motes of light. When one logged off, they could pick to come back at the position they'd left, or at one of the nearby Altars of Rebirth.

"What happens when they log off completely? Not just let their zombies go back?" Suzy, who stood next to Dave, asked.

Induca reached them, smiling at Suzy but not interrupting. She was also interested in the answer.

"Those motes of light is the system copying their patterns then transferring it to a brain held within a storage facility. When they log back on, their body is regenerated and their gear is moved to the Altar of Rebirth, where they revive. When we get a loading screen when logging on, that's because it's taking longer for the altar to recreate our bodies or for the gear to reach the Altar of Rebirth that we're entering the game from," Dave said.

Induca shivered slightly at these words.

Dave sighed and shrugged. There wasn't anything they could do about the current situation.

Induca and Suzy's hands found each other's as everyone prepared to fight the Affinity spirit-controlled shades.

***

Once again, the raid party stood from their rest, eyeing the Affinity shades. The Stone Raiders-led raid had been able to clear them out but hadn't advanced any further.

The numbers had thinned out as lower-leveled people who had barely made it to this level had left for the outpost, knowing that they would be a liability. Others looking to try to milk some experience and loot out of it, even if they were a lower level, stayed around.

They had confidence in their abilities. Some of them were ignored, however; their low level and the way that they were talking made the others doubt they would be anything but a liability. After gaming for a while, Dave, as well as other veteran gamers, had a very keen bullshit radar.

The group was much smaller than the first raid group; however, it was made up of mostly strong people. For this next stage, they were all going to group together to take out the first couple of shades, get a feel for the fighting, then they could possibly change into smaller groups so that they could share the experience around more.

Deia looked over everyone as the first Affinity shade was pulled from the front of the temple.

It raced after the Air creation Suzy had sent out. Its ethereal body unleashed powerful magical blasts.

"Air Affinity!" an observer called out.

Deia drew an arrow on her bow, pulling and releasing with ease. People started changing weapons and readying themselves for the shade possessed by an Air Affinity spirit.

Its speed left behind afterimages; it was but a few moments before it arrived. Thankfully, everyone had hotkeyed their different gear sets by the Affinities that they might fight. With the press of a button, everyone had weapons that were best suited to deal with Air Affinity creatures.

Mages unleashed their spells. Earthen lances shot outward as large flowers appeared from the ground, spraying a green gas at the Air Affinity shade.

Its speed was incredible as it moved its body in ways that a living being never could.

"Fire at the same time! Don't give them any way to escape!" Deia said.

Spells became more concentrated, mages working together, so that, although not all of their attacks hit, some of them did.

The ranged fighters did the same. Arrows came from several directions, boxing in the Air creation as it had to slow its forward momentum to try to dodge the incoming attacks.

After being held back for just a few moments, it charged forward again with a shriek. Spells and attacks hit its Mana barrier as its shriek turned into an attack. Waves of cutting air slashed out at the raid party.

Melee types raised their shields while the Air mages tried to defuse the Air attacks. Shields were pressed backward as the people behind them resisted the powerful attack.

The shade continued to scream. The tanks blocked the attacks, allowing the mages and ranged fighters the freedom to attack without worrying about defense.

Curses and hexes weakened the shade. The potency of the attacks increased as they were chained together by groups for the maximum effect as buffs further increased their striking power and reduced the times between calling up spells.

The shade's hands turned into claws and unleashed vicious Air blades outward. Its Health plummeted under the concentrated attack, until finally it slumped down. The last of its attacks drained out as it dropped to the ground, a pool of ectoplasm and a Mana core on top.

Everyone started to recover themselves. A number of the weaker Players who had boastfully barged their way into the raiding group now had pale faces. Just facing one of the Affinity shades showed just how strong they were compared to the Affinity animals they'd defeated before.

Even if someone was a Level 800 in stats, as the Stone Raiders and the other guilds recommended to fight these Affinity shades, these were not easy creatures to kill. For those hovering around the Level 500 mark, they were seriously re-thinking their plans. If they had been at the front with the other high-leveled tanks, then they'd been tossed away or outright killed by the Air Affinity shade.

"Check your quivers, Mana, and Health," Deia said to everyone. Most were already working on readying themselves for the next shade.

Although the experience gain hadn't been much over so many people, there were fifty of them standing in the Six Affinity Temple's grounds.

So, the grind for experience and loot continued within the grounds of the Six Affinity Temple.

By the time they got to the fifth Affinity shade, they were starting to come together, acting stronger and stronger. They were also opening up a bit more, using their more powerful attacks and not only relying on those that they had used for a long time.

People were experimenting, but only slightly. Although they had got into something of a rhythm, no one was overstepping their bounds so far that they might completely mess up.

If a creature was too powerful, then Dave would step in to help out with his suppressing magic. He didn't gain much experience, but for him, his strength came in using his abilities and creations in new and different ways. Just by suppressing creatures, he was able to gain insights into his gravity magic and refine the effects of it.

Deia looked over to Party Zero. They might be fighting hard but they weren't using their trump cards. All of them were testing out their new moves, spells, and strengths while not calling on their full power.

Deia felt that they could fight two or three Affinity shades as a party. If they were to do that, then they wouldn't be able to help out the other groups or could be easily overwhelmed if a fourth attacked them.

Also, it wouldn't allow them to refine their moves; it would simply make them have to fight with everything.

"The experience gain might not be much but people are still gaining a few levels here and there," Dave said from beside Deia. If he didn't have to, he didn't leave Deia's side. As the end of her pregnancy came closer, his protective instincts continued to make him stay around Deia as much as possible.

"These are pretty high-leveled beasts. Just by themselves, these creatures would be the boss monsters in most other dungeons," Deia said. The wind howled around her as a flaming arrow shot outward, a red flaming streak that slammed into a Light Affinity shade.

Dave cocked his head to the side suddenly. His eyes thinned and he looked up at the Six Affinity Temple.

Deia followed his gaze, her eyes widening.

There were thirty-seven remaining Affinity shades under the pillar-supported landing outside of the actual temple. These floating shades now slowly halted.

As one, the shades' faces whipped over to look at the raid party. The action made her scalp itch as Deia went cold.

A screech rose from all of the shades at the same time. Different attacks lashed out from the Affinity shades as they charged forward together.

Everyone's faces paled at the enraged wave of shades.

What the hell is happening? Dave waved his hand. Orbs appeared in a line and a Mana barrier formed between them as they covered the raiding party.

The attacks slammed into the barrier, making it flare with impacts.

"Deia, get out of here!" Dave yelled.

Lox, Gurren, and Steve, seeing the oncoming creatures, stepped up. They moved faster and faster, their images blurring as their attacks landed on the Affinity spirit that was holding their attention.

"Run!" Deia yelled to the raid party.

People raced away from the temple and toward the crack. Those who had been focusing on the battle looked around to try to figure out what she meant. Once they saw the shades, they raced after their fellows.

Malsour cast massive area of effect curses that should slow the shades as Anna appeared behind the Earth Affinity shade. Her sword cleaved it in two, revealing a Mana core.

Lox waved his ring, sucking up the ectoplasm as well as the Mana core.

Dave grabbed Deia's hand as they raced backward. Dave created a gravity field to hold himself and Deia so that the baby wasn't thrown around. The outer field pulled them along while the inner made it feel as if they didn't move.

The remaining fighters put on all their speed; support classes threw out speed buffs as if it were candy, not caring about depleting their Mana reserves.

"Why are they all attacking at once?" Deia asked.

"I don't know but I think we should ask Jung Lee when we get back. He might know more," Dave said, his face grim as they continued to pull back. The rest of Party Zero was cruising away with their magic except for Lox, Gurren, and Steve.

The Devastator armor allowed the two Dwarves speed that matched Malsour's surfboard.

"You'll never catch me—I'm the fucking gingerbread man!" Steve yelled at the shades, running backward as he threw his middle fingers up and shook them at the Affinity shades.

The shades, sensing their prey getting away, once again let loose with their ranged attacks. The Air Affinity shades were gaining on the group as they fled.

Dave's orbs that had been following the group once again flared to life, the runes on their bodies lighting up as the Mana barrier between them was activated. The Mana quickly changed colors dangerously.

"Need to work on that energy dissipation," Dave muttered to himself. With another wave of his hand, four cylinders were thrown out of his bag of holding.

These cylinders rushed outward. A whirring noise filled the air as the cylinders cut into the ground. They moved from place to place, carving something into the ground.

The Mana barrier behind the raid group continued to flash angrily with the shades' impacts.

A section failed as an orb fell from the sky, burnt out from the power consumption.

The other orbs moved their positions, compensating for the burnt-out orb, but the Mana barrier was much weaker as it lacked the support that it had just a few moments ago.

Deia eyed the floating cylinders that raced across the ground ahead of the fleeing raid party. The sounds that came from them were similar to when Dave was using a carver to create prototypes.

Dave threw out more orbs to reinforce the Mana barrier as more burnt out and fell to the ground.

The cylinders that had been moving erratically for nearly a minute stopped their movements and rushed toward Dave. They disappeared into his bag of holding, much like Suzy's creations did when she was changing them out or storing them for later.

Party Zero, who was acting as the rearguard, rushed over to the spot where the cylinders had been working. Deia saw the large runes that had been carved into the ground.

As they passed, Dave conjured a final rune within the floor. Power flowed out from Dave's Abscondita armor. The runes lit up.

The Air Affinity shades reached the rune-covered area and promptly collapsed.

Gravity manipulation formation.

Dave had coded out an area where the gravity would be greatly increased. The shades that entered the area dropped to the ground; they were simple creatures and rushed into Dave's trap. They recovered, circulating Mana to overcome the trap as they moved forward at a greatly reduced speed.

Party Zero passed the Affinity pools and jumped down the stairs.

They were halfway across the open area where the shades spawned when the light around Dave's armor fell away and an explosion rang out behind the group.

The Affinity shades had broken Dave's trap but the raid party was already exiting the Six Affinity Temple.

The shades continued to rush forward as the last of the raid party broke out into the bright day. The Affinity shades' faces went slack. It was as if a switch had been flicked: they stopped their movement before slowly turning back toward the temple, slowly making their way back to their original position.

Party Zero slowed down their pace to a walk.

"Just what the hell triggered them to all rush us?" Malsour said.

"I don't know." Deia shook her head.

"Been awhile since I had a rush like that." Suzy laughed.

The others in Party Zero smiled. They'd barely escaped but now that they'd made it out, they were excited.

Deia looked at them all and rolled her eyes.

"Shows that we're still not the strongest things here," Dave said.

"Well, we never thought that—others just said it," Lox said.

The others agreed. Seeing that, Deia's heart was a little lighter. She was scared that they would all get so overconfident in their abilities that it would make them a liability in the future. Having them out on the raid not only showed that they hadn't fallen back on their training, but that they still had coordination and more importantly, that they couldn't be lone rangers, taking on all comers by themselves.

It might be kind of a letdown that we got chased out, but, I think the lesson we learned from it was well worth it. Deia looked at them all with a smile on her lips.

"Okay, well, I've got to get back to work." Dave sighed.

Deia's hand found his. With the Jukal and the upcoming event, Dave had been pushing himself hard. "Well, how about instead of getting buried in work, why don't we go and check out the Dwarven tournament. Aren't the semifinals and finals tomorrow?" Deia looked to everyone.

"Well..." Suzy began.

"We'd love to!" Induca flew up next to Suzy and grabbed her hand.

"I'm in the mood to watch a fight," Malsour said.

"You know we're there." Steve's hands wrapped around Lox and Gurren's shoulders.

The clang of metal on metal made everyone wince.

"Great—got three metal heads now," Dave complained.

"Hey, you made these beauties!" Gurren's two thumbs pointed at his armored body.

"Why do I have a feeling that I'm going to regret it?" Dave looked to Deia.

She shook her head and giggled slightly. "Oh, Anna, bring Alkao as well. I'll invite Quindar and Fornau." Deia's words were more like an order.

"Yes, ma'am," Anna said dryly.

The others chuckled. As much as Anna said she didn't want to go out with Alkao, they all knew one another enough to read her and her emotions.

She was too stubborn for her own good. Thankfully Alkao was equally as stubborn.

Chapter 37: Dwarven Tournament's Finals

Dave smiled as Deia came through the portal. With her were Anna, Alkao, Quindar, and Fornau. The rest of Party Zero as well as a number of the Dwarven Master Smiths were already there and waiting.

The new arrivals and those waiting greeted one another as they set out from the teleport pad.

Dave had cleaned up after the fight, now wearing a simple set of pants and shirt instead of his armor and weapons.

Deia interlinked her arm with his, a smile on her face as she leaned against him.

He kissed the top of her head, the smell of freshly washed hair filling his senses.

They were all waiting in Terra. People were talking in excited tones, the different Dwarven Master Smiths boasted about the warriors who had come from their respective mountains and their achievements.

There was only one Dwarf left in the match, born and raised in Aldamire: Ondae was one of the hidden masters. He had a Weapon of Power but didn't use it in the matches to be fair to the other contestants.

Ondae was a name held in the hearts of the Dwarves. Many of the various hidden masters around Emerilia didn't want to join in on the fights; using their hidden trump cards would make it easier for other forces to defeat them in the future. They were the hidden strength of the Dwarves. Although Ondae was fighting for the sake of competition, many believed that he was hiding his own trump cards for just this reason.

The last couple of rounds were being held within Aldamire. It was the largest Dwarven mountain and hosted the last of the matches.

"It's hard to think that the prison is supposed to be opening up in just a few weeks," Deia said softly.

"I know. Though, I talked to Bob—it seems he will have somewhere safe for you and your cousin's children to go," Dave said.

"Me? I'm not going anywhere," Deia said angrily.

"If you're pregnant, you are." Dave's voice was icy. He didn't want to argue and if she was angry with him, he was fine with that. Otherwise he might lose her and their unborn child.

Dave's harsh words momentarily stunned her.

He looked at her with unwavering eyes.

Any arguments she had rose to her lips but never made them past in the face of his stare and the cold logic behind it.

"We will talk about this later," Deia resolved.

"No, let's finish it here. If you're pregnant, you're not going out and fighting. If I see you out there fighting, I will teleport your ass back to the laboratory, every damn time. I don't care if the Jukal notice," Dave said. "I'm not doing this to just fight you—I'm doing this because I love you too much to lose you and I'm willing to argue my ass off and piss you off as long as you're safe."

Dave's tone warmed, as he felt truly vulnerable. He had never loved someone as he loved Deia. Seeing her hurt, or with her and his child in danger, troubled his heart.

Deia's eyes softened and her chin quivered a bit. "Okay. If things turn bad, I'll stay with Bob. Otherwise, I'll stay down here doing what I can," Deia conceded, her words quiet. She understood Dave's love for her and his protective spirit. She could not ask for a better man to be at her side.

Dave turned her so she faced him and wrapped his arms around her. His powerful arms were gentle to as to not put pressure on the baby between them.

"Thank you, firecracker," Dave said, genuine relief in his voice as his entire body seemed to relax. He kissed Deia's head.

Deia looked up at Dave with a saucy expression, puckering her lips. Dave laughed and kissed her lips. She let out a content noise, turning and leaning against Dave's shoulder. He kept his arms around her, wishing that the moment never ended.

The crowd in Terra were all talking in excited tones as the teleport pad flared to life and the bustling streets of Aldamire came into view.

"Now connected to Aldamire!" an automaton declared.

The waiting group walked through the teleport pad and into Aldamire.

Dwarven shield bearers watched them all. Their commander bowed deeply to the mass of Dwarven Master Smiths who came through. The smiths nodded to the forces there and continued on their way, returning to their excited chatter, whether it was about what they had been working on, the match coming up, or just random conversation.

The commander's eyes went wide as Steve, Lox, and Gurren walked through, the last two wearing their Devastator armor.

The Dwarven shield bearers' stony expressions shifted slightly as they looked upon the two massive Weapons of Power.

Lox and Gurren's armor nodded to them as they continued to talk to Steve.

"No, I'm telling you, you've got to try using the Air enchantments on your joints!" Gurren said.

"Yes, we'll be faster, but then they're weaker," Lox said.

"Then we've just got to increase our Intelligence to compensate. If we can react fast enough, we can switch between Air and Dark Affinity enchantments. Move like wind, smack like Steve's axe," Gurren said, his last words stilted, as if impersonating a caveman.

"Thanks," Steve said with a wide smile.

"I don't know if that was a compliment or not," Induca said beside Suzy.

Suzy just shrugged. Lu Lu, resting on her shoulders, let out a complaining screech. "Someone's moody because I'm talking about my other soul-bound creature, aren't they." Suzy scratched under Lu Lu's chin.

Lu Lu's upset expression soon turned to pleased purring under Suzy's expert itching.

Induca giggled as her fingers scratched between Lu Lu's wings.

Under her two moms' petting, Lu Lu's expression turned to one of relaxed bliss, happy to have her two Human servants put their hands to real work!

***

Malsour watched over it all and he smiled. His heart had been tight with worry over the last couple of months. With the loss of members from his own family, a thread of anger had weaved its way into his heart. He had wanted to fight the heavens then and there, to go all out and attack the Jukal that dared to bring this pain to his family.

Over time, he had calmed down his emotions, dealing with them and holding them back, promising himself that later, he would deal with these issues in his heart, and he would make those who hurt his family pay for what they had done.

His analytical and calculating mind had returned, now that the pain within his heart unraveled a bit. Steve, Lox, and Gurren were talking with the various Dwarven Master Smiths, making plans for drinks as well as talking about the competitions and their different armors and weapons. Dave and Deia were talking to each other softly, glued to each other, in their own world.

Suzy and Induca were similarly keeping to themselves, relieving the stresses over the last couple of weeks and giving Lu Lu attention. The little lightning phoenix seemed very pleased with the state of the world.

Malsour looked to Quindar, Fornau, Anna, Alkao, and Jung Lee.

Jung Lee looked around Aldamire with surprise across his face. His face looked younger as he stared at these new sights. Jung Lee had spent his days moving around Terra. As a potion master, he had been excited and thrilled by the rare and powerful ingredients that passed through Terra. He'd spent days just walking through the various potion gardens located within the growing towers. He'd also been practicing with his sword in the various training areas.

Still, everything was a shock to him. Malsour hoped that he would join the Stone Raiders. They had helped Jung Lee escape, as they felt it was the right thing to do. Sure, he might help them later on, but that wasn't their main reason.

Jung Lee excitedly conversed with Anna, Alkao, Quindar, Fornau, and Malsour. They had all been around longer than most people on Emerilia. There was a thread of familiarity between them all.

Here, no one was rushing to work on a project, or training up fighters, or readying themselves for a fight. For just tonight, they could push those worries off. They were just a big group of friends going to see a grand tournament and have a night without worries.

***

The two semifinals were going on in the morning while the finals would be held in the afternoon.

All around Aldamire, people were in a festive mood. The mountain city's outer reaches, where people were allowed to roam, were filled with all manner of people. Food and drink flowed easily as bards sung of the great battles that had occurred and others talked of the upcoming matches.

The actual arenas had been erected around Aldamire Mountain. With thousands of Dwarves, it had taken a few days for them to make the arenas as well as the massive fortifications that could keep out anything that Ashal's wilderness produced.

Today, the group from Terra had come to see Ondae and Iswul fight. Ondae was an Earth-attribute melee fighter; Iswul was an Orc berserker, unlike the normal Earth or even Dark affinity Orcs, Iswul was blessed with an affinity for water. Among Orcs, it was rare to find another with this water affinity.

The arenas that surrounded the mountain now showed massive projections that would make it appear as if the fighters were within these arenas. The real fights would take place within two massive arenas that had been built on the two second-tallest peaks of Aldamire Mountain.

People swarmed through the mountain. Dwarven shield bearers kept order, not afraid to offend someone or throw them out of their territory for a moment. The Dwarves' temperament was well known and very few wanted to create a disturbance with them. It allowed the atmosphere to be festive instead of tense with people fighting outside the arena as well as within it.

The group navigated through the rising levels and different groups of vendors. It didn't take long until they reached the arena. The arena thrummed with energy and voices as they were escorted to an area that had been set aside for their group.

Everyone took their seats. People were talking excitedly as they pointed at members of Party Zero as well as the famed Dwarven Master Smiths.

It wasn't long after they took their seats that the contestants appeared.

The announcer was actually drowned out by the cheers and cries of the audience.

Ondae waved slightly before looking to Iswul. Ondae's armor looked simple but to Dave's eyes, he could see the great workmanship that had gone into making this armor.

Iswul's armor was much larger than Ondae's. It wasn't pretty but it was decently made. The massive set of armor made him look like a hunched moving tank.

His helmet was open, allowing one to see his scarred, green-skinned face. His right tusk had been broken off at the halfway point; both tusks had been carved into elaborate tribal markings. Above his right eye and on his left cheek, there was a scar that ended where his tusk was. The attack that had taken his tusk had also left a deep scar on his face.

In his hands, he held a small rounded shield as well as a sword that would have to be used with two hands by most people.

With his weight, Iswul didn't seem encumbered; instead, he seemed to be walking as if he were out on a stroll.

Ondae and Iswul's eyes were locked on each other's, eyeing their opponent carefully. To get to this stage, they both knew that the other was to not be underestimated.

They stepped onto the large stage set in the middle of the arena. The two ignored the crowd, totally focused on each other as a Mana barrier erupted around them.

The crowd's volume slowly got under control as the announcer waited for them.

"Welcome to the semifinals! From this battle, the two contestants for the first place in this here Dwarven tournament will be decided!"

Once again, the crowd erupted into excited cheers.

Everyone got themselves under control again as Ondae and Iswul slowly walked around the outside of the stage, studying the other for any sign of a weakness or possible advantage that they might have. They looked over the other's gear, their strides.

Both of them were great fighters; any shred of evidence that they could gain now might lead to victory later on.

"Let the battle begin!" the announcer yelled.

Ondae's shield jumped up as if it were sentient. The stones beneath his feet cracked as he surged forward.

Iswul leaped forward as well. Just before they were about to meet, Iswul moved out of the path of Ondae, perfectly anticipating his strike.

Ondae spun and turned; his shield, modeled after the same ones used by the warclans, had its tell-tale twin spikes slammed into the ground. Ondae braced himself.

Iswul, who had moved like an eel to escape Ondae's strike, moved as if there were not hundreds of pounds of armor on his body. His sword seemed to move slowly as it collided with Ondae's shield.

Iswul's movements flowed from one to the next, as if water drifting between boulders and then hit as if that water fell from a great height.

Ondae's shield rang with the impact. He was thrown back five steps as the twin pegs on his shield left deep grooves in the ground. Ondae's sword jabbed outward, so fast that it was but a silver blur.

Iswul once again bent and moved as if his body were boneless.

Dave's eyes saw the thin silver line that appeared across Iswul's shoulders where Ondae's blade had passed.

Iswul's eyes seemed to take on a red glow from underneath his helmet. His movements sped up, his blade once again darting out toward Ondae's shield.

The two clashed. Ondae turned, pulling his shield free of the ground as their swords and shields clashed. With every impact, the very air around them quaked with expended power; when a blow landed, the other's feet left deep impacts in the ground.

The crowd was completely silent, none of them daring to blink or look away as the two masters clashed.

Many were just watching the after images of the two as they came together.

They moved across the stage, exchanging blows with ferocious speed.

Dave felt a smile grow across his face.

Iswul and Ondae's hidden faces under their armored helmets were covered in massive smiles. To find an opponent with which they could go all out gave rise to an excitement within them both.

Ondae's hits and movements were strong and powerful while Iswul's were slippery and seemingly delicate.

"Ondae is using his strength in bursts, isolating it to parts of his body," Steve commented, his voice filled with respect. Ondae's control over how he augmented his body's strength told of a master of his Earth Affinity. He used it to augment different sections of his body instead of all of it to get concentrated power through every movement.

"Iswul is keeping the flow more constant but his strength is more than Ondae's. I wonder if it's because he trains in that armor," Alkao commented.

"Even though he's not moving his Mana around to buff his body as much, Iswul's attacks greatly vary in strength. He might have a few weak attacks but still Ondae has to fight with all of his power because he can easily hide his weak and strong attacks. His ability to internalize and control Mana is impressive," Deia said.

The others all nodded. They hadn't been able to notice this as their sensitivity toward Mana was nowhere as close as Deia's.

Ondae threw up a few earthen walls to block attacks, creating earth pillars under his feet to change the direction of his attack.

Iswul looked pressured but continued to dodge by the slimmest of margins, taking hits on areas he didn't need to worry about.

Knowing that he would be healed afterward, he was willing to take a few injuries.

Ondae increased his weight. Dropping under Iswul's counter-attack, he planted his feet and punched forward with the edge of his shield.

Even Iswul couldn't stop the short ranged brutal attack. He spat blood out of his helmet as Ondae charged forward. This one hit wasn't enough to take Iswul out.

A red mist seemed to gather around Iswul as his speed started to increase, his eyes glowing red.

"He's activated his berserker racial trait!" Alkao said with alarm. This racial trait was the same one that the Demons had.

Alkao leaned forward, interested in how Iswul would use it to his advantage.

Iswul met Ondae's attack, stopping his blade with his small shield. The attack's power was so great that Ondae nearly lost his blade.

Seeing the new red haze, Ondae retreated, his blade ringing violently.

Iswul flowed forward; Ondae attacked—his blade and shield moved, making whistling noises as they cut through the air.

The Mana barrier trembled with just the air from these attacks, the dust and debris getting whipped up in the attacks.

Iswul lurched to the side to avoid Ondae's blade, before coming back like a spring! He launched his sword at Ondae.

The air within the arena seemed to stir as those present took in an alarmed breath of cold air.

He had actually thrown his sword! Why would he do that? This thought resounded in everyone's mind.

Ondae was forced to dodge as Iswul closed the three meters between them before he recovered.

His right fist and left small shield moved so fast that it seemed that the air was constantly rushing past Ondae.

Multiple impacts could be heard, blending together as one. It sounded as if they were in a smithy, not watching a fight.

Ondae attacked here and there. His sword became ungainly at this range; his shield was nearly pressed up against his body.

Iswul didn't give him a moment to recover, to set his feet.

This was a Dwarven shield bearer's nightmare—losing momentum. If they lost momentum and weren't able to recover, then it was more likely that they would fall and open a hole within the formation.

Ondae's body became covered in a green glow as he let out a cry. He pushed his foot forward a half-step as Earth Mana surged through his body, reinforcing his actions. Unlike mages, both he and Iswul reinforced their bodies with the Mana they controlled.

Iswul's small shield slammed into this shield as it shot forward. Iswul let out a grunt of pain as he was thrown backward, actually flipping with the momentum imparted by Ondae's blow. He landed in a three-point stance, his right hand and feet leaving deep scars in the stage's floor.

Ondae hadn't been standing idle. Earth columns erupted from the ground, tossing him forward as he picked up speed.

Iswul jumped out of the scars left by his limbs and rushed to meet Ondae. Blue Mana circulated over his body as they clashed in mid-air.

The sound of metal hitting metal rang out as a shockwave of air from the two meeting blew out from between them, leaving a line of broken rocks in the stage and clearing the sky of debris and dust thrown up by their previous clashes.

Ondae got the upper hand, his sword coming down on Iswul.

Iswul got his small shield up in time to defend, but his body crashed down into the stage, a crater forming where he landed.

Ondae rushed downward, increasing his weight.

Iswul jumped out of the crater, dodging Ondae. His shield slammed forward, hitting Ondae's side.

Water met Earth. Ondae didn't have time to change his Mana from increasing his weight to defense. He was the one thrown. He turned in the sky, his shield coming down, twin spikes digging into the ground to slow him.

Iswul and Ondae once again flashed forward.

These attacks contained their full power. The barrier around them shook with the power of the attacks.

Iswul got behind Ondae; his leg flashed out and the air seemed to crack as Ondae shot forward.

Ondae slammed into the ground and tore up the stage. He started to climb out of the pit as Iswul appeared in front of him. His small shield moved in a blur of light, hitting Ondae's helmeted head.

Ondae slammed into the ground once again, a crater around him.

Dave let out a breath he didn't know he was holding. To get in that last hit, Iswul had created water jets under his feet to reach Ondae before he recovered.

The audience was quiet, looking at the destroyed stage and unconscious Ondae.

"And the winner is Iswul!" the announcer said.

Time seemed to start again as yells and cheers filled the arena.

Animals within miles of Aldamire heard the noise and fled. The audience had never seen something like Iswul and Ondae's fight in their lives!

***

Josh and the Stone Raiders leadership walked through Aldamire. They'd just seen the end of the fight between Zela and Kiona. The two semifinals had been held at the same time. They were just talking about the fight between the rogue fighter and Air Affinity mage when a voice cried out.

"Who let you bums out of Terra!"

They looked over to a restaurant they were passing, the doors and windows were open with a filled patio. It wasn't hard to see the metal idiot waving at them.

"Who brought this pile of bolts out?" Josh complained as the group moved to enter the restaurant, seeing Party Zero, Dwarven Master Smiths who worked at the Terra smithy and Alkao, Quindar, and Fornau.

They greeted one another and grabbed seats, taking up half of the restaurant as they talked about the matches that they had seen and the eventual matchup between Iswul and Kiona.

"I've got to say, I think Kiona has it," Kim said.

"You've said she's fast, and she's got a good cutting ability with her Air Affinity. Though Iswul is armored as hell and while he might not be as fast as Kiona, his dodging ability is crazy." Gurren waved a chicken leg to emphasize his point.

It had taken quite a lot of cajoling to get Lox and Gurren to show their faces.

Even the Dwarven Master Smiths were talking about the upcoming match instead of studying the new Weapons of Power that Dave had created.

"But you should see this—she can control tens of different wind spells at the same time! Her chaining ability is crazy!" Dwayne took a deep drink from his tankard.

Josh drank from his mug and snorted.

"So, who do you think is going to win?" Dave looked to the others.

"I think Kiona. If Iswul can get close, then she's going to be in trouble, but her movement speed is going to be significant. As long as she has the Mana pool and regeneration for it, this is going to be pretty one-sided," Quindar said.

"It looks like he can control his berserker state, which means that he can gain an increase in his abilities for a period of time," Alkao added.

"I'm just happy that I'm not fighting either of them," Josh said.

"Reminds me of something the Chinese say." Dave snorted and shook his head. "When you think that you're the strongest, you're really nothing more than a frog in a well. There are always stronger, more powerful people. Attaining the peak, it's a never ending progression."

"I have also heard a similar saying," Jung Lee said. The strange man seemed to have a calming aura, his every action refined.

Josh studied the man as he continued to talk.

"I think that Iswul has not yet used all of his moves. From what it sounds Kiona can do, unless she has some trump cards then Iswul will quite possibly win this."

Everyone had thoughtful looks on their faces.

So, this is the man that Dave and Party Zero saved from the Six Affinities prison. When trying to sense the man's aura, Josh seemed to be stopped by a metal wall. There was no getting past it and understanding the man beneath. It was alarming because even people who had the ability to hide their aura, a part of their aura leaked out. Jung Lee seemed to be a Mana-less child.

That kind of abnormality made Josh frown as he took a drink from his mug.

As time went on, they relaxed more, drinking and sharing stories. Even the Dwarven Master Smiths came to join their group, as well as a number of other Stone Raiders who had also come to see the tournament.

By mid-afternoon, they were happily buzzed as they all headed for the third match of the day: the finals between Kiona and Iswul.

***

Alkao smiled as the big group entered the arena, quickly moving to the boxes that they had gained access to.

Everywhere they went, they attracted looks of interest and mutterings.

"Is that a Demon? I thought they were all up in Devil's Crater," someone commented.

"Look at those Dwarven smith necklaces! I've never seen so many Dwarven Master Smiths together!" another said.

"Those are the leaders of the Stone Raiders! The number-one Player-run guild in Emerilia! I heard that they have equal alliances with the adventurer's and mage's guild!"

"Is that an Aleph automaton? It's huge, and talking!" The speaker sounded confused as Alkao snorted and shook his head at this comment and the others that rose in the group's passing.

They were allowed through a guarded section of the arena. There were many powerful men and women who were watching the Dwarven tournament. As such, security was high in these places.

They quickly entered their box, the majority moving to get closer to the action.

Deia, Fornau, Quindar, Malsour, Suzy, Induca, and Lucy quickly took seats to the back of the box. Although they might be fighters and this was indeed an interesting event, they didn't have the same hot blood as the others.

Alkao felt a small but powerful arm squeeze him from the side as they stopped next to the banister. He looked down with a wry smile at Anna's perky ears and her tail that swished from side to side.

"Someone seems to be happy today," Alkao commented, looking at Anna's tail.

She made a noise of complaint, making to pull back her arm.

Instead, he snuck around her and held her tight.

She struggled half-heartedly before giving up. She looked up at Alkao with a frown. Her hair had fallen down over her eyes, a glow on her cheeks from the drinking. She sighed, causing the errant hairs to shift slightly. She looked back to the fight and leaned into him.

"It's nearly perfect." Her words were quiet; it was only with Alkao's hearing that he was able to pick up what she said.

A wide smile spread across his face as he relaxed. Slowly but surely he was breaking down this stubborn wolf's walls.

The sound of a bell rang through the massive arena. Silence descended as everyone waited with anticipation.

"And now for the final round of the Dwarven tournament: Iswul versus Kiona!" The crowd's cheers were like a wall of noise.

From opposite sides of the arena, Iswul—wearing his massive armor—and Kiona—wearing a simple shirt and pants—walked out. A white staff with a clear orb nestled in its peak rested in her hands.

Kiona waved at the crowd with her free hand and the cheers increased. Iswul's steps were light but there was a power behind him as his hulking armored mass moved toward the stage like an unstoppable juggernaut.

Alkao felt his heart stir at the sight of these two competitors.

Everyone at the front of the box looked at them excitedly. There was no way that they could even try to talk—the volume was too much.

Kiona floated from the ground. The air around her moved as if it were a familiar coat. A Mana barrier enclosed the stage and the contestants.

"Let the final battle of the Dwarven tournament begin!" The announcer's voice was barely audible over the crowd's cheers.

Kiona opened her eyes, holding her staff to the side as the air was whipped up into a storm around her. Her eyes glowed white and her face became impassive and cold as power surged through the arena.

Iswul let out a low growl, flipping his longsword so it ran along his leg as he crouched. His small shield faced forward; blue lines and runes formed over him as he called down buffs onto his body.

Kiona gestured with her free hand; following it, a blade of Air whistled through the arena, carving a line in the stage's rocks.

Iswul tilted to the side. He exploded forward and a crater appeared under his feet as he dodged the Air blade.

Another was quickly thrown out.

Iswul dodged this as well. He was like a boat in a storm, rolling over these attacks.

Kiona's hand blurred as blades tore clean lines through the air and stage, leaving it in ruins.

Iswul made it within ten meters before he was hit by an Air blade. There was a shrieking noise as the Air blade cut into metal. Iswul appeared five meters back from where he had encountered the blades.

Since Kiona's first attack to Iswul's leap backward, Alkao had only taken a breath. *Their speed is incredible!* Alkao thought.

There was barely a pause before Iswul charged in once again. His body wove through the attacks Kiona unleashed.

Air blades shredded the stage apart while Air lances formed. As they passed over the stage, rocks were shattered and torn apart, leaving a path of destruction as the debris was thrown away wildly.

The Mana barrier stopped the whizzing debris from hitting the audience.

Iswul dodged one of these lances. His body blurred as he moved bonelessly through oncoming attacks. A shriek tore through the arena, making Iswul momentarily lose his concentration. A blade hit him as a lance surged forth. He used the momentum of the first blade to toss himself aside. He landed prone on the ground. With a growl, he slapped the ground, once again returning to his feet to meet Kiona's blades.

The lines and runes that covered his armor glowed brighter as he increased the power of the buffs on himself and on his armor. His speed increased dramatically. He surged forward. His body turned into a blue blur; his sword and armor glowed similarly. He used his blade to forcefully parry the Air blades, and divert them.

The corner of Kiona's mouth twitched at this sight as Iswul hurled himself forward.

A wall of Air blades met with Iswul. With his unnatural dodging ability and using his sword and shield to divert the blades or to take the hits on his bulky armor, he was closing the space to just a meter.

She raised her staff up and down. The air that surrounded her surged in power. The angry breeze that surrounded her before spun faster and faster. A tornado not dissimilar from the lances that she had thrown out grew around her body.

Iswul held up his shield. Thin wisps of air outside the tornado marred the surface of the shield as he was pushed backward by the tornado's force.

"Break for me!" Iswul yelled. A red aura covered the blue Mana that flowed through his buffs. A layer of water covered Iswul, mingling with this red berserker aura to make it look like fresh blood.

His sword flashed forward, covered in the mixture of aura and Mana. It slammed into the tornado. Water and Air Mana fought each other as the forces of Kiona's spell competed with Iswul's strength.

A shockwave exploded outward, and silver scars appeared where Iswul's armor had been hit.

Iswul let out a yell. Holding his sword into the tornado, Mana surged through his body. The surge of Mana broke the carefully constructed spell formation Kiona had created to hold up the tornado.

The tornado exploded outwards, quickly dissipating and revealing Kiona.

A bow and arrow made from air rested in her hands as the wind around her dissipated an arrow shot forth from her bow. Iswul barely had time to react as he raised his shield.

A loud noise rang out through the arena with the arrow's impact.

He was forced back half a dozen feet as once again the air around Kiona was stirred up into an angry tempest. Lances formed around her; her staff floated beside her in the air as she pulled back on her bow string again. An arrow once again turned into a spinning cutting wind.

Iswul moved out of the way of the arrow, a deep gouge in his shoulder armor.

Attacks rained down on him, faster and more furious than before.

The spells over Iswul's body disappeared, the Mana falling away as he jumped and twisted to escape and attack. As he was moving in the air, blades of water cut out from within his armor. His armor fell away. A lance turned his shin guard into scrap metal as pieces rained down from his body, revealing Iswul himself. He wore a simple cotton shirt and shorts with padding strapped to him to stop his armor from chafing. He held just his sword and shield.

What is he doing? He took off all of his armor—it was the only thing stopping Kiona from cutting him apart!

Alkao looked at the large Orc. He was about six and a half feet tall, with tribal blue tattoos that looked like waves, from calm to raging tsunamis, across his body.

These different designs glowed with blue Mana as magical circles appeared around Iswul as he applied buffs directly to himself.

Kiona unleashed attacks on him as Iswul turned into a blue and green shadow.

He weaved through the attacks. His blade swung out and slammed into the weak Air barrier around Kiona.

Without his armor, his speed had risen by nearly twenty percent. Where he had taken hits on his armor before, now he moved through Kiona's attacks with ease.

She pushed him back with a wall of blades and Air lances. It took time for her to call on more of the spells, which Iswul used to close in once again and strike out at her barrier.

The sound of raging wind and Iswul's sword impacting on Kiona's defenses rang out through the arena. Kiona started moving from her first spot, trying to create distance from Iswul.

As her image blurred, Iswul seemed to become faster. Hounding her again and again, his sword smashed against her Air barrier relentlessly.

Kiona's face turned from indifference to one of focus as she bit her lower lip, constantly creating and unleashing spells at Iswul. If just one of them landed on his bare body, then the fight would be hers!

Though, Iswul's uncanny dodging ability and the strength of his blows was making her go all out with chain casting spells. Even with her large Mana pool and regeneration, her face was starting to pale as Mana fatigue closed in on her. She dissolved her bow and grabbed her staff; the speed which she could make her Air attacks increased.

Iswul still hounded her again and again, a cold smile on his face as he started to laugh happily.

To viewers, it looked as if Iswul were playing a mad game, facing Mother Nature herself.

He had indeed clashed with a powerful goddess who rained down attack after attack down on him. Here, this was where he came alive.

Alkao and the members of the Stone Raiders were all watching the match with intense eyes.

The line that Iswul walked—between victory and defeat, between death and survival—it was a situation that they had all been in. It was a situation that these gamers came for: to feel alive, to feel the thrill of winning against the odds.

These were two impossible and powerful forces clashing with everything on the line.

Iswul's Mana surged as his attacks hit harder and harder.

The barrier, which had been also serving the function of pulling wind to Kiona in order to make it easier for her to cast more powerful spells, failed in a burst of wind.

Iswul was pushed back a few steps but he rushed to the side. As Kiona whistled, a bird seemed to form in the air. It was two dimensional and hard to see unless one was looking from above or below.

The bird tore through the air, making Iswul, who dodged the attack, spit out blood from the massive pressure wave that followed it.

Kiona twirled her staff, a cyclone forming in front of it.

The debris under Iswul's feet turned to dust. He seemed to disappear under his great speed.

Alkao's eyes weren't fast enough to catch Iswul's movements, only seeing his destination.

Iswul was behind Kiona, his large arm on her neck while his sword made her back arch as it poked her lightly in the back.

Immediately, Kiona's attack dissipated.

Alkao looked at the two combatants, whose chests were moving rapidly as they panted from their exertions.

The stage that had held their fight was a pile of rubble and dust. The strength of their attacks had torn it apart.

Finally, the announcer came to his senses. "Iswul is the winner of the Dwarven tournament!"

The crowd took a moment before they cheered.

Iswul released Kiona and lowered his sword.

No matter who the crowd had been hoping to win from the beginning, now they all stood and cheered till their lungs burned.

The fight was something that they would tell their grandchildren. The abilities displayed showed off the true fighting abilities of both parties. The match had been hard and at any moment one of them could have fallen.

Even Alkao, who was usually a rather restrained man, cheered the two competitors.

Epilogue

Kol tapped Dave's side, pulling his attention from the two fighters in the middle of the arena.

"What is it?" Dave yelled. The cheers had died down somewhat, but it was still incredibly loud.

"We've got work to do." Kol handed Dave a potion.

Dave recognized the potion that would clear someone's mind. It was commonly used to cure hangovers or to sober up quickly.

Dave drank the potion without hesitation. The other members of the Council of Anvil and Fire were also taking the potions. Their exuberant cheering from a moment ago was replaced by solemn smiles.

Kol led the way out of the box.

Dave waved to Deia.

She gave him a questioning look.

Dave raised his shoulders and hands in a shrug before waving to her, indicating that he didn't know what was going on but he'd catch up with her later.

The Dwarven Master Smiths were greeted by Dwarven shield bearers; they moved around them as protection. Even in the halls under the arena they could hear the wild cheering.

They were quickly escorted out of the arena and into the actual mountain, where only Dwarves stayed.

Dwarves had deep looks of respect as they moved out of the way of the group, nodding their heads in greeting as the Dwarven Master Smiths passed through and reached a bank of elevators. They dropped down deep within the mountain, exiting one elevator to get on another.

They entered a large facility that was carved into the mountain. There were Dwarven guards all over the place. Their auras were powerful—not as strong as Kiona's or Iswul's but if three or four of them grouped together, the two champions might have issues with trying to defeat them.

They entered the facility. The shield bearers who had brought them down turned and left as the Dwarven Master Smiths were checked and verified by guards no less than three times as they made it through different checkpoints.

Finally, they reached a massive vault door.

As Dave looked at it, he was stunned. His Touch of the Land spell didn't penetrate this door or the surrounding walls. It was like a black hole in his senses.

Hidden Dwarven masters stood on either side of the door, with others nearby if they were needed.

These individuals were as strong, if not stronger, than Ondae. All of them wore gear that was many times better than the simple armor and sword Ondae had used.

There were even a few who held Weapons of Power.

Dave continued to stare at the door as Kol came over.

"Within this vault, Weapons of Power from all over Emerilia are stored," Kol said.

"Why do we need a vault for them? There can't be that many," Dave said.

Kol looked to Dave with a crooked eyebrow. "There have been thousands of Dwarven Master Smiths on Emerilia, each having made a handful of Weapons of Power. There are also some weapons that come from Creatures of Power, or the Pantheon, or are made by people other than the Dwarves. While they weren't Weapons of Power, their strength is comparable. Once these weapons are recovered, then the Dwarven Master Smiths imprint these weapons, increasing their power but also adding in the safeguard that is their Willpower, changing them into Weapons of Power."

Dave's eyes went wide as he shook his head.

The Dwarven Master Smiths knew that their weapons were meant to cause destruction. Though it could be said that their true abilities didn't come out until they were creating a Weapon of Power.

This was because even if their weapon was passed around, it would only unleash its full power and strength when held by those who were accepted by the thread of the Dwarven master's soul.

Dave looked at the door with newfound respect.

The Dwarven Master Smiths' excited tones from earlier had dimmed somewhat as they stood outside the massive vault that held multiple Weapons of Power. The usually rambunctious group was much quieter than normal.

After some time, a large group of people were escorted into the facility and before the Dwarven Master Smiths. These people came from all manner of backgrounds. They had been fighters within the Dwarven tournament who had passed through the war council and the Council of Anvil and Fire's testing.

They might not have been the strongest of the fighters but they were people who had proved themselves in the eyes of these two groups.

These fighters, filled with excitable energy, showed deep respect when in front of these Dwarven Master Smiths. Their eyes flickered to the two hidden Dwarf masters who stood beside the vault door.

Iswul and Kiona, who were in the crowd, also looked to these masters with interest. These two hidden masters were much stronger than the people in this room, and used at least one Weapon of Power.

The room was tense as the Dwarven Master Smiths looked over the contestants and those who had been elected to take a Weapon of Power.

Endur stepped forward. In his position as head of the Council of Anvil and Fire, he had shown an inner steel that he had usually hidden with sarcastic remarks and flippant remarks.

All of the Dwarven Master Smiths stood behind him.

The contestants looked to Endur with questions in their eyes.

"My name is Endur. I am the head of the Council of Anvil and Fire. The reason you have been brought here is that you have tested your abilities in the arena and passed the tests of my own council and the Dwarven war council." Endur's voice rolled through the large hall. No one dared to make a noise.

"In a few weeks or months, the event known as 'Of Myths and Legends' will begin. This event is of the likes of which has not been seen in the history of Emerilia. This contest was made to not only see who the strongest people were in Emerilia. It was also to see which of you would help to lead Emerilia out of this event. Each of you has shown incredible fighting abilities, a strong heart, and a strong mind. While the gods have their own champions, so, too, does Emerilia need hers.

"I'm not saying that you're the best of people on Emerilia. Though I do say that when creatures start being released across this world, you will hurry to attack them, whether this be for fame, wealth, or a sense of duty."

The people in front of Endur seemed to relax. Some of them might be good people, but most of them had come to search for glory and riches. This kind of motivation was enough for the Dwarven Master Smiths as long as that person had a moral code that would make them search for those riches and power out in the light of day instead of killing their enemies and friends from behind.

"To this end, we will support you in your path." Endur looked to the two hidden masters.

They bowed their heads slightly before turning to the door.

They made a number of motions with their hands before cutting their fingers and pressing their blood to the door.

Locks started to release. The deep and powerful sound of these locks made everyone look at the door in shock. Even the Dwarven Master Smiths had a reverence in their eyes as the doors opened.

An ancient and powerful aura spread out from within.

"Follow your senses and if you pass the weapon's test, then you may take the Weapon of Power that chooses you." Endur waved for them to enter the vault.

Someone stepped forward; the others followed as they walked silently into the room.

Dave's face was dark as he looked over these powerful people as they entered the vault.

Weapon-filled racks, neatly stacked and displayed: it made any smith look in awe while a warrior would feel their hand itch to hold these weapons.

Dave sighed as he saw those weapons. The event that they had prepared for so long was finally coming near. Worries and fears rose to the surface.

He had prepared as much as possible for what was to come. If he just had more time, he could produce machines and weapons to protect Emerilia, not only from the creatures that were being released but from the Jukal Empire.

However, his time was running out. Although he could hope about using his different creations to save Emerilia and the people on it, he simply wouldn't be able to.

Dave took a deep breath, determination hardening his features.

He would persevere and see that Emerilia survived: for Deia, for his unborn child, for his friends and family.

***

Somewhere in Heval

A flash of light filled the cave, revealing a five-foot-tall metal spire that descended into the ground.

Runes covered the spire as a green screen appeared, facing out in every direction.

The screen read:

Spawn Point

Days	Hours	Minutes	Seconds
20	23	59	59

Emerilia will be continued in Beyond All Expectations.

Want a bigger map of Emerilia and the continents? Check out **http://theeternalwriter.deviantart.com/**

You can check out my other books, what I'm working on and upcoming releases through the following means:

Website: **http://michaelchatfield.com/**

Twitter: **@chatfieldsbooks**[1]

Facebook: **Michael Chatfield**[2]

Goodreads: **Goodreads.com/michaelchatfield**[3]

Thanks again for reading! ☺

Continue on for Character Sheet!

1. https://twitter.com/chatfieldsbooks
2. https://www.facebook.com/michaelchatfieldsbooks/?ref=hl
3. https://www.goodreads.com/author/show/14055550.Michael_Chatfield

In Alphabetical order

Ankol

Dwarf

Dwarven Master Smith. Smithing Art: Metal Spinner. Lives in Grorart Mountain.

Boran-Al

Lich

One of the Dark Lord's Champions. Works directly under the Dark Lord. Creates Creatures of Power and carry's out the Dark Lord's orders. His Citadel was destroyed.

Alastair Montgoa

Arch Lich aka former Lord Vailyn. Gave up his fellow Aleph to have everlasting life; used the centuries to build strength and knowledge

Barry

Dwarf

Dwarven Master Smith. Smithing Art-Unknown. Wandering smith.

Cassie

Elf/Human Halfling

Holy warrior. Leader of the Golden Sabres. In a relationship with Josh Giles.

Dark Lord

God

Embodiment of the Dark affinity. Created Demons. Normally an ally with the Earth Lord. Always looking a way to tip the power balance of Emerilia in his favor.

Dasano

Dwarf

Dwarven Master Smith. Smithing Art: Metal Press. Lives in Grorart Mountain.

Akatol Dracul

Dragon

Water Mage. Was the second Dragon, Denur's husband. Went mad and started a genocide, disappeared.

Denur Dracul

Dragon

Fire Mage Hailed as 'Mother of Dragons'. First of her race, a creature of power created by the Lady of Fire. Seen as her daughter. Sister to Oson' Deia.

Gelimah Dracul

Dragon

Dark Mage. Brother to Induca, Louna and Malsour

Fornau Dracul

Dragon

Earth Mage. Quindar's mate Malsour and Induca's grand-nephew.

Induca Dracul

Dragon

Fire Mage. One of the youngest from the first generation of Dragons. Sister to Malsour, daughter of Denur, aunt to Quindar, great aunt to Fornau. Member of the Stone Raiders and Party Zero.

Kinal Dracul

Dragon

Louna Dracul

Dragon

Induca, Gelimah and Malsour's sister.

Malsour Dracul

Dragon

Dark Mage. One of the oldest Dragons in existence, first born of Denur. Deia and Induca's Guardian, Stone Raider and Party Zero member. Brother to Induca. Great Uncle to Fornau Dracul and Uncle to Quindar Dracul.

Quindar Dracul

Dragon

Wind Mage, wife to Fornau, Niece to Induca and Malsour.

Wokui Dracul

Dragon
    Water Mage

Xednai Dracul

Dragon

One of the first Dragons, had several Dragons. Her son is Fornau.

Gorpal Dunsk

Dwarf

Dwarven Master Smith, lives in Aldamire Mountain, created 3 Weapons of Power - Mace of Fury, Tower Shield, Boots of Smash. Smithing Art: Paint Copy

Earth Lord

God

Embodiment of the Dark affinity. Created Earth Sprites.

Edmur

Dwarf

Dwarven Master Smith. Had been in the Dwarven War Bands as a Shield Bearer. Former pupil of Quino's Brother to Endur. Smithing Art: Metal's Song

Edwards

Human. Military scientist within the Deq'ual System. Friend of Sato's

Edwin

Beast Kin. Beast Kin representative on ruling council.

Endur

Dwarf

Dwarven Master Smith. Had been in the Dwarven War Bands as a Shield Bearer. Former pupil of Quino's, brother to Edmur, lives in Zolu Mountain. Smithing Art Hammer Blows

Esa

Human

Melee fighter. Member of Mikal and Jule's party. Fought at Boranl-Al's Citadel.

Member of the Stone Raiders. Going out with Jules. Works under Dwayne as a fighter. Being trained for a leadership position under Dwayne.

Lord Esamael

Human.

Lord of Emaren within the Gudalo Kingdom.

Ela-Gal

High Elf.

Warrior living in Aleph, married to Ela'Dorn. Persectued by high elves as heretic.

Ela-Dorn

Orc.

Researcher and professor at Aleph College. Aleph Council Member. Married to Ela-Gal

Fend

Dwarf

Lord Under the Mithsia Mountains.

Geswald

Human.

Trader's Guild Chapter head in Emaren.

David Grahslagg

Dwarf/Human Halfling, in-game character of Austin Zane. Dwarven Master Smith, Resident of Cliff Hill, member of Party Zero and the Stone Raider's Guild. Other names: Austin Zane

Josh Giles

Human

Rogue. Leader of the Stone Raiders. Was a investment broker on Earth, became an E-head. In a relationship with Cassie from the Golden Sabres.

Gimel

Human

Warrior.

Fellox Guild Master.

Gorrund

Dwarf

Dwarven Master Smith in Benvari Mountain with Jesal, teaching four apprentices. Smithing Art: Blood Bender.

Goula

Demon

On the Ruling council for Devil's Crater.

Gurren

Dwarf

Shield bearer, member of Dwarven War Band under Lox's command, sent to guide people to Cliff-Hill. Friend of David Grahslagg, Kol's Grandson. Member of the Stone Raiders.

Helick

Dwarf

Dwarven Master Smith.

Kim Isdola

Human

Cleric/alchemist. Lieutenant in Stone Raiders.

Ishox

Demon

On the Ruling council for Devil's Crater.

Arch-Mage Jekoni

Human/item

Soul bound to Staff of Growing, over 2,000 years old; missing legs. Held within Dwarven Vaults with other Weapons of power.

Jeeves

AI

Made by Bob to assist the Dwarven Master Smiths.

Jeremy

Human

Fellox Guild member.

Jesal

Dwarf

Dwarven Master Smith, Dave's master smith trainer. Smithing art: Nature's Guide

Jules

Human

Healer. Member of Mikal and Esa's party. Fought at Boranl-Al's Citadel.

Member of the Stone Raiders. Used to be an army medic, E-head without legs IRL. Going out with Esa. Works under Lucy as support, leads the healers of the Stone Raiders.

Joko

Dwarf

Shield bearer, member of Dwarven War Band under Lox's command, sent to guide people to Cliff-Hill. Friend and trainer of David Grahslagg.

Deceased.

Anna'Kal

Wolf Beast Kin/Administrator AI24681

Air mage. Originally a program meant to assist Lo'kal with the running of Emerilia. Anna was uploaded to a Player body and inserted into Emerilia. She became emotionally attached with her charges. When the Beast Kin people were wiped out from Emerilia she went into cold storage, waiting for her father to awake her when a chance came to fight against the prison they had created.

Member of the Stone Raiders and Party Zero. Daughter of Bob.

Lo'kal

Jukal

Scientist, created Emerilia. Awarded the position of the Gray God, maintains Emerilia, its people and Players. Other names: Bob, Bobby McMahnon, The Balancer, Gray God.

Kino

Demon

On the Ruling Council for Devil's Crater.

Kol

Dwarf

Dwarven Master Smith. Gurren's grandfather. Resides in Cliff-Hill. Taught Dave how to Smith. Runs his Smithies. Smithing art: Blind Man's Touch

Lady of Air

Goddess

Embodiment of the affinity Air. Known for causing mischief. Her Champions act as spies and information brokers, tilting the balance of Emerilia.

Lady of Fire

Goddess

Created Dragons, Mages Guild and College. Gave gift of 'knowledge' to the people of Emerilia. Mother to Deia, Lover of Oson'Mal and best friend with Bob.

Other Names: Ignil

Lady of Light

Goddess

Sent Players to kill/capture Dragons to make her own Creatures of Power. Created the race known as Angels. Large rivalry with the Dark Lord.

Lena

Demon

On the Ruling Council of Devil's Crater. Wife to Vrexu.

Lovan

Dwarf

Mithsia Mountain Warclan leader

Lox

Dwarf

Shield bearer. Was the commander of the War Band sent to guide people to Cliff-Hill. Friend of David Grahslagg. Member of the Stone Raiders.

Suzy Markell

Human (IRL)

High Elf (Emerilia)

Austin Zane's secretary and best friend. David Grahslagg's best friend and assistant with running Cliff Hill Smithy and Factory. Summoning Mage. Steven's contractor, member of Party Zero and the Stone Raiders.

Max

Dwarf

Shield bearer, member of Dwarven War Band under Lox's command, sent to guide people to Cliff-Hill. Friend of David Grahslagg.

Deceased.

Meda

Dwarf/Elf

Aleph Council member. Deals with the food within Aleph cities and facilities

Melanie

Human

Arch Mage Alamos' Wife.

Melhoun

Water snake made by the Water Lord.
Sealed away.

Mikal

Human

Rogue. Jules and Esa's party member. Member of the Stone Raiders. Friends with Party Zero.

Oson'Deia

Elf/Demi God Halfling

Elven Ranger and Fire Mage. Daughter of Oson'Mal and Lady Fire of the Affinity Pantheon. Resident of Cliff Hill and member of the Stone Raider's Guild, Leader of Party Zero.

Other names: Ouluv'Deia

Penelope

Human

Fellox Guild member.

Pete

Human

Geswald's secretary.

Queen Farun

High Elf

Queen of Raolor.

Queen Mendari Selhi

Human

Queen of Selhi.

Quino

Dwarf

Dwarven Master Smith, lives in Zolu Mountain. Trained the brothers Endur and Edmur. Smithing Art: Internal cutting.

Rola

Dwarf

Dwarven Master Smith. Smithing Art Puppeteer. Lives in Aldamire Mountain.

Sato/Communications officer Sato

Human

Lives in De'qual system.

Communications Officer, becomes Vice commander of Deq'ual military forces. Grandfather original settler.

Emperor Talis

Human.

Ruler of the Xeugrera Empire, located in the Ashal Continent.

Tounk

Dwarf

Shield bearer, member of Dwarven War Band under Lox's command, sent to guide people to Cliff-Hill. Friend of David Grahslagg.

Deceased.

Demon Prince Alkao/Alkao Travezar

Aerial Demon

Melee fighter. Commander of the Third Demon Horde and leader of Xerzit lands. Oldest of the five remaining Demon Prince's of Devil's Crater.

Dwayne Trebault

Human

Melee fighter. Lieutenant in Stone Raiders. Leads and trains the melee fighters in the Stone Raiders.

Venfik

Elf

Lady Air's advisor.

Lucy Vernia

Wood Elf/Human

Lieutenant in Stone Raiders. Spy master, deals with supporting the Stone Raiders and paperwork.

Vrexu

Demon

One of the seven Demon Princes. General in the Devil's Crater Army. Married to Lena, the youngest of the five remaining Demon Princes.

Water Lord

God

Embodiment of the Water Affinity. Created the Mer-People and water creatures. Created the Water Serpent Melhoun. Rival to the Lady of Fire.

Austin Zane

CEO of Rock Breaker's Corporation. Engineer specializing in space vehicles. Background in Astro physics. Other names: David Grahslagg

Wis'Zel

Wood Elf

Bard. Works for David Grahslagg, managing his Ceramics factories in Cliff Hill.

www.ingramcontent.com/pod-product-compliance
Lightning Source LLC
Chambersburg PA
CBHW070646310726
48982CB00001B/439
9781989377574